MARTIN HARBOTTLE'S APPRECIATION OF TIME

MARTIN HARBOTTLE'S APPRECIATION OF TIME

Dominic Utton

ONEWORLD

A Oneworld Book

First published by Oneworld Publications 2014

A CIP record for this title is available from the British Library

ISBN 978-1-78074-372-1
ISBN 978-1-78074-373-8 (eBook)

Text designed and typeset by Tetragon, London
Printed and bound by CPI Group (UK) Ltd, Croydon, CR0 4YY

Oneworld Publications
10 Bloomsbury Street
London WC1B 3SR
England

For my dad

'The human race has only one really effective weapon and that is laughter'

—Mark Twain

'I wasted time, and now doth time waste me'

—Shakespeare, *Richard II*

This is a work of fiction. Any resemblance to people or institutions, living or dead, is entirely coincidental and, to be frank, most likely the product of your own fevered imagination. You can probably blame the media for that.

Prologue

April 7

From: **DantheMan020@gmail.com**
To: customer.service@premier-westward.com
Re: Premier Westward service, Oxford–London line.

Dear Sir/Madam

I am writing to complain about the continued and many delays on this line. I have been getting Premier Westward trains to and from my work for five days a week between Oxford and London for the past 14 months. And, to be honest with you, I'm fed up.

I rarely go more than two or three days without a delay to one of my trains. Could you provide me with an explanation please?

Yours

Daniel

April 21

From: **DantheMan020@gmail.com**
To: customer.service@premier-westward.com
Re: Premier Westward service, Oxford–London line.

Dear Sir/Madam

Further to my email of April 7 (attached), I am writing once again to enquire about the many and continued delays to my service. I have heard nothing back from you about this. Could someone please do me the courtesy of giving me an explanation?

Yours

Daniel

May 31

From: **DantheMan020@gmail.com**
To: customer.service@premier-westward.com
Re: Premier Westward service, Oxford–London line.

Dear Sir/Madam

Please see the attached emails dated April 7 and April 21.

Hey! Oi! Cooeeee! Do you exist? Are you just a figment of my imagination? Am I shouting into the abyss here? This is the third email I've written to you and I still haven't heard so much as a peep, a whisper, an echo of a reply in return.

It's bad enough your trains are a disgrace – I was 32 minutes delayed this morning, 32 minutes late into work (and trust me, my boss is not the kind of man who lets these kinds of things slide) – but the fact that you, the so-called customer service department, can't even be bothered writing back to me is nothing short of shocking.

So you know what? I'm no longer going to waste my time with you. I've had it with the monkeys. I'm going straight to the organ grinder. I'm talking to the MD. Sure, I realise his email isn't anywhere on the website (funny that), but I wouldn't let that concern you. I can find his email easily enough. I'm smart like that…

So farewell, customer service monkeys. Have nice lives. I won't be writing to you again. I'll be writing to your boss.

Dan

Martin Harbottle's Appreciation of Time

Letter 1

From: **DantheMan020@gmail.com**
To: Martin.Harbottle@premier-westward.com
Re: 07.31 Premier Westward Railways train from Oxford to London Paddington, June 1. Amount of my day wasted: 12 minutes.

Dear Mr Martin Harbottle

Good morning.

I do hope you're well. My name is Daniel and I am a customer of Premier Westward trains. Every morning, five days a week, I catch a

Premier Westward train from Oxford to London and every evening I catch one home again. It's what I do. It's what I have to do, in order to get to work and back.

As Managing Director of the Premier Westward train company, I am sure you will be fascinated, concerned and most of all keen to hear about my experiences on your trains.

Oh, and before you just pass me on to your customer 'service' department, you'll notice I've attached a bunch of emails I've sent them over the last six weeks or so. Guess how many replies I've had, Martin? Go on, guess.

None. That's right. I don't feel very serviced. I don't feel very serviced at all. And so now I'm writing to you.

Because you must care, right? You must want to do all you can to provide a good service for your paying customers?

I'm writing directly to you – as Managing Director of PW – because, not to put too fine a point on it, the service you run is a shambles. And I thought you should know. Being the man in charge of the whole shoddy operation. The buck stops with you, right? Well, here it is. Here's the buck. Stop my buck!

I thought you'd like to know how awful it really is, having to catch two of your trains every day. You welcome feedback, don't you? You want to improve the customer experience, correct? Good.

But you know what? I've had a better idea than simply complaining. I've decided not to get mad – but to get even. My frustration at the appalling service you provide, at never going more than about three journeys without experiencing a delay, has prompted me into what I'm going to call a 'project'.

A project! That makes it sound exciting, doesn't it? Do you want to hear more about my project? You do! Oh goody! Here it is then. Here's my project.

From now on, every time I'm delayed on one of your trains I'm going to send you an email letting you know about it. Good, eh?

But wait! It gets better! Not only will I send you an email every time I'm late, I'm going to make the length of that email reflect the length of delay on the service you have provided for me. Because, after all, Mr Martin Harbottle, Managing Director, it is your job to be interested, concerned and eager to help with this kind of thing. Because you're anxious to provide the best service you can to your customers, right? Right.

Good. So, to continue…

The idea is that by sending you an email every time I'm on one of your delayed trains, I shall waste some of your time, just as you have wasted mine. If you've only wasted a few minutes of my morning (or evening) I shall accordingly send you a short, pithy, minute-or-two-wasting email. And if, on the other hand, you've wasted more of my time, so the email shall be longer, and no doubt far more tedious for you to read.

This morning, for example, you wasted 12 minutes of my time, when the 07.31 train from Oxford to Paddington slowed to a crawl between Maidenhead and Slough. I was late for work. I'll have to leave work late now. Thanks for that. Thanks for wasting my time, messing up my work schedules and wrecking my evening. My boss was annoyed with me when I arrived in London; my wife will be annoyed with me when I arrive home again in Oxford. And none of it's my fault. It's your fault.

The thing is: time is precious, isn't it? I'm sure you're not enjoying having your time wasted like this. I'm sure as a go-getting managing director about town (even if the town is Reading, or Slough, or wherever your head office is) you have fantastically busy working days. I'm sure you have a happy, healthy, fulfilling home life too. I'm sure that you wouldn't want unnecessary wastes of time to impact upon either your work or home life, would you?

Of course not. It's rubbish when that happens. It sucks.

In fact, I shall even be presumptuous enough to assume that the prospect of receiving many, many more emails like this from me – some of which, let's not kid ourselves here, will be longer and far more tedious to match the longer, more tedious delays that your train company will doubtless waste my time with – fills you with a kind of dread and ennui. Of course it does! And that's how I feel every morning at Oxford and every evening at Paddington. It's like anticipation in reverse. (What do you call anticipation in reverse? What's the word for when you're expecting something that you know will be rubbish? Something for us all to think about, perhaps. Something for us to return to, again and again. Anticipation in reverse. The feeling that what's coming is bound to be disappointing.) I think it could be a theme for these letters! I think it could end up being a – what's the word? A motif. A conceit.

And in the meantime, that's my project. Of course, it may be that by some happy miracle your train service suddenly starts doing what I'm paying you to make it do, and run according to the timetables. In which case, this will be both hello and farewell…

But I think we both know that's not going to happen, don't we? So, not farewell but *au revoir*. (That's French, by the way. It means 'until we see each other again'. I think. Truth be told, I'm hopeless at languages. I'm a total dumbkopf at languages. I'm *très stupide* at all that languages stuff. Except the English language, of course. I'm all right at that, Martin. In fact, I'm pretty good at it. It's what I do, you see. It's what I am.)

I've got a train to catch home tonight, after all. What do you think the chances of it running on time actually are? I mean, as Managing Director of Premier Westward you should be able to put a percentage on one of your trains running on time, shouldn't you?

Shall we say: 100 percent chance? No, of course not. Ninety percent? Eighty? Fifty? Twenty? Let's see, shall we?

Au revoir!

Dan

From: **Martin.Harbottle@premier-westward.com**
To: DantheMan020@gmail.com
Re: 07.31 Premier Westward Railways train from Oxford to London Paddington, June 1.

Dear Dan

Thanks for your email.

I am sorry you have had negative experiences with Premier Westward. I am well aware of the issues customers face each day and use the trains myself every day. When things go wrong I try and assist as much as possible so I feel I am as aware of the issues we face as I can be.

This morning, delays were frustrating for us. All delays are frustrating for us.

I share your view that reliability just isn't good enough right now and this is primarily an issue with Network Rail reliability. We are applying pressure for improvement.

Also, do you mind if I ask a question of my own? I'm curious as to how you obtained my email address?

Martin

Letter 2

From: **DantheMan020@gmail.com**
To: Martin.Harbottle@premier-westward.com
Re: 07.31 Premier Westward Railways train from Oxford to London Paddington, June 3. Amount of my day wasted: five minutes.

Hey, Martin! (You don't mind me calling you Martin, do you? It is how you signed off your letter, after all.)

Hey Martin! Thanks for your letter. Imagine that! The Managing Director of Premier Westward trains, writing to me! I feel… honoured, Martin. Humbled.

It was good of you to write back to me. I didn't expect it, if I'm being honest, but thank you very much for taking the time to do it. It was big of you. You're a gentleman.

Guess what? Yesterday I wasn't delayed at all! You got me to work, and you got me home from work, and all at the times you promised me you would. Well done! I'm proud of you, Martin. For a crazy moment I even wondered if it had something to do with my letter, my project – whether it really had spurred you into action, forced you to pull your finger out.

Silly of me, I know. I'm embarrassed just thinking about it. Because here we are, just the day after the day after my first letter, and I'm having to email you again. Admittedly, this morning's train was only delayed by five minutes, but still. Rules are rules. We have to play by the rules.

I'm a firm believer in playing by the rules, Martin. And for that reason, just as I promised, this letter will be correspondingly about half the length of the last one. Just as my delay was half the length.

One thing, however. You asked how I got your email address. I used my skills. Or as the kids say, my skillz! The skillz I've picked up from ten years of working in the seamier side of the media! I'm a journalist, you see. (Oh, I can sense your ears prick up already.) I work for the *Globe*. Yes… *THAT Globe*. (Was that a sharp intake of breath, Martin? We're not all bad, you know!) Finding people's email addresses – it's part of what I do. It's surprisingly easy. I could probably get your mobile number too, if I could be bothered.

But don't worry. I can't be bothered. Emails it shall be.

Oh, also: something else in your kind reply intrigued me. You try to help out when there are delays? Really? How do you do that? I have a vision of you, Martin, striding manfully through the carriages, ripping off your shirt as you go...

Au revoir!

Dan

Letter 3

From: **DantheMan020@gmail.com**
To: Martin.Harbottle@premier-westward.com
Re: 19.50 Premier Westward Railways trains between London Paddington and Oxford, June 3. Amount of my day wasted: 21 minutes.

Oh, Martin. You've only gone and done the double. Delayed me on the way to work this morning, and then delayed me again on the way home this evening. I do hope you're feeling proud of yourself. I can picture you now, high-fiving and thigh-slapping and whooping your way around the office. Double score! Two–nil to Premier Westward.

Twenty-one minutes tonight. What did happen? And, Martin – were you forced to assist? Did you rush to the scene of the delay, pants outside your trousers, cape billowing in the wind behind you? 'It's OK, citizens! I'm the Managing Director!'

We know you're the MD, Martin. And seeing as we have so much time together today, perhaps I'd better tell you a little bit more about myself.

My name is Dan (you know that bit already). I'm 32 years old and I live in Oxford with my wife, Beth, and our two-month-old daughter Sylvie. (Neither of us are French or anything – we named her after a St Etienne song. That alone should tell you more about me than anything else I write here: I'm the kind of person who names his children after St Etienne songs.)

I don't have any family other than them. My parents died a year or so ago, one after the other. Nothing dramatic, nothing out of the ordinary, nothing that doesn't happen every day all across the world. Mum from her dodgy ticker, Dad from a broken heart not two months later. She didn't have a chance to know what hit her, really, and as far as he was concerned, dying was just the next thing to do. There was no raging against the dying of the light – without her, he couldn't really see the point any more. He gave up: and why the hell shouldn't he?

It's no biggie, and, actually, I don't really want to talk about it.

Anyway: no parents, no brothers, no sisters. Just me and Beth and little baby Sylvie.

We moved to Oxford before I got the job at the *Globe*. I was freelancing then, you see, working from home. I was writing for everyone, for anyone who wanted a titbit or two. If they were willing to pay, I was willing to give them whatever they asked for. I grubbed around the grubby end of Grub Street. I wrote for newspapers high and low. I could tell you a tale or two. Perhaps I will, one day. But the point is, I wasn't in an office. I could live anywhere.

And once Beth finished her nursing course there was no reason to stay in London. People get sick everywhere, right? So five years ago, when Beth graduated and was offered a job at the John Radcliffe hospital, it made total sense to get out of our cramped little flat in London. We kissed goodbye to the flotsam and jetsam of Finsbury Park, caught a train to Oxford and did the whole grown-up mortgage–marriage thing.

I worked from home, on email and the internet and, well, PlayStation – if I'm honest, quite a bit of PlayStation – and Beth cycled to and from work every day. There was no commuting. My working day began about 20 minutes after I got out of bed and our family time together began the minute Beth opened the door in the evening. It was a good system. It worked.

And then… and then I only got offered a job, didn't I? I only got offered the chance of a regular income, of holiday entitlement, of sick pay. I only got offered a pension, a company healthcare scheme. (Memo to self: must look into that company healthcare scheme sometime.) After years of chancing it where I could, of hustling for features here, interviews there, celebrity nuggets and tittle-tattle everywhere, I was only offered a steady, secure, grown-up salary.

It's not a big deal, this job of mine. It's not a massive deal – not yet. It's a junior position on the showbiz desk, rewriting copy mostly, not a lot of bylined stuff. But it's a start: it's still a staff job in the newsroom of the biggest newspaper in the world. It's got potential. It could take me places.

So anyway: a year or so ago I was offered the chance to be a grown-up. Of course I took it. Even if it did mean commuting back to London every day. Even if working for a Sunday paper means my working week is now Tuesday to Saturday.

Can you remember the moment you decided to become a grown-up, Martin? Or were you one of those people who was always a bit grown-up? Were you one of those weird kids who had a life-plan way back when you were doing your GCSE options? Were you focused from an early age? Was it always going to be trains for you? Did you study hard, apply yourself diligently, work sensibly towards a long and steady career in train management?

I'm guessing that in your case, becoming a grown-up was simply the next logical stage in your development. I'm guessing it was inevitable. Like puberty. Like acne. I'm guessing you saw becoming a grown-up as nothing more dramatic than the thing that comes after leaving university.

And then what? Find a girl, settle down, if you want to you can marry? Look at me, I am old but I'm happy? Cat Stevens knew it. Despite it all, he knew what being a grown-up meant.

(Obviously Cat Stevens' life should not be taken as a literal model for how to be a grown-up. Let's not do anything rash now. Abandoning your career at the height of your success and vowing never to pick up the instrument of your success again is obviously – or rather, *obvs*, as they say in our magazine supplement – not that sensible, or responsible, or adult-like. It's not something many school career advisers would recommend. But you know what I mean. The lyrics to 'Father to Son': they're about becoming a grown-up, right? They're about the melancholy inevitability of having to become a grown-up. It's a song about accepting defeat. It's a song about surrender.)

Where was I? Oh yes. Growing up. I can imagine you were always quite a sensible boy, Martin. A sensible boy, and then a good bloke, and now a steady chap. And then what? A nice old gent… and then fondly remembered. That's life. That's the epitaph.

But that, I suppose, is how you get to be Managing Director of a company like Premier Westward. And not someone who writes about reality TV wannabes and scandalised soap starlets and disgraced pop flops and lecherous actors and priapic footballers and self-loathing WAGs for a living.

Oh dear. It doesn't sound much like I enjoy my job there, does it? It doesn't sound like I get off on what I do. Please don't think that! You couldn't be more wrong! It's just the delay that's put me in a bad mood, it's just your rotten trains that are souring my normally sunny disposition. The truth is, I love my job. You wanna hear a secret? I'd probably do it for free. I may not be getting the bylines or the glory every week, but still. I'd probably do it for free.

Don't get me wrong, I need the money. God knows I need the money – if it wasn't for the money I certainly wouldn't sit on these trains every morning and evening, an hour each way (when they run on time). If it wasn't for the money and the fact I need to be a grown-up now, after too many years of spectacularly failing to be a grown-up. If it wasn't for all that… I'd do it for free.

I'm a good bloke, obviously, a loving husband and father, but I'm also a tabloid journalist. And that makes me a professional bastard. I basically think I'm better than everyone else and at the same time worry that nobody else really realises it. It makes me think I'm always right (even when I sort of know, inside, I may be wrong). Because the *Sunday Globe* – it is always right, isn't it? It tells the world what's right – and more often, what's wrong.

We work in absolutes. Black and white and read all over. No grey areas for us! When I write my little bits and bobs, my news in briefs, when I lay it all out for our millions of readers, I can't afford to see both sides. It's not what they want – and it's not what my boss wants. They call it 'taking a line' in the tabloid game, Martin. We've got to take a line on every story. We've got to believe we're right, or we're scuppered.

And do you want to hear a secret? I may only wallow in the shallow end, but I'm absolutely in love with it. With the celebrity world. I'm obsessed by it. I live and breathe it. And I also hate just about everyone involved in it. I think they're vain, shallow, venal, self-obsessed, back-stabbing monsters. (And that's just the cast of *Hollyoaks*.) And I just can't get enough of them all. And that may be all of tabloid journalism in a nutshell for you right there.

And so I write about them. That's why I write about them. And now that I work for the most-read English-language newspaper in the world, and also the most notorious tabloid newspaper in Britain, what I write about them has an impact on their behaviour.

You know what that impact is? You wanna hear another secret? A secret about the world of tabloid journalism and celebrity?

For all the fuss we make about their bad behaviour, and for all the fuss they make about our reporting of their bad behaviour, all any of it does is makes their bad behaviour worse. That's how it works. That's the Faustian pact. That's the hidden symbiosis of tabloid and celebrity. Bad behaviour shifts newspapers, and shifted newspapers make reputations. Nobody remembers the nice, quiet, sensible family men and women, do they? Nobody remembers the good blokes, the steady chaps.

And, believe me – anyone who wants to be a celebrity wants nothing more than to be remembered. For whatever reason they can get. Being remembered – that's the point of it all. No matter what their publicists say.

It's a perverse sort of logic, isn't it? If I were to write in the *Globe* about the terrible service I get on your trains, for example, well, that would be seen as a bad thing within your company. The sort of thing you'd actively discourage me from doing. Normal people, normal companies, people like you and companies like yours – you don't want to be remembered. Not by the popular press. Not if that's what it costs. And quite right too.

Oh dear! Am I ranting, Martin? Do I rave? Am I beginning to sound like a tabloid monster? Like the worst, seediest kind of hack? Am I giving you the willies? Do excuse me. I'm just being honest.

Because that's another thing about me (we're going to find out so much about each other, Martin. We're going to become such confidantes!) – I'm disgracefully honest.

I've built a career on it. Or rather, I'm building a career on it. Because, while I'm being honest and before you get too scared, I'm no big shot. I may write for the biggest and baddest paper in town, but I'm no kingmaker or king breaker. I'm not the Fake Sheikh. I'm just a reporter on the showbiz desk. I write what I'm told. And – contrary to popular belief and stereotype – I make sure everything I write is true.

My mate Harry the Dog says it's going to be the downfall of me, my honesty. 'Don't be so bloody honest all the time,' he says. 'Don't start forming your own opinions, just write what you're told to think.'

His mate Rochelle (she's the editor of the magazine supplement – it's called *Amazeballs!*, I'm sure Mrs Harbottle is a fan) is even more perplexed by the idea.

‘Honesty? Totes yawnsville,’ she told me. ‘Like, seriously: whatevs.’

What about you, Martin? What do you think? Are you worried I’m going to write about you? About your trains? Is that why you wrote back to me? I can’t help wondering…

Tell you what, seeing as we’re here, why don’t you tell me about yourself? Do you love your job? Or do you grow frustrated? Do you sometimes feel like you’re no longer doing the things that fired up your passion for train management in the first place? Is being Managing Director of Premier Westward trains a bit like being headmaster of a very large and very complicated school? Are you one of those headmasters who first got into it because he wanted to teach, to feel the visceral thrill, the exhilarating responsibility of standing in front of a roomful of children and actually educating them… and now spends his days gazing at spreadsheets in an office by himself, balancing budgets and juggling timetables and stressing over staff quotas and never actually going anywhere near a classroom or interacting with any of the children except to send them home in disgrace?

Or do you love the power? Do you get off simply on being the man in charge? Do you prefer being the field marshal, safely miles behind the front, gazing at his models and blithely giving the orders?

Of course not. You’re the man of action! You’re there on the sharp end, helping out where you can. You told me that already.

Hey, guess what? Look at the time! *Tempus fugit*! Twenty-one of your minutes wasted. My work here is done… but I do look forward to you addressing my concerns. In fact, I can’t wait!

Au revoir!

Dan

From: **Martin.Harbottle@premier-westward.com**
To: DantheMan020@gmail.com
Re: 07.31 and 19.50 Premier Westward Railways trains between London Paddington and Oxford, June 3.

Dear Dan

Thank you for your emails concerning the delayed 07.31 and 19.50 of June 3. I do understand how frustrating being late for both your journeys must have been.

The problem in the morning was caused by a late-running earlier train in the Reading area which unfortunately had the effect of congesting many subsequent services, of which yours was one. The delay in the evening was due to faulty signalling in Southall. It is something we are continuing to address with Network Rail and I agree that it is simply not good enough.

On a personal note, I would like to assure you that as Managing Director I take all of our customers' concerns very seriously – and not just those who work for 'tabloid' newspapers! But on that note, I would also like to stress that I consider this a private correspondence and would not expect any of it to appear in print.

I do hope that, even if you are unhappy with the service we are providing, I can assure you on a personal level that as Managing Director of Premier Westward, I am striving to do all I can to provide you with the best commuting experience I can.

Yours

Martin

Letter 4

From: **DantheMan020@gmail.com**
To: Martin.Harbottle@premier-westward.com
Re: 07.31 Premier Westward Railways train from London Paddington to Oxford, June 8. Amount of my day wasted: five minutes.

Just a little one today, Martin. A small but perfectly formed five-minute delay. Pert – that's the word. A pert little delay.

So small, so perfectly formed, so pert, in fact, that I've not even had time to finish my crossword today (confession: I love a crossword, me. I'm a sucker for a wordsearch. I'm all over a good game of Scrabble. My dad used to make them up for me, when I was a kid – meticulously tracing out the grids, shading in the dark spots with the retractable pencil he kept in his jacket pocket, carefully writing in the clues underneath and always including a space for 'workings out'.)

Anyway. This isn't one of my dad's. This isn't in his league, sadly. This is the morning 'Commuter's conundrum' from my daily red-top. I've scanned it in for you and everything, Martin. See if you can finish what I've started.

Au revoir!

Dan

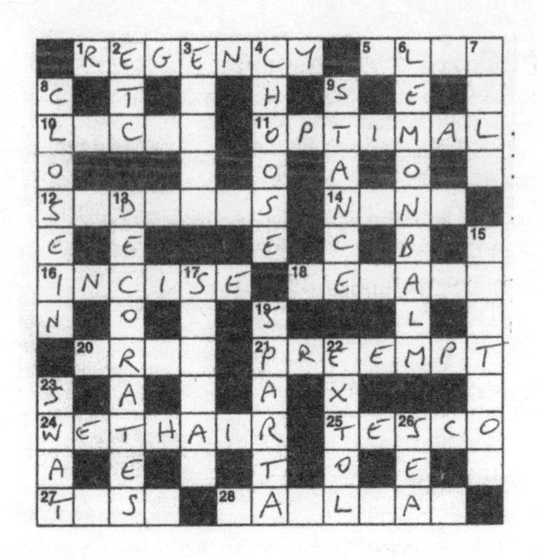

Across:

1. Period 1811–20, beloved of Dandies
5. Internet journal
10. Lawful
11. Ideal
12. Melancholy
14. Number in Frodo's fellowship
16. Cut
18. Keep in custody
20. Stuffy, uptight person
21. Take advance action
24. Dampened follicles (3,4)
25. Every little helps for this supermarket
27. Cricket exam
28. Mass-transit system

Down:

2. And so on
3. __ Nous – Between ourselves
4. Pick, select
6. Citrus-like herb
7. Impudence

8. Move nearer to target
9. Position
13. Improves through paint or wallpaper
15. Published issue
17. Indicator
19. Frugal home of Ancient Greeks
22. Sing the praises of
23. Fly-killing method
26. Large body of water

Letter 5

From: **DantheMan020@gmail.com**
To: Martin.Harbottle@premier-westward.com
Re: 19.50 Premier Westward Railways train from London Paddington to Oxford, June 14. Amount of my day wasted: seven minutes.

Dear Martin

Seven minutes. 'Oh come on!' you're thinking. 'Give us a break! Cut us some slack! Seven minutes? What's seven minutes?'

Seven minutes, Martin, is 420 seconds. It's over one tenth of an hour. It's a cigarette. It's the first glass of wine after another long day. A lot can happen in seven minutes. A two-month-old baby girl promised a kiss from Daddy before she falls asleep could drift off kiss-less in those seven minutes.

Seven minutes can be an age, an eternity. It all depends on context. E, as I'm sure you don't need reminding, totally equals mc squared.

Take the recent brouhaha in North Africa. All those protestors, stopped in their tracks, shot down, executed. The authorities there are saying it was self-defence, that the army was fired upon first, that they were reacting to a hostile situation. I'm hearing different in the newsroom. But the point is – it all happened in a few bare minutes.

In a few minutes – not even as many as seven – those 22 men went from just another bunch of chanting, protesting citizens uppity about some civil rights abuse or another to corpses. Bundles of rag and bone. Dead in the dust. Whether they were firing too, or whether they weren't.

Seven minutes can change the world. And if I'm any kind of journalist at all, I reckon those few minutes in the heat and the madness and the dust and the sand are going to cost an awful lot more than just those 22 bodies.

Oh, Martin! Look at us. We're getting far too serious. We need to calm down. We need to remember what we're here for. We don't want to hear about murder and mayhem in the squares of North Africa! Such talk can only bring us down.

Have you ever been on the radio, Martin? I have. And let me tell you, seven minutes on the radio can feel like an awfully long time. When you're on live radio, seven minutes can feel like all the time in the world.

So there I was, about six years ago, brought in to the studio to grace the airwaves with my insight and analysis on the new Oasis album. All of London was listening. The nation's capital city was agog! What would I, self-styled voice of the nation's youth (and at that time contributing rock and pop reviewer for the *Sunday Express*) have to tell this great city about *les frères* Gallaghers' latest? What would we all learn about the state of British rock?

London paused. London cocked an ear.

And I… blew it. I floundered. Early on in my allotted seven minutes, whilst trying to express my frustration with Noel's bandwagon-jumping critics, I jumbled up the phrases 'gets my goat' and 'I have a beef with' (I have no idea why those two phrases were in my mind to begin with) and I loudly declared: 'That really gets my beef.'

There was a terrible pause. And then I said it again. And then for seven minutes I couldn't think of anything else to say. All I could think was: 'What the hell does "gets my beef" mean? Why did I say that? What kind of idiot am I anyway? Gets my beef? *Gets my beef*?'

Martin, it was awful. It was seven minutes of abject misery. And it felt like an awful lot longer.

So please, don't tell me seven minutes doesn't really matter. It does. They do. Time is relative. Whether it's 22 men lying broken in the dust or one man making a prat of himself on the radio: seven minutes can feel like for ever.

Oh, and as I write, on a train in the morning (the morning following the delay I write of today. Did I mention time is relative?), inching past the golden suburbs of Reading, I see we're already eight or so minutes behind schedule again. Expect another letter later today. And if you thought that being seven minutes late got my beef… baby, you ain't seen nothing yet.

Au revoir!

Dan

Letter 6

From: **DantheMan020@gmail.com**
To: Martin.Harbottle@premier-westward.com
Re: 07.31 Premier Westward Railways train from Oxford to London Paddington, June 15. Amount of my day wasted: 17 minutes. Fellow sufferers: Guilty New Mum, Competitive Tech Nerds, Universal Grandpa, Lego Head, Train Girl.

How goes the war, Martin? Bad guys still winning? Hang in there, soldier. The sun also rises. Dreams never end. It's Glastonbury next weekend! That's something good, right? That's something to look forward to. Assuming it stops raining, of course.

So chin up, private. Eyes forward. Some day this thing's gonna end. I promise.

But not today. Today things don't look so peachy at all. Today you're going to have to kick back and listen to my nonsense for a good 17 minutes of your day. And what's more, now we're getting into the swing of things here, you'll see I've made a slight change to the format of my letters. Exciting, eh! More of that later…

But first things first. I do hope that you know how much I do appreciate you taking the time out to reply to me personally. Even when my letters veer towards the sarcastic, the hyperbolic. Even when it might feel like I'm giving you a bit of a slapping, literary-speaking. It's not personal. It's not bullying. That's just how I write, Martin. It's how I was trained to write.

And the fact you can understand all that and remain so polite makes you a big man. A Big Man. A man's man. A man's Big Man.

So. That's the polite stuff over and done with. Now to business. Much as I respect you as a man's Big Man, I find myself once again let down by you and your service.

I was 17 minutes late for work today. It meant I arrived late for an important meeting. It was a crisis meeting, one of an increasing number of crisis meetings we seem to be having on the showbiz desk. It was a crisis meeting about ethics. About integrity. (Of all the ridiculous things to have a meeting about on the showbiz desk of the *Globe*, for Christ's sake.) It was one of those ridiculous meetings where, thanks to the indiscretions and, ahem, eccentricities of our predecessors, we were getting a roasting. It was the whole newspaper in microcosm. It was one of those meetings where we were told not to be so fast and loose with our newsgathering tactics, but at the same time, in the same breath, we were told if we didn't keep getting the scoops we'd be out on our ears.

The police have been in touch, apparently. The whole unpleasantness could go beyond a few hacked-off celebs moaning about getting caught with their pants down. It could even get beyond the take-the-money-and-shut-up stage. It's bad, in other words.

And yet, we were getting a good going over for not getting more exclusive stories. For not catching more celebs with their pants down. Go figure that one.

Anyway. The point is: it was an important meeting.

And I had to walk in late, all elbows and knees, clutching a half-sipped coffee and dropping my notepad and mumbling apologies as everyone stopped talking and watched. In silence. In disapproving silence. I wanted to say: 'Don't judge me! Judge Martin Harbottle, Managing Director of Premier Westward trains! He's the Delilah to my David here! Be silent and disapproving towards him! It's his fault! It's all his fault!'

But of course I couldn't. I had to grin foolishly and take it like a man. And not a big man, either. Not a man's Big Man. I had to take it like a small man.

I don't understand why we're getting the blame for the sins of our predecessors at the paper anyway. I don't understand why this sudden need for self-flagellation. We are the Free Press, right? We have a duty to report the news, whatever it might be.

And I have no idea why the shadier newsgathering tactics of my forebears should be in any way relevant to my current job churning out salacious witticisms on the implied indiscretions of the celebrity world. I'm not breaking any laws. I'm not even in a position to break any laws. But I was told to be there. I was told to be there because that's how it works at my place. You do as you're told. And turning up late and looking incompetent is generally frowned upon.

So. Anyway. That was my morning. And I'm guessing this is an email you knew was going to come today, didn't you, Martin? I'm betting you turned up for work this morning; I'm betting you fired up the Premier Westward Super Mainframe Megacomputer and felt your little heart sink.

There was an incident this morning. One of your trains, Martin: it broke down! It totally broke down. Like it was too old or poorly maintained or something. As luck would have it, it wasn't my train, but still. That old or defective or poorly maintained train broke down and snarled up the line for everyone else.

I wasn't the only one, of course. It's not just about me! My train was, as always, packed. (Over-packed, some might say.) And, as always, it held many of the usual suspects, the same faces I see every day. We're a regular little community – united by habit and circumstance and frustration.

The thing about commuting is that it's a shared experience. We're all in it together, as someone once said. We're creatures of habit, making for the same spot on the platform, the same seat in the same carriage, every day – and so, naturally, commuting becomes something of a glimpse into the human zoo. It's like watching a David Attenborough documentary – and you start to recognise your fellow victims by their habits as much as their faces.

This morning, for example, from my usual spot in Coach C I counted five regulars.

There was Guilty New Mum, freshly (and early) returned to work after maternity leave, all of a flap, juggling laptop and Filofax and scalding coffee whilst phoning home to check on baby, muslin squares and nipple shields spilling out of her handbag...

Competitive Tech Nerds – two middle-aged banker types with weak chins and big suits – were arguing loudly about the relative merits of Cloud storage versus external hard drives. Which at least made a change from the interminable mobile phone discussions they seem to endlessly recycle (when the new iPhone came out they almost came to blows, so overcome were they by the excitement of it all).

On the seat opposite them was Universal Grandpa – wisps of snowy hair, white beard, M&S slacks, smart jacket, the kindest face you ever saw, copy of the *Telegraph*. No idea where he's going every day at this time: he looks too old and too nice to be doing this. And next to him was Lego Head: a huge, heavyset man in (I'm guessing) his mid-thirties about whom I know nothing other than that he has got on this train every single time I have, always makes for exactly the same spot, never says a word to anyone, never reads a paper or a book, never plugs himself into a laptop or iPod or mobile phone… and has hair that looks exactly like it's made out of Lego.

And down a little, on the opposite side to me, is Train Girl. I don't know much about her either, other than that she's easily the best-looking part of my journey to work every morning. Not that I pay too much attention to that kind of thing, obviously.

So there we all were. Delayed, late, in trouble with our respective bosses, thrown together by habit and circumstance, forced into daily unwarranted intimacy, and (with the exception of Competitive Tech Nerds) never once even acknowledging each other's presence, despite it all.

Does that make you feel a little worse, Martin, knowing the human cost of your incompetence? How would you explain such a pitiful service to us all? How do you communicate such failure? Enlighten me! Educate, inform or at least entertain me. Tell me why I'm getting a pasting at work for the bad behaviour of my predecessors, while you seem to be able to run a shoddy business with impunity.

Can you communicate that to me? Can you do it now? Can you do it, in the words of the Artist Formerly Known As Prince, like it's 1999? Or even in a manner befitting, say, the 21st century?

Yes? All right! Go Martin! I feel energised! I feel invigorated! I feel like… like a Big Man! This could be a new beginning for me and you! We gotta make it happen!

Yours, in breathless expectation,

Au revoir!

Dan

PS. Just read this back, Martin, and worried it may sometimes appear like I'm bullying you. Don't worry. I'm not. I'm not really threatening you with the diabolical power of the *Sunday Globe*. I'm a straight-up bloke, I keep telling you that. I've no intention of taking this conversation any further than between us. Trust me. (Though I am interested in whether that means your responses will stop. Are you only writing back to me because you're a bit scared of who I work for? Because of the power of negative publicity? Because we do look a bit scary at the moment, don't we? What with all these headlines we're generating about ourselves? Or do you write back because you really do care about running a good service? I wonder.)

Letter 7

From: DantheMan020@gmail.com
To: Martin.Harbottle@premier-westward.com
Re: 07.31 Premier Westward Railways train from Oxford to London Paddington, June 17. Amount of my day wasted: 13 minutes. Fellow sufferers: Guilty New Mum, Lego Head, Train Girl, Universal Grandpa.

Dear Martin

What's happening? You've gone all silent on me. I'm getting worried. Three letters without a reply. You don't really think I'm a bully, do you?

And I wanted to get your thoughts on the North African situation, too. I told you those 22 weren't firing on the army, didn't I? The *Globe* newsroom is rarely wrong! I told you they'd become a flashpoint for something far bigger. I told you those few minutes of madness would have major repercussions. And now… thousands. Thousands of angry men with flags where before there were barely two dozen.

What's going to happen out there? What do you think? It's a little bit worrying, a little bit horrible… but it's exciting, isn't it? It's news! News is happening!

Have you spurned me, cast me aside, left me in the lurch? I do hope not. Everyone I love goes away in the end.

(Actually, that's not strictly true. It's just a lyric from a Johnny Cash song I like. The people I love don't go away. Or at least they haven't yet. The people I love: they're going nowhere. At least, that's what they tell me. 'What am I doing, Dan?' they say. 'I'm going nowhere. I had a career, I used to have a life – and now I'm stuck in with the baby all day, surrounded by dirty nappies and dirty baby clothes and dirty baby, talking nonsense with someone who can't even understand what I'm saying because she's only two months old, watching Jeremy bloody Kyle and Eamonn bloody Holmes and Alan bloody Titchmarsh and not even bloody hearing them over the noise the bloody baby's making cos it won't bloody sleep and I think I'm going mad and there you are having fun at work all day with all your funny, clever, single, baby-less friends and here I am going bloody nowhere…' That's what they tell me. That's what the one I love tells me. She's not going away. She's going nowhere.)

Oh dear – is this sounding like therapy, Martin? Are you to be my therapist? Would you like me to tell you how I really feel? Would you like me to share?

OK then, I will. I've got a bit of time of yours to waste today, after all. Here's how I feel. Here's what I'm feeling right now.

Have you looked outside your window recently? Out beyond the usual view, I mean? There's a whole world out there. Look at North Africa. It's revolting! And it's not the only place – it's just the latest. Something's always happening somewhere. And that is why I became a journalist. To be a part of it. Not to read about the world on my

Twitter feed whilst sitting delayed outside Slough; not to scroll through websites while chugging at half-speed past Didcot Parkway; not to flick through other people's copy in other people's newspapers while stalled near Southall. I became a journalist to be a part of it all.

Outside it's all going on – and I joined the newspaper so I could watch it unfold from the inside. So I could be a part of it unfolding.

There's nowhere like a newspaper when there's news about. It's so exciting!

Watching it all get written up, being part of the process that moulds that raw information and unsculpted experience and makes it into news.

What could be better than that? Seriously. Even if the rest of the world largely thinks we're pond-life, even if the rest of the world thinks we're monsters. We're making the news. We may be rats, but at least we're not mice. We're doers!

Let me tell you another anecdote by way of illustration. (Don't worry, this one's not humiliating.)

Do you remember when Princess Diana died? Of course you do. Tall blonde lass, liked a holiday, married that odd feller with the big ears, unfortunate business with bulimia, three of us in this marriage, Queen of Hearts, landmines, Paris underpass, all that stuff. That's the one! Well, you may also remember that she died very late on a Saturday night. My boss once told me that when she died he received a panicked call from the night news desk – and he ran – literally ran – into the office, straight from the pub.

Everyone was called in – and everyone came in. They came from their beds, from other people's beds, from pubs, from clubs, from wherever they were. They came in the middle of the night and they put together a whole new newspaper in a matter of hours. Half of them were drunk, a good number were a good deal worse than drunk. But they worked like maniacs through the middle of the night, because it was the most momentous news story of their lifetimes and they didn't want to be anywhere else in the world than in the newsroom reporting it.

My boss – he said it was the best night of his life. He'll tell anyone who asks: the night Princess Diana died was the best night of my life. As you might guess, that sentiment often gets misinterpreted.

But do you understand what he means? Do you get it?

There's nowhere like a newspaper when there's news about. It's a thrill, a buzz, an adrenaline kick. Working in a newsroom: it's mainlining the zeitgeist. It's utterly addictive. Even when you're the story yourself. Especially so. All this unpleasantness alleged against the *Globe*... it's worrying (Beth is worried, for sure) and some of the details are undeniably unpleasant... but I can't deny it's exciting.

I want to be amongst the action, Martin! I want to be with all the stuff that's doing stuff! I don't want to be stuck in a crummy seat on a crummy train staring at some crummy town out of the window, thinking about the things I'm missing.

I at least want my life to be as exciting as my bored, frustrated wife thinks it is. That seems fair, doesn't it?

Au revoir!

Dan

From: **Martin.Harbottle@premier-westward.com**
To: DantheMan020@gmail.com
Re: 07.31 Premier Westward Railways train from Oxford to London Paddington, June 17.

Dear Dan

Thank you for your most recent letters. Of course I am always happy to hear of your concerns, if unhappy that you have cause to write at all!

Your train home on June 8 was delayed due to the slow running of a freight train in the Didcot Parkway area. On both the 14 and 15 June signalling problems on the Oxford–Paddington line meant that a 'go-slow' order was in force. On June 17 problems outside Reading meant many trains, including yours, were congested in and out of the station. We put the safety of our passengers above all other concerns at all times, even if it does unfortunately result in some trains running slightly delayed.

To address your other concerns: I hope you don't attribute my responses to any worry over negative press. I like to think that as Managing Director, I am receptive to the concerns of any Premier Westward passenger.

I am sorry you feel that your time on our trains is not as stimulating as it might be. And I imagine that life at a tabloid newspaper must be very exciting! I expect you have plenty of anecdotes to match that of your boss.

And yes, the situation in North Africa is very worrying. It puts things into perspective rather, don't you think?

Best

Martin

Letter 8

From: DantheMan020@gmail.com
To: Martin.Harbottle@premier-westward.com
Re: 22.20 Premier Westward Railways train from London Paddington to Oxford, June 22. Amount of my day wasted: ten minutes. Fellow sufferer: Overkeen Estate Agent.

How the devil are you, Martin? Well, I hope? In the pink? Good, good. Well done.

I gather you had a rough night of it last night. I hear that all Premier Westward services out of Paddington yesterday evening were – not to put too fine a point on it – up the spout. Down the Swanee. Round the U-bend. Nothing moved, as I understand it, for hours.

I monitored it all on the internet. I kept a window open on my desktop as I worked into the night. All those winking 'delayed' signs reproduced faithfully for the benefit of the world. Just as well I had to work late, eh? Just as well my sadistic boss was in an especially bad mood (the threat of legal action against one's employers can do that to a man, I hear). Just as well he wanted all my copy rewritten. Or I'd have been right round the U-bend myself.

As it was, I escaped with a mere ten-minute delay to my journey home. As it was, my wife was only moderately cheesed off with me. Lucky me!

Or rather – lucky us. Me and Overkeen Estate Agent. My sole regular fellow traveller on the night shift home.

He's an odd one, is Overkeen Estate Agent. I only ever see him when I'm on these later trains – and he always seems to have come straight from work. The shiny suit, the tie in a fat footballer's knot. (What is that knot? Like a quadruple-Windsor, far too big for any shirt collar, squatting there at the neck like a fat silk Buddha. Who decided that was a good look? And when did we start taking sartorial direction from footballers anyway?) He's always on the phone (a white iPhone – and that in itself speaks volumes. He chose the white model. He looked at the black version and said: No. I want a white one. I am male, I appear to be heterosexual… and yet still, despite all that, I'd prefer the white iPhone. That's the sort of person I am) and he's always saying things like: 'We need to drill this down', and 'Let's get that actioned asap'. He uses words like 'diarise' and 'bro' and 'PDQ'. He calls people 'legends'. He's about 14 years old. I'm simultaneously repulsed and fascinated by him.

But, to be fair to him, he rarely seems bothered by the train delays. He just keeps talking nonsense into his white iPhone and staring at his reflection in the window.

But then: I've been thinking. If I'm to write to you every time my train is delayed, and if a massive, will-to-live-sapping delay should therefore prompt an equally massively time-wasting letter to you in return, then there may be a problem in my otherwise brilliantly childish revenge plan.

Are these letters nothing more than me wasting even more of my time than you've wasted in the first place?

That, Martin, would make all this decidedly Pyrrhic. A Pyrrhic victory. Do you know what a Pyrrhic victory is? Of course you do – you must have benefitted from a classical education. Where was it? Rugby? Stowe? Where then…? St Andrews? Cambridge? Or have you worked your way up from nothing? Managing Directed your way out of the mean streets? Was it a case of sport and management directoring being the only legal options for a kid from the wrong side of the tracks?

I'm going with the classical education. The traditional route to the top. Born to rule, eh? Effortlessly schooled in the ways of casual superiority.

Anyway, no shame in that either way. We play the hands we're given, right? You am what you am! You need no excuses. You deal your own deck: sometimes the aces, sometimes the deuces. Dead right!

Where was I? Oh yes. Pyrrhic victories. Let me explain, just in case you skipped class that day.

A long time ago, in a country far, far away, there was a king called Pyrrhus. As Ancient Greek kings go, he was pretty tasty. Gave the emergent Roman Empire a bit of a spanking on more than one occasion. He took no lip off nobody. He was a born winner.

But there was a flaw. Old Pyrrhus, he was a bit over-keen. The way he saw it, winning was all that mattered. Victory had to be pursued – no matter what the cost. Until, after one particularly bloody encounter at a place called Heraclea, his defeat of the Romans was so absolute that it ended up costing him his whole army too. He won the battle, but he also kind of lost. And a certain Mr Plutarch, who was a leading tabloid scribe of the day, coined the term 'Pyrrhic victory' to describe that peculiar kind of victory that comes at a prohibitive cost to the victor.

Interesting, eh? But also, eye-opening. A Pyrrhic victory. Are my letters Pyrrhic victories? It gives me pause. Oooh, and it makes me wonder, as Robert Plant put it. Am I the real loser here? Twicefold? Firstly for giving you so much money for such pitiful service every day, and secondly for wasting my own time in order to waste your time writing about it?

Possibly. I'd welcome your thoughts.

But on the other hand… to hell with it. I'm with Pyrrhus.

Until next time,

Au revoir!

Dan

From: **Martin.Harbottle@premier-westward.com**
To: DantheMan020@gmail.com
Re: 22.20 Premier Westward Railways train from London Paddington to Oxford, June 22.

Dear Dan

Thank you for your email. I feel it's the least I can do to personally offer an apology when your journey home has been delayed.

I fully understand your irritation with your most recent delay. I suspect, however, that you did not realise that the delay was due to a particularly nasty fatality at Hayes and Harlington. It did take some time to reopen the line, partly due to the actions needed after any death on the railway, but also due to the driver having to be relieved from duty due to the trauma.

I am sure there are always things we could do better, and I expect that this was true last night. However, there are times when the circumstances are genuinely outside our control. Clearly last night's incident was not something you could be aware of, nor indeed would our customers have realised quite how difficult the situation was at Hayes.

Although we work closely with British Transport Police and Network Rail to prevent suicides, sadly we are not always successful. Line closures at peak time will lead to long delays due to congestion. We took a number of measures to reduce these, but there was a lengthy period where all trains were stopped and this inevitably caused problems for our customers. Delays then knocked on to later services such as yours.

I am sorry for the inconvenience this caused.

Martin

Letter 9

From: **DantheMan020@gmail.com**
To: Martin.Harbottle@premier-westward.com
Re: 07.31 Premier Westward Railways train from Oxford to London Paddington, June 23. Amount of my day wasted: 18 minutes. Fellow sufferers: Lego Head, Competitive Tech Nerds, Train Girl.

Martin: we've become penpals! We're totally e-buddies. I'm developing a more regular dialogue with you than I have with my own wife. I feel we're getting… intimate.

Guess what? My train this morning, as I scoured the papers for the latest on the worsening situation in North Africa, as I digested the details of the marches and rallies, as I read with increasing scepticism the assertions and proclamations of the men in charge (terrorists, Martin? Can those protestors really all be terrorists? I doubt it), as I made mental tallies of the dead (that bomb in the market place) and the rumoured dead (those shaky YouTube videos, the shuddery figures running away from the men with guns)… my train this morning, as the burnished rooftops of Reading town reflected the rosy-fingered dawn in all its glory outside the grimy windows and Lego Head sat staring into space as usual and the Competitive Tech Nerds talked loudly and without listening to each other about the Web 3.0 (nope, no idea either)… my train this morning was delayed.

What happened? I do hope it wasn't another particularly nasty fatality. I feel bad enough about the last one. And I also (sincerely) hope the driver of the train that hit whoever it was last night is OK. That's a pretty crappy thing to have to deal with and I'm sure you're not paying him enough to do so.

But on the other hand – don't you have contingency plans for such eventualities? I mean: people do jump in front of trains, don't they? They do it quite a lot. Isn't there a system in place, or does the whole flimsy façade crumble and fall away every time it happens?

Perhaps – and I'm no managing director, obviously, so take this with a pinch – but perhaps what you could do is concentrate on running a business that can cope with the occasional emergency. (I say 'occasional' but you know what I mean.) What you could do is put your energies, abilities and (whisper it) budget into making Premier Westward trains the kind of company that doesn't fall apart every time something awkward happens.

Or am I being hopelessly naive again? Am I applying disingenuous tabloid logic onto a very complicated situation?

Oh dear, I've just read this back and realised that now I'm sounding very cross. I'm not generally a cross person. You should see me normally. I'm lovely. I'm a pussy cat. It must be something about your trains that bring out the grumpy old man in me. It must be something about these letters that reveal the person I really am. I did wonder if this would become like therapy, didn't I? Are you really to be my therapist, Martin? Will you be my shrink?

I've got 18 minutes to fill today, and in the absence of anything else to talk about, why not? Let me tell you some more about my life.

I've been thinking: how much of our lives are just a succession of Pyrrhic victories?

You want to afford a comfortable, happy life? Fine: go get a job, work for a living. And the price of doing that is that your job will take up the majority of your time, your life, your happiness.

It's a Pyrrhic victory. Sure, you've got the security, you can provide for your family, you can feed and clothe and shelter the ones you love. But it comes at the price of never really seeing them.

Or take marriage. That's what we all want, isn't it? The Cat Stevens 'find a girl, settle down' thing we talked about before? One true love: that's what every poem, every pop song, every wish wished upon a star since the dawn of forever has been about. Find The One!

And what's the price of finding The One? Real life with The One.

Real life with The One – and knowing there'll never be another one. That's a Pyrrhic victory. It's a win that comes with prohibitively huge losses. Or if not losses, then at least a cost. A big old cost.

Don't get me wrong. I love Beth. I'm in love with Beth. I reckon she really is The One. But we've been together seven years now and the realisation that there'll never be another one is beginning to bite a bit.

Let's say, for example, just hypothetically and all, there was a girl who gets on the same train as me every day, who always stands at the same place on the platform at the same time, who always makes for the same seat on the same carriage, just as I do. And let's say, for example, just hypothetically, that that place and time on the platform and that seat and that carriage all happened to be right next to where I am every day. Let's call her Train Girl, for want of a better name.

So: hypothetically, my instinct is to check her out, right? I mean, she's actually pretty hot. If I were still in the market and on the lookout, I'd say she was definitely my type. She doesn't look much like Beth (bobbed dark hair to Beth's longish blonde locks, perhaps a little curvier to Beth's dancer's physique, a touch softer, more delicate around the eyes and nose compared with Beth's sharper features) but she's still my type.

If I was looking, I mean. If I was checking her out.

Which, of course, I'm not. Because I'm married, and the price, the cost, the Pyrrhic victory of marriage is that you're no longer allowed to check people out. Just as the price, the cost, the Pyrrhic victory of checking out someone other than your wife could be your marriage itself. The consequences are too great. The whole situation's too totally Pyrrhic for words.

Don't get me wrong. Please don't let me be misunderstood! I know it sounds like I want to cheat on my wife, but I don't. I'm just trying to make a point. The price of victory is defeat – in all things. And besides: it's nice to offload on you like this. I feel like if my train delays are going to have any upside to them, at least it might be that I can bore you with the workings of my mind without having to pay a shrink to listen to it all. You're listening because you care about your customers, right? Right!

Oh, hang on! What's the word count? Where are we at?

Ah. I've still got about six minutes to waste, I'm afraid. That's the deal. So. What shall I say? How shall I fill the time?

I know!

Just to reassure you about my marital steadfastness and matrimonial happiness, I'll tell you about how Beth and I met. Would you like to hear that? It's a beautiful tale. It's got everything. A real tear-jerker. An old-school romance. A bonkbuster!

We met eight years ago, in a bar in London's fashionable Central London. I was technically unemployed at the time, writing for a couple of music magazines for cash in hand (when they had some) and signing on to Her Majesty's Dole. I'd not been long out of university, you see: I was still finding my feet in the grown-up world.

Beth was still studying. She had just started her nursing degree, and was sufficiently young, naive and drunk enough to be impressed by my patter. We were introduced by mutual friends: my mate Trev and her friend Claire were seeing each other, and were at that slightly embarrassing stage in their relationship when they want all their friends to become friends with all their other half's friends.

So there we were. Both slightly the worse for wear, in one of those bars where the barmen pretend they're somehow better than the people they're serving – and from the moment we were introduced to the moment we were finally kicked out of the place long after everyone else had left, we didn't talk to anyone but each other.

I won't lie: she was the hottest girl I'd ever met. (And let's not forget, I'm on first name terms with most of the *Hollyoaks* cast.) A few years younger than me, a million times better looking than me, at least as funny and certainly as clever as me… I was properly smitten. She did this thing when she listened to me: her eyes widened. Her pupils actually dilated. You have no idea how much of a turn-on that is.

So, anyway, for the rest of the night, until the chairs were stacked on tables and the glasses were taken away and the uppity bar staff finally lost their tempers and turfed us onto the street, we didn't talk to anyone but each other.

And then… she went back to her place, and I went back to mine. Without so much as a kiss. She went back to her place, and her boyfriend, and I went back to mine, and my girlfriend.

Oh yeah: I had a girlfriend. Surprised? I already told you: I'm not the cheating kind. And evidently, neither was she. Nothing happened that night – nor the next time we saw each other, a few weeks later at Trev's birthday party… except that we talked and talked to each other again all night, and at the end of the night swapped email addresses.

Nothing happened that night or any other night, for a whole year.

But throughout that year, we must have exchanged over 200 emails. Two a week, each, at least. Throughout that year, I must have told Beth more about myself than I'd told my actual girlfriend. Throughout that year, we didn't even meet again. (Trev and Claire split up soon after his birthday. He lacked ambition, apparently. She lacked a willingness to perform certain acts Trev had read about in *FHM*. It was never going to work.)

And then, almost exactly a year after we first met, we met again. I was selling stuff to the nationals by then (and consequently no longer signing on); she was still studying. We were outside another one of those stupid trendy bars in Clerkenwell. We bumped into each other in the taxi queue. Literally. I was drunk and laughing. She was drunk and crying. She'd just split up with her boyfriend.

I'd been single for a month by then. She got into my taxi. And I've never looked at another girl since. (Well, OK, I suppose I have looked at Train Girl, but you know what I mean. I've never *looked* at another girl since.)

Oh dear, Martin. Are you OK? Are you crying? Don't worry! It's OK to cry! I know, I know, it's a beautiful story. But aren't they all, in the beginning? Isn't every story beautiful when it starts? It's what happens next that really matters.

Anyway! Time has caught us. Until the next delay…

Au revoir!

Dan

From: **Martin.Harbottle@premier-westward.com**
To: DantheMan020@gmail.com
Re: 07.31 Premier Westward Railways train from Oxford to London Paddington, June 23.

Dear Dan

Thank you for your email. Our 07.31 yesterday morning was eight minutes late arriving into Oxford after we were held up by rail enthusiasts in Banbury taking pictures of a steam train from beyond the safe part of the platform. This subsequently set us running behind another train, where we incurred an additional ten-minute delay.

Yours sincerely

Martin

Letter 10

From: **DantheMan020@gmail.com**
To: Martin.Harbottle@premier-westward.com
Re: 07.31 Premier Westward Railways train from Oxford to London Paddington, June 28. Amount of my day wasted: three minutes. Fellow sufferers: Train Girl, Lego Head, Universal Grandpa, Guilty New Mum, Competitive Tech Nerds.

Dear Martin

Ooh, it's another small one. They all add up though, right? Like drips in the desert slowly gouging the Grand Canyon, they all add up. The only question is: how shall I waste your time accordingly?

Perhaps by sharing how I spent my wasted time this morning…

Martin: I made a playlist. A mixtape, as those of us who remember *Top of the Pops* might say. I used to make playlists for Beth when we first started going out – a carefully crafted selection of songs that spoke about us, about how I felt about her. I'd spend ages on them, agonising over exactly the order the songs should go in. I've no idea where they are now. I've no idea if she's even kept them, to be honest.

Well, today I've made a mixtape for you. I took all the stations on the local stopping service between Oxford and London Paddington and I put them to music.

And you know what? It wouldn't be a bad album. Perhaps it's something you should look into?

'**Oxford** Comma' – Vampire Weekend
'Truly **Radley** Deeply' – Soundgarden
'Didcot Parkwaylife' – Blur
'I Don't Want to Go to **Cholsey'** – Elvis Costello
'Goring & Streatley Underground' – The Jam
'Pangbourne in the USA' – Bruce Springsteen
'Tilehurst Me Kangaroo Down, Sport' – Rolf Harris
'Red **Reading** Wine' – Neil Diamond
'Twyford a Little Tenderness' – Otis Redding
Anything by Iron **Maidenhead**
'Slough Deep is Your Love?' – The Bee Gees
'Shang-A-**Langley'** – The Bay City Rollers
'Iver Had the Time of My Life' – Bill Medley and Jennifer Warnes
'West Drayton End Girls' – Pet Shop Boys
'Hayes & Harlington You, The Rock Steady Crew' – Rock Steady Crew
'It Never Rains in **Southall** California' – Albert Hammond
'Sexual **Ealing Broadway'** – Marvin Gaye
'Paddington Dogs and Englishmen' – Noel Coward

Think of the franchising opportunities, Martin! I want ten percent of everything…

Au revoir!

Dan

Letter 11

From: **DantheMan020@gmail.com**
To: Martin.Harbottle@premier-westward.com
Re: 21.20 Premier Westward Railways train from London Paddington to Oxford, June 30. Amount of my day wasted: 11 minutes. Fellow sufferers: none that I recognised.

Dear Martin

Have you seen the news today? Oh boy! It's all happening, isn't it? Home and away.

The situation, as they like to say on the BBC, is worsening. Things have become grave. It's getting real. I did wonder how long it would take for it all to kick off properly, over there in North Africa. I did wonder how long it would take before the authorities stopped surreptitiously taking out a few supposed 'terrorists' and just started shooting willy-nilly. I did wonder how long it would be before they stopped pretending to be the good guys and opted instead for old-school horror tactics. That's proper shock and awe. You wanna protest? Fine. BAM BAM BAM. You're dead. And dead men don't protest.

I did wonder how long it would take before the killing began in earnest. You just can't have the squares of your capital filled with people waving flags – not if you're a proper dictator. It's embarrassing, apart from anything else. And so I did wonder how long it would take before it all went a bit horrible.

We all wondered, in the *Globe* newsroom. We had a book running on it, in fact. If only they could have held off another week I'd have made about 200 quid. As it was, my mate Harry the Dog, who also just happens to be deputy foreign editor, scooped the lot. Typical. Another reason not to trust tinpot regimes, eh?

Do you want to know why we call him Harry the Dog? There are a few theories floating around – that his nickname came from the notorious Millwall football hooligan of the same name, that it came from rhyming slang (he's always on the dog and bone), that it came because once he gets his teeth into a story he refuses to let go…

And the answer is: none of the above. Harry the Dog got his nick-name from the children's story. The story of the little dog that got so dirty his owners didn't recognise him any more. That's our Harry. Brought up as Harold by very well-to-do parents, sent to the very best schools, easy possessor of a first-class degree from yer actual Oxford University, tall, blond, louchely handsome, destined for great things, headed for a stellar career in politics, economics… and spurner of all of the above in favour of hacking along at the country's dirtiest, most notorious Sunday newspaper. Harry: drinker, smoker, gambler, shagger, tabloid journalist. Harry: now all-but-disowned by a family who only wanted the best for him. Harry: the dog that got so dirty his parents didn't recognise him any more.

He's a brilliant bloke – in both senses of the word. Brilliant in that he's a genius; but also, he's a brilliant bloke. My best mate and ally against the daily madness of our boss. And now two-ton richer.

Anyway. What was I saying? Oh yes, it's bad out there. What with the indiscriminate killing of peaceful protesters and all. But it's bad in here too. It's looking very bad! That half-wit Scottish crooner, the one with the famously bewigged hair and the refreshingly down-to-earth girlfriend (the same 'refreshingly down-to-earth' girlfriend he's been cheating on, by the way, regularly, methodically, blatantly, outrageously, with every starry-eyed casting-couch candidate or ingenuous young media wannabe he can get his manicured hands on) – he's definitely taking us to court, it seems.

(He's not taking *us* to court, Martin. He's got no beef with you and me. He's fine with us. We're cool, in his book. We're gravy.)

He's taking my employers, the *Globe*, to court. He doesn't like our methods. He doesn't like the way our methods have exposed him as the duplicitous, cheating liar he is. He thinks that by telling the world about his many and varied and predictable and often quite grubby affairs, we've somehow broken the law. And, more worryingly, it would appear that the Crown Prosecution Service agrees with him.

My boss is not a very happy man. His boss is even less so. And *his* boss is furious. And as for *his* boss… she's incandescent. And she only answers to one person. And he is not the kind of man anyone ever wants to see angry.

And, most pertinently for me, all of this anger does not bode well for the little guys, the rank and file. We're the bottom of the food chain, and we're the ones who bear the brunt of the men who bear the brunt of the big men's wrath. It's only a matter of time before they start the shooting too. Or the firing, at least.

It would probably be best if I didn't lose my job. You know, what with the mortgage and the wife and now the baby and all. I got responsibilities! And while I hate having to stand on your terrible trains every morning and evening, while I seethe every time I shell out hundreds of pounds for my monthly season ticket, I nevertheless don't want to find myself stuck in Oxford, at home and out of work.

I'll be honest, with you (I'm always honest with you!), things aren't exactly peachy at home. Beth's not happy. She's depressed, in fact. Postnatally so. A doctor told her. All that lethargy and listlessness, all those fuzzy-brained mornings in front of Jeremy Kyle and dreaded nights trying to get Sylvie back to sleep; all those zombie walks in the pre-dawn hours with wailing baby at her breast, struggling to latch on, struggling to go down, struggling to bring up wind… it's made Beth depressed.

I don't know if you're familiar with postnatal depression (do you have kids? How old are they?) but, basically, it's a proper ache. Because there's not much that can actually be done. Sylvie's not going anywhere. Sylvie's needs remain the same (constant, unrelenting). And when it comes to just about everything apart from the odd nappy and the occasional winding, I'm not really able to help. I've got to go to work to earn the money to pay for the nappies. I've got to get more than four hours' sleep a night so I can manage to actually do the work to earn the money to pay for the nappies. It's a vicious circle. There's nothing I can really do.

What can I do? Not about the North African thing, and not about the paper being taken to court thing (both are regrettably out of my hands) but about the postnatal depression thing. If you've got kids, tell me: what can I do? Don't tell me this one's out of my hands as well.

Oh – there's another thing, too. Before I forget. My trains. Your trains! They're not getting any better, are they? Another 11-minute delay to my journey home tonight. As if the slaughter and the suing and the miserable wife wasn't enough. I'm not getting home until half-ten anyway – and now you've bunged on another ten minutes on top of that. You're totally, as Shaun Ryder so eloquently put it, twisting my melons, man.

Au revoir!

Dan

From: **Martin.Harbottle@premier-westward.com**
To: DantheMan020@gmail.com
Re: 21.20 Premier Westward Railways train from London Paddington to Oxford, June 30.

Dear Dan

I am sorry to hear that you have been delayed again. It's really not good enough and you have every right to be angry. The 07.31 on June 28 was subject to mechanical issues and the 21.20 service from Paddington on June 30 was late arriving into the station and so subsequently late leaving the station again. I hope this helps ease your frustration a little.

To answer some of your other questions, yes, I have two children, both (thankfully!) grown up and at university now. I well remember the sleepless nights and endless nappy changes though!

Although I wouldn't claim to be any kind of expert on postnatal depression, I can tell you that after the birth of our first, my wife found the support of friends with babies who were in a similar position to hers to be very helpful. Perhaps your GP might be able to put her in touch with other new mothers?

I am also sorry to hear about the situation at your work. I must admit, to the casual observer, it does seem that certain sections of the press have overstepped the mark on occasion. It's interesting to learn of the crooner in question's colourful love life, however! Has this been reported?!

Best

Martin

Letter 12

From: **DantheMan020@gmail.com**
To: Martin.Harbottle@premier-westward.com
Re: 21.48 Premier Westward Railways train from London Paddington to Oxford, July 7. Amount of my day wasted: 11 minutes. Fellow sufferers: Corporate Dungeon Master.

Martin: it's been a week. No delays for a week. Well done! Outstanding work.

Thank you for your last letter – advice taken on board. Beth saw the doctor this week: she's got a flyer for some baby groups, some coffee mornings and whatnots. She thinks it's all a bit pointless, but like I told her: that's just the depression talking, right? (She didn't think that was very funny. Mental note: don't bother with the black humour and can the dark wit when you're dealing with a postnatally depressed woman. It's really not worth the tears and the apologies.)

Anyway, ta for the advice. We'll see if it perks her up any. Though between you and me, if the baby's making her depressed, I'm not sure that going someplace where there's going to be lots more babies is really going to help. If my dog was making me depressed (I don't own a dog, it's another metaphor. The dog is a metaphor for my baby. But not in a bad way, obviously. I'm not comparing my baby to a dog! What kind of monster do you think I am?) – if my dog was making me depressed, you wouldn't advise me to hang out at a dog show, would you?

If, say, sitting on trains was making me depressed (which, to be honest, it is), then you wouldn't recommend I catch more trains, would you? Would you? Actually, perhaps you would. Perhaps I'm asking the wrong man on that one.

Anyway. She's going to take little Sylvie to a baby group today. There's another tomorrow. We'll see if sharing the pain helps.

But enough about me. It's a bog-standard-length delay today – and what with the only other evening regular being Corporate Dungeon Master tonight (mid-forties, pin-stripes, thinning hair slicked back, actual briefcase containing immensely powerful-looking laptop on which he plays role-playing games all the way home; from what I can gather, surreptitiously glancing over the aisle or at the reflection in the window in front, his character would appear to be a barbarian wizard. I'm not entirely certain, but I think the game's called Ragnarok. Either way, I'm not sure how much he actually enjoys it as every journey seems to involve a steady stream of swearing at the other characters on his screen, all those little bare-chested, weapon-wielding avatars running around like headless chickens) – what with it just being me and Corporate Dungeon Master on the train tonight, I'll cut straight to the chase.

You asked me about our litigation-happy singing friend. The crooner and Blue-Mooner. The one with the spectacular syrup and the girl-next-door girlfriend (although they haven't actually had sex in years, take it from me – theirs is a union based on mutually beneficial publicity alone. Love has nothing to do with it). The one with the one massive song two decades ago and that other massive song five years ago and a lot of lucrative nonsense in-between. The one with the roving eye and the wandering hands and the entirely unfussy kilt etiquette. Oh yes. It's all true. And oh no, most of it hasn't been reported. Not because it's not true, but because the truth gets suppressed under injunctions, or super injunctions, or privacy rulings, or a significant 'favour' for the hapless girl who could prove it to be true (sudden celebrity boyfriend, appearance on reality TV, big fat pile of cash), or a significant threat to the hapless girl who could prove it to be true. Or even occasionally because the papers can't prove that it's true without implicating themselves in the process.

It's a tightrope. Finding the truth is the easy bit. Being able to tell the truth is another thing entirely.

Our crooning friend: let's say, for example, that it became known to someone on the news desk that he enjoyed the attentions of a pair of spectacularly young-looking Estonian girls at an establishment known as 'Slavs to Love' in a rather run-down part of London's once-fashionable Pimlico. Let's say it became known because another girl at this establishment was concerned that the two Estonians in question were neither there entirely consensually nor of a legal age to consent to anything that our friend might demand of them.

This is entirely hypothetical, by the way, Martin. You understand that, right? It's all entirely conjecture and I'm making no accusations against anyone. Good.

So: let's say someone from the news desk looks into it. Let's say she finds the girls, confirms that something is very rum indeed and arranges with them to set up a hidden camera and a mic the next time our priapic lounge lizard comes a knockin'.

And what happens next?

Nothing. Slavs to Love is suddenly and mysteriously no more. A police raid. An entirely coincidental police raid the day after our visit. A police raid that came courtesy of an anonymous tip-off. Our girls? Disappeared. Deported. Back to Estonia. The whistleblower who alerted us in the first place? Suddenly spotted out and about on the arm of hot young (gay, as it happens) boy bander Nero Duncan. And she won't return our calls. And Mr Duncan happens to share an agent with... yes, you guessed. I don't need to say any more, do I?

Shocked? It is shocking. And there's plenty more where that came from. There's a file of unprovable but entirely true dirt on the man as heavy as the Stone of Scone. And plenty more like him. No wonder he dislikes us so much. We know what he really is.

But what's this? Our word count has been reached! Fair's fair, you only used up 11 minutes of my and Corporate Dungeon Master's time, and so I'll take up no more of yours. But I'm sure we'll speak again soon.

Au revoir!

Dan

Letter 13

From: DantheMan020@gmail.com
To: Martin.Harbottle@premier-westward.com
Re: 07.31 / 07.52 / 08.06 Premier Westward Railways train from Oxford to London Paddington, July 12. Amount of my day wasted: err... Fellow sufferers: Lego Head, Universal Grandpa, Competitive Tech Nerds.

I'll be straight with you from the start, Martin, I'll level with you from the get-go: I don't know how to handle this one.

The thing is: I didn't even catch one of your trains this morning. I couldn't catch the 07.31 because it was *cancelled*. Why was it cancelled? We were never told. So anyway, undeterred and relentlessly optimistic as always, I stuck around for the 07.52 and guess what? That got cancelled too. We weren't told why about that, either.

When the 08.06 joined them in the by-now oh-so-fashionable cancelled club, I walked. I turned around and walked out of there, all the way to the bus station, where I paid a further £15 and caught a coach to London. I left Lego Head and Universal Grandpa looking serenely confused on the platform – Competitive Tech Nerds had already left, swearing at the useless information boards and talking about catching a taxi together (I think I caught them arguing about whether to get it as far as Reading or to take a chance on Didcot). There was no sign of Train Girl or Guilty New Mum: they must have bailed even earlier.

Don't get me wrong. Obviously I didn't have to catch a coach. I could have stuck it out and stuck around. A nice man at the station did tell me things were likely to get moving by about 8.30, but he couldn't promise. He confessed that he didn't know what was going on either.

Which sort of begs the question: who did know? Somebody must have known! Why didn't the person or people who knew why those three normally packed commuter trains had been apparently inexplicably cancelled, tell some other people, so they could tell the rest of the people in your company, so that those charged with keeping the passengers who pay to use your trains informed about where their trains might be could actually do so?

It's not rocket surgery, is it? It's not brain science.

So, yes, I could have stuck around and taken my chances on things getting moving again by 8.30, but the thing is, even if the nice man at the station was right, the platform was by then already full of (at least) three trains' worth of passengers anyway. The chance of getting a seat would be less than zero. To be honest, I didn't rate my chances of even getting on the thing at all. If it came at all.

So I left. I made like a Tom and cruised. I got me up and got me out. I got the coach, and arrived to work about an hour and a half late.

Do you have any idea how angry that made my boss? We're not talking about the most stable of men at the best of times. We're not talking about the most level-headed, hear-both-sides, judge-not-hastily, slow-to-react kind of man in even the most favourable circumstances. We are, in fact, talking about someone who was always borderline unhinged. A man who was close to the precipice even before all the current legal unpleasantness.

We call my boss Goebbels. That's his nickname. He's proud of it too. He has a reputation for unreasonable behaviour. He once sacked the entire graduate trainee intake (eight fresh-faced kids eager to work 14-hour days for minimal pay for two years just for a shot of a job at the end of it) because one of them refused to strip to her knickers and streak at an England v Sweden match (it was for a story, obviously – the girl in question bore a striking resemblance to an A-level student the England manager had been rumoured to have had an affair with. We couldn't persuade the actual girl herself to do it – the fact that she was 17 made things a bit tricky – but Goebbels thought it would still make a good page lead with a lookalike).

Of course she refused. I'd have refused too, and walked before he could sack me. But it was a bit harsh to sack all the other grad trainees just because of her unwillingness to whip her top off in front of millions and play ball.

He's been known to throw books, telephones, fax machines, computer monitors, once even a chair, at reporters failing to file good copy. He infamously made one of the sub-editors stand all day on a table in the canteen with a dunce's cap on, because he had used a split infinitive in a headline.

He is not, in short, a reasonable man.

And now his job's threatened. Now the police and the Crown Prosecution Service and even hacks from other newspapers are questioning his means, motives and methods – well, now he's gone full-blown psycho.

Turning up an hour and a half late with nothing but some phoned-in excuses about cancelled trains? It cost me a thwack around the head with a 1988 edition of *Who's Who* (a particularly fat year, that year, too. Just thank God it wasn't a hardback copy) and a promise that I would work at least an hour and a half late every night for the rest of the week.

I got off lightly. But my card's marked. There's a blot on the old escutcheon, as Harry the Dog might say.

And, of course, that's not all of it. I've got another problem.

My other problem is, how does this morning's marathon delay square with this pet project of mine? If the length of this email is to reflect the length of my delay, if I'm to waste a proportionate amount of your time (as you have wasted mine), then what do I do about today's sorry situation?

It's a test case, is what it is. It's – as our bewigged adversaries in the legal profession prefer to put it – a precedent. If, for example, I decide that a cancelled train is the equivalent of, say, 30 minutes' delay, then that's how it'll have to be from now on. The precedent will be set.

But does that mean that three cancelled trains require me to bang on for an hour and a half of your time?

I'm not going to bang on for an hour and a half today. To be frank: I don't think I could manage it. I haven't got it in me to keep you stimulated for that long. So I'm going to devise a formula. A secret formula! An equation involving the relative differences between scheduled journey times for the train I should have got and the coach I did get, factoring in an integer representing the cancellation of trains (multiplied by three) and with a little bit added on for the walk from the train station to the bus station. And a little bit taken off for the slightly shorter tube journey at the other end. And then a wordsearch right at the bottom to cover all the extra time I forgot to include in my original calculations.

What did happen this morning? The buzz in the station was that a train broke down. Could that be true? Again? How often does that happen? That trains break down, I mean? What's the lifespan of your average passenger train these days? How often do you replace them? And is that too many questions for one paragraph?

I await the answers with breath firmly baited. Or bated. And in the meantime, I'll leave you with a cheering thought. One ray of sunshine in an otherwise grey and overcast day.

I sat next to a lovely old American gentleman on my coach journey to London this morning. He was over for his holidays. He 'did' the Lake District at the weekend, he 'did' Oxford yesterday and he was 'doing' London today and tomorrow. On Saturday he was off to France to 'do' Paris, before tripping over to Deutschland to 'do' Germany – all of it, mind – on Sunday, Monday and Tuesday. He was one of life's doers. I really liked him. I liked his energy. He was about 85 and he was 'doing' Europe in about ten days. Europe was totally his lobster!

When I grow old I'd like to be like that. The doing bit/Europe being my lobster thing, I mean, obviously. Not the holidaying alone on a coach bit. When I grow old I'd like to be one of life's doers. How about you? Would you like to be a doer someday too?

And in the meantime, and in the absence of any doing to do – I made a wordsearch for you. It's not in the same league as my old dad's were, but it's something. See how many you can find!

Au revoir!

Dan

Wordsearch for Martin

p	i	d	l	a	t	e	d	p	d	y	e	h	s	a
r	f	n	e	n	n	o	r	a	r	n	s	a	l	g
i	s	f	c	l	y	s	a	d	a	y	u	s	o	n
v	s	e	o	o	a	i	w	d	b	n	t	f	w	h
a	s	r	s	p	m	y	t	i	m	n	a	d	e	m
t	s	d	e	u	i	p	s	n	a	o	f	v	a	r
i	e	e	n	m	c	r	e	g	s	e	e	r	f	s
s	n	a	p	a	o	x	w	t	i	r	t	o	t	o
a	e	m	i	r	p	t	e	o	e	i	e	t	p	d
t	r	o	u	b	l	e	s	n	n	n	t	m	e	a
i	o	x	f	o	r	d	y	u	t	e	c	e	n	t
o	e	c	a	r	g	s	i	d	c	e	r	e	i	f
n	g	n	i	d	w	o	r	c	r	e	v	o	t	t
p	r	o	f	i	t	m	a	r	g	i	n	s	l	j
l	a	y	a	r	t	e	b	t	i	c	k	e	t	n

Words to find:
betrayal, customers, dan, delays, disgrace, excuses, incompetence, inept, isambard, late, martin, overcrowding, oxford, paddington, prime, privatisation, profitmargins, refund, ripoff, slow, ticket, trouble, westward.

From: **Martin.Harbottle@premier-westward.com**
To: DantheMan020@gmail.com
Re: 07.31 / 07.52 / 08.06 Premier Westward Railways train from Oxford to London Paddington, July 12.

Dear Dan

I am sorry once again that you have had to write to me. The 21.48 on July 7 was late leaving Paddington due to a problem with the relief driver.

Yesterday we unfortunately experienced widespread disruption to our services in the morning due to vandalism on the line in the Banbury area. The theft of copper wiring is a serious and ongoing problem and one that we are working hard with Network Rail and the British Transport Police to prevent in future.

I am sorry that you felt you had to catch the coach to London, and also sorry that the delay caused problems when you arrived at work. 'Goebbels' sounds a fearsome chap!

Best

Martin

Letter 14

From: **DantheMan020@gmail.com**
To: Martin.Harbottle@premier-westward.com
Re: 21.20 Premier Westward Railways train from London Paddington to Oxford, July 15. Amount of my day wasted: 16 minutes. Fellow sufferers: Overkeen Estate Agent.

Top o' the pops to you, Martin. Phew! What a scorcher! Summer has arrived. Here comes the sun, little darlin'... and I say: it's all right.

Summertime – and the view from the window of one of your delayed trains as the sun sets over England...

London is a beautiful thing, isn't it? Not Tower Bridge or Buckingham Palace or St Paul's Cathedral or any of the other tourist traps, but the real London. The dirty jumble of it. The glorious mess. The triumph of human endeavour and failure and achievement that's written in every building – from the vaulted roof of Paddington Station to the sloppy tower blocks west towards Ealing Broadway. In the purple haze of a summer sunset, it all looks beautiful.

And the train line, Martin – it cuts right through it all. To gaze out of a smeary Premier Westward train window as you arrow west out of the capital is to see a sight you won't find advertised in any visitor brochures (well, maybe in one of yours, but you get the point) but it should be. It should be.

Those great slabs of building either side of the sidings around the

Paddington basin – every window holding its own human story, hidden behind nicotine curtains and pot plants; the brown brutal thrust of the Trellick Tower, burnished by the last of the sun, somehow looking something like its architects must have first imagined it would – like a symbol of hope, of aspiration. The goods yards and building sites and vast car parks of Acton and Southall – in the right light they speak of industry, of work, of progress… of getting things done. And there's nothing so gloriously human as the wonder of getting things done, is there? That's what we're here for: to do things. To get things done.

And then the slow slipping away of the city, the sporadic trees and parks of Hayes, and Drayton and Slough, until beyond – the gentle glory of the English countryside. In the dusk, in the last of the light, over and across and along the looping line of the River Thames towards Oxford. It's beautiful, Martin.

And after the sun had set and the skies had darkened? Well, then there's nothing to look at but your own reflection. Or those of your fellow passengers. Actual humanity. And, of course, actual humanity does tend to break the spell, somewhat.

So it's a sigh, an unscrewing of the cheap wine, an unconscious sniff of the collective sweat and the fractious soundtrack of Overkeen Estate Agent jibber-jabbering endlessly into his white iPhone about 'event horizons' and 'outsourcing the subs bench' and 'making the portfolio wash its own face' and all the various 'legendary' deals he and his 'bros' are setting up.

I'm on this train too much, Martin.

And if you think I'm annoyed about it, you should hear what Beth has to say. She doesn't know I'm writing to you, of course (she'd only laugh at me. She'd only call it a midlife crisis, these rants of mine. She'd think that – and she's supposed to be the depressed one. What does that say?) but she's not at all happy with the hours I'm away every day.

They're not helping the situation at home, let's put it that way. Me never being around, I mean. They're not helping convince my postnatally depressed wife that there is more to her life than attending to the every whim of the baby. They're not helping her believe that there was any point in marrying me at all actually, when we barely see each other, and less still when we're both awake.

They're not helping her believe that her life is in any way better now than it was before she married me.

All she does, she says, is feed, burp and change. Feed, burp and change. Her life is broken up into three-hour segments, 180-minute chunks, eight of them a day, during which she feeds, burps and changes the baby. Milk, wind and poo. That's all she's about now.

Do you know how long it takes to feed, wind and change a three-month-old baby? Beth reckons it takes about an hour and a half. Which gives her another hour and a half after she's finished before she has to do it all over again. Eight times in every 24-hour day, seven days a week.

She's sleeping in one-hour bursts, every now and then through the day and night. She's eating where and when she can: frantic, gobbled-down, quick microwavable bits of whatever she can get, any ideas of enjoyment or pleasure in food abandoned in favour of simply getting something down her in those brief, blessed moments when Sylvie's not screaming for attention.

Refuelling, that's what she calls it. Not eating. Refuelling. And she's low on fuel. She says she feels like she's constantly running on fumes. Like she can only put enough gas in the tank to get her through the next few miles.

And all the time, the constant, deafening, relentless, ear-piercing, heart-piercing, soul-piercing crying. The perpetual wail of the three-month-old; and the perpetual sobs of her mother. Neither seem to stop for very long. They're driving me crazy and I'm hardly ever even there.

So where am I? Where am I when all this is going on? I'm at work, mostly, or travelling to and from work, or sitting on one of your delayed trains fretting about it all. I'm barely at home for eight hours in every 24. Monday to Friday I'm around for two, maybe three, of those feed–wind–change routines. And always in the middle of the night, when normal people are sleeping.

Through the week I do try to help: doing the midnight shuffle with the screaming bundle, shushing and cooing and pacing the same six paces across the bedroom floor, up and down, down and up, shush, shush there, shhhhh… I put in what hours I can. But I can't breastfeed. Beth's still got to get up to do that. And I do need to get up and function at work the next day. We've got a mortgage to pay. I can't work all day and stay up with Sylvie all night.

Weekends are easier. For Beth, I mean. Weekends she'll at least sleep more, waking only to hoik her nightie down or pull her pyjama top up, latching Sylvie on half-comatose, mechanically, somnambulantly, refuelling her, filling her up, giving her the necessary, before her little flushed face finally turns away, lips still pursed like the tiniest rosebud, white drops like dew on them, and Beth will hand her back to me without a word and collapse back into bed and sleep again.

And despite it all – I can't help myself – I'll find myself thinking: is that the loveliest sight in the world? Is that the most beautiful thing I'll ever see in my life? And then the rosebud lips will tighten and widen, and the eyes will screw up into angry knots, and Sylvie will start with the screaming again.

Christ, it's hard, isn't it? How do people do it? Beth and I – we spend most of our time thinking: this can't be how it should be done. This doesn't make sense at all. There must be an easier way, there must be something we're missing here… After millions of years of evolution, we still have to go through this? Science and nature and the human race hasn't come up with anything better than this?

Not that we actually discuss it or anything. Not that we ever actually talk or anything. When I'm around, then I'm on the Sylvie shift, and Beth grabs the chance to do her own thing (sleep). She's not going to waste valuable sleeping time actually talking to her husband or anything. And even if she were to, I'd only be telling her about work, about my increasingly unhinged boss, about the culture of paranoia and fear that's beginning to creep into the place. About how we're all getting a bit worried this whole scandal might not blow over after all.

She's depressed enough already. No point in having her worry about me on top of it all, right?

Although there is one silver lining: at least she's no longer at home all day. The baby groups seem to be working. A bit. She's gone along three times now. She's making (tentative) friends at least. She's no longer spending all day every day feeling her mind turn to mush in front of *Antiques Hunt* and *Murder She Wrote*. If it's a comfort to the miserable to have companions in their misery, then perhaps she's getting something out of it, at least.

And in the meantime, I just get on with it. I just get on with work and travel and the utter weirdness of home life (it's no life really. It certainly doesn't feel like married life, much). I just get on with it and don't burden my depressed wife with the details.

And instead… I burden you with the details! Sorry about that.

Still. Tomorrow's Saturday. Last day of the working week for me. A day off for you. How will you be spending your weekend? As if I needed to ask! You'll be at Silverstone, right? On another corporate jolly. The British Grand Prix. Zoom! Zooooom! More champagne! More *petits fours*! More hobbing and nobbing with all your other managing director chums! What super fun!

Is it exciting? The Grand Prix, I mean. All that engineering. All that technology. All that speed. Do you look at that engineering, that technology, that speed and ever think, we could use some of that here? No? Oh well. Enjoy the fizz, eh?

Au revoir!

Dan

From: **Martin.Harbottle@premier-westward.com**
To: DantheMan020@gmail.com
Re: 21.20 Premier Westward Railways train from London Paddington to Oxford, July 15.

Dear Dan

Thank you for your email yesterday. You can be assured I value all feedback on our service.

Unfortunately the 21.20 was delayed outside Southall due to problems caused by the sudden hot weather. I hope the situation is resolved now.

Best

Martin

Letter 15

From: **DantheMan020@gmail.com**
To: Martin.Harbottle@premier-westward.com
Re: 07.31 Premier Westward Railways train from Oxford to London Paddington, July 21. Amount of my day wasted: five minutes. Fellow sufferers: Train Girl, Guilty New Mum, Lego Head.

Just a short one today, Martin! A welcome change for both of us, after the lengthy ravings of my last few missives. A breath of fresh air in this stifling heat, this heatwave, this hot, hot summer we're having.

This is the summer, isn't it? It's been a week now, this heat. That makes it summer, all right. A week's unbroken sun? That makes it a memorable summer. That makes it a classic. A loooong hot one! Snappers will be dispatched to Brighton Beach to catch candid shots of sun-soaking lovelies. Should it continue for another week, the records will tumble. The old 'since records began' phrase will be wheeled out in the *Sunday Globe* newsroom. (Incidentally: do you know when records actually did begin? It was only, like, a century ago. It's not that impressive, is it? The hottest July since women got the vote! The hottest July since the invention of the toaster!)

Anyway. It's still hot, that's the point. I do hope you've managed to adapt to the unexpected conditions. I do hope you won't continue to be caught out by the 'sudden' heat.

I'll tell you one thing, though. It's not all bad, this heat. It has its upsides. The girls! The girls in their summer clothes. The bare legs, and bare arms, and bare shoulders. The crop tops and micros and minis. The toning and tanning… even Train Girl's at it. The best-looking person on the morning commute looks even better than before. Her business suit seems notably skimpier. Her business skirt is definitely shorter. It almost makes one happy for a slight lengthening of the scheduled journey time. Almost.

Not that I'm looking. But like Harry the Dog says: it doesn't matter where you get your appetite, so long as you eat at home. Right? Right.

Besides. My thoughts are on higher things than checking out the chicks in their ever-decreasing hemlines. I'm above all that bare flesh, all that sudden skin. I'm all about the news. The real news, I mean, not the tittle-tattle I write about. The serious stuff.

It's getting worse, isn't it? The North African situation. It's headed for civil war. Take it from me. Take it from Harry the Dog, who knows about these things.

On the one side, the old dictator, funny headgear and ludicrous, medal-bedecked outfit still intact. On the other, a raggedy uprising with no discernible leader leading them. And in the middle, the army. Which way will the army swing?

This is what happens when nobody listens, isn't it? This is what happens when nobody learns. And nobody is learning. Nobody's looking at the bigger picture. The whole region's about to go up like a petrol bomb and nobody in charge can see it.

I tell you what, Martin. I'll tell you— Oh, hold up. No I won't! Not right now, anyway. Look at the time! It's time to say *au revoir*.

Au revoir!

Dan

Letter 16

From: **DantheMan020@gmail.com**
To: Martin.Harbottle@premier-westward.com
Re: 07.31 Premier Westward Railways train from Oxford to London Paddington, July 26. Amount of my day wasted: 18 minutes. Fellow sufferers: Train Girl, Lego Head, Guilty New Mum, Competitive Tech Nerds.

Hey hey, you're the Martin! People say you Martin around! But you're too busy singing, to— What's that you say? You don't think that's working? Martin/Monkee? No? Oh, suit yourself then.

No matter. Because I'm in a good mood today! Nothing's gonna bring me down. Not the fact that things at home are still too weird for words, not the fact that my wife and I still continue to live like two strangers in the same house, passing our baby between us while the other sleeps (her) or works (me). Not the fact that full-blown civil war has indeed begun in North Africa. (It was the tanks that did it, in the end. Those two tanks – and the moment that one turned on the other. When the turret slowly swung around. When that single tank broke ranks. When it stopped rolling towards the crowds with the others; when it stopped, and paused, and the turret swung slowly around. That was the moment that did it. That was the moment the army split in two and civil war began. It was just about the maddest thing I've ever seen on the ten o'clock news. And captured brilliantly, I might add, on pages six and seven of last Sunday's *Globe*.)

None of it's bringing me down today though. Not even the fact that you've delayed my journey to work again. Not even that you did so by 18 minutes.

No! Screw all that! I'm in a good mood today. I'm in a good mood because two brilliant things have happened to me since last I wrote. Two totally egocentric things. Two of those all-important boosts to the old self-esteem that confidence players like myself need in order to perform.

I got the splash! My first splash! I only went and knocked those rebellious North African tank commanders off the front page of the most-read English-language Sunday newspaper in the world. I only went and bumped the dead bodies and the bloodshed to pages six and seven. The splash! My name all over pages one, four and five of the *Sunday Globe*.

Did you see it? Did it scream out of the newsstands at you on Sunday morning, in black and white and red on top? OOPSY DAISY! KING OF DRIBBLE IN IGGLE PIGGLE PICKLE!

What a story! 'Premier League crook Jamie Best was exposed last night as a compulsive thief – with a bizarre addiction to stealing cuddly characters from the children's TV show *In The Night Garden*. Light-fingered striker Best, 24 – on a reported £100,000 a week salary – said: "I don't know what comes over me. They're just so cute. Iggle Piggle's my favourite. But I feel gutted now. Sick as a parrot."'

What an intro! What a scoop! Are you proud of me?

I got the tip late Friday – someone at a Manchester branch of Toys R Us who reckoned he had England's Number 9 on CCTV. I was the only one still on the desk – I took the call, I claimed the tip, and so I was the one who got the job.

I was on the last train out of Euston (not one of your trains, no offence) and first thing Saturday morning I was watching it myself, in grainy black-and-white but unmistakeably the boy with the golden boots, open-mouthed, notebook out, chequebook ready. It was a story – it was a story all right. But it wasn't a splash – not yet, not without Jamie himself.

And do you know what happened then? Just as I am about to name a price and take a copy of the footage back to London with me, I only get a nudge from the kid who called me in the first place. He's jumping up and down. He's buzzing like a mobile phone. He's so excited he can barely speak. And he's pointing at the monitors. At the ones showing the live feed, at what's happening in the store right now. And there he is! England's Jamie Best, handsome and tall in his designer threads and plumped-up quadruple-Windsor knot, sauntering down the aisles to the pre-school section!

He doesn't even have kids!

One sharpish text to Goebbels back at the office ('story big, send snapper, more to follow'), and I was out of there like a whippet, like a young Maradona, showing blistering pace, with the kid from security hot on my tail. And as we streaked down to intercept the boy Best, we talked tactics.

It was a classic move. We sprung the old inside-out, the onside-offside trap. The give-and-go. Security hung back, out of sight, behind our man's back… and I took up a position on the wing, off the ball as it were, but close enough to see his every move.

It worked like a dream. I watched England's hottest young prospect in 20 years hoover up Iggle Piggles and Upsy Daisys and Makka Pakkas. I witnessed him shovel in armloads of Tombliboos and fistfuls of Pontipines. I saw the precocious Boy Wonder fill his bag with Ninky Nonks and Pinky Ponks. It wasn't shoplifting: it was theft on a grand scale, every bit as audacious and extraordinary as the 30-yard screamer against Italy that marked his England debut just eight or so months ago. And if his goal that day filled me with wonder and joy and heart-bursting belief in the future of this country, Jamie Best's performance in the aisles of Toys R Us on Saturday made me feel a million times better.

After that it was easy. A tap on the shoulder, an introduction, a flash of the press card, a nod towards the security guard and the offer of a deal. My heart was hammering and I felt sick with terror at what I was about to do… but I kept my voice calm, I kept my gaze steady, I held my nerve. I did it all by pretending to be Harry the Dog.

Talk to me now, Jamie, I said, tell me everything I want to hear. Lay it all out in heartfelt detail, in sentimental, remorseful, sincere tones, in the simplest, most easily understood terms. Fess up to the crime. Give me the skinny on every cuddly toy you've taken and every children's plaything you've pinched. Don't spare a single detail.

And then, tell me and my eight million readers about the terrible pressure you've been under, about your troubled childhood, about your need to get professional off-the-pitch help. Plead with us to show you some compassion, to let you get your head together so you can get back to doing what you do best for club and country next season. Pose for the photos, promise us the exclusive follow-up chat in a week's time and another after that should it ever happen again…

Do all that for me, Jamie, play ball, give the *Globe* everything you've got – and I think I can persuade my boy in the uniform over there, and the other lads watching in the security office, to do the decent thing and not press charges. I think I can convince them that the best and most compassionate thing to do would be to let you seek the help you need, on your terms, and not according to the ruling of some judge in some crown court. I think I can leave the police out of it, pretty much.

What do you say, Jamie?

Oh, and we need to have this chat right now. (I need to file my copy by three p.m.) The snapper's on his way. He'll meet us at my hotel. And you need to not tell a soul until the first editions hit the stand tomorrow morning. And then not talk to any other papers about it. Not ever. Or at least not until we say it's OK.

Are we cool with that, Jamie? Are we game?

Of course we were cool with that! He never stood a chance. I took England's Jamie Best on, and I totally *owned* him. It was a stellar performance. Textbook tabloid journalism. A classic. I nearly threw up with relief when he nodded and followed me out of the shop.

(Goebbels, needless to say, was over the moon. A proper scoop, willingly and lawfully obtained. When I called him, when I breathlessly filled him in on developments in the cab on the way back to my Travelodge, with a frowning, furious, terrified Jamie Best sitting next to me, taking in every word, he sounded so happy he could have cried. I swear if he'd been there he would have kissed me.)

After that it was easy. Autographs for the boys in security, autographs for me and the photographer and Goebbels and Harry the Dog back in London, contracts hastily drawn up and emailed over and signed, two hours of chat, another half-hour of pictures, hand-shakes all round and Jamie got back to his club in time for training. And I sat at my desk in my Travelodge with my laptop, shaking – literally shaking – as I bashed out the copy.

So did you see it on Sunday morning? Did you splutter into your cornflakes? My name, right there on the front page of the *Globe*. And better than that: my photo! A page one picture byline! That's about as good as it gets, in my filthy trade.

Did you see it? I'll tell you who did see it. Because that's the other reason I'm in such a sunny mood on this beautiful sunny day.

You remember Train Girl? The only good thing about the 07.31 from Oxford to London Paddington? The girl with the bobbed dark hair and the soft eyes and the winningly short business skirts just now? The girl I always see at the same spot on the platform, who always sits in the same seat opposite me in Coach C every day? The girl I've never actually spoken to but have, um, noticed?

Today, she didn't sit in her usual seat opposite me. Today she sat down next to me. She sat down next to me in that too-short skirt and bare legs, and she spoke to me.

She pulled out a copy of Sunday's *Globe*. She'd saved it to show me! She smoothed it out, put it on my lap, pointed at my picture byline and said: 'It is you, isn't it? I *knew* it was you!' And she burst out laughing. In a good way. And then we talked, all the way to London. And she's funny. Funny and smart and quick. And it was nice to actually have a conversation with a girl that didn't revolve around how unhappy she is or how difficult everything is or how if only I was around more/listened more/cared more then perhaps her life wouldn't be so rubbish. It was nice to make a girl laugh again. It was really nice.

And I hardly looked at her legs at all. Even when she bent over to pick up her ticket from the floor and her skirt hitched right up at the back. I hardly even paid any attention at all to how smooth her skin seems to be. Because I'm married, right? Because – as we've already discussed – I'm not that kind of person.

It was nice to make a friend. Good old Jamie Best and his odd cuddly-toy-centric peccadilloes. Jamie Best and his Iggle Piggle pickle! He's given me my finest career moment and he's made me a new friend.

(Sadly, he hasn't managed to make the trains run on time. But he is only one man. And, believe it or not, and don't take this the wrong way and get any funny ideas, for once I welcomed the delay. Eighteen minutes extra chatting to Train Girl this morning? It flew by!)

Au revoir!

Dan

From: **Martin.Harbottle@premier-westward.com**
To: DantheMan020@gmail.com
Re: 07.31 Premier Westward Railways train from Oxford to London Paddington, July 26.

Dear Dan

Thank you for your letters of 21 and 26 July. I'm sorry to hear that once again our service has not been up to the standard I expect. The five-minute delay on the 21st was due to minor congestion and the lengthier delay on the 26th occurred because of the late arrival of a driver to another service in the Reading area. Unfortunately that left that particular service stuck on the platform – which then impacted upon a wide number of other services, yours included.

On unrelated matters, I'm afraid I don't take generally take the *Sunday Globe* as a rule, though I have been known to pick it up on occasion. I am very pleased to hear that you scored a 'scoop' however and I do hope it makes things a little easier for you at work. I am more of a rugby than a footer fan myself, but I also hope Mr Best receives the professional help he so clearly needs. He would seem to be a very troubled young man.

Best regards

Martin

Letter 17

From: DantheMan020@gmail.com
To: Martin.Harbottle@premier-westward.com
Re: 20.50 Premier Westward Railways train from London Paddington to Oxford, July 27. Amount of my day wasted: nine minutes. Fellow sufferers: Corporate Dungeon Master.

Martin, I've been thinking again.

What you want to do is take inspiration from the people of North Africa. Look south. Look beyond Paddington station and over Europe and into the streets and the squares of North Africa. There's change afoot. There's a revolution going on – and for once, it looks like the good guys are winning.

It's inspiring, isn't it? It only takes a spark. It only takes a moment to change everything about everything.

We've got another sweepstake running in the *Sunday Globe* newsroom. This war will be over by Christmas? Forget that: this war will be over by Halloween. (Although I'm not sure they celebrate either Christmas or Halloween down there.) When will this war be over? You know where I've put my money? I've put £50 on this war being over by the August Bank Holiday. I've put half a ton of my hard-earned on this war being over by the Reading Festival. They'll be dancing on top of those tanks before September – you watch.

And if that's not inspiring enough for you, take a look at the streets of Athens! Have a butchers at the piazzas of Naples! Get yourself an eyeful of what's going down in Seville and Murcia! The people are taking control again. There's agitation. Aggravation. There's anticipation of change. Strikes and barricades, marches and demonstrations: all across southern Europe.

What are they getting up and angry about in our holiday hotspots? Who cares? Isn't it enough that they are at all? Taxes, unemployment, corruption, student rights, agricultural policies… whatever. The point is that they're putting down their cappuccinos, they're abandoning their kebabs, they're spurning their siestas and they're shouting about it. They're trying to make a change. They're trying to make a *change*.

Still not inspired? OK, try this. How's this for a tale of changing fortunes? You can keep your civil wars and revolutions, you can pooh-pooh your populist uprisings – this one's a doozy. This one came straight out of left field.

It's about me.

It seems I'm the man these days. At work, I mean. (I'm not the man at home. I mean, I am the man, the only man in the house, the only one of the three of us there with a Y chromosome – but I'm still not the man. I'm still the one to blame for everything, back at home.)

But at work… at work, I'm the man. Since my adventures with England's Number 9, I'm the new darling of the news desk. It may even be that my days of non-bylined NIBs (News In Briefs, Martin, do keep up) might be numbered. It may even be that all those hours I spend getting the stories and standing up the stories, only to hand the stories over to someone more senior, might be over.

Goebbels is practically in love with me right now. It seems my scoop has eased the heat on him a little. Sales were up on Sunday, every news channel and Monday paper followed our lead, and for the first time in months, people stopped talking about us as a scandal-hit rag, or a shamed tabloid, or a crumbling empire, and remembered what it is we actually do. And that made everyone happy.

So Goebbels has gone all sweet for me. It seems I can do no wrong in the misty eyes of the deranged old psychopath. He even wants to take me out to lunch. (I say lunch – there's unlikely to be any actual eating involved. In the best Fleet Street traditions that men like Goebbels were spawned from, 'lunch' means 'pub'. And only women and children eat in pubs, right?)

Goebbels taking out a junior showbiz writer for lunch? It's unprecedented. It's unheard of. It's, frankly, unbelievable. It's about as predictable as a civil war in North Africa, about as rare as a pan-Mediterranean protest. And it's certainly as exciting as both. (Well, for me, anyway.)

I'll let you know what he says. I'll let you know what comes of it all. But in the meantime, stay tuned – and hey! Don't get so down on yourself! So my train was nine minutes late home tonight: that's better than the 18 minutes it was delayed yesterday, right? That's twice as good.

Au revoir!

Dan

From: **Martin.Harbottle@premier-westward.com**
To: DantheMan020@gmail.com
Re: 20.50 Premier Westward Railways train from London Paddington to Oxford, July 27.

Dear Dan

Many thanks for your letter and thank you for your encouraging words. Although your service on July 27 was unfortunately a victim of an incident involving the disturbance of a badger sett in the Taplow area, it is reassuring to know that it has not put you off continuing to use Premier Westward.

Best

Martin

Letter 18

From: **DantheMan020@gmail.com**
To: Martin.Harbottle@premier-westward.com
Re: 21.18 Premier Westward Railways train from London Paddington to Oxford, August 3. Amount of my day wasted: 14 minutes. Fellow sufferers: Corporate Dungeon Master.

Dear Martin

What about you, big man? Are you well? Are you good? (Don't you just hate it when you ask someone how they are and they reply 'good'? I'm not asking after your moral health. I don't care if you're good or bad. Or even, as Corporate Dungeon Master's little on-screen alter-ego would appear to be, 'Chaotic Neutral'. I was enquiring about your physical and mental wellbeing. Are you well? Or unwell?)

I hope you're well. Both physically and mentally. I hope you're in a better state (physically, mentally and most likely morally) than the company you're supposed to be running, at least.

As for me, I'm OK, thank you. You know, mustn't grumble. Work is still going well, at least. I'm still the news desk's golden child. Did you see the paper on Sunday? Three bylined pieces! (Plus all my usual guff, the stuff that doesn't get my name attached to it, the titbits and teasers and gossipy asides.) Goebbels is still smiling at me. Creepy though that is.

And there's the England match to look forward to. I'll be working Saturday afternoon of course, but I'll have the radio on. The first England match of the season. Against the European champions, too. How will our plucky lads fare against the continental pass masters? How will our gritty determination play out against their silky skills? All eyes will be on Jamie Best. All of England will be looking towards the troubled young striker and sometime soft-toy kleptomaniac…

I, personally, cannot wait. It will be a match to savour, one way or the other. Will you be there? In your box at Wembley, quaffing Chianti and eyeing up the prawn sandwiches? Of course you will. England expects!

But, you know, it's not all wine and roses, is it? Nothing ever is. What's that we were saying about Pyrrhic victories? Work, for example, is going well – but it's coming at a cost, of course.

I hate to keep asking your childcare advice, but do you ever cease arguing, once you become parents? Do you ever stop it with the nagging and the sniping and the snapping? Do you ever get back to how things were before the birth, when you used to enjoy talking to each other?

And so we have these arguments, over and over and over and over (like a monkey with a miniature cymbal, as someone smarter than me once put it) and the end result is always the same: I don't understand. And she's always crying. And I feel frustrated and angry and misunderstood, but also like a bully and a bad husband and a bad man. And it breaks my heart.

I don't want to be a bully and a bad husband and a bad man. I don't want to argue with Beth. Why would I want to do that? I want to help her. I love her. I want it to be like it was before, when we never argued, when we spent most of our time laughing, when we could make fun of each other without immediately taking offence, taking it personally, taking it the wrong way. I want to come home and have her happy that my career looks like it might be going somewhere.

And instead… take my scoop. Take the weekend's adventures, my moment of triumph, my big break. What was my wife's reaction? A weak 'Well done' and a week's worth of resentment. It's all very well for me to go off gallivanting to Manchester chasing stupid footballers, you see – but some people have to stay at home and look after our baby. It's all very well for me to drop everything at a moment's notice to go enjoy myself writing about celebs – but some of us have to live in the real world, the world of feeds and nappies and endless exhaustion.

My Sunday scoop: the way you'd hear it in my house, you'd think it was an entirely selfish act. Can you credit it?

Oh, and now I feel worse. Because now I've read this letter back to myself and it sounds like I hate Beth. I don't. I love her. It's just… I wish I wasn't always in the wrong. I wish she'd appreciate what I have to go through too.

It makes me wonder what they talk about at these baby groups she goes to. (Three times a week now.) She's made friends there, which is great, obviously, a couple of older mums I know from sight, one on her third and the other on her second, living proof that it must get better, that people must go back for more of the same; plus some single dad type from up Jericho way, where the houses are nicer and the pubs are all 'bars' and the shops are all 'delis'.

He's a *Guardian* reader, apparently. Just him and his baby boy in an end-of-terrace. With basement and loft-conversion, natch. No doubt tastefully decorated in stripped pine and neutral colours and a hint of the exotic. Just him and his baby boy… oh – and the cleaner three times a week, obviously.

Seems he got disillusioned with working in the city and now freelances for charities. No idea where the mother is. (Part of me wonders if she got sick of the sheer smugness of it all: you see his type round Oxford a lot – sipping on their fairtrade lattes and rustling their *Guardians* and banging on about the shanty towns and slums of New Delhi and Buenos Aires, talking earnestly of their internet campaigns and letters to the editors of worthy magazines nobody actually reads, and all the while sitting on mortgage-free half-a-million-quid houses and planning to send their kids to public schools.)

Let's just say he's not my type. He's rugby more than football, if you know what I mean. He probably even calls it 'footer'. (No offence, Martin.) He's not the sort of person I would choose to hang out with, but of course I'd never say that to Beth. It's great she's got a friend. Good for her.

But I can't help wondering, great though it is she's got someone to talk to during the day… what is it they actually talk about? We never talk, not in a meaningful way. What is it my wife and the other mums, my wife and the single dad (let's call him Mr Blair. It's not his name but I can't help thinking it suits) actually talk about?

Does she laugh, when she's with Mr Blair? Does he make her laugh? Does she listen to tales of his work? Is she impressed by them? Is she interested in what he has to say?

Would you believe me if I told you I hope he does make her laugh? Because, believe it or not, I do hope he does. I don't want her to forget how to laugh completely, you know.

Oh dear. I'm sorry. What a downer of a letter! And after all the excitement of my last letter too. I promise to make the next one better. I promise to keep my woes to myself. Next time I'm delayed, Martin, I shall stick to talk of trains. You have my word.

And enjoy the match! Come on England! Come on Jamie Best!

Au revoir!

Dan

From: **Martin.Harbottle@premier-westward.com**
To: DantheMan020@gmail.com
Re: 21.18 Premier Westward Railways train from London Paddington to Oxford, August 3.

Dear Dan

Please accept my apologies for the late running of the 21.18 yesterday. The train was held up due to a strange sound being heard underneath one of the coaches after it arrived at Slough. Subsequent investigation proved it to be a false alarm, but the train was unable to make up the time lost before it reached Oxford.

I am also sorry to hear things continue to be difficult at home. The first months after the birth of a child do place enormous strain on a couple, and clearly the long hours necessitated by your career don't help. In my experience (for what it's worth) there is little to be gained by arguing with your wife, no matter how unjust you feel any accusations might be. As I'm sure you appreciate, she is in a very heightened emotional state, with all sorts of hormones flying around her body, and as such may say things that she would not mean otherwise.

I remember clearly my own wife repeatedly threatening to 'take an axe and a can of petrol' to my shed in the early days after the birth of our first. My tactic was simply to shrug and tell her she must do what she thinks best, despite the shed housing my irreplaceable collection of ultra-narrow-gauge vintage replica railway engines. Of course she never carried out her threat. My collection remains safe!

I do sincerely hope things improve at home, but if you want the advice of someone who has been through all that (twice) many years ago, then I would suggest you simply stick it out. It does get easier!

Best

Martin

Letter 19

From: **DantheMan020@gmail.com**
To: Martin.Harbottle@premier-westward.com
Re: 20.03 Premier Westward Railways train from London Paddington to Plymouth, August 6. Amount of my day wasted: 14 minutes. Fellow sufferers: no regulars (Saturday).

How's life treating you, Martin? Crumpets and honey, I hope. Whiskers on kittens and, er, what was it, bright copper kettles? You get the idea, anyway. I hope you're well.

Today's letter, as promised, will stick to the facts. Just the facts, ma'am! I promise not to bore on about my boring home life. Today, we're going to get back to our roots, back to our original *raison d'être*, back to the real reason we're here. Today, Martin, we talk of trains!

But first… today's letter is going to need a little explanation. Some clarification. You'll observe from the lines above that I caught the Plymouth train last night. I didn't go to Plymouth last night. (Why would I want to go to Plymouth? What is there in Plymouth anyway? Apart from Plymouth Hoe, I mean. And the National Marine Aquarium. And the National Armada Memorial, the Mayflower Steps, Crownhill Fort and Smeaton's Tower. And of course Home Park, stamping ground of Plymouth Argyle Football Club and a veritable am-dram venue of dreams. But apart from that, really, what is there in Plymouth?)

So I didn't go to Plymouth.

What I did do was go to Reading. (Again.) What I did do was try to be clever.

Now I know what you're going to say. You're going to say exactly what Mr Morrison, my old head of Sixth Form and as fine a chap as one might ever encounter, said. He said: 'You're clever, Daniel, but you're not as clever as you think you are. And if your cleverness doesn't get you in trouble, your lack of cleverness will.' Pretty deep, eh? He was a deep guy.

And guess what? He was right, too! It's only taken about 15 years, but bless me if the old feller wasn't proved on the money in the end! Here's how, and listen closely, it's a properly fascinating tale. And we've got 14 minutes to waste together in the telling…

So. Last night, I got out of work early. I was out by seven. On a Saturday. Amazing. It seems I'm still the darling of the news desk. I'm still in Goebbels' good books (we're lunching (drinking) next week. There's talk of promotion. There's talk of putting me on the fast track once all this unpleasantness with the high court dies down. Once that crooner sees sense and shuts up, once the other celebs stop bleating and the police stop sniffing around and the other newspapers get back in their boxes. Things are looking up!)

Still buoyed by an impressive England performance (to hold on for a draw like that, after the boy Best's early dismissal, was impressive. To dig in as they did, after the tempestuous Number 9 was sent for an early bath, showed real grit) I headed west with head held high.

And having just missed the 19.50 (one word: tourists. Actually, eight words: tourists standing still in front of ticket barriers. And escalators. Ten words, then) I looked at the timetables, I did a few quick mental calculations, I weighed up the options, balanced the probabilities, bounced around the maths, crossed the i's and dotted the t's and made what I thought was a clever decision.

I decided to hop on the 20.03 to Plymouth, jump out at Reading at exactly the allotted time it was due to arrive there (according to your timetable) of 20.32 and then, after a merry skip up the escalators, over the footbridge and down the steps to Platform 7, leap gaily onto the 20.41 to Birmingham New Street, due in to Oxford at 21.05.

Brilliant! And, with the bonus of having to only endure a Premier Westward train for half my journey home.

Oh, can you imagine the sheer scale of self-congratulation that was happening in my tiny mind last night? Can you? I all-but-swaggered on to that train, so confident was I that I'd finally cracked the system. After all, with nine minutes to spare at Reading, I was assured of making that connection, right? Right?

Wrong.

I blame myself. I was obviously too clever. Or not clever enough. Or not as clever as I thought I was. Or some horrid Mr Morrison-vindicating combination of the three. Of course I should have guessed that the train would not arrive at Reading at the time it was supposed to. Of course I should have known that nine minutes' grace would not suffice. I felt so stupid!

I stepped off that train at Reading a broken man. And then I waited 15 minutes or so for the next fast train to Oxford. And instead of arriving energised and optimistic into the city of dreaming spires at a credible 21.05, I trundled in weary and dreary at 21.19. A victim of my own half-cocked attempts at cleverness.

You know what happened? I flew too close to the sun. I got my wings all melted off. I'm like that Greek lad. Whatsischops. Icarus. I'm exactly like Icarus.

So how did I recover? How does one bounce back from a thing like that?

All I can say is, thank the Lord for *Celebrity Big Brother*. I shushed Beth to bed, settled down with Sylvie on my lap and a cooling bottle of beer in my hand (this heat! When's it going to break?), tuned the television in and all was well with the world again. Do you watch? Are you addicted? Oh, you should. It's brilliant. It's a tonic.

Why, if it wasn't for the hilarious antics of those cringing C-listers and desperate D-listers (and in a few notable cases DD-listers... actually, that's rather a good joke, isn't it? DD-listers? I might use that next week, in the new *Celebrity Big Brother* column the editor wants. There's no official word on whose name will go at the top of it, but Goebbels has been making some seriously encouraging noises), if it wasn't for their adorable stupidity, their puppyish willingness to impress, to jump through hoops, to sit and stand, beg and roll over for our amusement... why if it wasn't for these brilliantly desperate, wonderfully awful people, then I would have gone to bed with all my previous intellectual confidence shot.

I say it again. Thank the Lord for *Celebrity Big Brother*! Thank the Lord for celebrities – for being so venal and self-obsessed and narcissistic that we all can't help but shine in comparison.

What do you think? Are you in love with the antics of adorable Essex girl and stunning tabloid lovely (she's my DD-list celeb) Nikki Nyce? Do the post-rehab ramblings of washed-up-by-her-mid-20s American actress Candy Crush give you hope for humanity? Do the macho poses and Neanderthal postulations of former-player-turned-pundit and the man they call football's Mr Controversy, Graeme Green, make you laugh out loud?

Will the stream-of-consciousness gibberish and preening, fatuous codswallop they all spout – and actually seem to believe – reset all our disoriented moral compasses and revitalise all our flagging intellects?

If there's one thing the *Celebrity Big Brother* house is teaching me, it is that no matter how stupid I am, or how stupid I do, I'm never going to be as stupid as some. And that, my learned friend, is a beautiful lesson to learn.

It almost gives me hope!

Au revoir!

Dan

Letter 20

From: DantheMan020@gmail.com
To: Martin.Harbottle@premier-westward.com
Re: 07.31 Premier Westward Railways train from Oxford to London Paddington, August 9. Amount of my day wasted: 19 minutes. Fellow sufferers: Train Girl, Lego Head, Universal Grandpa, Guilty New Mum.

Martin, I very much hope you're well. Are you well?

Believe it or not, I ask that sincerely. I want to know. I don't get to talk to anyone properly, not really, not these days. Work is work and home is… well, home.

I used to talk to my mum and dad, of course, but they're no longer around. Not that they'd offer solutions or anything – but that's not what people talk to their parents for anyway, is it? When you talk to your parents, you just want them to listen. And listen some more. And nod and tut and sigh in the right places. And then tell you it will all be all right in the end. And by talking to them, by having them listen, you kind of work it out for yourself.

At least, that's how it was for me. Is that what you do with your kids when they call home from university? Do you just let them talk? Do you listen – or do you try to offer advice, too?

I used to have quite long chats in this way, with my dad. Me doing all the talking, he doing all the listening. Seems quite odd, in retrospect, but at the time it felt completely natural. And I'd always feel better afterwards.

Actually, I lie. He would offer advice, in his own way. He'd make crosswords for me, wordsearches, meticulously drawn little games for me to play, one with every letter they'd send to me at uni or, later, in London. And the clues, the answers… often as not they'd have their own advice. Just words, Martin. But the right words.

I miss that. I miss those crosswords. I miss being told the right words.

But look at me – I'm getting soft! I'm not writing to you to harp on about my dead dad. I'm writing to complain!

For example, I spent 19 minutes more on your train this morning than I had originally intended (or you'd originally promised, when I paid for the ticket). Nineteen minutes! What's all that about, Martin?

But on the other hand, my morning trains aren't so bad these days. Not now I have a friend. Train Girl and I: we sit together now, side by side in Coach C (a third of the way up, on the right, facing the direction of travel). We sit and we talk, and we laugh, all the way from Oxford to London. So perhaps I do have someone to talk to properly, after all. Perhaps.

She works in PR. That's why she was looking at bylines in the paper three weeks ago. That's how she recognised me. She's funny and smart and actually rather beautiful (not that I'm looking or anything, not that her looks have anything to do with our friendship at all) and she gets my jokes and she makes pretty good jokes herself. She lives in a little flat in the city centre, she's single, she says she prefers it that way. She says she never has to go looking for a date – she's always got plenty of options. She says that if she's in the mood for a, er, 'date' then she rarely has any trouble finding a suitable candidate. She's cool. She's funny and smart and independent and liberated and cool. And she's got good legs. (Not that I've noticed, really.)

And she listens to me. (You listen to me too, of course, but you don't really have any choice in the matter. Train Girl listens to me through choice. She chooses to sit next to me and listen – there's a big difference there.)

When I talk about the ups and downs of work and the weirdness of home, she listens. She even seems interested.

And home is weird. Home is still weird. Beth and I – we're still not talking, not really, not much besides baby updates, Sylvie headlines, 24-hour rolling Sylvie news… but she at least doesn't seem to be as depressed as she was. Those coffee mornings are helping. The coffee mornings and the afternoon playdates. Most afternoons she's over at someone's house now, eating biscuits and drinking (more) coffee and watching Sylvie make friends. Most afternoons it's Mr Blair's house, in fact, with Mr Blair's one-year-old son. Apparently it doesn't really matter that he's eight months older than Sylvie: it's the stimulation she's getting that's important. And the stimulation Beth's getting too, I guess.

Actually, you know what? I tell a lie. We are talking, Beth and I: we're talking about Mr Blair. About how brave he is, to carry the burden of single parentdom after his wife upped and left (so I was right about that). About how much he cares for his little boy, how he's given up everything to look after him. About how committed he is to the environment, and to fair trade, and to the rights of Taiwanese factory workers (or whatever). About how he not only reads the *Guardian*, he regularly writes letters to the *Guardian*. About how beautiful and tasteful and fashionably minimalist his charming half-a-million-quid house in Jericho is.

Yes, we talk about Mr Blair. Good old Mr Blair, eh?

(We don't talk about Train Girl. What would be the point? Beth would only get funny about her. She'd only get depressed again.)

So there are some positives. And work too: there's some good stuff happening at work. We can take inspiration from that. I've got my *Celebrity Big Brother* half-page – and it's got my name on the top of it. Three hundred bylined words every week guaranteed: and a chance to show I can handle a column. I'm no longer writing anonymous NIBs and I'm no longer the news desk's whipping boy. It's all good. It's all coming together.

But then, as we know from our discussions about Pyrrhic victories, there's always bad stuff to go with the good, right? There's always good stuff and bad stuff together. That's the way the world works. Take North Africa: there's the good stuff we already know about, but then there's the flipside. The recent stuff. The refusal of the vicious old dictator to go. The urgings to fight to the death. The... well, the death. All the deaths.

All these deaths... and the fact that the whole thing is possibly not going to be over by the bank holiday and I may have lost my £50. That's the worst bit. About the only person who does seem to be happy is Harry the Dog. He's ecstatic, he's loving it all. He spent ages last week lobbying Goebbels to run the pictures un-pixelated.

'Nothing like a good suicide bomber,' he told me in the pub last Friday, as we popped in for a quick one after work and he lined up the Guinness. 'The readers go wild for a bearded nutter in a Semtex vest. Can't get enough of the crazy old buggers. In a better world we'd have a suicide bomber every week. Throw in a dodgy government and a conspiracy theory and some proper clear shots of the carnage and you have yourself the perfect spread, my friend. Now, I'm nipping out for a crafty smoke – why don't you line up another couple of jars of the black stuff while I'm gone, eh, there's a good chap.'

The worst thing is: he may be right. When our readers engage with politics, it does tend to involve a fair amount of blood.

So what about the marches and the strikes and the barricades across the Mediterranean – that's all good, right? Power to the people! Up the workers! But then, look at what they're protesting about, look into the issues, and it's not so good. It's not so good at all, that they have to march, and strike, and man barricades. It's not so good that it has to come down to this.

And there is bad stuff at work, too, to go with the good stuff. And the bad stuff at work is looking pretty goddamn bad.

The crooner with the false hair and the Highland flings – he's not going to drop his suit after all. He's got his court date. He's taking us to court. And the word is he might win. The word is that regardless of how true the stories we printed about him may be, the methods we used to get them may have been unsound. Or, in fact, illegal.

And if he does win, don't expect it to end there. If the sex-mad Scot does get the verdict he's after, then expect the floodgates to open. Every famous face we've ever exposed is going to want a slice of the action. Every celebrity we've ever shamed is going to want their revenge.

Worrying, eh? It gets worse.

There have been whispers. Whispers of much worse. I mean, celebs: they're one thing. Who gives a flying front-page splash if we look a little too closely into the affairs of film stars and television personalities and self-appointed rock gods and washed-up crooners and whatnots? It's what they signed up for. And as we already know, there's no such thing as bad publicity. Not only is all publicity good publicity, but a lot of the time (unless it's *really* bad publicity), bad publicity is better than good publicity. Bad publicity gets you remembered, and that's what the publicity game is all about.

So, no, to hell with the celebs. They can take it. They get no sympathy from me.

But the whispers, however, are of a different kind of scandal. A different moral dilemma altogether. The whispers are that it may not just be the celebs who have come under the unwavering and occasionally not-strictly-legal scrutiny of the *Globe*. The whispers are that some of our, ahem, targets may be real people. Normals. Civilians.

It's one thing fighting a moral battle with a multimillionaire serial-cheat heartthrob – it's another thing entirely if the person you need to smear in court is a victim of crime himself. Or herself. Like, say, for example and just off the top of my head, if that person's son was a victim of the infamous Beast of Berkhamsted, the still-at-large home counties' serial killer who struck seven times six years ago. In that kind of situation, the moral weight shifts pretty significantly. In that kind of situation, we could begin to look like the bad guys.

But, y'know, like I say – it's just whispers. And newsrooms are full of whispers, 90 percent of which are usually rubbish. Let's not get too worried just yet. Let's not upset the applecart, just as things are looking brighter. Let's make like Harry the Dog, and see the positives in the terror, the sunny side to the horror.

After all, Martin, this letter was supposed to be inspiring you. I'm supposed to be firing you up here, filling you with passion, steeling your resolve to get your trains sorted. Nineteen minutes' delay this morning – what are you going to do about it? How are you going to fix it?

Au revoir!

Dan

Letter 21

From: **DantheMan020@gmail.com**
To: Martin.Harbottle@premier-westward.com
Re: 20.50 Premier Westward Railways train from London Paddington to Oxford, August 12. Amount of my day wasted: six minutes. Fellow sufferers: Corporate Dungeon Master.

Martin. Those whispers in the newsroom I mentioned? I shouldn't have mentioned them. Forget about them, Martin. They really are just whispers, the paranoid mutterings of over-stressed hacks over-keen to see conspiracy theories and worst-case scenarios wherever they can. And what would really not be good is if those whispers left the newsroom and reached the wider world and thus gained a kind of spurious credence, if you know what I mean. As any good tabloid journalist will tell you, it rarely matters if a rumour is true or not: a good story is a good story. And as I'm sure you don't need telling, there are some out there who would consider those whispers to be a dynamite story.

So, mum's the word, eh, Martin? So to speak.

The other thing I wanted to correct, or redact, or at least qualify, was my position with regards to Train Girl. Re-reading that last letter I can see how one might get the impression of impropriety with regards to my intentions towards her.

Martin, I'm not going to have an affair with Train Girl. I'm a married man. I have a wife. I have a four-month-old baby girl. I've got principles. I spend my days exposing cheats and outing liars and pouring scorn and outrage on the kinds of men who go sleeping around while the missus looks after the little 'un at home. And I am not that kind of man, Martin.

Which is not to say, of course, that none of what I wrote about Train Girl is true. It's all true – she is funny and smart and sort of beautiful. She does make me laugh and she does make that morning commute a little more bearable. We're friends. But that's all – and that's all we'll ever be.

Believe it or not, I'm sort of growing to like you (despite your trains) and I actually would hate you to think of me like that. (And also, on a more practical level, I'd hate for you to inadvertently let slip some newsroom gossip and end up getting me the sack.)

Au revoir!

Dan

From: **Martin.Harbottle@premier-westward.com**
To: DantheMan020@gmail.com
Re: 20.50 Premier Westward Railways train from London Paddington to Oxford, August 12.

Dear Dan

Thank you for your letters. I take all delays very seriously and so always welcome feedback, positive and negative. So in that sense I am pleased to hear that you are enjoying your journeys into London more, as well as being saddened to learn of further delays to your journeys.

Please don't worry about my discretion with regards to your letters. I consider our correspondence personal and although I log the pertinent facts from all your complaints in the proper manner, I would not divulge anything of a more personal nature that you tell me.

And I have no doubt your intentions towards 'Train Girl' are nothing but honourable.

Once again, I can only apologise for the latest delays and assure you we are striving to do better.

Best

Martin

Letter 22

From: **DantheMan020@gmail.com**
To: Martin.Harbottle@premier-westward.com
Re: 07.31 Premier Westward Railways train from Oxford to London Paddington, August 17. Amount of my day wasted: 14 minutes. Fellow sufferers: Universal Grandpa, Guilty New Mum, Lego Head.

Hey, Martin! Marty! (Did anyone ever call you Marty? At school maybe? Marty? Marto? Martinho? Martorelli? The Big M? No?)

Guilty New Mum is on the train again today, Marty, and she seems to be having some sort of crisis. She's packed in the breastfeeding and feels terrible about it, but then after the 'incident in the Putin meeting' (her words, Martin, and we can only wonder what that incident might have involved and what part her breasts might have played in it – even if, hilariously, she works with someone called Putin) she's decided it has to be formula from now on. She doesn't want to take any unnecessary lactation-related risks again. Except that now she spends all day and night wracked with guilt over poor baby's nutritional intake. It's a dilemma, Marto! It's keeping her awake at night!

How do I know all this? Not because she told me: don't be ridiculous. We're commuters – we don't talk to each other. We pretend each other don't exist, most of the time. I know this because she told Sue all about it, in stage whispers on the phone, all the way from Didcot to Slough this morning. Who is Sue? Absolutely no idea. But, given from the way the conversation ended ('No, Sue, you're not listening! It's not as simple as that, Sue!'), given the length of the sigh, the muttered curse and the rolling of the eyes immediately following the conversation, I'd say Sue don't know shit from shinola where breastfeeding's concerned. Even if she has had three of her own already.

Lego Head – who was sitting next to her today – remained inscrutable throughout, staring into the middle-distance; but I'm sure I caught Universal Grandpa suppressing a smile at the 'incident' anecdote. He caught my eye, there was a flicker of something like shared amusement, and then we both looked away again – me at my little laptop, he at his trusty *Telegraph*.

Either way, I'm in no mood for on-train bonding today. I'm hungover. My head hurts. My arms ache, my legs buckle, my chest throbs and my stomach rolls and lurches. I feel like death. I feel like I may even still be drunk. And, most alarmingly of all, I didn't even have a drink last night. I didn't have a drink last night, because of all the drinks I had at lunchtime.

Yesterday I finally went for my long-promised lunch. Goebbels and I, breaking bread and raising a glass together. Goebbels and I! As the clock struck half-past-noon, we left the newsroom floor and took a walk to a local place of refreshment, and we didn't leave again until well after five. (I say well after five – it was actually 7.30.)

We had lunch together, Goebbels and I, for seven hours. And do you want to know what we ate for lunch? That's right! We ate nothing. A

Goebbels lunch revolves around the three major alcoholic nutritional groupings – the protein, carbohydrates and fat of the booze world. Whisky, wine and beer.

Though not necessarily in that order. Things started traditionally enough: the credit card slapped on the bar, the nod and wink and careful instruction to the barman to keep safe all the receipts, the request for two pints and two scotches ('sharpeners, Daniel'). These were naturally consumed at the bar, standing, as befitted our status as real men, proper blokes, seasoned drinkers – along with another two like them – before we repaired to a cosy corner of the pub with a bottle of wine and the real business of lunch could begin.

Martin, don't get me wrong – I'm a drinker. I like a drink. I could tell you stories about me and drink… but yesterday was another matter altogether. Me a drinker? Yesterday I was a rank amateur, a Sunday League clogger compared to the real drinking talent on show, the expert, ruthless, Premier League drinking displayed by Goebbels.

I lost count of how much wine we'd had after about the third bottle. By the time the whiskies were being lined up again I could barely count at all. I could barely speak.

But as it turned out, that didn't matter. I wasn't there to speak. I was there to listen. And, whatever other basic human functions I may lose when I'm drunk, my memory is not one of them. I never forget a thing. Goebbels talked up a storm; I listened. And I remembered it all.

Do you want to know what he told me? Of course you do! You want all the dirt! You, Martin, who profess never to buy the scandalous and scandal-ridden *Globe*… you're getting a taste for the scurrilous tale or two, aren't you? You're learning to love the indiscretions I keep dropping your way. Of course you are. That's the way it works.

So how about the one about the famously hirsute actor caught wandering around a notoriously rough gay pick-up spot in Edinburgh at three in the morning. You may remember that. And you may also remember his defence: 'I couldn't sleep,' he said, 'I was walking my dog.' Far-fetched, maybe, but also plausible enough to get him off the hook. Except… do you know who he called from the police station, after he'd been picked up and hauled to the holding cells, along with several other men who also just so happened to be in the area at the same time?

He called his personal assistant. And here's what he told her: 'You need to do two things: first, get my lawyer. And second, go buy me a dog. I REALLY need to own a dog right now.'

Or there's the primetime TV mogul who likes nothing more than to lie under a see-through coffee table while specialist ladies (how can I put this?) squat on the glass and, well, relieve themselves.

They do number twos, Martin. Goebbels has seen the photos. There's even rumours of a video, somewhere.

He told me – and this is the crucial bit, Martin, this is when we'd changed up from wine to whisky – that there was absolutely no way the paper was going to go under. He told me that too many people were too terrified of what we had on them to dare take us on properly.

There is a vault, you see. All this information – it's in the vault. We haven't run these stories because, dynamite though they are, they're worth more existing as threats. They're great leverage. They keep us, in Goebbels' words, 'literally above the law'.

Even our litigation-happy crooner friend. Goebbels reckons even he's not stupid enough to follow it through all the way. Goebbels reckons it's a bluff, and the whole sorry business will blow over by Bonfire Night. Not because the paper's not guilty. Because the collateral damage of taking on the *Globe* would prove catastrophic to all involved.

And then do you know what he told me? He told me, with an actual pat on the back, that I could be a part of all that. He told me my

Jamie Best scoop was the best thing we'd run in years. He told me I was a natural. He laid it all out – like this was all I'd ever wanted.

And then he told me he didn't want me as junior showbiz reporter on his paper any more. He told me I'm moving to the news desk – and I'm to report directly to him from now on. He wants me chasing stories. Proper stories. Because this, of course, is all I've ever wanted.

And I… I nodded. It was about all I was capable of, by that time. I nodded, and I smiled, and I clinked glasses with him and I slurred something like 'Cheersennn'.

But here's the thing, Martin. Is this all I ever wanted?

Au revoir!

Dan

Letter 23

From: DantheMan020@gmail.com
To: Martin.Harbottle@premier-westward.com
Re: 07.31 Premier Westward Railways train from Oxford to London Paddington, August 23. Amount of my day wasted: 12 minutes. Fellow sufferers: Train Girl, Lego Head, Universal Grandpa.

Dear Martin

It's been, what, six days without delays? Well done indeed. Keep this up and people will start thinking you run a competent train service. Keep this up and I won't need to write to you at all.

You know who has been reading my column? You'll never guess. Get this: Universal Grandpa – he's been reading my column! It seems that along with his daily *Telegraph*, he likes to partake of a guiltily pleasurable *Globe* on a Sunday. Who'd have thought it?

He nodded to me last week, the day after Guilty New Mum's recounting of the incident in the Putin meeting (still can't get over that name!), and then on Friday he caught my eye and actually smiled at me as he sat down in his usual seat. At the time I thought he was smiling because Train Girl was running down the carriage with two cups of coffee howling 'Ow! Ow! Ow! Ow!' as it splashed on her hands (she gave me mine with 'That's two quid and a skin graft you owe me,' which was quite funny, to be fair). But no! It turns out he was smiling for another reason!

This morning, Universal Grandpa said hello. More than that! He nudged me and with a twinkle in his eye whispered: 'Very funny column you had there on Sunday, son. You're a cheeky devil but it made me and my daughter laugh.'

How about that? Fame, Martin! The adulation of the British public! It's why we do it, isn't it? It's why every journalist insists on a byline. For the glory. For the glory of making a twinkly old man with a white beard laugh at my *double entendres*.

He winked again as we arrived in Paddington and shuffled our way through the corridor to the train door. Train Girl did a double-take. I think she thought he winked at her. She didn't look quite as unhappy about that as you might have thought, either.

So. Eight million people including Universal Grandpa and his daughter are reading my column! Do they include you? I hope so. And if you're not… well, what else is there in the news to keep your pecker up and engines stoked?

North Africa! Here we are, barely a week off the August bank holiday, the Reading Festival, and my deadline for the newsroom Victory in North Africa sweepstake, and it looks like the rebels are coming good for me. Lord love 'em, it looks like they might actually win this after all! And by default net me a grand or so in the process. Democracy – it's a beautiful thing, right?

Newsnight is amazing at the moment. Twitter is electric. The blogs and YouTube posts coming out of the area are as gripping, action packed and loaded with drama as anything I've ever seen at the cinema. Harry the Dog is on fire. And our picture desk... it's a wonder they're researching anything else. Every day the shots come in – from our men out there, from freelancers, from adventure-seekers, fortune-hunters, aid agencies, mercenaries – and every day we hear the gasps and exclamations from the picture desk, the whistles and swear words muttered with eyes wide and heads shaking.

I've no idea how those boys out there are doing it. Only the capital remains, Martin! Only the mad old dictator in his mad old imperial palace with his mad old imperial guard remains. They're nearly there! Like I say: amazing. Inspiring.

And how's it inspiring me, Martin? As I schlep to and from my desk at the world's most famous (and now infamous) newspaper?

Oooh, as Robert Plant once said, it makes me wonder. It makes me wonder what I should be worrying about. It makes me wonder if the average bleeding freedom fighter in the dust and desert and blood really gives a damn about the affronted privacy of some bewigged fool of a crooner back in London town. It makes me wonder what the arguments Beth and I are having are really about. It makes me wonder, when I look at little Sylvie's perfect little face, just what will become of us all, lost here on our little rock in space.

It also, if I'm being honest, makes me wonder what I'm going to spend that thousand quid on, when they storm the palaces in a week's time. But maybe that's just me.

Au revoir!

Dan

Letter 24

From: **DantheMan020@gmail.com**
To: Martin.Harbottle@premier-westward.com
Re: 22.21 Premier Westward Railways train from London Paddington to Oxford, August 27. Amount of my day wasted: 13 minutes. Fellow sufferers: no regulars (Saturday).

Dear Martin

It's Saturday! Saturday, Saturday! Saturday night's all right! Old Elton knew the score, right? Or, to bring things up to date: Saturday night's all right for hanging around West London's dreary Paddington Station after a 12-hour shift with nothing to look forward to other than a sad pasta meal for one and a mini plastic bottle of wine from M&S on the train home. And hanging around longer than usual because the train's delayed. Saturday! Saturday, Saturday! Etc.

I say nothing to look forward to… there is the loving bosom of my family, of course, once we've finally boarded the train (actually, I'm on the train now; I'm writing this on the train, having polished off my pasta and wine before we reached Maidenhead and, for the record, we're currently nine minutes late and counting), once we've made our torturous way through England to Oxford in the night. There is that.

And, to be fair, my family will be waiting up for me. Beth will be pleased to see me. She'll say something like 'Thank Christ for that' as I walk through the door, she'll hand me a wailing, bawling, howling little bundle of love and she'll turn around and go to bed. Relieved, happy, pleased I'm finally home.

Yes. Saturday nights might be all right for Elton, but for me Saturdays are difficult, Martin. Saturday is press day. Saturday is when the editors decide that all the work we've done from Tuesday to Friday is basically worthless and pointless and the whole paper needs to be rewritten from scratch in order to make Sunday's *Globe* worthy of the title. Somehow, for some reason, every Saturday is the same.

Every Saturday there's a panic. Do we have a scoop? Is the scoop we have really a scoop? What does everyone else have? What do the lawyers say? But what do the lawyers say? Listen! What do the lawyers say?

(There are an awful lot of lawyers these days. The lawyers have more say than Goebbels does at the moment. The lawyers are setting the news agenda right now.)

Saturday was bad enough before. There is an unspoken rule on Sunday papers that any work you do on a Tuesday or Wednesday is essentially pointless, that any story you uncover before Friday (or at a pinch Thursday) will never make it through the weekend, either because someone else will have uncovered it too, or else because after four or five days of being mentioned in morning news conference everyone will have become so bored of it that it will feel stale by then regardless.

But now that we know we're going to court, now the big cheeses know they're going to have to justify themselves, their methods, their working culture, Saturdays have become seriously acrimonious.

It's no longer enough to have a story – or even to have a story that survives the week, or even a story that survives the week and stands up – these days it seems every story has to survive the kind of legal scrutiny that would make Atticus Finch throw in his wig and give up.

It is, for want of a better word, intense.

Still, at least the column's going well. Are you enjoying the column, Martin? Are you enjoying its expansion away from just *Big Brother* and into the whole of reality television? Are you enjoying it as much as Universal Grandpa, my new biggest fan, the man who told me yesterday that his daughter 'couldn't believe I catch the same train as you'. (His 42-year-old daughter, before you ask, and before you start down the same thought process that Harry the Dog went down when I told him. The one that ended with him drawling, 'Well if you don't want to cash in on your fame with her, send her my way. Tell the old duffer you know a real journalist...')

Do you get a kick out of my *bon mots* and pithy puns and puerile put-downs; my searing dissection of the lows and blows of the more lurid end of the television schedules every week? I hope so. Everyone else is. I mean, modesty forbids but... everyone else is. Except perhaps the hopeless, helpless lot of 'celebs' I'm taking the rise out of. I dare say they're hating it. But who cares what they think, right? They can take it.

And, of course, it is the weekend. Two days away from the nonsense. Two days in the warm, enveloping embrace of my family. And as it happens Beth is feeling generally better about things. She's still depressed of course, but not as depressed as before. Those coffee mornings and playdates and toddler groups are helping. Her afternoons watching Sylvie and mini-Blair and all the other babies bond – they're helping too. They, apparently, are helping most of all.

And then... next week. And we do it all again. That's the way the world turns, Martin. That's the way the mop flops. That's the way the cookie's consumed. And who knows what might happen next week? Anything could happen! When there's news about, when there's news in the air, anything might happen. The future, as Sarah Connor so perfectly put it in *Terminator 2*, is unwritten. Why, you might even manage a week without a delayed, congested, broken-down or otherwise busted train! Can you imagine such a thing?

I'll tell you one thing that is happening next week, Martin. I'll let you in on a secret. Me and Train Girl – you know, my new almost-beautiful friend, the one I don't fancy in the slightest – we might be going for a drink.

An actual drink, in an actual pub, after actual work. As actual friends. She mentioned it, all casual-like, yesterday morning. 'We should have a drink,' she said. 'It seems mad we only ever talk for an hour at half-seven in the morning each day. We should have a drink. We should go for a drink.'

And do you know what I said? I said, that sounds like a great idea. I said, let me clear it with the wife and get back to you… but that sounds like a great idea.

Have I cleared it with the wife? Of course not. Will I this weekend? Of course not. Like I've told you before, there's no point in starting another pointless argument. So I won't clear it with the wife – but I almost certainly will be going for a drink with Train Girl next week. Why not? Two friends can have a drink together, can't they? It's… civilised.

It's not like I'm planning any funny business. If I were that way inclined I'd be going for Universal Grandpa's star-struck daughter, wouldn't I?

Oh! Hello! Check it out, Martin! The cooling towers of Didcot loom into view out of the dark, we're 13 minutes behind schedule, and according to my patented delay-to-letter-length formula I've pretty much reached my limit for the evening.

Farewell and *adieu*, Martin! Have a lovely weekend, you hear?

Au revoir!

Dan

From: **Martin.Harbottle@premier-westward.com**
To: DantheMan020@gmail.com
Re: 22.21 Premier Westward Railways train from London Paddington to Oxford, August 27.

Dear Dan

Many thanks for your letters of August 17, 23 and 27. I am sorry for not replying sooner to any of them, but I have been away from the office on annual leave. Mrs Harbottle and I are lucky enough to have a holiday home in Spain.

Your train on August 17 was late due to a problem with a relief driver before it left Oxford. On August 23 we were the unfortunate victims of a failed Cross Country train congesting the area around Reading, and on August 27 the train was late leaving Paddington due to its late arrival into Paddington. This lateness subsequently caused it to lose still more time on its journey to Oxford.

On another note, I would like to reiterate that anything of a non-train-related nature that you tell me in these letters will be considered strictly between us. And so, with reference to your letter of August 17, are you able to give me a further clue as to who the TV mogul in question might be?!

Best

Martin

Letter 25

From: **DantheMan020@gmail.com**
To: Martin.Harbottle@premier-westward.com
Re: 07.31 Premier Westward Railways train from Oxford to London Paddington, August 31. Amount of my day wasted: seven minutes. Fellow sufferers: Train Girl, Competitive Tech Nerds, Lego Head, Guilty New Mum.

Martin! *Hola*! *Buenos días*! *Hasta mañana*! How were the *sangría* and the *señoritas*? How were the sun and the sand and the silence? I hope you had a lovely break. Sincerely. I hope you got away from it all.

Thanks for your most recent reply. It makes me feel so much better to know that the reason my train was late on Saturday night was… because it was late. That's some serious zen you've got going there, Martin. That's some major Buddhist mind-bending philosophical shizz you're spouting.

And I'm sorry – much as I love a good gossip, I simply can't tell you any more about the exact identities of our misbehaving celebrities. If I know anything about libel law (and believe me, I know a great deal), I know enough not to go committing stuff like that to paper. Not without the weight of the world's most-read English-language newspaper behind me, anyway. But I'm sure you can work it out. I'm sure if you put your mind to it, you'll get there eventually.

Talking of libel… I'm in a funny old mood this morning. I've got stuff to look forward to, and stuff to dread. On the one hand, tonight's the night I'm meeting Train Girl for that civilised, just-friends drink. After a weekend of rows with the one I love, tonight's the night I remember what it's like to make a girl I don't love laugh. And to be honest, I can't wait. We talked it over on the train this morning (the train I'm writing about now, the one that was seven minutes overdue arriving into London). We're hooking up in Soho. We're going to sink a few cold ones in the warm August evening, watch the hustlers and bustlers around Dean Street and Old Compton Street, chat about this, chat about that, clink glasses and go our separate ways. She's staying at her friend's empty place in Clapham tonight (her friend is in Machu Picchu right now, just so's you know); I'll be on one of the late trains home.

Don't worry, Martin. I will behave myself. I will not stoop to the level of those I write about. I'll make that train all right.

So that's good. That's something positive. But on the other hand, I've got a meeting this afternoon. A meeting with Goebbels. And it's not going to be one of those meetings where he drunkenly tells me I'm the future of this newspaper. In fact, it has all the makings of a good old-fashioned bollocking.

I'm assuming you saw the news over the weekend? The England squad for next Saturday's qualifier against Azerbaijan? The very notable omission? Your friend and mine, England's erstwhile Number 9, the young, precociously talented and as we now know closet kleptomaniac Jamie Best – dropped.

Well, it was hardly a surprise, was it? After his red card in his last outing, his poor start to the season in Manchester… his mind's clearly not on his game. Only right to give him a rest. Probably best for the boy, in the long run.

The only thing is – Jamie's not seeing it that way. Jamie's blaming us for his below-par playing at the moment. Jamie's saying we set him up. Or, more specifically, that I set him up. Jamie's saying the CCTV's been doctored, that we got a lookalike, that we bullied and blackmailed him into giving us the story. Jamie's saying he's just another hapless victim of the worst excesses of the *Globe*.

And yesterday Jamie's lawyers wrote a letter. A letter threatening legal action, defamation, slander, emotional distress, loss of earnings even. (Loss of earnings! The boy's on more per week than I'd earn in three years!) And today I'm going to find out just what we're going to do about it. So it looks like I really may need that drink tonight after all.

But don't you worry, Martin. I'll keep you informed. And I can't wait to hear more about your wonderful summer holidays!

Au revoir!

Dan

Letter 26

From: **DantheMan020@gmail.com**
To: Martin.Harbottle@premier-westward.com
Re: 20.50 Premier Westward Railways train from London Paddington to Oxford, September 2. Amount of my day wasted: nine minutes. Fellow sufferers: Corporate Dungeon Master.

Dear Martin

How's tricks? How's the tracks? Keep on truckin', that's the spirit!

I expect you're looking forward to the weekend. I'd like to do that – have a weekend worth looking forward to, I mean. I need a holiday. Beth and Sylvie and I, maybe that's what we need. A holiday.

And in the meantime… here we are again.

So what's occurring? Well, there's Corporate Dungeon Master, slaying and spell-casting his way around his virtual universe. I caught a sneaky peek at his screen when he attempted the train toilet (a move brave enough for any universe, virtual or otherwise). Do you want to know what his character is called? This middle-aged city worker with his pin-striped suit and briefcase, his beer belly and his moobs, commuting between the Square Mile and his comfortable home and (no doubt) loving family in rural Oxfordshire? Do you know how he's known in his alternate universe? He's known as Sauron Flesh Harrower.

That's his alter-ego. That's what he's chosen to call his virtual self. Sauron Flesh Harrower. That's the image he wants to portray every day, to and from work, in these hours (plus delays) away from the drudgery of real life. Sauron Flesh Harrower. A nod to *Lord of the Rings*, a childish bit of horror, a name that would embarrass even the nerdiest of schoolboys. I was almost too amazed by it to laugh as he came huffing and puffing back from the (flesh-harrowing) toilets. Almost. Not quite. Sauron Flesh Harrower!

Do you know what I would call myself, if I was playing an online sword and sorcery game? If I was controlling a virtual warrior wizard in battles with socially inept American teenagers every night? If I was trying to portray myself as a dungeon master not to be messed with? I'd call myself after former Chelsea striker Didier Drogba.

Drogba! Say it out loud. Drogba. DROG-BA! I am Drogba, destroyer of worlds! Look on my Champions League record, ye mighty, and despair! It's a name, Martin! It's a name to strike fear into portly middle-aged men and emo kids everywhere.

Until that time, however, I'll content myself with watching Corporate Dungeon Master mutter and curse his way around the dragons and dungeons on his computer screen. Although I may rename him: Corporate Dungeon Master no more – arise Sauron Flesh Harrower!

But I digress. I've got news! You want the scoop! And there's just enough time to tell you about my drink with Train Girl before I let you get back to hobnobbing with the rock gods and flesh harrowers of the Reading Festival.

So. Here's what happened. We… went for a drink.

We had a few drinks. We went to a few places. We started off standing outside a pub in Dean Street, cradling pints and smoking fags (she drinks pints, Martin! She smokes Marlboro Red!), we ended up working our way up that road, back down Wardour Street and halfway along Old Compton before calling it quits.

She looked great. She looked like she'd worn something especially. She stood out in the Soho crowds: her bare legs, her strappy shoes, her strappy vest; the way she carelessly held her drink forever on the edge of spilling (but never quite); the way she kept brushing her hair out of her face when she laughed.

We had a laugh. We had a real laugh.

And you know what else? That's all that happened. At the end of the night, when I had a train to catch home… I caught my train home. With nothing more than a peck on the cheek by way of goodbye. Nothing more than I might give any female friend with whom I'd been sharing a drink and a laugh. Nothing inappropriate at all.

You see: I am a good person. I totally told you!

Au revoir!

Dan (aka DROG-BA)

From: **Martin.Harbottle@premier-westward.com**
To: DantheMan020@gmail.com
Re: 20.50 Premier Westward Railways train from London Paddington to Oxford, September 2.

Dear Dan

Thanks for your letters. Unfortunately on both occasions this week your trains were late due to congestion. And for the record, the correct term for online 'Dungeons and Dragons'-type games of the kind you wrote about is MMORPGs, or Massively Multiplayer Online Role-Playing Games. And contrary to popular prejudice, they are not the sole preserve of 'portly middle-aged men and emo kids', whatever an emo kid might be, but rather one of the fastest-growing phenomena on the internet, with whole societies (we call them 'guilds') and communities dedicated to social interaction, as well as 'swords and sorcery'. I feel it is a shame that you feel compelled to judge Sauron Flesh Harrower purely on the basis of his avatar's name and I must say I do consider it rather 'tabloid' of you.

Regards

Martin

Letter 27

From: **DantheMan020@gmail.com**
To: Martin.Harbottle@premier-westward.com
Re: 17.21 Premier Westward Railways train from London Paddington to Oxford, September 6. Amount of my day wasted: seven minutes. Fellow sufferers: No regulars (far too early).

Martin. Oh, Martin. What a day. Have you seen the evening paper yet? Have you caught the news? Christ, where to begin?

Here's how it began, Martin.

I arrived in work this morning as usual, dumped my stuff, logged on, checked my emails as usual, nipped up to the canteen for a coffee as usual, grabbed the morning papers, sat at my desk, scanned the wires, double-checked my emails... all as usual. The ordinary office chatter was going on (football, telly, kid troubles, wife troubles), Goebbels was swearing at some sad sack from IT on the phone, nothing worth reporting, when suddenly, all hell broke loose.

Have you ever seen a police raid, Martin? I mean, in real life? I'd seen two before today, both in the line of duty, both from the outside looking in, as it were, both times on the side of truth and justice, notebook and Dictaphone in hand. Today, I saw my third. And this time, I was on the inside.

There was a shout, a clatter by the lifts, something getting knocked over. We all looked up, and suddenly the newsroom was full of policemen. They were all yelling at us to stay where we were (where exactly were we going to go? We're four floors up here) – and they were all striding around to man themselves at each bank of desks: news, features, showbiz, city, foreign, sport (sport?), two to each department. They were kitted out in the full shebang: black combats, boots, high-viz jackets, truncheons swinging from utility belts. They were acting like they were busting the secret mountain stronghold of al-Qaeda; they were loving the self-importance of it all.

And behind them all, striding in like Napoleon Bonaparte, the boss. Chief Super, or whatever. (Is 'Chief' not enough? Or 'Super' not enough? He has to be both Chief and Super?) He was actually holding his truncheon. He was barking orders: 'Nobody move! Put your hands where we can see them! Do NOT touch your computers!'

About six people stood up – Goebbels amongst them – and were promptly pushed down again. The editor came flying out of his office at the far end of the floor – and was promptly told to get back in. Bonaparte followed him and shut the door. And meanwhile, we all sat there like spare parts, staring at the riot squad.

The only sound was the faint clicking of a dozen different camera phones surreptitiously being turned on to video mode and subtly slid around to point at the policemen. (If you're going to try it on with tabloid journalists, Martin, you better make sure you stick to the rules.)

And so... we all waited. Goebbels must have tried to get up and been told to sit down half a dozen times. The rest of us contented ourselves with eyeballing the coppers. Harry the Dog offered his policeman a cigarette. The sports editor told his exactly what he thought of him, mostly in words of one-syllable and four letters. A terrified-looking trainee asked if she could phone her mum. (That'll be a no, love.) The tension grew.

From her office we heard *Amazeballs!*' editor Rochelle call out: 'How long exactly is this all going to be? I've a spray tan booked and a Dior launch later...'

After 20 minutes or so the editor's door opened again. He didn't come out. Bonaparte came out, puffed-up and self-important like a peacock; he marched straight up to the features editor, told him to get his things and asked him to accompany them to the station.

Pin. Drop.

And then smiling – actually smiling, the sadistic so-and-so – he turned to address the newsroom. 'Acting upon information received,' he said, 'we are apprehending this man in the course of our enquiries to possible lawbreaking at the *Globe*.

'And as for the rest of you: nobody touches anything until my team has conducted a search of these premises. You all make yourselves scarce. Out of consideration for your working practices, we're doing this at the start of your working week so as not to disrupt the production of your newspaper too much – but we will need you to leave the building. And anyone who objects,' and he turned to Goebbels as he said this, who was physically shaking with rage, 'will be arrested for obstructing the law and wasting police time.'

And then what? And then we all filed out, stunned, and we went to the pub. And after four or five hours of sitting listening to everyone getting increasingly furious, I bailed and caught the train home. Tomorrow I'll turn up at work as usual and see what's what.

And so I get on the train home. And then what do you do, Martin? You screw that up as well. Another seven pointless minutes of my life wasted. Nice one. Well done.

Au revoir!

Dan

PS – I got a text from Goebbels as the train drew in, by the way. They released the feats ed without charge. But the company have dismissed him anyway. Lovely.

From: **Martin.Harbottle@premier-westward.com**
To: DantheMan020@gmail.com
Re: 17.21 Premier Westward Railways train from London Paddington to Oxford, September 6.

Dear Dan

I'm sorry to hear of your latest delay. Seven minutes is unacceptable and we shall endeavour to do better in future. The problem on this occasion was a faulty signal box in the Taplow area. I have been on to Network Rail about infrastructure maintenance several times already this week, but rest assured I shall bring the matter up again with them as a matter of urgency.

Once again, please accept my most sincere apologies for the time this delay took out of your evening.

Best

Martin

Letter 28

From: **DantheMan020@gmail.com**
To: Martin.Harbottle@premier-westward.com
Re: 07.31 Premier Westward Railways train from Oxford to London Paddington, September 8. Amount of my day wasted: 11 minutes. Fellow sufferers: Guilty New Mum, Lego Head, Universal Grandpa, Competitive Tech Nerds.

Thanks for your letters, Martin. Most informative. But… that's all they are. Did you not read what happened on Tuesday? We were raided. By the police. A man was arrested. Our computers were examined. Some plod probably scanned all my emails. (He wouldn't have scanned these emails, of course: these all come from a separate computer, an independent laptop, through an entirely non-work-related webmail address. I'm not completely stupid, you know.)

Are you not interested at all? Are you not appalled? Aghast? Martin, I thought you'd be as outraged as I am – or if not that then at least sympathetic. Do you think I seriously give a damn about faulty signal boxes in the Taplow area? Democracy is under threat here! The enshrined right of a free press is being torn up, and your reaction is to blather on about signal boxes?

I despair.

Look up, Martin. Look about. Raise your head and gaze out of the window and check out what's happening – out there, outside the train, on the other side of the tracks, beyond the sidings, in the real world. Get out of your seat, Martin, get out of the train, and step into reality.

The world: it's screwed. It's falling apart. The centre cannot hold. The North African revolution is stalled and stuttered and suffocating under shellfire, and after those two Médecins Sans Frontières guys disappeared last week, even the aid agencies have all scarpered.

Greece and Spain are still revolting; now Paris and Amsterdam are looking to go the same way. The French students are back on the streets, marching through the Marais on the way to the Bastille; expect them to be joined by the farmers and the fishermen before too long. Maybe even the railway workers. Can you imagine that, Martin? Railway workers downing tools and making a point about the world?

And what are we doing? We're doing nothing. We are not doers at all. We're wasting time, Martin – and it's only a matter of time before time doth waste us in return.

Oh, you know what? Forget it. The train this morning was 11 minutes late, but I just can't face writing a letter that long to you this morning. It was 11 minutes late. And, I'll be honest with you (as ever), without Train Girl on, it felt a lot longer.

(She's ill: she texted me – did I not mention we're texting now? We swapped numbers on our night out last week. Don't read too much into it or anything, I've got hundreds of numbers on my phone, and, you know, seeing as we're friends now it seemed silly not to swap numbers. So we're texting. She texted me this morning. She said she was ill. Something she ate, apparently. She also said how shocked she was by the events of Tuesday morning. She said it was a disgrace and a scandal and she hoped I was OK, and if I wanted to talk about it or go for another drink or anything, just shout. Like I say: she's a friend. She gets it, Martin.)

And what were the rest of them doing this morning, as the world falls apart?

Guilty New Mum was in a flap about nursery schools ('All I'm saying is we need to be thinking about it now,' she whispered into the phone, loud enough for most of the carriage to hear. 'It doesn't make us pushy parents. I only want what's best for her. Of course I won't ask that. I can't ask that. You know how it works. I've only just come back and I can't go round trying to call in favours off the likes of him, for crying out loud.') The Competitive Tech Nerds were getting all Alpha Male about Smart TVs ('Motion capture remote control IS the future.' 'Nonsense, motion capture was over before it began. It's the next Betamax, the next Blu-Ray, the next HDTV.' 'Are you comparing Betamax with HDTV?' 'Absolutely! HD has gone the way of the dodo, my friend. HD is yesterday...' and so on, *ad infinitum*.)

Universal Grandpa was chuckling over something in his *Telegraph* crossword – though only after our now customary wink on the platform, as one of us holds open the train door for the other – and, in the midst of it all but somehow totally separate from it all, Lego Head sat perfectly still, doing his daily nirvana thing.

And I looked at them and of them all, it seemed only Lego Head was anything like close to getting it. Of them all, with their worries and pointless arguments and half-a-century (or whatever) of the same commute, the same paper, the same crossword, only he was opting out. Lego Head: the Buddha of the morning commute.

So anyway. My train this morning was 11 minutes late – but I'm just not in the mood for wasting that much of your time today. I'll owe it you. I'll put it on the slate. I'll make it up to you next time, OK?

And in the meantime: seriously, Martin. Open your eyes.

Au revoir!

Dan

From: Martin.Harbottle@premier-westward.com
To: DantheMan020@gmail.com
Re: 07.31 Premier Westward Railways train from Oxford to London Paddington, September 8.

Dear Dan

Thank you for your letter of September 8. I am sorry you feel my responses are lacking something. I am endeavouring to always explain the reasons for your delays in each of my responses to your complaints. It may interest you that, as on September 6, the continuing signalling problems at Taplow were once again responsible for the slow running of your service.

On other matters, I was of course sorry to hear of the events of Tuesday in your office. I am sure, however, that the authorities acted with due diligence and that if there is a suspicion of illegality then no one – not even the country's best-selling newspaper! – should be considered above the law.

On a personal note, I am glad to hear again that your journeys with Premier Westward are made more enjoyable thanks to your friendship with 'Train Girl'. And do you really have hundreds of numbers in your mobile phone? I think I must have no more than a dozen! And the only texts I ever receive seem to be from my mobile service provider offering 'sim updates'!

Warm regards

Martin

Letter 29

From: **DantheMan020@gmail.com**
To: Martin.Harbottle@premier-westward.com
Re: 20.50 Premier Westward Railways train from London Paddington to Oxford, September 14. Amount of my day wasted: 12 minutes. Fellow sufferers: Sauron Flesh Harrower.

Dear Martin

Tally ho! Look smart, old boy! Best blazer and tie on, shoes polished, buttons buffed and hair properly combed! It's rugger time! The Rugby World Cup starts tomorrow, and I can only imagine the near-hyperactive levels of excitement in the Harbottle household.

It's your thing, isn't it? Rugger, I mean. You don't consider it to be a bunch of public schoolboys prancing about in the mud, all repressed homoeroticism and hearty elitism and fat, posh bullying at all, do you? Of course not. Why should you? We built an empire on that game. (And we possibly lost it for the same reasons.) I bet old Isambard Kingdom saw the value in rugby. I bet he'd have taken some time out from creating the Great Western Railway in order to cheer our boys on against the might of Tonga and Western Samoa. As I'm sure you will too.

Thanks for your letter. And apologies if the tone of my last to you was a little… terse. I've been under a lot of pressure, as they say. Things have been getting on top of me, at home and away. Your seeming inability to do what I'm paying you so handsomely to do (get me between Oxford and London on time) is just another straw bending the camel's toe. (That is the phrase, isn't it? Or am I thinking of something else entirely?)

At least there's been no further news at work. No further incidents. All's quiet on that front. Though of course the court case starts next week. The fellatious warbler and his fallacious accusations – he's getting his trial and it's going to be dynamite all right. He'll have his say. But the real question is: will we have ours? How far is the paper prepared to go in its own defence?

At home… well, things at home ain't what they used to be. There's trouble in paradise. Beth's getting better, getting less depressed – and that's good at least. She's starting to feel like a person again, as opposed to a baby-slave, a martyr to nappies and feeding time and teething troubles.

(Oh, did I not mention – Sylvie's started teething. Just as she showed signs of occasionally wanting to sleep at night, she's got a little tooth or two coming through. And it's giving her no end of grief. Dribbling, drizzling, screaming grief. Sodden sheets and blood on her bib. All this anguish over a few teeth, and it's not like they're even going to last the decade. These same teeth that are causing little Sylvie so much pain – they're all going to fall out again and get replaced by new ones. I mean, really. Is someone taking the mickey here?)

Where was I? Oh yes. Beth's starting to feel like a person again. A woman, even. But it's nothing to do with me, guv. It's her new social circle that's responsible: the mums and the dads and their shared responsibilities and experiences. The baby mafia. Me? I'm just the bloke she hands over to at home. The one she married.

And now I'm in the bad books still further. There is a weekend happening, apparently. A baby-bonding weekend, at the end of this month, organised by the NCT – twelve babies and their parents in a Travelodge near Milton Keynes for three days and two nights, learning how to grow and develop and share and relate and sympathise and empathise and all that other jazz. It turns out it's been on our calendar for a while now, it's been booked and paid for for weeks.

Except, here's the thing. I never look at the calendar. I can't remember ever being told about this weekend away. And, given the state of war at work at the moment, there's no way I can get a Friday and a Saturday off to go and sit in a room full of depressed women learning about baby sign language. There's no chance, I told Beth. I'm really, truly sorry – but it just isn't going to happen. It's not my fault. Be reasonable.

Between you and me, Martin, I don't think I should have told her to be reasonable. In my experience, telling someone to be reasonable almost always incites them into direct unreasonable behaviour. Cue a lot of tears and slammed doors and accusations. And I just had to stand there and take it while she screamed at me, Sylvie gently dribbling watery blood on to my shoulder.

So, yes. Things, as I say, ain't what they used to be.

How do things get like this, Martin? How can it be that something like Sylvie – Sylvie, who, we agree, is the most beautiful, extraordinary, heart-stoppingly perfect embodiment of what Beth and I mean to each other; Sylvie, a living apotheosis of love – how can it be that it's Sylvie who's the driving cause of all this awfulness between us?

We never used to argue. You want an anecdote? I've not told you an anecdote for a while, have I, Martin? OK, here goes.

When Beth and I had been officially dating about six months, we went on holiday together. It's a big deal, your first holiday with a new girlfriend, it's a dry run for living together. It's when you first find out all those odd little quirks and habits that seem amusing or endearing in isolation are actually not that cute, not that adorable after all. It's when you have your first proper argument.

So, there we were, Beth and I, young and clever and newly in love, on a budget flight to Crete. And we're talking about how we never argue, as you do when you're young and clever and in love and the only thing you ever talk about is yourselves and how young, clever and in love you are… and Beth makes me a bet.

She bets me £20 I can't manage two days without arguing with her. I argue with everyone else, she points out; there's no way that I'll manage 48 hours of non-stop, inescapable proximity to anyone – even her – without sniping about something.

Nonsense, I say. I'm young and in love… and besides, I don't argue with everyone. Only idiots. So I up the bet – a further £5 for every subsequent 24 hours we go without arguing.

It took about seven months until the bet was finally settled. By that time she owed me about 1,100 quid. (Oh, and the argument, for the record, was over the official recommendations for units of alcohol one should consume per week. She said they were set in stone. I said that, on the contrary, they were completely made up, plucked out of thin air, they were medically entirely unproven. So I actually won that argument as well.)

Anyway, the point is, we never argued. And now… it's all we do. It can't just be Sylvie, can it? That wouldn't make sense at all.

And you know what the other point is? We need that holiday. We need to go on holiday again. We need a weekend away, together. Just not a baby-bonding weekend, that's all. Or not this particular baby-bonding weekend.

Oh, and while we're at it: 12 minutes today, Martin – that's how much of my life you've taken from me this Wednesday. Twelve minutes spent on your train that should have been spent at home. And after I let you off three or four minutes the other day too! Shame, Martin. Shame on you.

Au revoir!

Dan

Letter 30

From: DantheMan020@gmail.com
To: Martin.Harbottle@premier-westward.com
Re: 20.20 Premier Westward Railways train from London Paddington to Oxford, September 20. Amount of my day wasted: nine minutes. Fellow sufferers: Sauron Flesh Harrower.

Dear Martin

We're in the dock, old boy! It's the court case of the century. It's the eternal struggle, the classic showdown: it's good versus evil. ('Good' in this instance being represented by a multimillionaire egomaniac singer with a history of illegal and semi-legal vice to his name; and 'evil' being the world's most-read English-language newspaper, dedicated to, amongst other things, exposing the illegal activities of multimillionaire egomaniac singers.) It's exciting, isn't it? Two days in and already it's unmissable.

All the rolling news channels are covering it. Most of the newsroom are streaming live blog updates on their desktops, too. Twitter feeds are being monitored, the newswires are being constantly refreshed – all for the latest word from inside the Royal Courts of Justice.

Are you watching too, Martin? Is that why my train is late again? Have you been distracted by the case for the prosecution? Can't say I blame you. It's sensational stuff. But just in case you haven't been following (in which case, why is this train delayed?), I'll sum up for you.

First big surprise? It's not going to be the short, sharp shock everyone predicted. No in-and-out job, this. We're up for a long haul. On day one, both lawyers laid out their respective positions. And if the case for the prosecution went on a bit, then our bewigged boys did so right back.

Is this to be about one priapic crooner and his outrage at being outed as such? Apparently not. The way our synthetic-blond, Bravehearted friend is going about it, this is going to be the whole *Globe* on trial: our means, our methods, our motivations. His QC was pretty clear about it; he said so right at the start. 'We have not sought to bring this case because of the way my client has been treated by this newspaper,' he declared. 'We are here today because my client is just one of many hundreds of victims of this newspaper's endemic and systematic culture of bullying and abuse. The difference is, he has chosen to stand up to them. He has chosen to say "no more". Over the course of this trial you are going to hear about how the activities at this newspaper have frequently shown complete disregard to the law of the land. And, might I add, not just where my client is concerned.'

Fierce stuff, eh, Martin. Crikey! I don't know about you, but when I heard that I thought: well, I'd send them down. Guilty as charged, your honour.

Do you do that thing, when you watch *Perry Mason* or *A Few Good Men* or *To Kill A Mockingbird* – that thing where you change your mind about the verdict depending on who's speaking? I do. When the prosecutors are doing their thing I'm all for taking the accused away right there and then. No further evidence needed. And then, when the defence gets up, suddenly it's as if the veil has been lifted from my eyes and I'm finally seeing the truth for the first time. Suddenly the only possible verdict one could deliver has to be 'Not Guilty'!

Every time. I do it every time. I'd be hopeless on jury service.

So... although it was looking bad right then, although that opening salvo had me wondering if my whole career really was a colossal mistake, it only took the afternoon session and our opening statement to turn it all around for me.

The threats were implied, Martin, that was the clever thing. The suggestions were planted: the newspaper knows more than it has let on already. We laid our strategy out plain and clear. It was all: 'This newspaper has secured the convictions of murderers, paedophiles, gun runners, drug cheats, benefit cheats, bent MPs, bent cops, war criminals, drug pushers and sexual predators,' and then it was all: 'We report the news. We do not fabricate the news,' and then there was a bit of: 'What stories we may have run on the man who is charging us with this list of crimes have all been demonstrably and provably true. He may not like it, but if he doesn't like it he shouldn't do it,' and then, best of all, right at the death: 'We intend to defend ourselves, the honour of the world's greatest newspaper and indeed the honour of all the world's journalists, the honour of journalism itself, against the self-seeking, self-serving, self-interested motives of men like this who would seek to muzzle the truth for his own ends.'

Rock and roll! There was actual whooping in the newsroom! Stick that in your sporran and play with it! It's going to be a fight – and what's more, it looks like it's going to be a dirty fight.

And do you know what the moral of the story is going to be, Martin? It's going to be this, the same as it always is: don't take on the tabloid press. Don't take on the tabloid press because, eventually, in the end, you'll always lose.

Au revoir!

Dan

Letter 31

From: **DantheMan020@gmail.com**
To: Martin.Harbottle@premier-westward.com
Re: 07.31 Premier Westward Railways train from Oxford to London Paddington, September 24. Amount of my day wasted: seven minutes. Fellow sufferers: no regulars (Saturday, innit).

Dear Martin

What's this? Another delay? That's two in the same week – you're getting sloppy again. You've fallen into those bad old habits once more. You want to look at that, Martin. You don't want that to develop into some kind of culture of incompetence at Premier Westward, do you?

Because that, as we're finding out, is what happens at institutions. They develop 'cultures'. As the Trial Of The Century™ has told us this week, repeatedly, big institutions develop cultures: of incompetence, or arrogance, or deceit or illegality. (Never positive things. Never a culture of excellence, for example. Or a culture of rigorous investigation.)

It's all gone a little flat, hasn't it? After the explosive opening salvos, I mean. There's been an awful lot of legal jargon and points of order and boring closed sessions between counsel and the judge. There has, to be blunt, been no dirt.

Would you like some dirt, Martin? Something filthy and titillating to wallow in while we wait for events to pick up again? You would! I thought so. How about another little tale from the vault, another little dirty secret that never got to see the light of day. Another reason why the man spearheading the crusade against the *Globe*'s culture of deceit is about as amoral as they come.

Let's keep it hypothetical, of course. Let's not make any black-and-white accusations. But let's also suppose that a decade ago, just about the time that our libidinous and litigious friend hit the big time, a certain newspaper received a tip concerning his activities in Argentina.

You may remember his adventures in Argentina. They were splashed all over the (quality) papers, featured in BBC documentaries, raised a fortune in donations. You may remember how he had been recording over there (later turned into a documentary, as you may also recall, and responsible for a remarkable resurgence in his popularity) and had been struck by the terrible conditions in which so many children were forced to live.

In the favelas of Buenos Aires, we learned, our sensitive friend found his calling. Those grubby-faced urchins running barefoot through the shanty towns acted upon him in the most profound way. A campaign was formed, awareness was raised, a foundation set up – and, with his famous face earnestly peering out of every promotional bit of bumpf, millions were raised to help drag those kids into something like a better life.

It was a truly wonderful, heart-warming story. And it made the man behind it massive. Global. And you know what else? The whole thing was a sham.

So. Like I say, a certain newspaper received a tip about what was really going on. And what was really going on was this: the whole thing had been set up, planned in advance, the most photogenic urchins selected and kept safe months before he 'happened to chance upon them', every heartfelt utterance and exasperated sigh and dewy-eyed expression of regret and despair that we could live in such a cruel and uncaring world carefully scripted and committed to memory. There was a triumvirate of conspirators – a record-company boss with eyes on our boy for a career-resurrecting documentary, a leading charity director with an ends-justifies-the-means mentality and, of course, our friend himself. They had cooked it all up between them. There are emails. One of them even allegedly contains the following: 'People are bored of Africa. Africa isn't sexy any more. India's too dirty and Eastern Europe too ugly. Nobody wants to see any more backwards Romanian orphans – and besides, the music's shit. Whereas South

America… it's sexy, the samba's superb, the kids are beautiful, and there's enough guns and sunshine to keep it all photogenic.'

Cynical, eh? What a cynical so-and-so! And yet, it worked a dream. It showed our man to be both talented and caring. It melted a billion hearts worldwide – and sold almost as many CDs. The documentary shifted more DVDs than could be stocked – both sides of the Atlantic. And, to be fair, it raised a lot of dough for the charities involved.

But that's not all of it. There are other rumours too. I'm sure you can guess. But I wouldn't want to go there. Not without proof.

So. Nice chap, eh? No wonder he wants to shut us up.

Anyway! Enough about all this nonsense, Martin. I do keep boring on about work stuff, don't I? I do keep banging on about newspapers. I'm sure you couldn't give two figs: I'm sure the intricacies and intimacies of the Premier Westward running schedule and the continuing difficulties with signal boxes in the Taplow area dominate your thoughts, night and day. And quite right too. So they should.

One more thing though, before I go. Do you remember that baby-bonding weekend that sparked such a row last week? The one I either wilfully forgot about or didn't know about, depending on your point of view? The one I can't go on? Well, it seems Beth and Sylvie are going anyway. With or without me.

What do I think about that? I guess you're just going to have to wait until the next delay to find out. I've overrun this email enough already. But don't despair! Something tells me that you probably won't be holding your breath for too long…

Au revoir!

Dan

Letter 32

From: **DantheMan020@gmail.com**
To: Martin.Harbottle@premier-westward.com
Re: 20.20 Premier Westward Railways train from London Paddington to Oxford, September 28. Amount of my day wasted: eight minutes. Fellow sufferers: Sauron Flesh Harrower.

Dear Martin

Comrade! *Viva la revolución*! *Forza* insurrection! A new dawn rises, the tattered flag of protest still flies and all is not lost!

What? No, I'm not talking about Sauron Flesh Harrower and the nightly fights for the Dungeons of Azkhabar (or wherever). I'm not even talking about work and the battle for a free press that's happening right now in the Royal Courts of Justice. I'm talking about the news! The real news! The rebels have stormed the citadels of power – literally. In the dust and the despair and the blitzed-out remains of what was once the capital, through the rubble and the smoke and the abandoned bodies of dead men, the battered remains of the free people's army of North Africa have broken through the dictator's last defences.

They're in, Martin! They've taken the Imperial Palace. And the footage… the footage is incredible. It's just about the worst-quality, most poorly recorded, lowest-production-value recordings I've ever seen passed off as any kind of news report. But it's incredible. Shaky, hand-held, cheap Nokia action; blurry, distorted, out-of-focus satellite-phone coverage; a mess of people running and shouting and firing into the air, sandalled feet and filthy robes, beards and big hats and sudden faces – and a weird soundtrack of part-singing, part-yelling, gunshots and muffled crashes. And back in the studio, grave-faced presenters trying to make head or tail of it, but all agreeing on one thing: it's the end for the old regime. Unbelievably, incredibly, despite all the odds, freedom looks like it's won the day.

Except for one thing. There appears to be no sign of the old dictator himself. The main man, the *Grand Fromage*. Where is he?

We're counting on them finding him by Saturday. Goebbels has been doing his nut about it, he's not happy with the situation at all. 'We need closure!' he's been screaming at Harry the Dog. 'We need them to find him and we need it to happen before we go to press! Make it happen! Get on the phone and make it happen now! I want his head on a pole by Saturday afternoon! What's wrong with these people? How hard can it be? You've spent four months liberating the bleeding country and now you go and lose the man in charge? Idiots! Idiots!'

He's this close to sending one of us over there to go and do the job properly. 'Anyone with a camera would do,' he's been screaming at the picture desk. 'I can't use this crap! Find someone with a camera and get them to hold it still and point it in the vague direction of something interesting!'

He's not exactly filled with revolutionary fervour then, Martin. Not like us.

Or are you? Hang on: when was the last time you gave me your opinion on anything? When was the last time you wrote back to me, Martin? I need to know where you're at on all this. I need to know why my trains are so screwed up of course (first and foremost, in fact), but I need to know what you think of all this other stuff that's going on too. And actually, while we're here, and seeing as I did ask you a letter or two ago, I also need your worldly wise, avuncular advice re the whole Beth situation.

She's definitely going on this weekend thing on Friday. She's set on it, unrepentant about it. She said if I can't be bothered getting my priorities right, then perhaps it's best I don't come after all. But there's no way I can stop her going. So I said something like, it's only going to be mums there anyway, to which she replied that Mr Blair was going for a start.

Of course Mr Blair's going. Mr Blair, with his well-thumbed copy of the *Guardian* and his vegan coffee blends. Mr Perfect, with his perfect house and perfect child and perfectly balanced viewpoints. How could he not be going?

And so that settles it. If Beth's going for her weekend, then I'm going to do something nice with one of my friends too. Train Girl mentioned having another drink and I told her Saturday night would be good. Saturday, after we've put the paper to bed (with or without the dictator's head on a stick). And with no wife and child to get me up on Sunday morning, so much the better, right?

Au revoir!

Dan

From: **Martin.Harbottle@premier-westward.com**
To: DantheMan020@gmail.com
Re: 20.20 Premier Westward Railways train from London Paddington to Oxford, September 28.

Dear Dan

Thanks for your letters of September 14, 20, 24 and 28. I am sorry you have had the need to write to me again and I would like to take this opportunity once more to extend my deepest apologies. I would like to point out, however, that only the delay of September 14 was over ten minutes – ten minutes being the marker by which we class a train as being 'officially' delayed. But nonetheless, I fully understand how even the shortest lengthening of your journey can prove frustrating.

To address your other points: I have been following the news from North Africa with great interest, though I must confess the court case which your paper is defending has not captured my imagination to quite the same extent. Nevertheless it is fascinating to hear your stories of the 'crooner' in question. Quite the dark horse, as they say!

I am also flattered you consider my advice 'avuncular'! For what it's worth I can offer little else other than to repeat myself. The first years after having a baby are very difficult, but you must try to allow for your wife's hormonal imbalances and mood swings. Things will get better!

All the very best

Martin

Letter 33

From: **DantheMan020@gmail.com**
To: Martin.Harbottle@premier-westward.com
Re: 07.31 Premier Westward Railways train from Oxford to London Paddington, September 29. Amount of my day wasted: ten minutes. Fellow sufferers: Lego Head, Guilty New Mum, Train Girl, Universal Grandpa.

Oh, Martin. This is no good. I write to you last night, and now I'm having to write again this morning. The very next day. The very next train. It was delayed coming into Oxford, it dawdled a fair while on the platform at Oxford, it was overdue leaving Oxford. Is it any wonder it got into London ten minutes late?

Which apparently barely counts as a delay at all! Are you serious? Are you redefining the English language? Are you redefining the very concept of time itself? Tell you what: let's just stick with my definition of delayed. Let's just say, for argument's sake, that 'delayed' means 'didn't arrive on time'.

So. My train to work this morning was delayed – whichever way you choose to define it. And I really could have done with arriving on time today, too. Given what happened last night and all. Given I was up all night, watching it happen live on the news channels, Sylvie balanced on my lap, chubby little cheeks lit blue by the light of the three a.m. telly, alternately gurgling, screaming and sleeping. (That's

Sylvie gurgling, screaming and sleeping, not me.) Given it's going to mean a big day at work today. (Even for us showbiz types. It'll be all hands on deck, even for those of us who wallow in the shallow end.)

But it was mental stuff, all right. It was worth staying up for. The pursuit, the chase, the capture. The execution. When I tuned in, reports were filtering through of something afoot in the Imperial Palace and by the time they'd got their man on the ground in amongst the action, a full-scale hunt was in progress. Hundreds of men legging it through corridors and bursting into rooms, robes and sandals and bare feet and everyone clutching some kind of weapon. Battered automatic guns, machetes, kitchen knives, sticks, bricks, bottles... anything that could do a bit of damage. Rushing from one room to another with deadly intent and our lone western reporter right in the thick of it.

Word had got out that the old dictator was still around. He hadn't scarpered too far after all. He didn't even make it off the premises. In one of the thousand nooks and crannies and secret places of his old palace, the most hated man in the world was holed up. Elvis had not left the building. And now everyone who could find something to hurt him with was ripping the place apart trying to find him.

Do you know what it reminded me of? Do you remember back when English football hooligans used to tear up foreign cities? Like a ragged, shambolic, sunburned militia, running through the streets hurling whatever they could find at whatever they could reach, seemingly completely chaotic yet all oddly guided by the same instinct, the same unarticulated plan: left here, right there, up against the *Carabinieri* there, and more often than not with a breathless, half-scared, half-exhilarated reporter amongst them, ducking the debris and the beer spray. Well, it reminded me of that, in a strange way. There was no strategy to the chase – but you just knew that with every ransacked room and smashed-up corridor they were getting closer.

And then they found it. The secret door. An actual, real-life, secret door! Those things really exist! Not only that, but the reporter, the man with the only live camera feed back to the west, was right there with them when they uncovered it. And then… and then it got quicker. Things sped up – and things turned brutal.

Door smashed in, stairs charged, camera almost dropped in the crush, a room uncovered, a moment's pause as they took it in – and then howls of protest, cries of anguish, screams of absolute rage. The old dictator's old torture chamber. His personal torture chamber, for his personal use. Manacles and shackles and electrical cable. Bloodied tables and bins full of… stuff. Tool kits. Meat hooks. Bodies and bits of bodies. Horror.

And, finally, the money shot. A shaky zoom towards one of the torsos still hanging on a wall – and there, what's that, behind it, a glimpse of beard, two terrified eyes and a mop of matted black hair. Cowering behind a mutilated corpse was the man this whole thing was about. You couldn't make it up, Martin. Hollywood couldn't do it justice.

That glimpse was all we got before the crowd, the mob, saw him too and the shot was lost in an angry blur. And then the awful bit. Thank Christ Sylvie was asleep. Just the noises alone could give you nightmares. The hacking and slicing and bashing and crunching and breaking and squelching and screaming and, underneath it all, our man on the ground, our eyes and ears, pleading, begging, sobbing at them to stop. But never taking his lens off the action.

There wasn't much left in the end. And when they cut back to the studio, there was horrified, unbelieving silence for at least 30 seconds before someone remembered what they were supposed to be doing. And I have never ever seen anything like it in my life.

These are the good guys, remember. These are the ones we've been cheering along all this time. Those guys being broadcast committing murder last night, those boys literally beating the life out of someone live on TV – they're the ones we've been calling heroes all summer long. Little wonder the bods in the studio weren't sure what to say.

So: it's going to be a big day at work today. I've had next to no sleep and it is what I think can safely be called a major news day. I'm going to be lucky if I leave my desk before at least ten hours have passed. And starting the day late thanks to ten minutes spent kicking our heels at Slough isn't exactly ideal, is it, Martin?

Au revoir!

Dan

Letter 34

From: **DantheMan020@gmail.com**
To: Martin.Harbottle@premier-westward.com
Re: 07.31 Premier Westward Railways train from Oxford to London Paddington, September 30. Amount of my day wasted: 15 minutes. Fellow sufferers: Train Girl, Lego Head. (Where is everyone?)

Oh hello, here we go again. Back once again with the renegade station master. Three delays in three days, Martin! The hat trick. That means you buy everyone a drink, right? Everyone in the Premier Westward Imperial Palace gets a glass on the house, courtesy of the MD's Wednesday to Friday treble of delays. And you saved the best to last. Fifteen minutes this morning.

Standards. That's what it's all about. Standards, and making sure you keep hold of them. That's the thing: in work and in life. Those North African rebels – it rather looks like they may have lost their standards a little, doesn't it? What with the way they ripped apart the man who used to be in charge of them. What with the dismembering and the beheading and whatnot. The dispassionate observer might say they let their standards slip a smidgen there. Even if their motives seemed understandable. Tricky to set yourself up as a champion of freedom and justice when you're physically ripping the bowels out of someone with a kitchen knife.

It's got everyone in a bit of a flap. It's got a lot of people unsure just what they should be thinking. (Not us, though: we've got a very clear line on the whole messy business. Do you want to know our angle? Shall I give you a world exclusive scoop of this Sunday's front-page splash? We're running with: GOOD RIDDANCE. That's what we do, Martin: we take a complicated problem and make it beautifully simple. Good riddance. You won't find a better headline all weekend. It's one of Harry the Dog's finest. He's as proud of those two words as he ever was of anything achieved at Oxford.)

And talking of standards, the *Globe* has always been a newspaper that sets standards, right? One way or another. It's the biggest-selling paper, that's for sure, the most-read. It's almost certainly got the biggest budget. It gets the biggest scoops, the best stories. It nurtures talent and pays talent and poaches talent and looks after talent. It's got standards, all right.

But then it's also got a certain standard of ruthlessness too. It's quick to judge, slow to forgive. It doesn't tolerate slackness, or incompetence, or weakness – from politicians, public servants, celebrities or, to be honest, its own staff. It takes no prisoners.

That's the standards we set, right? That's what's expected of us, as the scurrilous, scandalous, standard-bearer of tabloid journalism. That's what we do.

Except maybe it isn't any more. Goebbels pulled me aside yesterday afternoon, into his office, cleared space among the million fuzzy pictures of what was left of the old dictator, the bits of him they strung up on that flag pole, and motioned for me to sit down. He wanted my opinion. He was worried. This court case, he said, was in danger of diluting everything the *Globe* stood for. Our standards, he said, were under threat.

Take a look at the paper, he said. What have we been splashing with lately? This Sunday aside – nothing. Nothing worth the title it's printed under. Nothing that wouldn't ordinarily make a page seven lead at best. Or a mid-paper investigation. An *Amazeballs!* feature. We're scared, he said. While this legal nonsense is going on and the attention of the world's media is focused on us, examining our every move through forensic eyes, we're bottling it, too frightened to take a risk on a great story. We're becoming scared of pissing anyone off. The *Globe* has become timid, he said, and it was breaking his heart. And he wanted to know what I thought about it.

I said I thought that it was better to be careful now. I said we were right to play the long game. And given what we know about the way some of the things around the place used to work (Did I tell you the story about the reporter who regularly filed expenses for prostitutes and cocaine? Do tell me if I repeat myself!) perhaps it was better to calm it all down a bit.

And then do you know what he said? He said nothing. He threw a mouse at me. (Not a real mouse, a computer mouse. And it only made it about a foot out of his hand before being jerked back by its cable and falling on his desk.) And then he stood there and glared at me for what must have been a full 90 seconds.

And then, finally, he started shouting. 'Listen, sunshine,' he yelled, 'do you know what paper you work for? Do you know the history of this place? The standards we set? If you've not got the balls for this job, if you've not got what it takes to be a proper journalist, then I suggest you go buy yourself a tweed jacket with patches on the elbows and head over to the bloody *Guardian* and spend your days chewing lentils and writing about sodding Danish dramas nobody watches or cares about.

'But as long as you're here, and as long as you want to be a journalist, you do what I say. And I'm saying this: the fightback starts here. Let's get inspired by these boys in North Africa. Let's come out swinging. Specifically, with your column. You're too… nice,' (he spat the word). 'You started promisingly, but it's getting boring. Dig up some dirt. Say something that's going to get people talking. Make me laugh. Make me wince. Write something that's going to get quoted by other people.

'Listen, Dan,' he continued, voice softer now, but if anything even scarier than before. 'You've got real promise in this place. But you need to show me you can cut it. Jamie Best was a great result – but it's over now. And until you find me another splash like it, make your column something this paper can be proud of.'

And then he walked out, leaving me alone with all those photos. He'd even tacked one on the wall above his computer screen. It was (most of) the dictator's head: half-scalped, missing an eye, beard matted with blood and bits of brain. As I came out he saw me and pointed at it: 'If I had my way,' he said, 'that would be our front page. Head on a stick, son: that's what they want. Head on a stick.'

So, yes, Martin: standards. These are the standards of the world's greatest newspaper. And I'm being told to set the bar high once again. Today is Friday, and I'm going to have to spike this week's column and start again. I'm going to have to hit the phones and find a story. Something Goebbels will like. Something nasty.

What do you think about that? Do my standards matter? Do I even have any standards any more? My wife doesn't think so, for a start. I told Beth about it, of course. I asked her the same question last night, and do you know what she did? She started crying.

She said, 'You sold your standards when you started working for that paper.' And then she said, 'Whenever they tell you to jump you always jump. You don't ask how high, you just jump as high as you can and hope it's high enough.' And then she said, 'What's happening to you? What's happened to us? We used to laugh, we used to have a laugh. And now… you're always stressed and I'm always in a shitty mood and all we do is argue and worry.'

And then she told me she loves me. And I told her I love her too. And we both started crying because it's true but we keep forgetting it, what with life and everything getting in the way. How did that happen? How did life get in the way?

When we first moved here, Martin, to Oxford, out of London and into our dream little terraced house, it was always better. I might have the rose-tinted aviators on here, but the way I remember it, everything was better then. How is that? It can't just be about Sylvie – and it can't just be about my job. Can it?

The thing is, we don't do stuff now. We used to do stuff. We even went punting once. (Actually, I lie: we went punting twice. The first time was on a glorious afternoon in May, the kind of afternoon where every cliché about Oxford in the spring is duly ticked off – the students in black tie swigging champagne after their exams, the thwack of leather on willow in Christ Church meadows and University Parks, the dons asleep in the Botanical Gardens, and on the river, sparkling in the sun and drifting gently with the apple blossom down to Folly Bridge, dozens of punts, filled (mostly) with the young and beautiful and carefree. And us with them, sharing a bottle of white and zigzagging our way along. The second time… well, the second time was later that night, after the pubs shut, when we were good and plastered and decided to nick a boat and punt our way home, like pirates. We got about eight feet downriver before I overbalanced and took us both overboard.)

We used to go to gigs together, Martin. We even went to the theatre. We hung out in the cafe at the modern art gallery and walked out to little pubs in the country. We did couple stuff, the stuff couples do. And if love is an endless afternoon, it felt like an endless afternoon. An endless afternoon in the summer.

And now she's away this weekend and I've lost my standards. And as if to prove it, today I'm going to write something gratuitously nasty about a bunch of stupid kids on a reality TV show and tomorrow night I'm getting drunk with Train Girl.

Standards, Martin. Always the standards.

Au revoir!

Dan

From: **Martin.Harbottle@premier-westward.com**
To: DantheMan020@gmail.com
Re: 07.31 Premier Westward Railways train from Oxford to London Paddington, September 30.

Dear Dan

Thank you for your two most recent letters, I am sorry to hear your morning commute to work has been disrupted again. The problem on Thursday was related to communication issues at Network Rail's end of things, and on Friday all of the trains were delayed after a malfunctioning door at one of our depots resulted in some carriages being unable to be put in to service until later in the day. As I'm sure you appreciate, both events were the kind of unforeseen problems that one simply cannot plan for.

I do hope, however, that such 'acts of God' will not put you off continuing to travel with Premier Westward, and I can assure you that we strive every day to maintain the standards for which we have become rightly famous.

Best

Martin

Letter 35

From: **DantheMan020@gmail.com**
To: Martin.Harbottle@premier-westward.com
Re: 07.31 Premier Westward Railways train from London Paddington to Oxford, October 4. Amount of my day wasted: 13 minutes. Fellow sufferers: Train Girl, Lego Head, Competitive Tech Nerds, Universal Grandpa.

Dear Martin

Are you OK? Did you write that last letter to me drunk? Are you having some kind of episode? What on earth are you talking about? Acts of God? Have you lost your marbles completely?

I think perhaps it's best if we forget you ever wrote that last letter to me at all and simply agree to move on and never mention the whole embarrassing business again. But really: acts of God? As the editor of *Amazeballs!* might say, WTF?

Besides: there are so many more interesting things to talk about. There's news to report, home and away. And as well as all that, there's dirt to be dug!

(Did you see my column on Sunday? What did you think of this new slant we're taking, this aggressive new stance we're adopting? Did you like the bit where I described that unfortunate girl with the eating disorder as 'Moominmamma with a meat-feast pizza for a face'? Or the way I basically outed that over-aggressive Geordie lad as a secret bisexual by judicious employment of the phrase 'a real man's man'? Were you impressed with the sarcasm? With the use of fair comment to disguise a load of unsubstantiated insults? Did it tickle you how I appeared to have not only thrown away my standards but done so with gay abandon and, actually, appeared to have rather enjoyed it? I do hope so!

Universal Grandpa seemed to be impressed, anyway. 'My daughter liked your column again on Sunday,' he told me, as we waited for the train to arrive this morning. 'She said to tell you you're a saucy devil.'

'Well, in that case,' I replied, 'tell her it takes one to know one.' And then I thought: what am I doing? Flirting with an old man's daughter I've never met – and doing it through the old man himself? That's got to be wrong on soooo many levels.)

Anyway, we'll see today what the fallout is. We'll see what the lawyers made of it. Goebbels seemed to like it, anyway. 'It's a start,' was his text on Sunday morning. That was all. A start.

Actually, perhaps we won't hear from the lawyers today. The lawyers look set for a busy time of it again; it looks like the lawyers may have bigger fish to pull out of the fire and back into the frying pan. If yesterday was anything to go by, the court case is picking up pace again. There were developments, Martin!

It seems our syrup-sporting friend is rather enjoying his moment in the sun. Or rather, his lawyer is. (It seems to me that his lawyer sees himself as a bit of an amateur entertainer himself. There are too many verbal flourishes, a little too much grandstanding, for an ordinary performance. I can't help thinking that he's seeing this as his chance to impress, to be noticed, to make a name for himself. Lawyers, singers, byline-hungry journalists: we're all the same, really, aren't we? All hopping up and down, desperate to be seen, shouting 'look at me, everyone' to anyone who'll listen, ready to drop our standards at a moment's notice.)

So. That stuff in the Royal Courts of Justice yesterday. That talk of iceberg tips and avalanches (I love a good mixed metaphor!), of this case 'not being extraordinary, but, rather, horribly ordinary', of all the crimes (are they crimes?) we supposedly inflicted upon the poor helpless pup – the listening, and following, and fabricating, the interceptions and investigations and harassment and honey traps – being 'standard practice' and 'accepted practice' and 'just another day at the *Globe* office'.

And then the specifics. That nosy-neighbour-type they wheeled out, the net-curtain-twitching lady of a certain age who told how she used to see photographers hiding in the bushes; the postman who fessed up to taking a bung for the loan of his uniform for an hour one afternoon (oldest trick in the book – everyone trusts a postman at the door); the florist who said the same of her van (who can resist flowers?); the parade of doe-eyed, flicky-haired girls who recounted the huge sums of money they were promised for a camera-phone snap of our man *in flagrante*. (Notice they only called up the ones who turned the money down. There were plenty who didn't.)

And after all that, rather brilliantly it has to be said, the dismissal of all their evidence – by the man who had called them to the stand in the first place – as 'trivia' and 'hardly worth bothering with'. These aren't the real crimes, he said. The dynamite is still to come. The dynamite in this case… and in many more cases after this.

'If anyone thinks for a moment that my client is the only man to have suffered such shocking treatment at the hands of this "organ", then do please think again,' he said, waving a piece of paper. 'I have here a list of names several dozen long who have all approached me for similar representation. This case may be the first to be brought, but it will not be the last. And it almost certainly will not be the most shocking.'

It will not be the last. That's not good. That's going to get everyone nervous. But what was that last line about? Not the most shocking? What's the story there?

I can't help wondering who he's got on that list. I mean, if it is just a bunch of has-beens and wannabes and nearly-weres all out to make a buck on the back of a little press intrusion, that's one thing. And even if it's proper celebs, or public officials, or MPs… I reckon that's dealable with too. A Public Interest defence goes a long way. Everyone's got skeletons to expose.

But if it's something else… well, let's not go there again. Like I said back in August, that stuff about the mobile phone of the mother of the best-known victim of the Beast of Berkhamsted – it's just rumours. Just newsroom paranoia. Not even the gutter-dwelling, scum-wallowing *Globe* would stoop to hacking the families of murder victims. We wouldn't bother with normals at all. What would be the point? Where's the Public Interest defence in that?

No, despite what some are muttering, I don't reckon there are any ordinaries on that list of his. I'm sure it's just another flock of whining, over-pampered, double-standard-touting celebs looking for a bit of publicity, cash, and revenge. Although it will be interesting to hear what the older boys on the news desk make of it.

And meanwhile, back in the real world, things are moving again too. The newest government in the world (to be accurate, I'm not sure they're actually a government yet, as opposed to a rag-tag people's militia who've found themselves in charge) are trying to find their feet. Job one: make sure that victory's not Pyrrhic.

You remember Pyrrhic victories, right? When the cost of winning makes victory worthless? Well, it seems that's where our brave revolutionaries seem to be finding themselves. I'm not even talking about the whole moral side of things – despite the whole head-on-a-stick unpleasantness back in the Imperial Palace last week. I'm talking about the actual physical cost of taking the country.

Harry the Dog told me on Saturday that the real action's not even begun yet. Keep an eye on the borders, he reckons. Those neighbouring countries – with leaders every bit as nasty in their own way as the man we saw ripped apart on live TV last week – are eyeing up events with interest. They could have intervened, one way or another, months ago. They didn't. And the question is why?

They've got standing armies. And, according to Harry's sources, all leave has been cancelled. Those standing armies aren't going to be standing for too much longer. There's a whole nation there with borders wide open, a bunch of peasants in charge and seemingly no international community interested in backing them up.

There are three neighbouring regimes eyeing the place up, Martin. And according to Harry the Dog at least, it's going to simply be a matter of who reaches the capital first.

So, as they say in California, like totally Pyrrhic, right?

Au revoir!

Dan

Letter 36

From: **DantheMan020@gmail.com**
To: Martin.Harbottle@premier-westward.com
Re: 07.31 Premier Westward Railways train from Oxford to London Paddington, October 5. Amount of my day wasted: zero minutes. Fellow sufferers: Train Girl, Guilty New Mum, Lego Head, Universal Grandpa, Competitive Tech Nerds.

Check it out! High drama on the morning train! It all went off on the 07.31, as someone once said. (OK, nobody's ever said that, but you know what I mean.)

Today's the day Lego Head cracked. And it was pretty terrifying. (There's also swearing, Martin, just so you're warned. If you're of a sensitive disposition, look away now.)

I know that technically there was no actual delay on this train, but I couldn't wait to tell you all about it. It's huge, Martin. It's amazing. Unprecedented. And I've got to tell you about it now. You don't mind, do you? You probably owe me a few minutes from somewhere along the line.

So. Things started as usual. Everyone in their usual places on the platform, the Coach C regulars rooted to the same spots as always, shuffling forwards to the yellow line (do not cross the yellow line!) as the train heaved itself heavily alongside. The nod and the wink to Universal Grandpa at the door, the sympathetic smile to Guilty New Mum as she bustled and panicked her way down the aisle, dropping a diary and a bottle of Calpol out of her handbag, phone glued to the ear as usual, letting Sue know all about her latest troubles with the croup ('And now I've only brought the pissing Calpol to work with me and left my glasses on the bathroom shelf. Which means I'm not only blind all day and am going to have to bluff it through the whole stupid G8 thing but we're going to have to get another bottle of Calpol in case she worsens this morning...').

Train Girl turned up late, like always, flying down the platform and blowing a kiss at the guard as he held open the door for her and tried to look stern, landing on the seat next to me with a laugh and a pair of scalding coffees. And before we'd cleared the outskirts of Oxford, the Competitive Tech Nerds were at it again, showing off home music studio apps to each other on their iPads (like either of them have any need for a home music studio anyway. Who do they think they are? Brian Eno?).

And opposite them, next to Guilty New Mum, Lego Head. In the aisle seat. Facing opposite the direction of travel. And, as per, straight and calm and still in his seat, gazing at nothing, focusing on nothing. In a state of nirvana. The Buddha of the morning commute.

Until...

'Yeah, but I'm talking mic and plug-in recording options. That's what's really important, not whether you've got 16 or 32 tracks to record on.'

'Not true, mate. It's all about the mixing desk. And with more tracks to play with, the better the mix. Any producer will tell you that. Any.'

'You're falling into the classic trap there. *Sergeant Pepper* was recorded on an eight-track, as well you know.'

'Sixteen-track, mate.'

'Wrong. Eight-track.'

'Listen, mate, don't talk to me about *Sergeant Pepper*, OK? I must be the biggest Beatles fan there is, I've got all the albums, I've seen McCartney twice and the Bootleg Beatles half a dozen times and I am telling you that *Pepper* was recorded on a 16-track deck in Abbey Road Studios in 1968. You are way out of your league, my friend, way out.'

'I'm way out of my league? You're way out of your le—'

And then it happened. I watched it all unfold, surreal and in slow motion.

With an almost perceptible snap, Lego Head's eyes came back into focus, he lowered his head and fixed the Competitive Tech Nerds with a look so full of contempt, so loaded with scorn and disgust, I couldn't quite believe what I was seeing. First one, then the other noticed, and the conversation petered out. And then he spoke. For the first time in all these hundreds of journeys we've shared, Lego Head opened his mouth and spoke.

'*Sergeant Pepper*,' he said, slowly and carefully and in a surprisingly low tone and with, of all things, a Scouse accent, 'was recorded in 1967. On a four-track recorder. Four. Not eight, not sixteen. Four. So why don't you both shut up until you know what it is you're talking about. Or better still: shut up altogether.'

One of them started to say something and Lego Head held up a hand for silence. 'I haven't finished. Nobody cares about your music studio apps, or your GPS apps, or your content delivery apps, or whether you view them on Apple or Android or fucking Microsoft devices, or what MP3 players you use, or what headphones you plug into them, or what sort of dock you plug them into, or what fucking phone you use, or what laptop, desktop, tablet or fucking CALCULATOR you fucking use, or how many fucking megabytes or gigabytes or FUCKING TERABYTES you have or whether your fucking TV is a fucking smart TV or a fucking HDTV OR 3DTV OR A FUCKING TARDIS. NOBODY CARES, DO YOU UNDERSTAND? NOBODY FUCKING CARES ABOUT ALL OF YOUR USELESS SHITE. SO SIT DOWN, SHUT YOUR MOUTHS AND IF I HEAR ANOTHER WORD ABOUT ANY OF IT I'M GOING TO SHOVE IT ALL DOWN YOUR FUCKING THROATS. ALL RIGHT? ALL RIGHT?'

He was screaming by the end. Standing up in his seat like some huge, furious Scouse rhinoceros, screaming at the top of his voice at the cowering pair. The rest of the carriage was in dead silence.

When he finished he simply sat down, closed his eyes, tilted his head back and resumed his former position, as if nothing at all had happened. And, given that this was, of course, on a train in Britain in the morning, everyone else pretended nothing had happened too. Guilty New Mum made another call, Universal Grandpa resumed his crossword. It was like a paused DVD had started again – everyone just picking up where they'd left off. Carrying on regardless.

All except me and Train Girl. I stared, open-mouthed. She burst out laughing. 'Bravo!' she shouted at Lego Head. 'Well said, that man! A fucking Tardis! Ha!'

I kept my eyes on the Competitive Tech Nerds. They both looked like they were about to burst into tears. Can't say I blamed them either, and I told Train Girl to keep it down. Yes, they're idiots, and sure they're annoying, but nobody deserves that kind of humiliation, do they? Not in front of everyone?

And besides, I was a bit scared Lego Head might turn on us too.

The rest of the journey to London was sort of the same as usual. I say sort of, because it was like we were all pretending it was the same. Something fundamental had changed (Buddha had turned into… I dunno, Thor?) but everyone kept up the pretence that all was normal. All except Train Girl, who kept glancing over at them and laughing. Too much so, if you ask me.

So, like I say, sorry for the letter when there's no delay. But I bet you're glad I did write, eh? Whatever next!

Au revoir!

Dan

Letter 37

From: **DantheMan020@gmail.com**
To: Martin.Harbottle@premier-westward.com
Re: 20.50 Premier Westward Railways train from London Paddington to Oxford, October 5. Amount of my day wasted: three minutes. Fellow sufferers: Sauron Flesh Harrower.

Oh, Martin. Isn't this just typical? There I was this morning, dashing off a letter to you when there was no delay to speak of, and here I am this evening, slumped and frustrated and reeking of cheap wine outside Reading, subject to a proper, real-life delay. I could have saved that stuff from earlier, couldn't I? I could have written it all down now – and at greater length, in better detail, with more vivid colour.

Whatever shall we discuss? There's so much to say! Life is very long.

Life is very long, when you're lonely. Morrissey said that, as you well know. (You remember Morrissey, don't you? Lead singer with chirpy cockney bubblegum pop outfit Steve Morrissey and the Swinging Smiths. Had a string of Stockhausen–Waterman produced hits in the 1970s. Famously played their last gig on a rooftop in Jimmy Savile Row. Drummer only had one arm. Bassist sacked to be replaced by Sid Vicious. That's right! That's the one! Steve Morrissey! Had a well-publicised affair with Kylie Minogue. Enjoyed a Britpop chart battle with Oasis. Replaced Cheryl Cole as a judge on X Factor USA. Steve Morrissey! Good old Steve Morrissey!)

What's that? I'm talking rubbish? Well yes, perhaps I am. I may have had a drink. I may have spent the afternoon getting good and sauced with Harry the Dog at the pub over the road from work; we may have gone for lunch and never come back… but nevertheless. My train is delayed and a letter must be written. You have a duty to listen, right?

No? OK, I'll shut up. Was only three minutes anyway, right? See if I care.

Oh: one more thing. Sauron Flesh Harrower is on this train, and you know what? I'm beginning to think I recognise him from somewhere. Is that mad?

Au revoir!

Dan

Letter 38

From: **DantheMan020@gmail.com**
To: Martin.Harbottle@premier-westward.com
Re: 22.50 Premier Westward Railways train from London Paddington to Oxford, October 8. Amount of my day wasted: ten minutes. Fellow sufferers: No regulars (Saturday).

Dear Martin

Apologies. I may have been a little over-emotional in my last letter to you. I may have let the drink do some of my talking. Believe it or not, shambolic and disgraceful as your trains are, and despite how much I wish I wasn't delayed so much, I do (sort of) enjoy writing these letters to you. It's nice to talk to someone about stuff.

It would be nicer if you wrote back a bit more, obviously. I'd still love to know what you made of Lego Head's outburst the other day, for a start.

But then also, I'll confess, it is nice to have someone to talk to. Someone who doesn't know me, I mean. Someone away from the madness of work and someone away from the difficulties of home. I've only really got two proper friends – I married one, and the other… well, the other is Harry the Dog. He is a mate, of course, but I wouldn't actually tell him anything serious. He's a drinking mate, a laughing mate, a swapper of tales and creator of anecdotes. He's not someone to confide in.

And then there's Beth. She's both a laughing mate and someone to confide in. That's what she's always been – that's why I married her. But lately, we've changed. I don't know why, or even how exactly, but I wish we hadn't.

Are we having a crisis, me and Beth? I hope not. I don't want to have a crisis. I want things to be the way they were. I don't want to have to go through everything that couples having crises go through. Can't we just stop all the nonsense and start again? Press pause, rewind, record over all this new stuff?

Maybe. I hope so. I want to. I just don't know how to. Let me explain. Let me tell you about last weekend. What with everything else that's happened, I still haven't told you about last weekend.

Let's put it this way: Beth and I both had a great time last weekend. Though not with each other, obviously. She was away at her baby-bonding thing; I was out in London town with Train Girl. (My new friend, I guess. My third friend.)

What happened? Well, my wife came home full of enthusiasm and energy. She had a spring in her step and a smile on her face and a sparkle in her eye. The baby-bonding stuff was amazing, she said. She felt she really got closer to Sylvie, that the pair of them really connected, and that as a result from now on she was sure things would be easier for Sylvie at night. She was full of talk of baby massage and baby sign language and eye-to-eye and nose-to-nose and skin-to-skin contact. It was brilliant, she said, I should have seen it.

And what did I say? I said: great! Fantastic! So pleased! I even asked how Mr Blair did, as the only man there. 'Oh him,' she said. 'Dunno. I didn't really notice him, we were in different groups, mostly.'

The thing is, I was genuinely pleased she had a good time. I am genuinely pleased, I mean. And it was lovely to see her smiling again, to see the spark and the bounce and the energy back. She is still the girl I fell in love with, you know. That's not changed. She's still the coolest girl I've ever known, despite it all. And of course I missed little Sylvie when she was away – I missed our own bonding time, those late nights and super-early mornings on the sofa, her snoring on my chest, me watching atrocities in North Africa.

But then, I also had a pretty good time last weekend. I met up with Train Girl again, we hit Soho again, we got good and trashed together again. And we didn't talk about work, or about babies, or about how little sleep we were getting, or how the kitchen tap needs fixing. We talked about… actually, I can't really remember what we talked about. We talked rubbish. We talked and talked, we talked non-stop – and it was all fun, and most of it was funny (most of it hilarious in fact) and then when the pubs were kicking out she led me to this illegal basement bar off the Tottenham Court Road where there was a full-on Northern Soul party going on and an ancient man with dreadlocks who looked like a prophet and stank of ganja was selling cans of Red Stripe at a quid a go, and we danced like idiots to early Motown classics until about four in the morning.

And all that night, Martin, even when she tripped on Old Compton Street and fell – literally, movie-star-like – into my arms and I caught her, instinctively, one hand cradling her head and the other round her waist so I could feel the skin (soft, warm) where her shirt had ridden up from her jeans; all that night, even when we were mock slow dancing together to the Supremes in that basement bar and both her arms were raised around my neck and her hands were locked together at the back of my head and we were so close we kept stepping on each other's feet… all that night, we didn't even kiss. Not so much as a peck, except when we said goodnight, and I sloped back to Paddington to get the morning train home.

We didn't kiss. Of course we didn't kiss! Because, ludicrously, ridiculously, even in the midst of it all, even in the heat of the moment and under the influence of a good deal of alcohol, I kept thinking about Beth. My first thought on entering that basement bar was 'Beth would love this'. Despite it all, Martin, she's always on my mind. And the oddest thing of all is, I can't exactly tell her so, can I?

Au revoir!

Dan

From: **Martin.Harbottle@premier-westward.com**
To: DantheMan020@gmail.com
Re: 22.50 Premier Westward Railways train from London Paddington to Oxford, October 8.

Dear Dan

Thank you for your four letters this week and please accept my apologies for the three delays you experienced. The problem on Tuesday was entirely a fault of Network Rail, Wednesday evening saw us fall victim to vandalism of a signal box near Acton, and the delay to your journey on Saturday was the unfortunate result of a knock-on problem caused by earlier congestion from a cross-country train in Reading.

And please do not apologise if your letters occasionally veer towards the over-emotional. The truth is that while of course I am always sorry that you have to write to me at all, I do experience a little guilty pleasure at reading of the 'inside track' at the *Globe*! Your job – although I'm sure rather difficult in the present circumstances – does sound very exciting!

As regards the incident you mentioned with 'Lego Head': I have filed an official report on his behaviour. Regardless of provocation, foul and abusive language cannot be tolerated on any Premier Westward train – further incidents may lead to the beginnings of disciplinary action. Thank you for bringing that to my attention.

Best regards

Martin

Letter 39

From: **DantheMan020@gmail.com**
To: Martin.Harbottle@premier-westward.com
Re: 07.31 Premier Westward Railways train from Oxford to London Paddington, October 12. Amount of my day wasted: 14 minutes. Fellow sufferers: Train Girl, Lego Head, Guilty New Mum, Universal Grandpa.

Tally ho, Martin! Buck up there! Keep the old spirits high! Awful rotten luck in the rugger, of course – for England to go out like that, in the quarter finals, to a team as flaky and flukey as the Argentinians. Worse luck still to see our chaps so humiliated; and positively despicable sportsmanship of the victors to all peel off their shirts after the game to reveal 'Malvinas' t-shirts underneath. Terrible. Just not cricket at all. Not cricket and not rugby.

Still. Never mind, eh? Let's not dwell on what might have been. Let's move on!

Thanks for your reply, Martin! I'm so pleased to hear you're pleased to hear from me. Strictly speaking I wasn't really reporting Lego Head for anything, but I guess you're welcome anyway. And to be fair to the man, since it all happened he's been back to his usual self: implacable and unmoving in his seat all the way to Paddington. Competitive Tech Nerds have swapped carriages, however: I see them in the morning a little further down the platform, skulking with the amateurs at Coach E. (I say amateurs because, as I'm sure you know as well as I do, Coach E is the first of the standard coaches we all cram into, and as such tends to fill up much quicker than the others as the non-regular commuters panic and jump on the first available carriage they can find.)

I'm also pleased to hear that my troubles at work are proving so entertaining. Not sure I see it that way exactly, but still. It's nice to make someone else feel happy, right?

So what have I been up to? Well, Harry the Dog and I have been in the pub a fair bit. He's got his eye on one of the trainees and we've been entertaining her with tales from the tabloid front line, some dirty stories of the filthy trade. To be honest, it's the sort of thing we talk about anyway, but it's always nice to have a new audience. She's tiny, Scottish, shy, keeps her eyes down, but files remarkably good copy. We call her the Wee Tim'rous Trainee.

Last night we were joined by the editor of *Amazeballs!*, the magazine that comes with our paper: the 60-odd pages of celebs and fashion and beauty and those unbelievable real-life features ('I married my daughter's first boyfriend', 'My goldfish is possessed by Satan', 'Meet the women turning lesbian for God', etc) that supposedly give the girls something to read on a Sunday too.

Anyway. The editor of *Amazeballs!* is Rochelle – but everyone calls her Bombshell. (Don't worry, Martin, it took me a while to work out, too.) And the thing is: she is, too. Five foot four of pure energy. Swears like a soldier, drinks like a docker, looks like a film star. She's amazing. She's also terrifying. And last night she was on top form.

'We ran a feature last week,' she said, holding aloft a pint of Guinness in perfectly manicured hands. 'Wash in/wash out hair dyes, right? Get the look. One model, four glossy pages, four different hair colours. Looked totes amaze. I mean, sodding beautiful. Like, utterly spesh, right?

'But you know what,' and she took a pull of her pint and winked at the trainee. 'The model was blonde. She stayed blonde. In all the shots, she stayed blonde. We didn't dye her hair at all. Of course we didn't! WTF? We can't go round dying models' hair four different colours! We totes did the whole shizz on Photoshop!'

Wee Tim'rous Trainee stammered something about ethics, and Bombshell burst out laughing.

'Like – oh em gee! Ethi-whats? Darls, it's not exactly PCC stuff, is it? And anyway, we totes matched the colour to the colour on the pack.

Happens all the time. If you're shocked by that then you've got a lot to learn, sweetie. Like for example that piece we ran a few months ago, our Naked Beauty spesh. Nine top stars, *sans* make-up! Not any old desperadoes either – strictly A-list, strictly as nature intended. Well, maybe not A-list as in Hollywood A-list, but as A-list as *Amazeballs!* is going to get, right? No reality saddos, anyway.'

She turned to Harry. 'You remember that, don't you, darls? Everyone went totes crazy over it. Massive pick up. World-freakin'-wide. Showed just how beautiful we can be without all the slap. And nobody could quite believe we'd persuaded all those girls to do it.'

She grinned and winked at us. 'Do you want to know how we persuaded them? What our secret was? Promise you won't tell?'

We all nodded.

'The secret was, they weren't without make-up at all. Don't be ridiculous. Of course they had make-up on, you silly fuckers! Just very, very well-applied make-up. Make-up so beautifully subtle that it gave the impression of there being no make-up at all. Do you really think anyone in their right mind would do a shoot without any make-up? None of those stars are going to pose without make-up – that would be totes massively insane.'

She laughed and drained her pint. 'Tell you what, sweetie,' she said, fishing out a credit card and sliding it across the table. 'Get another round on there and I'll tell you a real journo trick, something you can use, a secret about doorknocks. About how to get into the house that mad bastard Goebbels sends you on, about how to get that line he's going to go totes apeshit if you come back without. Oh – and don't forget the receipt for those, darls.'

Drinks duly replenished, she continued.

'Three things. First: you have to remember these are real people you're dealing with. Normals. Ordinaries. They don't know the game, and chances are they think all journos are scum, right? Right. Second: at the end of the day you've got Goebbels screaming down the phone at you to get something, and so you have to get something or it's your ass totes getting whipped around the newsroom. Third: sadly you can't just make it up any more. So what do you do to get in?

'I used to always turn up without a coat. And a potentially see-through blouse. Major bonus if it's raining, actually. Nothing like a pretty girl looking forlorn in the rain to get some of that sympathy going. For really difficult ones I used to keep an onion in my bag. First time you're knocked back, you scootle around the corner and take a big bite from it. Hurts like fuck, actually – but once you're crying you're well in there. Give them some fluff about what an insane cocksucker your editor is and Fanny's totes your aunt.'

Harry started laughing, but she ignored him. 'But here's the really clever bit,' she continued, pointing her glass at each of us in turn. 'As well as that onion, always carry a bottle of wine in your bag. Everyone likes wine. Grieving people most of all. You're turning up with something they actually want! And the best bit of all? Once they've had a drink they're more likely to talk. Simples! Cheers!'

Harry and she clinked glasses, but the trainee and I looked at each other uncertainly. Here's the thing, Martin. Everyone who's anyone has been on doorknocks, they're like a rite of passage every journalist goes through. And everyone has their little tricks to get through the door.

Except me. I've never done one. I managed to skip that whole part. Because of the way I got into the paper, through the celebrity route, missing out any kind of trainee scheme, dodging that whole journalism qualification thing, I've never had to use those tabloid tricks like everyone else.

And thank God, too. I hate writing about normals. I may work for the *Globe*, but – and let's keep this between ourselves – I'm actually pretty uncomfortable with the way we treat the normals sometimes. Leave the real people alone, that's my philosophy. Take out the celebs, go after the wrong 'uns… but leave the ordinaries be. They've not signed up for any of the stuff. They don't know how the game works. And treating them like they do… well, it's just not fair, is it?

Beth used to call it my saving grace. Or at least she did before Goebbels ordered me to start getting so vicious.

Now? Well, like I say, she's worried about my standards. She's not the only one, if I'm being honest.

Au revoir!

Dan

Letter 40

From: **DantheMan020@gmail.com**
To: Martin.Harbottle@premier-westward.com
Re: 20.20 Premier Westward Railways train from London Paddington to Oxford, October 14. Amount of my day wasted: eight minutes. Fellow sufferers: Sauron Flesh Harrower.

Dear Martin

I made a resolution last night. Or rather, Beth and I made a resolution last night, and then I made another one this morning. Beth and I: we had a chat last night (I was home on time for once) about us, about us and Sylvie, about what's happening to us all – and we resolved to have a proper, longer chat over the weekend. We're even – and this is huge, Martin, this is massive – going to go out.

A table for two is booked, a babysitter secured, and on Sunday night the pair of us are going to leave the house together and go out together and eat together and have a good long chat together as man and wife. As a couple. I can scarce believe it.

It's been so long since we've done anything together as a couple I've almost forgotten we are a couple. It's been so long since we had a drink, and a laugh, and a meal out together, I've almost forgotten we ever did. And it's been so long since we sat down and had a good long chat together – about us, about what we're feeling, about what we feel and how we feel about each other – that I'm not even sure I'll know what to say. But I am pretty sure that it's a pretty good idea. After all these months of arguments and sullenness and simmering resentment, I reckon it can only be a good idea to do something nice together again.

So that was last night's resolution. This morning's came on the train. I sat, as usual, next to Train Girl (this recent dip in temperature doesn't seem to have affected her dress sense much, by the way. The arms are still bare, the skirts are still short; when we sit together I can often see the mark left on her knees where my suit trousers have accidentally scratched the skin. But I digress…) I sat, as I always do when she's there, next to Train Girl and after the usual hellos and the coin-toss to see who pays for the coffee, we also had a chat.

The thing is, Martin: you and I and she know that nothing has happened between us – and of course that despite her extreme hotness and her funniness and cleverness and the fact that we get on so well and have such a good time together, I don't fancy her because I'm a married man and not that kind of person at all – I've nonetheless been a bit worried about the whole Train Girl situation in general.

I'm a bit anxious that my relationship with her might be misconstrued. I'm concerned that it all could be taken the wrong way. And not least of all by Train Girl herself. I know it's ridiculous of me to even think that she might fancy me, but nevertheless I can't help the niggling, gnawing fear that I might be leading her on a bit.

So, we had a chat. I told her that what I was about to say might sound weird, and that saying it was a bit awkward, and that she really shouldn't take it the wrong way, and that if anything I was only saying it at all because I think she's so brilliant… but that maybe we shouldn't go out drinking together again. Or even sit next to each other on the train so much. What with her being so hot and me being so married and everything.

Do you know what she did, Martin? She laughed. And then she kissed me on the cheek. And then she said: 'Of course, darlin', don't sweat it. You take care of yourself, all right? And I'll maybe see you around.' And then she picked up her coffee, swung her bag over her shoulder and tripped off down the carriage and sat next to Universal Grandpa. Who – unbelievably, outrageously – looked her up and down from over his *Telegraph* and then shot me the sauciest wink I think I've ever seen.

So, I guess you could say it went well, right? I mean, a little disappointment on her part would have been nice, but at least she didn't cry or anything. She didn't look in the slightest bit bothered, to be honest. Which is good, I guess. Better than the alternative.

So there you have it, Martin: we're talkin' about our resolutions. Make that change!

Au revoir!

Dan

From: **Martin.Harbottle@premier-westward.com**
To: DantheMan020@gmail.com
Re: 20.20 Premier Westward Railways train from London Paddington to Oxford, October 14.

Dear Dan

Thanks again for taking the trouble to write to me. I do hope the very minor inconveniences you experienced this week did not upset your plans too much.

To address your other concerns, I'm pleased to hear that you and your wife have resolved to sit down and address any difficulties you might have been having. I did tell you that things would look better once her hormones had calmed down, didn't I! I am of course sorry that you feel your friendship with 'Train Girl' can't continue, however. She sounds like a fine young lady.

As for your startling revelations concerning the underhand goings-on of the press: I must confess I am rather shocked. Mrs Harbottle will be especially disappointed, as I remember her pointing out the very same 'stars with no make-up' article to me – she was very impressed with it at the time, though I dare say will be markedly less so now.

So you see – we sometimes do get the *Globe*! Mrs Harbottle does confess to a guilty love of the 'real-life' features in *Amazeballs!* magazine. But surely they can't be real, can they? I just assumed they were made up.

And I'm afraid I was rather sorry to see England 'crash out' (as you newspaper types like to say!) of the Rugby World Cup. Regardless of what happened in the game or your feelings towards rugby in general, I do feel that the conduct of the Argentinian team with regard to their anti-Falklands slogans was nothing short of disgraceful and surely deserving of ejection from the tournament and a lengthy ban. If I had my way we'd send the aircraft carriers down that way to show them who's boss all over again!

Best

Martin

Letter 41

From: **DantheMan020@gmail.com**
To: Martin.Harbottle@premier-westward.com
Re: 07.31 Premier Westward Railways train from Oxford to London Paddington, October 20. Amount of my day wasted: 11 minutes. Fellow sufferers: Lego Head, Guilty New Mum, Train Girl, Universal Grandpa.

Morning, big man. It feels like ages! It's been nearly a week. Just imagine: nearly a whole week without delays! The mind is quite literally blown.

Tensions keep rising in North Africa, where nobody really knows who's in charge and the new boys in the Imperial Palace can't decide on the colour of their new flag, let alone how to start rebuilding a smashed and shattered state.

And meanwhile, along the borders, the friendly troops keep amassing. There have been skirmishes, incursions, a little gunfire and a strengthening of positions. And, of course, it's all been in the name of stability.

Because, Martin, let's not forget that the Neighbouring Regime is friends of the raggle-taggle new government. They welcome the people's revolution; they applaud the passing of the old order. And the army lining up along the border like so many angry dogs straining against an invisible leash… it's there to help.

There are no hard and fast numbers coming through as yet, Martin. We're woefully short on facts. It's tricky to stand up a story when it's coming across thousands of miles of desert and through a media blackout. But what we're all hearing in the newsroom, what Harry the Dog's sources are telling him, is that the friendly soldiers are taking control of the border towns. They're in North African territory now. Keeping the peace. Looking towards the larger towns.

How long before they stop pretending and just start invading? I pulled out Christmas Day in Harry the Dog's latest sweepstake. I reckon that's a duff choice. I reckon it'll all be long over by then. We'll be on to the next thing.

And meanwhile, the world keeps turning; forever smoothly, forever flawed.

In the Royal Courts of Justice, the accusations mount up, the charges amass. The way they tell it you'd think we were actual criminals. And there's a new whisper buzzing around the place too, a new panic.

According to the word in the pubs and the bars and the less-discreet emails (seriously: when will people learn about emails? You'd think they would realise that, given all that's happening right now, undeletable electronic records are perhaps not the best medium for communicating indiscretions. You'd think that, like me, they'd not only open up new email accounts for that kind of thing, but also get new laptops like the very one I'm using right now to write them on), according to industry gossip, one of your so-called quality papers is lining up something against us. They've got themselves a story, apparently. Something related to but not directly concerned with the court case. Something big. Something horribly big. Something that could cause more trouble than our litigious friend could imagine in the wettest of his dreams.

I think you can probably guess what the worry is in the *Globe* newsroom. When we're not all placing bets on the future wars and extent of bloodshed of innocent people thousands of miles away in the dirt and sand, when we're not trying to dig up something new and nasty about our crooner friend, when we're not busying ourselves with the business of putting out the world's most-read English-language newspaper every week... we're bricking ourselves about where this whole thing might lead.

Where will it lead, Martin? If you want my opinion, I'll tell you: nowhere. The world will keep turning, the accusations and allegations will come and be proved or disproved and sooner or later the whole thing will be forgotten. Today's news: tomorrow's chip wrapper. That's the way it's always worked.

And in the meantime, I'm going to be 11 minutes late for work. And, it being Thursday today, that gives me 11 minutes less to prepare for conference; 11 minutes less to get a list of stories together to take into our morning meeting, the meeting where we decide what's going into the paper, the meeting where Goebbels traditionally rips to shreds any ideas not meticulously researched and properly stood-up. As it stands I've got one solid line on the secret stripping past of a soap star, a couple of super-flimsy leads on the extra-marital shenanigans of a couple of bonking headmasters at a top public school, and a potential cracker on a Conservative MP, the school friends of his three teenage daughters and what could only be described as a highly improper use of taxpayer's money. But I need more time, Martin. I need more time to make it tight before I can show it to my boss.

And you know what? Eleven minutes might have at least helped a bit. It would have been a start. And Lord knows we all need one of those, eh?

Au revoir!

Dan

Letter 42

From: **DantheMan020@gmail.com**
To: Martin.Harbottle@premier-westward.com
Re: 20.20 Premier Westward Railways train from London Paddington to Oxford, October 25. Amount of my day wasted: 11 minutes. Fellow sufferers: Sauron Flesh Harrower.

Evening, Martin. As our dungeon master friend opposite me on this evening train might say: Hail weary traveller! Thine, I dunno, staff looketh bent and haggard and thine sword hangs heavy in the sheath. What news of the war, fellow adventurer?

Truth be told, Sauron Flesh Harrower isn't looking himself tonight. Something's changed. Something's wrong, something's not quite right. It's almost as if he's… happy? He keeps grinning at the screen, making amused little noises to himself; I swear I saw him actually rub his hands together in glee.

I wish I could see his screen. I wish I could see what's made this normally fed-up, harassed, curse-mumbling escapist suddenly look so cheery. Can it just be a particularly successful orc-slaying session? Or is he up to something else on there? What do you think, as a fellow role-playing adventurer? What do you know about Sauron Flesh Harrower that you might be able to share with me?

So. Anyway. What's been occurring round your neck of the woods these last five days or so? (Again, so close to making the week, Martin! The mythical week without a delay!) Did you enjoy last Sunday's paper? Were you pleased I managed to get a solid line on the bonking sirs of St Mark's School for Boys? I've got to say, getting that former pupil to talk like that is what made it in the end. The things he said! The naked honesty! You can't beat a good old angsty posh boy with an abused past, can you, Martin? The public love it; they can't get enough.

But what am I saying? I sound like Goebbels. Don't get me wrong, Martin: I think it's awful what happened to that guy. And you should hear him – he's still bearing the scars, 20 years down the line. It's terrible. He was only a boy: having to watch that. Having to film it. Of course it's terrible. You don't need to tell me that: I'm the one who talked to him; I'm the one who got him to get it all off his chest, to name names and date dates and do it all on the record. (He was nervous at first, he wasn't sure to begin with… but once we'd got through the tears and the stammering and the reassurances and the general stressing of the importance of the whole business, he was more than fine. In the end I couldn't shut him up. In the end it was all I could do to get rid of him. What did he think I was – his therapist? Did he not realise I was on a deadline? Some people, Martin!)

Anyway. As usual, I digress. And we haven't much time today. No space for chit-chat! Every word must count! So. What's been happening with me (tearful and abused ex-public-schoolboys aside)? Well… Beth and I went out last week, didn't we?

Do you remember? It was the only story in town! We left little Sylvie in the capable (and expensive) hands of a nursery teacher friend of a friend, we left the house, we caught a cab and we had dinner in a restaurant. Like a proper married couple does. And just for a couple of hours we actually felt like a proper married couple too. For the first time in ages we enjoyed being with each other again.

Picture the scene. A little restaurant in East Oxford, a hop and skip from the colour and bustle of the Cowley Road, crammed and noisy with students and couples in tables of six and four and two, and in the corner, knees touching and with a sputtering little candle in a wax-ridged Chianti bottle between us, me and Beth, my wife and I, out like a couple. Like any other couple on a date.

And we talked. We talked and talked. We talked about why we never really talk any more. And we promised to try to talk some more. And it was great. It was like old times. It reminded me why I love her. She told a funny story about a mother at one of her coffee mornings who nearly gave her kid a spoonful of calamine lotion instead of Calpol (you'll have to believe me when I say it was funnier than that when she told it). She told me another funny story about a play she took Sylvie to see at the Community Centre called 'Bathtime for Bubbles' which involved two men jumping in and out of, well, a bath, and how at one point one of them slipped and fell over, half-in and half-out of the tub and one of the other children shouted 'I can see his winky-pops!' and sure enough, everyone could…

There's a whole world I'm missing here, Martin. Being in London, I mean. Being at work. Being at the scandalous and scandal-ridden and sometimes downright stupid *Sunday Globe*. While I'm freaking out about phone hacking and stressing out about sexually deviant schoolteachers and laying bets on the outcomes of civil wars thousands of miles away, there's a whole other world back here, at home. And it's all happening without me. And somehow, I keep forgetting to ask about it.

This other world of mine, the one with Goebbels and Harry the Dog and Rochelle the Bombshell: it's not real, is it? I get so caught up in it I sometimes feel like I'm in danger of losing myself, of forgetting what I am, who I am. I'm a tabloid journalist, sure, but is that actually what I am? Is that all I am?

Or am I a husband, a father? Am I the man Beth fell in love with, the man who fell in love with Beth? Can I be both? I hope so. I hope I don't have to choose. But if I did have to choose… I'd choose my wife, right? I'd choose my daughter. Of course I would.

Of course I would!

But I'm going off-track again. The point is, we had a lovely time. Genuinely. We had a real time. We talked and we laughed and none of it had anything to do with all the nonsense that dominates my life the rest of the time. It was like going away. It was like going away on that holiday we need so much. And as a result – lucky for you, given the length of this delay again – I'm in a good mood for once. All good!

Au revoir!

Dan

Letter 43

From: **DantheMan020@gmail.com**
To: Martin.Harbottle@premier-westward.com
Re: 20.20 Premier Westward Railways train from London Paddington to Oxford, October 27. Amount of my day wasted: nine minutes. Fellow sufferers: Sauron Flesh Harrower.

Dear Martin

I have news! Better news than all that stuff you get in the real world. Much more interesting than tabloid nonsense or death in the dust!

Sauron Flesh Harrower has been on my train for the last three nights, and if two days ago I was frustrated by the mystery of his newfound chucklesome demeanour, last night I got a sniff of the reason why, and tonight I cracked the story good and proper.

He's got a new friend! A lady friend! Not in the real world or anything (don't be silly!) but in the Dungeons of Diabolo, or whatever they are. A lady adventurer!

He has been sitting in the seat in front of me these two nights past, and I've been able to see his computer screen in the reflection of the window. It's a bit tricky to make much out at first, but you get better with practice – and then tonight I had the excellent idea of using the zoom function on my phone to enhance the picture, and then by actually taking photos, to study in more leisure what's actually going on.

And what's going on is this: Sauron Flesh Harrower (by whom I mean his avatar, his little computer character) has been hanging out with a statuesque, Amazonian, barbarian princess-type chick. They've hardly been going adventuring at all – but seem to be spending most of their time in some kind of virtual pub, drinking virtual goblets of mead together. Her name? Elvira Clunge. I kid you not.

In the real world, on my train heading west in the night, he's a middle-aged businessman in a pin-striped suit with thinning hair, sitting here chuckling and grinning at his computer screen like a loved-up teenager who can't believe he got lucky with the captain of the netball team – and in his other world, the unreal world, he's only got eyes for, he's perched on a chair in a tavern called something like the Slaughtered Magi next to someone rejoicing in the name Elvira Clunge. The pair of them sitting stiffly and awkwardly, all loincloth and bikini fur and oversized weapons. And it's making him deliriously happy. It's… surreal.

He has a chat box open. (That's what I needed the phone to read.) Do you want to know what they've been talking about? Do you want to know what the word from the Slaughtered Magi is? What sweet nothings Sauron Flesh Harrower and Elvira Clunge whisper together?

I'm going to copy it down verbatim for you. Seriously, I couldn't make this up. Here we go (obviously this is a snapshot of a much longer conversation):

<Sauron Flesh Harrower>: I have shed the foul blood of many fell beasts to drink with you tonight.

<Elvira Clunge>: *blushes* I'm glad you have done so, sire.

<Sauron Flesh Harrower>: Your beauty is worth it. For this moment I would have faced even the fabled Hounds of Hades.

<Elvira Clunge>: And for a kiss? What trials would you undergo for the promise of my lips, softer and plumper than even the legendary pillows upon the beds of the courtesans of the Emperor Carnus the Rampant?

<Sauron Flesh Harrower>: For your lips? Nothing more. There is no need. You are my woman now. Your lips are mine. Your body is mine. You are mine.

<Elvira Clunge>: No man has ever touched my womanhood. I am pure as the virgin snow upon the misty peaks of the Jagged Mountains of Montezuma.

<Sauron Flesh Harrower>: That is as it should be. When I take you I must be the first.

<Elvira Clunge>: Will you take me, my lord?

<Sauron Flesh Harrower>: Verily I say that I shall. Like a battering ram upon your palace gates I shall be. Like a mighty axe swinging through the trees in your forest. Like a

<Elvira Clunge>: When?

<Elvira Clunge>: When?

<Elvira Clunge>: When?

<Sauron Flesh Harrower>: proud tower thrusting into your clear blue skies.

<Elvira Clunge>: When?

And that's as much as I got.

Um. What are we to make of that? This man in his mid-forties, with his suit and shiny shoes, his slicked-back hair and briefcase, talking of battering rams and thrusting towers to a warrior princess in a virtual pub in a game called Ragnarok. This man in his mid-forties who chooses to call himself Sauron Flesh Harrower when he's not at work in (no doubt) middle-to-senior management somewhere, engaging in borderline-violent sex talk with a total stranger on a computer screen on the 20.20 train from Paddington to Oxford? I don't know whether to laugh or cry.

But also: when is he going to take her? I need to know! Martin, I never thought I'd say this, but tonight's delay: it's not long enough. I need more time. I need more time to find out how and when Sauron Flesh Harrower and Elvira Clunge are going to do the dirty with each other!

The only person more frustrated than me when we finally rolled into Oxford some nine minutes behind schedule was Sauron Flesh Harrower himself. With a sigh he snapped the laptop shut, slid it back into his bag, straightened his tie, slicked back his hair and gazed at his reflection in the window… preparing himself physically and mentally to face the real world again, the family, the wife who no doubt does not call him 'my lord', who perhaps isn't as pure as the virgin snow upon the misty peaks of the Jagged Mountains of Montezuma and whose lips, I'd wager, are not softer and plumper than even the legendary pillows upon the beds of the courtesans of the Emperor Carnus the Rampant.

We trudged off the train together. And if he was going to keep quiet about his doings in the Tavern of the Slaughtered Magi (as I'm sure he was) then I couldn't wait to get home and tell Beth all about it.

What did Beth say when I told her? She thought it was hilarious. She thought it was a scream. She fired up our own laptop and tried to join Ragnarok – she wanted to log on and find Sauron Flesh Harrower and Elvira Clunge and see the action for herself.

And so that's exactly what we did. We found the game all right, we downloaded the drivers… and then it asked us for our credit card details. Do you know how much Ragnarok costs to play? Fifty quid a month! That's what they're paying, for their dirty talk in virtual taverns – 50 smackers a month. Six hundred quid a year!

Obviously we didn't sign up. But we did go to bed still laughing, Beth jumping into the covers and whispering, 'You have a mighty weapon, my lord…'

And, just to add to the jollity, Sylvie didn't wake once, either.

Au revoir!

Dan

Letter 44

From: **DantheMan020@gmail.com**
To: Martin.Harbottle@premier-westward.com
Re: 19.20 Premier Westward Railways train from London Paddington to Oxford, November 1. Amount of my day wasted: 14 minutes. Fellow sufferers: None (odd time of night).

Trick or treat, Martin! Surprises or sweeties? I hope the spooks didn't spook you. I hope the ghoulies stayed away and nobody gave you the willies. And most of all, I hope the feral kids who seem to hunt in vicious, legitimised little packs like ASBO-flouting legions of the undead on that one particular night of the year did not do too much damage to you or your property.

I hope your house remained unegged. I hope your car has kept its full complement of wing mirrors and windshield wipers. I hope, in short, that the traditional Halloween teenage zombie apocalypse did not upset your evening too much.

Round our way, of course, we like to train 'em young. We prepare our children for their adolescent delinquency by getting them dressed up and trick or treating as soon as they can walk. Or even, in fact, earlier.

Last night, Martin, my baby daughter went trick or treating. We all did: Beth and Sylvie and I, our little nuclear family. We all dressed up, we got a little bag for sweeties, we carved ourselves a pumpkin, and we hit the haunted streets of old Oxford town. I wanted to go as Sauron Flesh Harrower and Elvira Clunge, but the weather just wasn't with us. Wrong time of year for bikinis and loincloths.

Beth still cut a dash as a rather saucy-looking Cruella de Vil (I don't know about you, but the slashed red dress and high heel does it for me, Martin), I was a rather rakish Dracula, and Sylvie was the cutest little toffee apple you ever saw (the costume was actually a Sainsbury's baby Christmas pudding outfit, cunningly adapted).

We hooked up with a bunch of other parents and babies and we went out in search of loot. And proper fun it was too: just about everyone had dressed up… everyone except Mr Blair, of course, who said something arch about Halloween being an ancient English pagan tradition that had been co-opted, corrupted and commercialised by the Americans. Didn't stop him grabbing a handful of fun-sized Milky Ways when they were handed out, mind.

Anyway: like I say, it was fun. Sylvie had a whale of a time – it basically combined the four most exciting things in a young life: staying up late, dressing up, hanging out with Mum and Dad, and getting lots of nice things to eat. Or look at, in her case, as she's still too little for chocolate.

Someone had brought a hip flask with them, and by the time we'd covered three or four of the closest streets to our house, we were all pretty well up for the pub… which is exactly where we ended up. Adults, dressed like unwanted extras from the 'Thriller' video, sitting around a couple of big tables; children, dressed almost unbearably cutely and massively overexcited, running, crawling and bum-shuffling in and out of our legs and around the pub.

The only slight downer came when Mr Blair tried to engage me in a conversation about the media (look, he started it!). I tried to be nice to him, Martin, honest I did – he is Beth's friend, after all, and all the other mums seem to like him too (though not so much the dads, which is interesting) – but, really, I couldn't resist sharing a few tales from the front line with him.

I confess: I was deliberately trying to shock him. You can't blame me for that, can you? I'd had a drink and all, and he was claiming some kind of spurious authority (I mean, what does he actually know? He may be the man when it comes to babies, he may be able to attend bonding weekends, but when it comes to the workings of Her Majesty's press, he's as ignorant as a baby himself.) So all I did was tell some of the more outrageous stories I've heard. The odd thing is, they're all true.

I told him the one about the Sunday broadsheet that decided to run an investigation into the Lesbian Avengers pressure group – and sent two male reporters to infiltrate the organisation (their reasoning being, astonishingly, that these particular chaps made for more realistic lesbians than any of the women in the office).

When the men were exposed as not only journalists, but inept drag queens (which could admittedly look like someone was taking the mickey), there was nearly a lynching – the two guys ended up being chased down the Holloway Road in London, holding their high heels and hitching up their skirts, pursued by a mob of 50 or so righteously furious women, before finally seeking sanctuary in a pub showing an Arsenal–Spurs game. Their pursuers burst in after them, punches were thrown, someone got glassed, and the police were called before a full-on lesbians v football hooligans riot broke out.

I told him the one about the reporter on another paper who was told to dress up as a schoolgirl and buy some crack in King's Cross – just because someone there thought that the idea that crack was being sold to schoolgirls in King's Cross would make for a good headline. She duly got dolled up and hung around for a while, fending off propositions from all manner of unsavoury characters, getting increasingly terrified, before finally someone offered her some drugs. Grateful, she handed over £50 and hot-tailed it back to the office, thankfully still in one piece.

But when they got a lab to test it, it turned out not to be crack at all. She'd been sold flakes of crystallised ginger. So what did the paper do? They ran the story anyway. The point was, she thought she was buying crack, right? And the comment editor took home the ginger and cooked it on her salmon for tea.

And after that, seeing as I'd had yet another drink and I was in full flow and on the subject of crack anyway, I told him the story about the features journalist who was told to babysit the crackhead heiress who was ready to spill the beans on her rock star boyfriend. She duly put her up in a hotel room overnight, stayed in an adjoining room, and in the morning went to rouse her. Except she wouldn't answer the door. There was no sound at all. Panicked, she got the hotel manager to break in, and found the girl shivering and blue-lipped and in the first stages of severe withdrawal. Between fainting fits she managed to tell the journo that the only way she'd be able to make the interview and photoshoot was if she got hold of some more drugs, and fast.

So of course she calls the news desk and asks them what she should do. The answer?

'Buy her some fucking crack!'

The desk gave her the address of a crack den in Hackney and she drove there, with the addict semi-comatose in the back of her Micra, knocked on the door, bought some rocks, asked for a receipt for her expenses, was told to get lost by the dealer.

Halfway to the shoot, with the car filled with crack fumes, she got another call from the news desk. The editor had changed his mind, the story was dropped and the shoot was off.

'What do I do about the junkie in the back of my car?' she asked. The only reply was a virtual shrug on the other end of the phone, and she ended up pulling over somewhere in Shoreditch, wrestling the confused girl out of the car, stuffing £20 into her hand (all she had left) and speeding off before she could work out what was happening.

I must confess I got a bit carried away by that stage, Martin. As Mr Blair's expression turned from amazed to shocked to downright disgusted, Beth had to tell me to shut up. People were getting uncomfortable. Most of the rest of the pub had gone quiet. She stood there in the middle of the room, in her blood red dress, black stockings, killer heels and hair piled up and falling down over her eyes, telling me in a low voice that perhaps not everyone is so amused by these stories as I am… and she looked pretty goddamned amazing.

That's my wife, I thought. And I left Mr Blair with a big old wink to let him know so, too.

So, yes, Martin. Halloween was a success, all told! The important thing was that we all had a good time together, as a family, like the old days.

Au revoir!

Dan

From: **Martin.Harbottle@premier-westward.com**
To: DantheMan020@gmail.com
Re: 19.20 Premier Westward Railways train from London Paddington to Oxford, November 1.

Dear Dan

Many thanks again for your continuing correspondence. Your train was delayed on the morning of the 20 October due to overnight vandalism. Such mindless defacing of Premier Westward carriages is unfortunately an ongoing problem for us, and one to which I confess there would not appear to be a solution. Why anyone would choose to write such things on a train is quite beyond me; and I must say that even their seeming inability to spell the profanities they're writing makes the whole business even more disheartening.

On the evening of the 27th your service was held up at Reading when a passenger was temporarily locked in the 'quiet zone' toilets and on the evening of November 1 you were late leaving Paddington when a pregnant lady refused to leave her seat in first class, despite only possessing a standard-class ticket. (She was eventually allowed to stay and let off with a warning, given that she was the only passenger in the first-class carriage and the conductor could not find a free seat in any of the standard cars.)

I must confess, however, that I have no record of any delay on the 25 October. Could you please check your records again?

Finally – some good news! As you may know, we at Premier Westward pride ourselves on the punctuality and reliability of the service we provide, and as such periodically carry out 'spot checks' on the performance of trains used by season-ticket holders. After performing one such spot check on your season ticket (you must believe me when I say that yours was chosen at random and is in no way related to our correspondence) I am happy to confirm that you are entitled to some compensation from us for your delays.

Premier Westward Railways are delighted to offer you a pair of Standard-Class Off-Peak Super-Advance Tickets from your home station (Oxford) to Torquay, to be redeemed at any time between now and December 31. The usual restrictions apply, of course, and you will need to specify exactly which services you intend to take. Once specified the tickets are non-transferable and non-refundable.

Congratulations, Dan! I hope you feel this shows just how seriously we do take passenger satisfaction, and on a personal note, perhaps it means you can take Beth and Sylvie on that holiday at long last! I hear Torquay is best visited during the winter months, before the 'holiday hordes' descend!

Many thanks

Martin

Letter 45

From: **DantheMan020@gmail.com**
To: Martin.Harbottle@premier-westward.com
Re: 20.20 Premier Westward Railways train from London Paddington to Oxford, November 8. Amount of my day wasted: five minutes. Fellow sufferers: Sauron Flesh Harrower.

Dear Martin

We did it! A week – a whole week – without delays! Oh frabjous day, callooh, callay! Pop the party poppers, unstream the party streamers, mix up the Premier Westward punch and let's do the locomotion! I hope you're proud, Martin. A week without delay: I hope you're properly proud of yourself.

On the other hand, a week without delay has meant a week without one of our little chats. And I do enjoy our little chats (sorry, I know that sounded sarcastic, but it really wasn't meant to: I do genuinely enjoy them).

It has also meant a week without the chance to thank you for the outstanding, one-in-a-million prize I've won! The letter arrived yesterday, Martin, confirming our non-transferable super-off-peak standard-class returns to Torquay! Beth, needless to say, was giddy as a child at Christmas. 'Torquay!' she kept whispering, eyes shining, face lit up. 'Torquay in December! Imagine that!'

And all I could do was shake my head and marvel at the wonder of it all. It really does make those above-inflation ticket price rises every year worth it, after all. It really does make one feel that perhaps all those lost hours gazing out of a window as life passes one by aren't lost at all, when one is presented with a pair of non-transferable super-off-peak standard-class returns to Torquay to be taken between November 8 and December 31.

Totes air-punch, as Bombshell might say.

But on the other hand… thanks. I'm deeply suspicious about being picked 'at random', and I'd take a few less delayed trains in exchange… but on the other hand, thanks. We do need a holiday. And perhaps Torquay is as good a place as any for a weekend away. In the cold.

I'll be sure to tell you all about it, of course. I'm certain I'll have plenty of opportunity.

And in the meantime: someone wrote something rude on the side of a carriage? Someone fell asleep on the toilet? A pregnant lady sat by herself in first class? For these reasons I arrive late at work and late home from work? Can you not do any better than that?

Oh – and as for the other delay, yes, I have 'checked my records', Martin, and yes, the delay did occur. I didn't imagine it. I didn't make it up. And if you don't believe me, ask Sauron Flesh Harrower. He'll tell you what for! He'll give it to you straight!

Au revoir!

Dan

Letter 46

From: **DantheMan020@gmail.com**
To: Martin.Harbottle@premier-westward.com
Re: 23.20 Premier Westward Railways train from London Paddington to Oxford, November 12. Amount of my day wasted: 23 minutes. Fellow sufferers: None (probably. Can't see properly).

Martin. I write this very drunk. I'm in Coach C on one of your trains in the middle of the night, we've stopped for what seems like for ever somewhere east of Reading, I've got half a bottle of bitter red wine and a packet of crisps left, and I'm fairly comprehensively slaughtered.

I'm also not in the best of moods. Today has not been a good day. Today has been a bad day. The worst, possibly.

I expect you've heard the news. You must have. You couldn't miss it. Splashed across the front page of your favourite quality paper (and inside, pages four to seven, plus a focus piece on 18–19 and a special op-ed at the back), picked up by every news channel and radio bulletin in the country, and doubtless dominating the news agenda tomorrow. The shit (excuse my French) has hit the fan. Buckets of the stuff. Whole portaloos of it. Toilet blocks' worth. Vast cesspits brimming with the most rancid effluence imaginable flying into a wind-farm-sized ocean of fans, spraying everywhere, covering everything.

We're up to our necks in it, Martin. We're drowning in it.

I woke up to the news on Radio 2 this morning. I'd got through a nappy change, half a cup of coffee and an Adele song before I knew about it. And then, the newsreader's voice, with that perfectly pitched mix of jovial and serious for 6.30 on a Saturday morning, saying just about the worst thing she could have said.

'Britain's biggest-selling Sunday tabloid has been hit with fresh allegations of privacy invasion, this time involving the family of the victims of one of the country's most notorious serial killers…'

And my stomach lurched. I almost dropped the coffee. I almost dropped the baby. And I grabbed my phone (I'd put it on silent last night so as not to wake Sylvie after she fell asleep in our bed again) and I checked my messages (eight missed calls, 12 missed texts) and it was all I could do not to throw up.

The rumours were true. The whispers were right. The *Globe* was being nobbled. Good and proper. The first seven texts were from Goebbels – increasingly frantic/furious/drunk variations on 'wake up and call me immediately' – and the other five from Harry the Dog (increasingly frantic/terrified/drunk variations on 'wake up, the shit has hit the fan'). I couldn't face the voicemails. I knew they'd just be more of the same.

Instead I rang Goebbels.

'Finally,' he snarled. 'I don't know what time you call this, but in case you haven't realised yet, we're right up the creek. I've been in the office all night. Get here now.'

I was about to hang up when he continued. 'Oh, and Dan, don't speak to anybody. If you must speak to your wife then tell her not to speak to anybody. I don't need to tell you why.'

And so I spoke to Beth, shaking her awake as I handed Sylvie over – fast asleep again now it was daytime – pulling on my clothes, jamming a toothbrush around my mouth. I did all these things simultaneously; I told her something very bad had happened at the paper; I told her to turn on News 24 and not to speak to anyone about it, about anything I might have said; and even before she had woken up enough to properly register what was happening, I had my bag over my shoulder and I was out of the door.

The office was packed. The newsroom rammed. Some (like Goebbels) had been there since the first editions had dropped at midnight the night before; others (like me) had rushed in as soon as they woke and heard this morning. But before it was nine a.m., everyone was in. Staff and casuals and contractors and freelancers and stringers and anyone who had ever had anything to do with the paper – they were all there, milling around like so many hopeless sheep, waiting for someone to tell them what was going on.

Goebbels was in his office with the editor and the lawyers and the managing editor and the editorial director and a bunch of scary-looking people from the board of directors. Only the lawyers were talking. Everyone else looked serious. Some nodded occasionally. Goebbels did neither. He stared at his hands, his clenched fists.

And we all watched them – and tried to look like we weren't watching them. And across the low murmur of furtive chatter was a soundtrack of bleeps and dings and bells and chimes and whistles and horns and xylophones and merry little tinkles that signalled incoming emails, arriving texts, fresh voicemails. All asking the same questions – and all ignored. Nobody was picking up.

Eventually the office door opened and the suits strode through the newsroom, followed by the editor (meeting nobody's eye) and the managing editor (who tried an ill-advised smile before ducking his head and scurrying on) until finally we were left with Goebbels and a couple of lawyers. He stood literally shaking with anger. The lawyers did the speaking.

'Colleagues,' one of them began, and in contrast to Goebbels' fizzing rage he was as smooth as warm butter. I hated him instantly. 'You will have seen in the news this morning some very serious allegations against this paper. The first and most important point to make is that they are not true. I repeat: not true.

'This newspaper has never illegally accessed the private voicemails of any member of the public. During the missing persons enquiry for Barry Dunn, and later when that enquiry became a murder investigation, nobody at the *Globe* ever sanctioned any intrusion into his privacy or the privacy of his mother, or that of any members of his family.' He paused, looked around the office at all the faces, all the crossed arms. 'We did not access voicemails, we did not hack into emails, we did not intercept texts or Twitter accounts or Facebook profiles or Myspace logins or school records or anything else anyone can think of. Not at that time, nor after. Or at any time. Ever.'

He nodded to us all, in a gesture that was presumably supposed to express solidarity, comradeship. 'I understand that these allegations have been a very great shock to you all. As they have to me. And to us all – right to the very top of the company. But if there is one thing this newspaper has always stood for, it is the truth. And we will get to the truth in this matter. Remember that. We will find the truth. We always do.

'And in the meantime, you may find yourself the subject of some media attention yourselves. Shoe on the other foot and all that.' Stony silence. 'Ahem. Well, I hardly need to tell you all, of all people, of the importance of saying nothing. Nothing at all. Not even "no comment" – we all know how just saying "no comment" can in itself look like one has something to hide. No head nodding, no head shaking, nothing. Some of the people who ask you questions will doubtless be friends, former colleagues now at rival news outlets. Please – I cannot stress this enough – do not talk to them. They are not your friends now.'

He clapped his hands together and glanced at Goebbels. 'Before I go, let me just say this: the next few weeks are going to be difficult. We will be under the kind of scrutiny and subject to the sort of outrageous speculation that will make the last month or two seem like nothing. But as long as we stick together, as long as we remember that we have done nothing wrong, we'll be fine.'

And then he left, to silence, and Goebbels cleared his throat. 'Right,' he growled, still looking like he was about to explode. 'You don't need me to tell you how bad this is. But that's not our business. Let the suits and the legals sort it out. All I care about right now is the fact that it's Saturday morning and I've got a newspaper to get out tonight.'

He pointed to me. 'And as of this morning we don't have a splash any more. The tax-fiddling Tory and his teenage totty is spiked. He's untouchable now – or at least till this is all over. That's what I've been told. Orders from the top. It would look petty, apparently. Like sour grapes.

'So it's gone ten, we've got no front page, no investigation and the rest of the news list is crap. What are you doing all standing there looking at me? Get to work.' And he turned and strode into his office, slamming the door behind him.

Heavy, eh, Martin? What do you make of it? It was reassuring to hear that all those allegations were false though, eh? It was good to have the lawyers insist that they were categorically untrue. That we'd done nothing wrong at all. Phew! What a relief!

Except, of course, every single person in that room knew the lawyer was lying. We'd all read the story by that time. Most of us had already spoken to at least one former colleague about how things used to work around here. And given that the rumours had been floating around since the summer anyway... regardless of what I might have felt a month or two ago, or a week ago, or yesterday, as of this morning there has been no doubt in my mind, or the minds of just about everyone there, that the newspaper was almost certainly guilty on all charges.

You know what I think, Martin? I think someone at the paper did listen to the phone messages, read the emails, access the Twitter and Facebook accounts of poor little Barry Dunn. I think we got into those of his mum, too. And his sisters, his dad, his aunts, uncles, grandparents, his friends, teachers, neighbours... of anyone and everyone, in fact, we could think of who might have had any connection to the lad at all. Who might provide a clue, a lead, on his disappearance. And afterwards, when he was found, lying in that ditch, I believe we kept at it – hoping for a steer on the identity of the man who murdered him. Your so-called Beast of Berkhamsted.

We did it, all right. And so the question, Martin, is not whether we did it – but why we did it.

The answer? Because we needed stories, of course. It was before my time at the paper, but even I remember that little kid was the only thing in the news for weeks. The pressure to get something new for the splash must have been huge. The need to get a fresh line, an original angle, must have been immense. Those reporters – callous as it sounds – they were just doing their job. They were just looking for leads, same as journalists always have done.

But you know what else? What if they had found something, in those first few days after his disappearance? What if their under-the-radar investigations had uncovered a vital clue? What if they had led to the kidnapper himself? Or afterwards, to the murderer? What if little Barry had been saved? If that case, still open, still unsolved, was successfully wrapped up, all thanks to a *Sunday Globe* hack with a notebook full of shonky numbers and dodgy passwords?

He'd be a hero, right? That hack: he'd be front-page news. We'd be front-page news. We'd be the ones who rescued little Barry Dunn, the ones who caught the Beast of Berkhamsted. There'd be champagne and handshakes and visits to the Queen all round.

And now? We might as well have killed him ourselves. That's how it feels tonight, 24 hours after the story broke, at the end of a day in which it's only gained momentum, a day in which the line of people queuing up to condemn us (politicians, personalities, public figures of all colour and creed) has only lengthened, and whose condemnations only grown stronger.

And believe me, Martin, this is not the end. It's barely the beginning. I know a story with legs when I see one… and this one's just getting started. It's barely out of the blocks yet. This one's going to run and run and run.

Anyway. We got our own paper out in the end. We'll be the only organ on Fleet Street not splashing on us. (We've got some rubbish about Jamie Best's new hairdo. Though to be fair, he does look a prat: dreadlocks on white boys have never been a good idea.)

We were going to go to the pub straight after signing off our pages (of course) but word came back that the pub was full of rival hacks. Of course. So Goebbels sent a couple of trainees down to the supermarket with the company credit card and instructions to buy as much booze as they could fit into their trolleys.

And so we got trolleyed. We stayed in the office after work and we got trolleyed.

And what am I doing now? I'm in Coach C on one of your trains in the middle of the night, we're finally coming into Oxford, I've got no red wine and no crisps left, and I'm fairly comprehensively slaughtered.

And you know what? I've got nothing left to say. We're running over 20 minutes late, I'm nearly home, and I've got nothing left to say. Except thank God I've got the next two days off.

Au revoir!

Dan

From: Martin.Harbottle@premier-westward.com
To: DantheMan020@gmail.com
Re: Out of Office Reply

Dear Sir/Madam

Thank you for your email dated November 12 this year. I can confirm that Mr Harbottle has received it and will endeavour to respond as soon as possible. Your concerns are of utmost importance to us.

Thank you again for writing to Premier Westward.

pp Martin Harbottle, Managing Director

This is an automatically generated response. Please do not reply

Letter 47

From: **DantheMan020@gmail.com**
To: Martin.Harbottle@premier-westward.com
Re: 22.20 Premier Westward Railways train from London Paddington to Oxford, November 15. Amount of my day wasted: seven minutes. Fellow sufferers: Overkeen Estate Agent.

Where are you? What's happened? An automatically generated response? That's new. When did you work that one out? Or – and perhaps I'm getting paranoid here – did you actually write that 'automatically generated' response yourself? Are you just pretending not to be about?

I do hope not. It wouldn't be the same, writing to you like this, if I thought you weren't interested in what I had to say. There's the train stuff, obviously, but also all the other jazz I bang on about. The stuff at home, the stuff at work. Sauron Flesh Harrower and the virtual romance of the virtual century. Aren't you supposed to be my shrink? Aren't you adopting the role of father figure, adviser, therapist? I'm trying to get it all off my chest here, Martin, I'm trying to work all this stuff out with you, and it wouldn't feel the same if you were to start making up automatically generated responses in order to avoid having to write back.

So. Stay with me. Please don't go. Please don't pretend to be a computer program to avoid speaking to me. Please listen to what work was like today.

Martin: work was… weird. You know that phrase 'siege mentality'? Well, it's a siege mentality at our place right now. And that's because we're under siege. Literally.

The TV crews, with their tripods and cameras and big furry mics, their tie-smoothing presenters with slicked-down hair and nervous glances at notes, their rows of vans with great awkward aerials and outsized satellite dishes plonked on top. The radio reporters, with their huge earphones and their faraway frowns and their scurrying about with bulky battery packs slung round their necks. The print journalists, lounging in packs, smoking fags, flicking through pages of shorthand, cracking cynical jokes and swearing.

They're all there. Outside our office, front and back. From first thing in the morning to last thing at night. Every now and then one will attempt to make it inside the building, sauntering to the door all casual-like, spinning a line about coming from this PR firm or that, trying it on with a story about being sent from IT to look at a problem with the servers in the newsroom, before being bundled back out again by security, to laughter and applause from all the other hacks.

They're enjoying themselves out there. They're having fun. And I completely understand why: it is fun, when you're after a story, when you've got the whole pack with you and there's a pub just round the corner and you're all agreed on what the official line might be (unless something really newsworthy happens – and then it's every man for himself). It's a laugh.

It's not such a laugh watching it from the other side though.

It wasn't so much that I felt harassed, or hounded, or any of those other words people use about press attention. I didn't feel like anyone was invading my privacy. I didn't feel violated or abused by the press attention. To be honest, I didn't mind it at all really – the camera lenses and flashes and faces with notebooks thrust forward; the shouted questions and accusations – I was fine with all that, actually. They're only doing their jobs, after all. I know quite a few of them and they're OK lads, mostly.

No, not harassed. I felt… jealous. I wanted to be out with them, on the scent of a good story. Not stuck in the office, the subject of the story. It didn't seem fair, somehow. Why should they have all the fun?

It's an odd feeling, Martin, when you're right there in the midst of the biggest story of the year, and you can't write a word about it. It's an odd feeling being part of the story, being on the inside looking out. I don't want to be on the inside looking out. I want to be where I usually am: on the outside looking in. Reporting. Bringing the news to the masses. Not being the news. Not having to rely on other people's version of events.

Anyway. I've used up my word count for the day, I've accounted for all the time in this particular delay. Till next time, Martin – or Martin's automatically generated email response system. Whichever one of you feels most compelled to write back.

Au revoir!

Dan

From: Martin.Harbottle@premier-westward.com
To: DantheMan020@gmail.com
Re: Out of Office Reply

Dear Sir/Madam

Thank you for your email dated November 15 this year. I can confirm that Mr Harbottle has received it and will endeavour to respond as soon as possible. Your concerns are of utmost importance to us.

Thank you again for writing to Premier Westward.

pp Martin Harbottle, Managing Director

This is an automatically generated response. Please do not reply

Letter 48

From: **DantheMan020@gmail.com**
To: Martin.Harbottle@premier-westward.com
Re: 07.31 Premier Westward Railways train from Oxford to London Paddington, November 17. Amount of my day wasted: seven minutes. Fellow sufferers: Lego Head, Universal Grandpa, Guilty New Mum.

Oh, Martin. Maybe you really have gone. Maybe you really are ignoring me. Maybe the joke's worn thin. Maybe since last weekend I'm no longer the sort of person you want to be receiving letters from. Maybe you no longer care about the train company you purport to run.

Well, whatever. I'll carry on regardless. My trains are still getting delayed, your company is still not doing what I'm paying you to make sure it does, the principle remains and I shall keep going. I've got used to it now. And since Train Girl and I no longer sit together in the mornings, it's not like I've got anything better to do.

Talking of Train Girl… I told Beth about Train Girl last night. As you know, things have been better at home recently. We haven't had an argument in weeks, we've started going out together a bit again, started talking again, started laughing again… and so I thought I should tell Beth about Train Girl. Because I don't want us to become the kind of married couple who keep secrets from each other, the kind of married couple who've stopped bothering, stopped trying, stopped making the effort to impress each other. And also because nothing actually happened between me and Train Girl anyway.

As we sat down to dinner together (and that's a new development too), as the pasta steamed on our plates and the glass of wine dully reflected our happily married faces back at us, I told my wife all about Train Girl.

And here's what I told her. I told her that back when we were barely talking to each other, back when things felt like they weren't going so well, when she spent more time with Mr Blair and the other mums than she did with me, I told her that back then, I made a friend.

I told her that my friend and I sat next to each other on the train every morning, that my friend and I had even gone out drinking a couple of times in London together. I told her my friend was funny and smart… and then I told her that I had decided we shouldn't be friends any more.

'And this is the really funny bit,' I said. 'You'll love this, Beth, this'll really crack you up. I decided we shouldn't be friends any more because I actually think she might have fancied me! Can you believe it?'

Turns out she could believe it. Turns out she believed I fancied Train Girl right back. Or that I at least encouraged her. And so for the rest of the evening, the rest of the night in fact, as the pasta was left ignored, slowly congealing and rubberising on our plates, as the glass of wine became a bottle, and then another bottle, my wife went into a major sulk. And I, her loving husband, sulked back.

Great, eh? It's good to talk. It's lovely that a man and his wife can sit down over dinner and discuss their relationship, their feelings. I feel so lucky that I don't keep secrets from my wife.

At least I've still got you, Martin. You wouldn't sulk at me, would you? You wouldn't accuse me of things I hadn't done with beautiful girls I'd deliberately turned down because I love my wife. Would you? Of course not! That would be unreasonable of you, for a start. And for another thing – you're just an automatically generated email response. It's not like you care, or anything.

Au revoir!

Dan

From: Martin.Harbottle@premier-westward.com
To: DantheMan020@gmail.com
Re: Out of Office Reply

Dear Sir/Madam

Thank you for your email dated November 17 this year. I can confirm that Mr Harbottle has received it and will endeavour to respond as soon as possible. Your concerns are of utmost importance to us.

Thank you again for writing to Premier Westward.

pp Martin Harbottle, Managing Director

This is an automatically generated response. Please do not reply

Letter 49

From: **DantheMan020@gmail.com**
To: Martin.Harbottle@premier-westward.com
Re: 22.20 Premier Westward Railways train from London Paddington to Oxford, November 23. Amount of my day wasted: nine minutes. Fellow sufferers: Overkeen Estate Agent.

Hi, Martin's automatically generated response system! Hope your hard drive remains uncorrupted. I must say, you may not have the eloquence of your human namesake, but at least you reply every time I write. That's something. That's a start.

It's still open season on the *Globe*. The reporters, the TV cameras, the satellite vans are still laying siege to our offices; the papers and radio reports and news bulletins are still full of juicy details about our shameful practices. And now the commentators are getting in on the action. The columnists. And there's nothing a good columnist likes better than making it personal. (That's what a good columnist does, of course: he makes the universal human. He takes the big experience, the big story, and finds the everyday angle.)

What has that meant in today's papers? Ooh, only a big piece in one of the 'qualities' about the 'ongoing culture of nastiness' at our place. A culture the columnist feels is illustrated best by... my column.

'A carnival of nastiness' is how she described it. 'A sarcastic parade of snide jokes and sneering double-entendres.' Also: 'bullying', 'arrogant' and 'an exercise in sailing as close to the legal wind as possible, while simultaneously implying and insinuating as much as the defamation laws will allow'. Oh – and before I forget: 'An example of how the very worst of the *Globe*'s old attitudes still exist at the paper.'

A bit harsh, I thought. A touch over the top. Sure, I go after some people a bit – but only ever celebrities, only ever those who signed up for the whole deal in the first place. God knows they make enough money hawking out their own lives. They started it: I'm just redressing the debt a little.

Anyway, screw them, There's bigger fish frying in the world right now. There's more important stuff going down. (Is it arrogant and bullying of me to mention myself before the new war in North Africa? Have I unconsciously elevated myself above a whole nation's tragedy?)

Christmas: that's what I had in the sweepstake. And they didn't even make it to the end of November. What the hell's wrong with them? Could they not see the writing on the border walls? They only managed to depose a whole dictatorship a few months ago, now they can't even hang on to what they've got. Last night, Neighbouring Regime blinked.

And by 'blinked' I of course mean 'invaded'. All that talk of guarding their own borders, of acting against the threat of terrorism... last night they stopped pretending and just steamed in there. The tanks, the heavy guns, the air support, and behind them the ground troops. Streaming through the sand like battalions of furious beetles. Village after village across the desert fell (they could hardly do anything else) and even as NATO and the UN and the EU and all the others protested, they powered on, claiming all in their path for the glory of Allah. You'll be reading about the war crimes later, about what they did to those in their path, about the human cost. And I lost my money again.

By the time I write, some 20-odd hours since the invasion began, only the capital remains. A country nearly twice the size of France and they just cut through it all in less than a day – and it would have been even quicker too, if their tanks could only move a bit faster. Only the capital to go, and in the capital, in the old Imperial Palace, what's left of the raggle-taggle revolutionary army are bedding down and digging in and preparing for the worst.

It's going to be a long night. A long night in front of News 24 for baby and me. (Just as well I'm sleeping in the front room at the moment then, eh? Just as well there's a war to watch, in between updates on the latest lows in the history of the scandal-ridden *Globe*...)

Au revoir!

Dan

From: Martin.Harbottle@premier-westward.com
To: DantheMan020@gmail.com
Re: Out of Office Reply

Dear Sir/Madam

Thank you for your email dated November 23 this year. I can confirm that Mr Harbottle has received it and will endeavour to respond as soon as possible. Your concerns are of utmost importance to us.

Thank you again for writing to Premier Westward.

pp Martin Harbottle, Managing Director

This is an automatically generated response. Please do not reply

Letter 50

From: **DantheMan020@gmail.com**
To: Martin.Harbottle@premier-westward.com
Re: 07.31 Premier Westward Railways train from Oxford to London Paddington, November 29. Amount of my day wasted: four minutes. Fellow sufferers: Train Girl, Lego Head, Universal Grandpa.

Oh, you know what? If you can't be bothered writing properly, neither can I. Let's play a game instead. Let's play Scrabble.

Here's a screenshot of one of the many online Scrabble games I have going at the moment. What's the longest word you can make?

Au revoir!

Dan

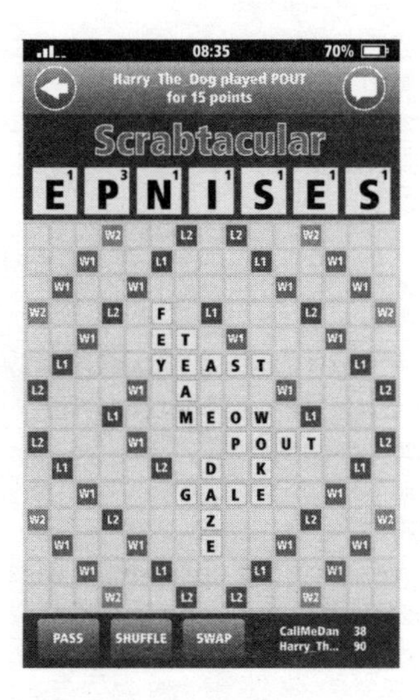

From: Martin.Harbottle@premier-westward.com
To: DantheMan020@gmail.com
Re: Out of Office Reply

Dear Sir/Madam

Thank you for your email dated November 29 this year. I can confirm that Mr Harbottle has received it and will endeavour to respond as soon as possible. Your concerns are of utmost importance to us.

Thank you again for writing to Premier Westward.

pp Martin Harbottle, Managing Director

This is an automatically generated response. Please do not reply

Letter 51

From: DantheMan020@gmail.com
To: Martin.Harbottle@premier-westward.com
Re: 07.31 Premier Westward Railways train from Oxford to London Paddington, December 2. Amount of my day wasted: 14 minutes. Fellow sufferers: Lego Head, Guilty New Mum, Universal Grandpa, Train Girl.

Yeah, hello, whatever. Greetings and salutations.

Me… I'm in a bit of a state, as it happens. I'm all over the place. I don't know if I'm coming or going. Work is still surreal. Work is like a dream. We go in, past the vans, the cameras, the shivering huddles of reporters cradling cups of coffee, we get our security cards checked and double-checked by men in high-vis vests (why have they started wearing those? Have they been saving them for a crisis?), we sit at our desks in the office and we try to do what we're paid to do.

I've finally persuaded my Tory-tupping teenagers to go on the record, at least. We can't run the story just now, obviously, given his high-profile 'war' on our paper, his daily interviews, his rocketing opinion polls, his new status as the darling of the broadsheet press... but we will. We'll get it all together and we'll hold it in the safe, ready to run when the time is right. And if his newfound popularity should take him right to the top of his party – well then, so much the better. The story will be so much the bigger.

That's how we roll: we look to the future. We play the long game – and we always win in the end.

Anyway, both girls have signed the necessary legals; both have agreed to the full on-the-record interview, both will pose for the obligatory photoshoot. In their school uniforms, of course (skirts a little shorter than usual, obviously, with legs bare and shirts untucked and at least one button too many undone), in suites at Claridges and the Ritz, sipping champagne. And when it does run, a nation will look at them and feel simultaneously outraged and envious. And when it does run, his career, his credibility, his family life, are shot.

But like I say, not just yet. For the moment, we've got nothing decent on at all. For the moment, while we are the story, we've got no stories.

But enough about work. Work, believe it or not, is not really the problem. It's my home life, my own life, that's got me in a spin. Beth is still in the weirdest of moods – and coming so soon after I made that resolution that work should not be as important as home, that all the excitement and madness of generating the news should not be as exciting or as mad as the goings-on of my wife and daughter – to take a step back like this just seems a terrible shame.

We are talking though. That's good. We talked last night. The problem, Beth says, is not that I made friends with Train Girl. That's fine, of course it is. The problem is that Train Girl wanted to be more than friends. Like that was something I could control.

Like that was something I actually wanted to happen. Like that wasn't something I nipped in the bud as soon as I realised what was happening because, actually, I love Beth and I didn't (don't) want anything to threaten that.

The thing is: Beth believes me, too. She believes nothing happened, she believes that I broke it off before anything could happen. She believes I wouldn't cheat on her. And yet... she keeps on about it.

And I don't get it. It doesn't make sense. And between you and me, I'm pretty pissed off about it. I've just about had enough.

So, you know what I did this morning? On the (very) delayed train of which I'm writing to complain as we speak? (I'm writing this letter at work, by the way: there's nothing else to do, after all). This morning, as I boarded the 07.31 express service from Oxford to London Paddington, as I shuffled forward to my usual seat in Coach C... I shuffled on past my usual seat until I got to Train Girl's seat. And then I sat down next to her.

'All right?' she said. 'You took your time. You lasted far longer than I thought you would.'

And so, guess what? Train Girl and I are friends again. Well, why not? If I'm going to get all kinds of grief from my wife for being friends with her in the first place, I might as well be friends with her now, right? I mean – why not?

So. Anyway. Train Girl and I are friends again. And I asked her what she meant by 'you took your time'. And do you know what she said? She said this: 'I meant you held out for longer than most of the other boys ever do. All the ones who tell themselves they shouldn't be friends with me, who start off all keen and then run away. They all come running back – and almost always quicker than you did. So well done. You managed to resist me for an impressively long time.'

And then she winked. Because she was joking, of course. About me resisting her: of course I'm still resisting her!

Although, as it turns out, not many do. She wasn't joking about that. On our delayed train to London this morning, Train Girl passed the time by filling me in on her love life – not the full story, of course, we'd need a decade of delayed trains for that, but the edited highlights. I think I mentioned before how she doesn't believe in 'boyfriends' as such… well, it seems her list of non-boyfriend conquests is impressive both for its length and its variety. She sees people she fancies, she has fun with them in whatever way they both fancy, and when she fancies something or someone else, she moves on. She's had young and old, students and professors, city boys and dropouts, lawyers and barristers and benefits cheats and just about everything in between. She's consorted with single men, bachelors, married men. Quite a lot of married men. It turns out that married men are quite her thing.

'The thing about married men,' she said this morning, smoothing out a wrinkle in her tights and adjusting the hem of her skirt. 'The thing about married men,' she continued, idly dangling a shoe from her toe, 'is that they're almost a better option than single men. Single men are an unknown quantity. And more often than not they're single for a reason, if you know what I mean. When I meet a single man, the first thing I ask myself is: "why hasn't he got a girlfriend?" Whereas a married man…' She smiled and pointed at me. 'A married man is married for a reason. Someone has decided she wants to spend the rest of her life with him. That's amazing. I can't imagine liking anyone so much I actually want to spend the rest of my life with him. Say what you like about married men – but they've all got that.'

I couldn't deny it. I do have that. And I reminded her, despite myself, that it was kind of something I wanted to keep – no matter how much I moan about it. But I also told her I wanted to be friends. She's cool, Train Girl, she's not like anyone else I've ever met. The irony is I think Beth would really like her too.

Anyway, she was fine. 'Of course you do,' was all she said.

Of course I do. Right? Even if my wife wouldn't approve. Of course I do. I still do.

Au revoir!

Dan

From: Martin.Harbottle@premier-westward.com
To: DantheMan020@gmail.com
Re: Out of Office Reply

Dear Sir/Madam

Thank you for your email dated December 2 this year. I can confirm that Mr Harbottle has received it and will endeavour to respond as soon as possible. Your concerns are of utmost importance to us.

Thank you again for writing to Premier Westward.

pp Martin Harbottle, Managing Director

This is an automatically generated response. Please do not reply

Letter 52

From: **DantheMan020@gmail.com**
To: Martin.Harbottle@premier-westward.com
Re: 22.20 Premier Westward Railways train from London Paddington to Oxford, December 6. Amount of my day wasted: 0 minutes. Fellow sufferers: Overkeen Estate Agent.

Jesus, are you still here? What have you done with Martin, you evil email program? Where have you buried the Managing Director, you cold-hearted computer? I need to speak to him! Not just about the ongoing delays, the general incompetence, the conspicuously poor service his company is providing, because, to be fair, I've not been delayed for a week (I'm not even delayed now). No: I need to speak to him about everything else.

Overkeen Estate Agent's here and he's talking turkey (choice phrases tonight: 'Going forward, we need to nail our colours to the mast'; 'Give me an idea bomb!'; 'There's no reason not to be a product evangelist about this'; 'Let's loop back and think offline'; 'Let's fire up the Flymo before the grass grows too long on this one'; 'Think low-hanging fruit first, yeah?'). I've been listening to him since we left Paddington, I still have no idea what he's on about and I don't think I can bear another moment of his nonsense.

It's just not the same, talking to an automatically generated email response. It just doesn't have the same heart.

I'll tell you what? Can you at least pass a message on? Can you tell him I wrote? Can you tell him I miss him?

Au revoir!

Dan

From: Martin.Harbottle@premier-westward.com
To: DantheMan020@gmail.com
Re: Out of Office Reply

Dear Sir/Madam

Thank you for your email dated December 6 this year. I can confirm that Mr Harbottle has received it and will endeavour to respond as soon as possible. Your concerns are of utmost importance to us.

Thank you again for writing to Premier Westward.

pp Martin Harbottle, Managing Director

This is an automatically generated response. Please do not reply

---

From: **Martin.Harbottle@premier-westward.com**
To: DantheMan020@gmail.com
Re: 22.20 Premier Westward Railways train from London Paddington to Oxford, December 6.

Dear Dan

First of all, please accept my apologies for the recent lack of responses from me. It was in no way intended as a personal snub, or an indication that as Managing Director of Premier Westward I don't take every single one of your concerns very seriously. I was merely away from the office, using up some annual leave with my family before Christmas. We like to go to Germany at this time every year. The markets there are wonderful!

I did set up an automatically generated email response system to deal with any correspondence while away. I see from your letters that you did receive those notifications. I hope you found them reassuring!

I'm afraid that it may take some time to find out exactly the cause of all your delays while I was out of the office. Please be reassured that I shall devote my time to it as soon as I am able to.

In the meantime, it seems like I did pick quite a time to be away! I'm not quite sure where to start. I do hope you haven't been caught up in any of the shocking practices being uncovered at the *Globe*, although I'm sure you're made of better stuff than that. And likewise, while I was initially pleased to hear that you and your wife had patched things up and made a new start, as it were, I am very sorry that you seem to be having difficulties again. I must confess that I feel perhaps renewing your friendship with 'Train Girl' (especially given her penchant for married men!) is not the best way to rebuild that particular bridge.

But as I say, your wife's jealousy would seem to be a little extreme. I wonder if there are any other underlying issues influencing her anger?

Warmest regards

Martin

Letter 53

From: **DantheMan020@gmail.com**
To: Martin.Harbottle@premier-westward.com
Re: 07.31 Premier Westward Railways train from Oxford to London Paddington, December 14. Amount of my day wasted: 10 minutes. Fellow sufferers: Train Girl, Guilty New Mum, Lego Head, Universal Grandpa.

Martin! You're back! Like a great fiery phoenix-train rising from the ashes of the engine sheds, you return! And everything is going to be OK again. The atrocities in North Africa, the horrors at work, the sadness at home… you're here, to make it all better. Or to at least make the trains run on time.

Thank you for your most recent letter, Martin! Thank you a thousand times. And Germany, eh? The Fatherland! The Christmas Markets, the spiced wine and sauerkraut pastries. The lederhosen-clad girls and jolly fat *Bürgermeisters*. Ice skating on the old *autobahns* of Munich and Baden-Baden! It sounds wonderful. It sounds almost as wonderful as a winter weekend in Torquay. I hope you had a wonderful time.

Meanwhile, I've been thinking about what you said about Beth. It is weird, isn't it? The more I consider it, the weirder it is. The way she's gone so weird over the fact that someone may have fancied me.

Over the fact I told her about it. It's almost as if it's the telling that has upset her so much. And that doesn't make any sense.

Why should she get so upset that I share that? Surely, as man and wife, we're not supposed to keep secrets from each other. Surely, as man and wife, we should be all about sharing. Everything. Even the things we may not want the other to hear. Why should the fact I'm doing that be so difficult for her?

Beth is not the jealous type. Never has been. She's never once suspected me of playing away – even knowing what my colleagues are like, even having met Harry the Dog and listened to his tales of debauchery and casual infidelities. When I went on a stag do last year she demanded to know all the details – not because she was worried I might misbehave, but because she wanted a good laugh.

(The stag party was in Berlin, Martin, on the weekend of Guy Fawkes' night. The Fatherland! You could have been there at the same time as us last year! We may have drunk in the same bars! Although predictably, of course, we ended up in a strip bar – unpredictably, the strip bar also turned out to be a brothel (who knew prostitution was legal in Germany?). I remember one stripper/prostitute taking a particular shine to me, even after I'd run out of money. I told her I couldn't pay for any more drinks, let alone anything else; she just shrugged, adjusted her bra strap (she was at least wearing a bra) and told me 'Hey, that's OK, I like you anyways. We chat, ja?' So we chatted. As Harry the Dog and the rest of the boys ogled and groped and a few of them slipped away with the girls, me and my *fräulein* sat and chatted. Which was fine, of course… except that after about an hour I couldn't think of anything else to say. So I ended up trying to explain that back in Britain that night there would be fireworks, bonfires, parties. She didn't understand why. Have you ever tried to explain to a German stripper why the British celebrate a plot to blow up Parliament every year? It's tricky, even before the language issues. 'But this man is bad, ja?' she said, frowning. 'Is not a good thing to put a bomb in the government? In Germany this is a very bad thing.' (Well yes, I had to concede, and yet nevertheless…)

Anyway, when I told Beth she thought it was the funniest thing she'd ever heard. She thought it was brilliant. She told me I should pitch it as a TV show – how long can you engage foreign prostitutes in small talk about British cultural traditions before they get bored? It didn't occur to her that I might have even thought about actually doing anything other than talking nonsense with the girl. She knew I wouldn't.

So now… why is she suddenly being all jealous now?

I've been thinking. I've been thinking about Mr Blair. I don't hear much about Mr Blair these days. Not since Halloween, not since that weekend away. Before then, he used to be all I ever heard about. His perfect house, his perfect opinions, his perfect child, his perfect parenting techniques. The way half the mums in the mums-and-babies groups used to go a little weak at the knees at his strong-yet-sensitive nappy-changing style.

But now… now Beth doesn't mention him at all. Why do you think that is, Martin? Why would my wife suddenly stop talking about a man who she has previously been so keen to eulogise? Why would she then go so crazy when I mention I'd broken off a friendship because I suspected my friend had inappropriate feelings towards me? Are those two things connected? Am I missing something massive here? Am I not catching the real story, the real scoop?

I've been thinking. And I'm not sure I like the direction my thoughts are headed in. But then, perhaps I'm just being a journalist about it. Perhaps I'm being too tabloid. Looking for the scandal, searching for the conspiracy theory, paying too much attention to the whispers. It's just that, well, recently, as we've seen, the whispers have tended to be right. The newsroom gossip, the outlandish theories, the hidden deceits – recently they've all turned out to be pretty well true.

You know what I'm going to do, Martin? I'm going to ask Train Girl about it. She knows her stuff where this kind of thing's concerned. She's clued up on the whole relationships thing. I'll present it to her as a hypothetical, a friend at the office, a story I'm working on – and I'll see what she makes of it.

Yes, that's it. That's the plan. Thanks, Martin! It's so good to have you back – I feel like I can think properly again!

Au revoir!

Dan

Letter 54

From: DantheMan020@gmail.com
To: Martin.Harbottle@premier-westward.com
Re: 22.20 Premier Westward Railways train from London Paddington to Oxford, December 17. Amount of my day wasted: 17 minutes. Fellow sufferers: No regulars (Saturday, innit).

Martin! Old friend! Brace yourself, son, this is going to be a long one. It's late at night on a stretch of track near Slough, we were late setting off, slow to get going, and now we've stopped altogether. We've got a lot to get through today, and (it seems) a lot of time to get through it together. So brace yourself. Hold tight.

We got a tip from the police today. A heads-up. Advance warning of a story that's going to break around 11 tonight. Around about now, in fact. (The police do that just to annoy the papers, by the way. Make announcements so late, once the first editions have gone, once the night staff has settled down and is hoping for an uneventful shift. They save up their big ones until such a time as will inconvenience as many journalists as possible. I'll tell you for nothing, Martin: there's a few hacks are going to get unwanted, panicky calls tonight, just as they're settling in for the evening; just as they're contemplating bed, or last orders from the bar, or one more digestif before going home to relieve the babysitter. Though not us, obviously. Not anyone from the *Globe*. Not because we've got our heads-up, our courtesy call, but because it's not a story we're going to be reporting. It's not a story we're keen on telling.)

And what is the story? What's the scoop? Tomorrow's news today, Martin, is that Her Majesty's constabulary are going to formally prosecute the *Globe* over the illegal accessing of civilians' private data – the civilians specifically being the family, friends and associates of poor little Barry Dunn, that most high-profile victim of the notorious Beast of Berkhamsted. The Crown Prosecution Service has concluded that the law has indeed been broken and that it will, for want of a better phrase, see our asses in court.

The CPS reckons it's got us bang to rights. And that will mean two court cases in simultaneous synchronicity. A war on two fronts. A pincer movement. On one flank, the petulant millionaires and their whining about the right to consequence-free bad behaviour, and on the other, a nation righteously (and correctly) outraged by the looting of a dead boy's most private information.

Tricky. In fact, a nightmare. If the case against us is as strong as everyone seems to think it is, we're going to get annihilated. Destroyed. The country's most popular newspaper recast as public enemy number one? There will be a feeding frenzy. It doesn't bear thinking about.

But then, things could be worse. (Could they? Really? Well… yes. Let's take a step back and look with a little clarity here. Let's get a little perspective. Yes, things definitely could be worse.) We could be in North Africa right now. We could be caught up in the latest developments there. And that really is a nightmare. They really have been annihilated, destroyed.

Happy Christmas, as somebody once said, war is over. The invasion, so swift, so laser-like in its infancy… and then so slow and dogged and brutal in its denouement, is finally concluded. The third flag in as many months (give or take a week or two) flutters above the tattered remains of the Imperial Palace. Neighbouring Regime is a neighbouring regime no longer: now it's simply the regime.

And what have they got for their trouble? The capital comprehensively smashed to blocks the size of Lego bricks. The rubble piled so high not even the tanks could get in. The thick layers of concrete dust in the air like a fog. The terrible silence. Terrible in contrast to the awful noises of the attack before… but terrible also because there is no human sound. No crying, no screaming, no wailing, no groaning. No mewling, no moaning, no pleading, no feeble begging for mercy. No sound… because there's nobody left to make a sound. That's the terror of that silence.

And then, the new leader. Astride a tank, in full military fatigues. Arms raised and palms outstretched. Magnificently bearded and with aviator shades. Talking of peace and unity and a new stability for the whole region, and later, why not!, the whole continent! The new leader – and his plans to bulldoze the old order away (both old orders – the old old order and the shortlived new old order). Literally bulldoze it all away. Starting with the capital city, starting on Monday. He's going to shovel everything up and shovel it all out and build a new city in its place. And with the rubble and the bricks and the sticks and the stones will doubtless be the bodies of the thousands of people who used to live there. And it doesn't take a genius or a cynic or a tabloid journalist to work out that they'll be bulldozed and shovelled up too. 'Cleansing', was the word he used. And we've heard that before, haven't we?

And then the contrasting shots of the adoring crowds back in the mother country. The jubilant scenes in the streets and the squares. The desperate declarations of love for their glorious, triumphant leader. The banners, the huge posters, the guns fired in the air in celebration. A nation united in victory. A nation doubled in size. And any thoughts of ever trying any funny business ever again as comprehensively flattened as their newfound territory's former capital.

So, yes. Things could be worse, I guess. When you look at the big picture. Things could definitely be worse. But it doesn't mean things can't be bad here too, right? There is no quantity theory of unhappiness. There are levels, sure. But things are still bad here too.

Oh, and you know what else? (I still have a few more minutes left of your time to use up tonight. Sorry about that, Martin: but then – you started it. You started it the moment this train stopped.) Talking of how bad things can get, I spoke to Train Girl. About the whole Mr Blair situation, I mean. I told her everything, except I changed the names to protect the innocent and guilty alike. I pretended it was a mate of mine worried about his wife's sudden and irrational jealousy.

And do you know what she said? 'This mate of yours? His wife is jealous because she's been shagging this other feller on the side.' That's what she said.

'Your mate's wife is cheating on him,' she said, with an authoritative nod of the head. 'That's why she's acting so weird. Think about it. She's there, having it away with this other guy, and although she feels bad about it, she doesn't feel bad enough to stop shagging him. Until your mate goes and tells her how he had the chance to shag someone else himself and didn't because he loves her. And what does that do? That makes her feel doubly bad. Super bad.

'So how does she react? She takes it out on your mate. She tries to make him feel like he's the bad guy here. And all because of her own guilt. All because he did what she couldn't by turning his free shag down. It's your basic guilty transference – she's transferring onto him all the anger she unconsciously knows he should be feeling towards her. She's not really furious with your mate; she's furious with herself. But now she's trapped.

'In a weird way, you know,' and this was said with a wink, 'it would have been better all round if your mate had shagged his sure thing. At least then they would have been even-stevens. As bad as each other.'

So there you go. That's not exactly the best news either, is it? Train Girl thinks Beth has been having it away with Mr Blair. Train Girl thinks my wife has been cheating on me with a *Guardian*-reading, tweed-wearing, latte-sipping, holier-than-thou Jericho socialist.

And you know what almost the worst bit is? I wasn't surprised she thought that. Because I've been thinking the same. And even thinking about thinking about it makes me feel dizzy and blind and sick. Even thinking about thinking it drains my blood and raises my bile and fills me with reeling horror, with lurching panic.

What if it's true, Martin? What if it's actually true? What do I do then? You really want to know? You really want to know what I'd do? I'd kill him, that's what I'd do. I'd kill the bastard.

Au revoir!

Dan

Letter 55

From: **DantheMan020@gmail.com**
To: Martin.Harbottle@premier-westward.com
Re: 07.31 Premier Westward Railways train from Oxford to London Paddington, December 22. Amount of my day wasted: 10 minutes. Fellow sufferers: Train Girl, Guilty New Mum, Lego Head, Universal Grandpa.

Oh calm down, Martin, I'm not really going to kill him. I couldn't kill someone. I couldn't kill anyone. The truth is, I don't know what I'd do. But don't worry. I wouldn't actually kill him.

Anyway. I haven't done anything yet. I haven't talked to Beth. I've just watched. I've watched, and listened, and made mental notes. Oh: and I looked at the messages on her mobile phone, too. Obviously. (There was nothing incriminating there.) I got into her Twitter account (likewise) and checked her Facebook (ditto). I haven't cracked her Gmail account, but I'm sure I can. But still. My mind is not exactly what you might call at ease about it. I'm going to have to confront her with it.

But not today. And not tomorrow, either. Tomorrow we're going to

Torquay, while we still can. While our non-transferable off-peak super-advance standard-class return tickets are still worth the paper they're printed on. We can't afford to spend the night (not even in midwinter), but it should still make for a nice day out, right? It may not be an actual holiday, but it's a start. A chance to forget all the awfulness right now and actually enjoy each other's company. And even I'm not stupid enough to ruin it by asking my wife if she's been having an affair.

Meanwhile... back in the land of the living, things have been nothing short of ridiculous at work. It's a ridiculous week this week anyway – with Christmas being on a Sunday there will be no newspaper and so we've literally nothing to do. Nothing to do except ignore calls from other journalists to tell our (anonymous, off-the-record) stories from inside the most notorious newsroom in the world. Nothing to do except scan the web for mentions of ourselves and all we've supposedly got up to. Nothing to do except patiently, systematically, methodically trawl through all our internet caches and email archives and delete anything that might be in the slightest bit incriminating. Nothing to do but photocopy contacts books and then destroy the originals. Nothing to do but transfer all messages, phone numbers and email access from work-provided company phones to newly bought Pay As You Go handsets. And then wipe the work ones clean.

Nothing to do but exactly what the police told us we shouldn't be doing. But then, you know, we're not stupid, are we? And who knows what might get taken out of context when presented as evidence. Better to be safe than sorry.

Anyway. What was I saying? Oh yes: I'm not going to kill Mr Blair. Of course I'm not. Even if he has had it away with my wife. Which we don't know if he did. Because I haven't asked her yet. But I will. I will ask her.

And meanwhile... I'm friends again with Train Girl. I haven't told Beth, of course, but every morning, like old times, we seek each other out in Coach C, we sit and we shoot the breeze all the way to Paddington.

She hasn't mentioned our conversation of last week (my fictional friend, her unerringly apposite advice) and I haven't talked about home either. We don't talk about much, truth be told. We speak a lot, we speak non-stop, but we're not saying much. It's like the opposite of me and Beth – there we don't do any speaking, but the silence… the silence shouts. The silence shouts all manner of suspicions and accusations and resentments.

What do we speak about, Train Girl and I? Well, her love life, mostly. I can't say I'm not intrigued. She's coming to the end of a relationship, as it turns out. I say relationship – as close to a relationship as she gets. There's some bloke she's been seeing (on her terms, at her place, at times convenient to her) and, not to put too deep a gloss on it, she's thinking of stopping seeing him.

He's an architect, apparently. Has his own practice. Married, of course, two kids. The oldest is 22. He's a few months shy of 60 but in good shape. Works out a lot. Body of a man two-thirds his age. What you might call a 'silver fox'. And good in bed, too: just the right mix of arrogance, experience and a rather eager gratitude that someone half his age and so obviously beautiful should even be giving him the time of day, let alone getting him in the sack. (Train Girl is remarkably candid about these things, Martin: she sits there, with her legs crossed and slightly sidewise, so her knees are pointing at an angle towards mine, one hand resting on my arm, squeezing every now and then to make a point, the other fiddling with her hair or a button on her jacket, her eyes dancing, her lips always moving, her mouth more often than not turned up in a smile… she sits there in the mornings and she talks quite openly about just how good or bad in bed the men in her life are. What they like, what she likes, what she wished they liked…)

But anyway, she's thinking of finishing with him. The problem isn't his age, or his wife. The problem is the sex.

'All we do is have sex,' she said. 'And that's great, it's fun… but it is just sex. You know? I tell him when to come round, he comes round, we do that thing with a bit of dinner and a bottle of wine, and then we have sex, and then I pack him off again. And although it's good sex – and good wine – it's just sex. We don't talk; we don't laugh. We don't go out and have a laugh, you know? Not like me and you did. There's no falling over in Soho in the rain.'

There isn't, is there? There's not much laughing at all, anywhere, right now. There's not a lot in the way of falling over in Soho in the rain. Not with Train Girl, and not at home either. And as for sex… well, that's the million-dollar question, isn't it? That's what we'd all like to know.

Au revoir!

Dan

From: **Martin.Harbottle@premier-westward.com**
To: DantheMan020@gmail.com
Re: 07.31 Premier Westward Railways train from Oxford to London Paddington, December 22.

Dear Dan

Thank you for your recent letters. I feel very touched that you seem to be so pleased I've returned from holiday, although of course I will be out of the office again for a week for the Christmas break!

I am sorry, however, that you have once again experienced a few minor disruptions to your services. All bar Saturday December 17's delays were as a result of the ongoing service improvements we're implementing on the Oxford–London line. Unfortunately, the implementation of any improvements to our service does mean an attendant dropping off of reliability and punctuality.

On December 17 your train was sadly disrupted due to a suspected sighting of an intruder on the line. It later turned out to be a false alarm – a scarecrow had in fact blown onto the sidings from some nearby allotments – but as I'm sure you'll appreciate, it took some time to establish the facts and secure the area. After that, of course, it was smooth sailing all the way to Oxford!

I sincerely hope you have a magical time in Torquay and I'd like to wish you and your family a peaceful and very happy Christmas!

Martin

Letter 56

From: **DantheMan020@gmail.com**
To: Martin.Harbottle@premier-westward.com
Re: 10.01 Premier Westward Railways train from Oxford to Torquay, December 23. Amount of my day wasted: all day. Fellow sufferers: wife, child.

And so the morning broke, Martin. The holiday. The city break. The trip to Torquay in the deep midwinter. On the day before the day before Christmas, Beth and Sylvie and I loaded up our bags (full of things for Sylvie, of course, nappies and nappy bags and two complete changes of clothes in case of accidents; baby food and water and spare water and spare baby food; wipes and wet wipes and tissues and muslin squares; three favourite cuddly toys and a blanket), strapped them all to the pram, strapped the baby in the pram, and set off through the weak and watery morning light to Oxford station.

Two hours and 47 minutes of travel lay ahead of us, and at the end of it: Torquay. Torquay! Just for one day. Two hours and 47 minutes each way, just for an afternoon in Torquay: it seems a long time, doesn't it?

You know what? It's not so long. It's not as long as, for example, six hours.

Six hours, Martin! Six hours on one of your terrible trains and we didn't get anywhere near Torquay. We didn't even make it to Reading. Six hours, and you know how close to the seaside we got?

Radley. We made it as far as Radley. That's about eight miles east of Oxford.

Here's what happened. Here are the edited highlights. Here's what we did on our holidays…

Beth and I had called a temporary truce. We decided, in as few words as possible, with as little in the way of reconciliation as manageable, that we would have 'a nice day out', free from all the tension of recent times. For Sylvie's sake, mostly. We decided to behave like adults, like a proper family.

And so there we were on the platform, our little nuclear family, ready for our grand day out. The train came on time (well done!), we boarded, we found a pair of seats together, we packed up the pram and loaded up the luggage racks, we wedged Sylvie onto our laps, and we got ready to go. Go!

No. The train made a half-arsed limp out of the station, struggled along the line for a bit, and then, with a sigh and a shrug, slowed and stopped before Oxford's spires were barely out of sight. And there we stayed.

We stayed there until the sun started to set again. On a draughty chugger train with no catering trolley. Cramped into a carriage with a baby on our laps. And if the initial delay gave us something to talk about (something other than ourselves, our problems, our suspicions and mistrusts) then once 20 minutes or so had passed, we fell silent again.

After an hour Sylvie started crying.

After an hour and a half I went forward to try to find out what was going on ('Oh, like he's just going to tell you,' said Beth, 'when he's not bothered to let any of the other passengers know what's going on, he's just going to open the door to his cab and invite you in and explain the whole situation to you…').

After an hour and a half and three minutes I came back none the wiser and sat down with a sarcastic sort of smile in answer to Beth's raised eyebrows.

After two hours the driver finally told us what was up. The train had failed. It had failed, Martin. It had failed at being a train. We couldn't move forwards or backwards. We also couldn't get off the train as that would be dangerous, apparently. We would have to wait until a relief train could be found to shunt us back up the track towards Oxford. They were currently trying to source one, but due to the delays that our failed train was causing across the whole network, that might take a while.

After three hours, Sylvie had eaten all of her food and drunk all of her water and had started on the spare food and spare water.

After four hours we were told a relief train was on its way. 'With a bit of luck we might be home for teatime!' joked the driver. Nobody laughed.

After four hours and ten minutes, Beth and I started arguing. I don't know whose fault it was, really (it was probably mine). I can't even remember what it was about… it was about everything except the one thing we really did want to argue about – whether I was having an affair, whether she was having an affair. I think it began with a suggestion we save some of Sylvie's food, just in case, which was obviously a thinly veiled attack on Beth's mothering abilities, which then became an assault on my lack of contribution as a father, which then escalated into a full-on three-way tantrum between two adults and a baby over which of us was the most hard-done-by and least appreciated by the other two.

And the other passengers? They pretended not to hear. They did that British thing: they engrossed themselves in their books and magazines and mobile phones. They pretended it wasn't happening at all – as though if they concentrated hard enough we would simply cease to be there, ruining an already terrible experience for everyone.

After five hours and 15 minutes we stopped arguing for a while to consider that Sylvie was now on her last nappy. 'I told you she shouldn't have eaten so much,' I said, somewhat unnecessarily.

After five hours and 17 minutes we started arguing again: in whispers now, furiously hissing at each other like demented geese.

After five hours and 35 minutes the relief train finally turned up. Someone attempted a cheer. Someone else told them to 'shut the fuck up, nobhead'. Beth started to laugh. I started to laugh too. Sylvie stopped crying and regarded us suspiciously.

We laughed almost all the way to Oxford. 'Shut the fuck up, nobhead!' That person had managed to endure over an hour and 20 minutes of Beth and I ripping shreds out of each other, had dealt with over four hours of Sylvie's wails and screams and soiled nappies… and yet one little attempt at a cheer for the relief train was just too much for him: shut the fuck up, nobhead! Perfect!

At six hours we jerked back into Oxford station, loaded up the pram again, loaded the baby into the pram again, and wearily walked home. In silence, again.

Torquay, eh? Magical. Thanks, Martin. Thanks for a wonderful day out.

Au revoir!

Dan

Letter 57

From: **DantheMan020@gmail.com**
To: Martin.Harbottle@premier-westward.com
Re: 19.50 Premier Westward Railways train from London Paddington to Oxford, December 28. Amount of my day wasted: eight minutes. Fellow sufferers: No regulars (away for Christmas, obvs).

Merry Christmas, Martin. I hope you got everything you wished for. I hope all your dreams came true. I hope the baby Jesus came down your chimney and filled all your sacks with holy spirits. I hope you had a good one.

How was my Christmas? Well, I'm back at work, so technically it was only two days long, but nevertheless, that was long enough. We ate, we drank, we made merry hell. How was Christmas in my household, mine and Beth's first Christmas with baby Sylvie? Pretty awful, actually, since you ask.

On Christmas morning, as we all three woke in the same bed – little Sylvie stretched diagonally between us, arms above her head and legs bent wide, as if to maximise the distance, as if to keep us as far apart from each other as possible – on Christmas morning, as we opened our eyes to the wails and demands of another day; on Christmas morning, as we parted the curtains and gazed at the grey drizzle, the freezing fog, as we trudged downstairs to our little tree and its little huddle of presents (all for Sylvie, of course, bar two little ones at the back. As is traditional, we both broke our pact not to buy each other presents), on Christmas morning, Beth and I had the biggest argument of our marriage. Of our whole relationship.

I mean, there've been some whoppers lately, some doozies, some proper stand-up screamers, but this beat the lot. It knocked them into a cocked Santa hat. And we haven't spoken since. Presents: silence. Turkey dinner: silence. Afternoon Bond film: silence. God bless us, every one.

What was the argument about? What do you think? The argument was about Mr Blair. It was about Beth and Mr Blair. It was about whether there is a Beth and Mr Blair. I finally decided that, without actual evidence of any wrongdoing, I'd go for the full confession. Ask her straight. Get it all out in the open, once and for all.

So that's just what I did. I came right out with it, as Sylvie crawled in and out of the cardboard boxes and across the wrapping paper and ignored the presents they'd recently contained. 'Beth,' I said, looking her straight in the eye. 'Are you having an affair?'

What do you think she said, Martin? Yes? Yes, Dan, I'm having an affair. I've been seeing someone else. It's not you, it's me. I've made a terrible mistake. Please forgive me?

She didn't say that. She told me, in no uncertain terms, that I was a terrible person for even asking. She told me she was horrified I even thought so. She burst into tears and then she slapped me and then she turned away and wouldn't let me near her. She said she was disgusted with me for thinking that way. She said she felt betrayed I even asked her. She shouted and she yelled and she screamed that I was a shocking excuse for a husband for daring to harbour such thoughts. She went on for ages. Until the wailing of Sylvie got to be louder than she was. And then… the silence. And she's not spoken since.

But you know what, Martin? Amidst all that shouting, all that shock and outrage and disappointment she expressed, she didn't actually answer the question. She didn't deny it. My wife did not tell me whether or not she's having an affair with Mr Blair.

And so we haven't spoken since. We spent the rest of Christmas with the baby between us, Beth sobbing, me cold. And as the two of them went to bed early, I kept sitting there, silent in front of the TV, drinking, thinking.

And meanwhile, on the box, Europe rose up in protest. Europe was outraged. Europe couldn't believe this stuff. In Rome and Madrid and Paris and Amsterdam, once again, they're up in arms. They're furious about the lack of action in North Africa, they're outraged by the inability of the West to do something about it all, to act in the face of such hideous behaviour. 'Betrayal' said the banners. 'Shame'.

And watching them, I wished I could get a banner and go marching myself. I wished I could kick up a storm too. Betrayal. Shame.

Au revoir!

Dan

Letter 58

From: **DantheMan020@gmail.com**
To: Martin.Harbottle@premier-westward.com
Re: 22.50 Premier Westward Railways train from London Paddington to Oxford, January 4. Amount of my day wasted: 20 minutes. Fellow sufferers: Fuck knows.

Martin. She was lying. She adtmitted it. She told me on New YEar Day, after one whole week of dead ssilence. She was lyinghf.

It only happened once. On that baby-bonding weekemnd. It was a mistake. She regretted it immediately. She loves me still. Even thouggh. Despite. She still ca'nt believe it. She still can't beleive it happened. She still can't believe she evber did it.

She wants me to forgive her. Can I forgive her? She's a lair, Martin. She's a liar. I'm so drunk I can barely see the screen, but I know that much. Sgjhhe's a liar.

Au revoir

Dan

PS – Ohhhh my trains 20 minute delayed but loike I said I cant see teh screen

properly. Ill owe you, ok> There's a pal. I'lll owe you one.

From: **Martin.Harbottle@premier-westward.com**
To: DantheMan020@gmail.com
Re: 22.50 Premier Westward Railways train from London Paddington to Oxford, January 4.

Dear Dan

I am sorry you have once again had to write to me. Over the Christmas period many trains are subject to revised timetables due to essential engineering work, and it seems that your service on December 28 was the victim of some over-running engineering work around the Reading area. On the evening of January 4 there was a problem with a malfunctioning heater unit in the driver's cab and the train was unable to leave Paddington until an engineer could be called to stabilise the thermostat.

I am also sorry to hear that your trip to Torquay was marred slightly by problems on the network. Unfortunately trains do on occasion fail. Another 'act of God' if you like! I am afraid, however, that the conditions of your complimentary tickets do mean that I am unable to reimburse or recompense you in any way for the inconvenience.

On a personal note, I would like to express just how sorry I am about your situation at home. But please, do not give up on your marriage too easily. Think of your daughter. Think of what might happen to her without you. I am sure that with some work on both your parts this is something you can overcome together, for the good of little Sylvie. It has to be worth a try, surely.

With warmest regards

Martin

Letter 59

From: **DantheMan020@gmail.com**
To: Martin.Harbottle@premier-westward.com
Re: 22.20 Premier Westward Railways train from London Paddington to Oxford, January 6. Amount of my day wasted: nine minutes. Fellow sufferer: Overkeen Estate Agent.

All right, I'll start with the good news. I'm drunk again. (Not too drunk. Not too drunk to at least run a spellcheck this time. But drunk nonetheless. Filled with booze! Replete with liquor! Stuffed to the gills with alcohol! Oh sweet, sweet beer, as Homer Simpson so poetically expressed it; cause of and solution to all of life's problems!)

OK? Happy? Good. That's the glad tidings done and dusted, the happy stuff out of the way. Now let's get on with real life.

Real life, in the real world, isn't going so well. Real life, full of questions and answers that can't be asked or found at the bottom of the glass, kind of stinks. Home's rubbish; work's gone fully fledged mental. Chicken oriental.

Oh, Martin. I wish I hadn't written that now. Chicken oriental, I mean. It's gone and made me hungry. I'd kill for some chicken right now. Some Chinese chicken. I'd murder for some. That's the problem with drinking on an empty stomach: your stomach stays empty. You try to fill it up with booze – God knows I've tried! – and it just stays empty. And then you get to Paddington and there's no time to get a Burger King and you get on the train and there's no buffet car and you get home and there's no chips in the freezer and besides by that time the headache's kicked in and all you want to do is sleep. And you wake up even hungrier. Oh, Martin: what I wouldn't do for some chicken oriental right now! Sweet, sweet chicken oriental!

Sorry? What was I saying? Oh yes: home – rubbish. My wife, in case you didn't get the message last time around, slept with Mr Blair. She cheated on me. She betrayed me. She played away. She gave it up and gave it out and made a mockery of everything I thought we were.

So, you know, home – rubbish. Toilet, in fact. Home: toilet. And that's all I'm going to say about it. Toilet.

Work – mental. Chicken oriental (oh God, I've done it again. I'm so hungry, Martin! So hungry!)

Do you want to know what happened at work today? Shall I tell you? OK. Here's what happened at work today. The police came round again. At first we were all like, all right officer, you again is it, let yourself in, you know your way around, what's it this time… until we realised they looked a bit more serious than the last couple of visits. This time they didn't do any of that standing around awkwardly stuff they usually do. This time they looked purposeful.

And their purpose? It didn't take long to find out. A pair of them marched up to the showbiz editor's desk. Even as he looked up from the seven mobile phones he was furiously texting between (and they were lucky to catch him here, in truth: he's never in the office, the showbiz ed, he's always out wining or dining, schmoozing or boozing, glad-handing or back-scratching. He doesn't do any of the actual writing in his column, he just phones in the facts and gets the rest of us to file it. His job, as actual showbiz editor, involves no editing and all showbiz. His job is to live the life and our job is to repeat the resultant anecdotal evidence), he looked up from his phalanx of phones and just managed to get out a 'What the f—' before they arrested him.

They only arrested the showbiz ed, Martin! In broad daylight! On a Friday morning! With handcuffs and everything! They only went and read him his rights and confiscated his phones and took him away for questioning and that! And even as Goebbels came barrelling out of his office shouting blue murder and they kept walking him out of the door with his arms behind his back, we all just sat there and gawped. The most cynical, the smartest, the most embattled hacks on Fleet Street, collectively gobsmacked.

So: first the features editor (he was never charged, you'll remember, they were just content to throw the mud, sully his reputation, make him all-but unemployable and then hang him out to dry) and now the showbiz ed.

He has been charged, however. They've charged him with the illegal accessing of private information. They're saying he's been listening in where he shouldn't, reading what he's not allowed to. They're saying that some of those stories of his were not the result of good honest journalism.

And you know what the strangest thing of all is? After we watched the Old Bill lead him out of the office (arms behind his back, officer at each shoulder, just like you see on the telly) we all turned to the telly. And watched them emerge from our building again. We watched them walk out into the scrum of reporters, the bank of cameras, the stroboscopic glare of the flashbulbs, pause, and give a statement.

And that's the moment Goebbels lost the plot completely.

They wouldn't tell us why he was being arrested, but they would tell every other news organisation on the planet? And do so outside our own offices? It's taking the mickey, Martin. It's properly having a laugh at us. He picked up a stapler, drew his arm back, and launched it at the screen. And now there's one less TV in the office too.

So what did we do? We went to the pub. I got drunk with Harry the Dog and Bombshell and the Wee Tim'rous Trainee, who's turning into a bit of a star, as it happens, but more of that later. What else are we going to do? Tomorrow's going to be a horror show… but today we went to the pub.

Au revoir!

Dan

Letter 60

From: **DantheMan020@gmail.com**
To: Martin.Harbottle@premier-westward.com
Re: 22.20 Premier Westward Railways train from London Paddington to Oxford, January 10. Amount of my day wasted: eight minutes. Fellow sufferer: Overkeen Estate Agent.

Dear Martin

Beth and I haven't spoken a word since she admitted sleeping with Mr Blair. Don't get me wrong: she's spoken. I just haven't spoken back to her. But yes, she's spoken all right. She's spoken, and shouted, and pleaded, and sobbed, and shouted again. She started off by telling me it was a mistake (well, durr), that she regrets it with all her heart, that she was a bit drunk and a bit overemotional and he was just kind of there and it just kind of happened and immediately afterwards she ran away back to her own room in tears…

And I didn't know what to say. So I said nothing. So she started crying. She's been crying since the weekend, in fact.

And am I happy about it? No. Am I happy I found out what happened? Yes. Better that than not know, right? Better to live with the awful truth than with the blissful lie. Right? Right? Better the Pyrrhic victory than the ongoing humiliation of ignorant defeat. Right?

Or am I wrong? Or should I stop with this whole right or wrong business, with always insisting that everything has to either be right or wrong, black or white, and acknowledge the grey areas, admit things sometimes aren't as simple as newspaper sub-editors and headline writers like to pretend they are?

The only problem is, I don't know how to do it. I'm like Overkeen Estate Agent here, in the shiny suit and tie in fat footballer's knot, shouting clichés into my phone. Trying to 'push things forward', trying to 'be first to the endgame' without a clue as to how to do it.

I've no idea what happens next. I've no clue as to where we go now. Where do we go, Beth and Sylvie and I? Now the evening is spread out against the sky…

Hey! I'll tell you what, Martin! I'll tell you something to cheer us both up. To give us both a hollow laugh. Goebbels: he's going mad. My boss, the man I look to every day for professional guidance, the man with the power to make or break careers… he's losing it. I mean, he's always been unhinged, he's always been on the edge – but now he's definitely fallen off the edge. He's strayed from the path. He's got off the boat. Never get off the boat, Martin!

You know how I know he's got off the boat? He's only gone and offered me the showbiz editor's job, that's how. The poor guy's barely been given bail and already Goebbels has taken me aside, sat me down, looked me in the eye and told me he needs me to be showbiz editor of the *Globe*.

(Oh, did I say he'd 'offered' me the job? Apologies. Not strictly true. He didn't offer me the job at all. He told me the job was mine. In much the same way you might tell someone their shoelace is undone. 'I need a showbiz editor today,' he said, 'and you're the best man for the job. Congratulations etc. I can't pay you more until this whole nonsense blows over, and you can't move desk because everything in his bit of the office has been sealed off by the police, and I can't actually announce it or anything as that might look a bit heartless, but for all intents and purposes, you're showbiz editor of this paper now. Once all this is over we'll make it official. Now go get me some stories.')

So there we are. Showbiz ed! Looks like my career really has taken off. Showbiz editor of the most-read English-language newspaper on the planet… at a time when we're being taken to court on the one hand over our showbiz reporting, and investigated by the police on the other over all our other reporting. Showbiz ed of the *Globe*… just as MPs and fellow journalists are calling for our muzzling. Pyrrhic, Martin! It's too Pyrrhic!

Au revoir!

Dan

Letter 61

From: **DantheMan020@gmail.com**
To: Martin.Harbottle@premier-westward.com
Re: 07.31 Premier Westward Railways train from Oxford to London Paddington, January 14. Amount of my day wasted: five minutes. Fellow sufferers: no regulars (Saturday, innit).

The kids are revolting, Martin! They want a riot of their own! All last night they were out, smashing seven shades out of the Seven Sisters Road, firing up Finsbury Park and tearing down south Tottenham. Wasn't it extraordinary? Christ, I love a good riot. Nothing like a good riot for filling a newspaper!

(Don't get me wrong, Martin. I'm not a fan of riots *per se* – I disagree in principle with the principle of civil unrest, of course: arson and looting and vandalism are all thoroughly bad things and to be wholeheartedly condemned… but in this instance, at this time, this riot is a godsend.)

Yesterday morning we had nothing to put in the paper. Nothing worthy of our paper, anyway. No big hits at all. And then, as the freezing cold dusk drew in on another January afternoon, some stupid (white) copper happened to thump some hapless (black) street-corner hash-peddler a little too hard (we're hearing it wasn't even real hash he was selling, Martin; we're hearing it was melted and refrozen chocolate), he happened to do it in full view of all the kid's mates, without any back-up, and then made the whole situation worse by attempting to calm things down by standing on the boy as he tried to get up again. He actually stood on him, Martin!

Well, the rest was inevitable. A thrown brick, and then another, the cop chased down the road, the kids suddenly drunk on the power they had (they chased an actual policeman off their manor!), one shop window stoved in, then another, and another, a fire lit, a few phone calls made, texts sent, BBMs back and forth… and before the moon was fully up all the way through to dawn; the whole borough in flames.

I'm hearing they plan to kick it all off again today, Martin. Pick up where they left off. I'm hearing the boys from the neighbouring boroughs fancy a bit of the action too. What I'm hearing is that today's going to be worse than yesterday, that tonight's going to make last night look like a tea party.

I can't even imagine what Goebbels is going to be like today. Kid in a sweet shop. It wouldn't surprise me if he got out there with a meths-filled milk bottle and a broken brick himself, just to make sure the story had enough legs to last till Sunday's paper.

And what am I going to do? I'm going to work late, of course – it's Saturday, after all – but then I'm staying in London tonight. Why not? There's nothing to go home for, is there? And I might as well enjoy the riot while I can…

Au revoir!

Dan

From: **Martin.Harbottle@premier-westward.com**
To: DantheMan020@gmail.com
Re: 07.31 Premier Westward Railways train from Oxford to London Paddington, January 14.

Dear Dan

First let me please apologise again for the slow running of some of your trains. As I believe I have pointed out before, any disruption of less than ten minutes does not actually register as an official delay on our records.

However, I did want to reply to your letters to reassure you that I do take even the smallest inconvenience to your journeys with the utmost seriousness. And also because I wanted to check that you're OK. And to remind you that it is an offence to be drunk on a Premier Westward train.

Best regards

Martin

Letter 62

From: **DantheMan020@gmail.com**
To: Martin.Harbottle@premier-westward.com
Re: 07.31 Premier Westward Railways train from Oxford to London Paddington, January 18. Amount of my day wasted: 12 minutes. Fellow sufferers: Train Girl, Guilty New Mum, Lego Head, Universal Grandpa.

An offence to be drunk on a Premier Westward train? Are you serious? Have you ever been on one of your trains back from London after 9.30 at night? Everyone's drunk. Old men and young men, businesswomen and students, tourists and day trippers – they've all had a drink. How else could they cope with the awfulness of it all? How else could they pass the time before they get home?

And, Christ, those later trains… I guarantee to you now, Martin, that on any given train after ten p.m., somebody will fall asleep and miss their stop. Head down, tie askew, dribbling onto their shirt, or else slumped over the remains of their Burger King, hands and chin and suit pockets shiny with grease.

There'll be cans rolling on the floor between seats, Martin, little rivulets of lager running down the aisles, and outside the toilets a pool, where the booze meets the overflow from the dripping, stinking bowl. And on that last train, more often than not, somebody slumped in it all.

So it's an offence to be drunk on a Premier Westward train? You know what I think? I think the most offensive thing about the drunks on

Premier Westward trains is the fact that they're stuck on those trains at all, paying massively over-the-odds fares for a service that rarely gets them to where they're supposed to be going in the time in which it promised it would. That's what I think is offensive.

Anyway. Martin: I'm not drunk now. It's not even eight in the morning. The sun is struggling to rise, I'm muffled up and huddled up and on my way to work and life is getting back to normal. Creeping in its petty pace. Even the riots are over.

Those riots – they're all done for. On Friday night they tore up the Seven Sisters, by Saturday they'd set fire to great swathes of Zones 2, 3 and 4… and by Sunday they were finished. And now? The blame game. Now the politicians will wade in, with talk of zero tolerance and outrage and lessons that must be learned. (Will one of those lessons be that it's generally a bad idea for white policemen to go knocking over and then stamping on black kids? I'm no professor of law, but I'm thinking probably not.)

It was good while it lasted though, eh? I mean: it was terrible, it was frightening, it was awful and reprehensible and totally unacceptable… but it was exciting at least.

What did you do during the riots, Martin? Did you watch them at home, eyes wide as the buildings burned, mouth agape at the streams of angry youths pouring in and out of TK Maxx and Topshop, stumbling in with hoods over their heads and jumping out again with jackets stuffed with loot? Did you marvel at the depth and breadth of consumer electronics swiped and stolen? Did you wonder that the only shops left alone seemed to be the bookshops? Did you have your own little riot party in the Premier Westward nerve centre?

I had a riot party. I stayed in London on Saturday night, as you know. I wasn't about to venture out to Paddington when I finished up in the office at 10 p.m. Edgware Road was in flames, the locals were out with knives defending their turf – and the word was that the boys were coming up from the wrong end of Shepherd's Bush to take them on. There were battles on Praed Street, Martin, and I didn't fancy that one bit.

Also, I didn't really fancy going home too much anyway. And Train Girl had suggested that if I was going to be in London anyway and needed a place to crash…

So out we went, she and I, and had our own riot party. London was in flames, but central London was partying. Zone 1, Martin, Soho, Covent Garden, where the people with money are… there were no riots there. Just people having a good time. We hit four pubs – each with their big screens tuned to News 24, each crammed with drinkers watching the action unfold like a crowd watching a big football match, noisy, raucous, cheering and groaning. It was like a cross between the Blitz and the World Cup semi-final. Everyone drinking like there was no tomorrow, raising toasts to their burning city.

We went to four pubs, and then we went clubbing. The DJ was playing riot-appropriate tunes. We got smashed. Train Girl and I – we got properly, paralytically drunk. We drank and danced and laughed and laughed and danced some more and drank some more and told each other everything. I told her about Beth and Mr Blair (like she hadn't guessed about my 'friend' and his 'wife'). I told her I had no idea what to do. She told me she'd finished with her architect. She told me not to think, not to worry, not to beat myself up, not tonight; she told me to have another drink and have another dance… and so that's what we did.

I don't remember leaving the club. I don't remember going back to her friend's place in London. And when I finally got back to Oxford, some time on Sunday afternoon, I went straight to bed again. By the time I woke, the riots were over and the clean-up had begun. And now… the blame game.

Au revoir!

Dan

Letter 63

From: **DantheMan020@gmail.com**
To: Martin.Harbottle@premier-westward.com
Re: 22.51 Premier Westward Railways train from London Paddington to Oxford, January 21. Amount of my day wasted: 14 minutes. Fellow sufferers: No regulars (Saturday).

Hey, Martin! Guess what? I'm drunk on one of your trains! How offensive! Are you shocked? Are you offended? I do hope so! I do hope I've caused offence by being drunk on this dingy train of yours in the night.

So. You know how I said how pleased I was about the riots, journalistically? How great they were, in terms of knocking our problems off the front page and giving us something we could report on too, on equal terms with the rest of the country's media (which, of course, what with us being the *Globe*, means 'better' – when we report on equal terms, we report better)? You know how I said all that? Well, it's a week later and I'm unhappy about the riots now.

Martin: in tomorrow's paper there should be a brilliant scoop of mine – my first as showbiz ed – and although it still will be there, it's been bumped right back. It's on pages 12 and 13 now. Why? Because the riots are taking up pages one to 11.

And it's not even the riots themselves, now. It's the fallout. The aftermath. The trials. Seventeen years for the boy who started it all, the one whose mate got stamped on, the one who cast the first stone, so to speak. Nine years for the stamped kid himself. None for the copper who did the stamping. Not even a reprimand. Understandably, Martin, there is some outrage. Naturally, people are asking if this is strictly fair.

And guess who's asking loudest, who's whipping up as much outrage as they can? We are, of course! We're leading the charge on this one –

we're sticking up for the hopeless youth against the bullyboy cops like we're the liberal Left or something. We're demanding answers! We're asking for resignations at the highest level!

Why do you think we might be doing that? Why do you think one of the key heads we're insisting should roll might coincidentally happen to belong to the very same Dibble who's been so enjoying himself marching in and out of our offices recently? And, more to the point, do you think anyone else is going to make the connection?

And – and this is the one I really can't work out – is this attack on the police an example of Goebbels' genius, or of his madness? Is taking the fight to the Old Bill an act of tactical brilliance or a kamikaze mission? It's a hell of a thing, either way.

You want to know what else it is? It's a bit of a pain in the proverbial, where I'm concerned. Because it's all knocked back my scoop to the page 11–12 wilderness.

My scoop! My revelation! My undercover reporter in the West Kensington branch of Narcotics Anonymous. The people she saw there! The stories she heard! Martin, it's the oldest, the stupidest trick in the tabloid journalist's book, so naturally it's brilliant. And it's all thanks to my most junior reporter, young Wee Tim'rous Trainee, a girl barely up from the regionals, a girl who this time six months ago was reporting planning permission applications and the squabbles inside local councillors' meetings. When she came to me and said she'd had this idea, to enrol at NA in swanky and celeb-filled West Ken to see who turned up, to see what might come out of it – well, the first thing I did was laugh, of course.

The second thing I did was tell her how I've heard that story told a dozen times before – and how each time the journo's been sussed within about five minutes of walking through the door. And then the third thing I did was tell her to go for it. Why not? It shows the girl's thinking, at least.

I tell you – she may look like she'd be terrified of her own shadow, but that girl's got serious skills.

It took her precisely two meetings, Martin. Two sessions with the smackheads and dope fiends of West London, two meetings with the chaz-monkeys and pill-poppers of Kensington town. She went there twice and she got me four Class A names, with pure, uncut confessions to their ever-so-secret habits.

Four! An actor's wife, a high-street heiress, a high court judge and, to kick it all off, a royal butler. An actual butler to the actual monarchy! All standing up there, believing the whole 'anonymous' shtick, unburdening themselves, letting it all out, telling my girl with the tape recorder all about their secret sessions with the pills and pipes and powders. Unbelievable.

We're running with the butler first, of course – he's the man who squeezes the toothpaste for the man who ties the shoes of the man who would be king! And he's also nosing up five grand a week's worth of the old Colombian marching powder. It's a brilliant story. And now it's going on pages 11 and 12. Justice, Martin! Where's the justice?

I'm just hoping for a better show in the coming fortnight. We'll go for the wife and the heiress a week tomorrow, and hit the judge the week after. Build the whole thing up into a kind of high-society drugs ring. Stretch it over three weeks and make the story look like a genuine phenomenon. Like everyone in swanky West Ken is at it. Plus, of course, by doing so we may have more names to add by then, more establishment figures with their noses caught in the till, so to speak.

(Oh, and in case you're worried about that 'anonymous' thing – it's not a problem. We're not going to say where we got the story from, obviously, and if the good people of Narcotics Anonymous – or even the man himself – work it out, what are they going to do? It's a true story. We're reporting a true story. You can't argue with the facts, Martin!)

Anyway: suffice to say I'm more than pleased with the scoop. I might even take Wee Tim'rous Trainee out for a drink – show my gratitude the old-fashioned way, the Fleet Street way, by getting her good and sloshed one lunchtime. She's got initiative, after all. She's got nerve. And you know what else? She's young and she's keen and both Bombshell and Harry the Dog have told me she's one to watch, too. Although in Harry's case that may be as much because he fancies her as anything else.

Oh, and Martin, don't worry. I've got no designs on her. My wife might be prepared to sleep with just anyone, but not me. I've still got principles.

And, just so you know, I didn't sleep with Train Girl last Saturday night, either. I mean, I did sleep with her. But I didn't, you know, sleep with her. We slept in the same bed, but we slept.

She told me all about it (I couldn't remember, remember). We came home from the club, we fell into her flat, I started crying (I really must stop doing that when I'm drunk)… and then I fell on the bed and fell fast asleep. It was all she could do to get my shoes off, get my shirt off, roll me over a bit and fall asleep next to me. And when we woke in the morning, we shared nothing more intimate than a bacon sarnie and a mug of coffee before I went home.

So: nothing happened, right? And don't start talking to me about intent, either. About what might have been, had I not been so offensively drunk. The point is: nothing happened. That's the story. Those are the facts.

Also, the crying thing. Don't tell anyone about that either. It's a bit, well, embarrassing, isn't it?

Au revoir!

Dan

Letter 64

From: **DantheMan020@gmail.com**
To: Martin.Harbottle@premier-westward.com
Re: 22.20 Premier Westward Railways train from London Paddington to Oxford, January 26. Amount of my day wasted: five minutes. Fellow sufferers: Overkeen Estate Agent.

Dear God, Martin, can we not go a bare week without someone important leaving the paper, one way or another? You know, just for the sake of a little stability? Just for the sake of allowing us to get on with doing our job properly? Or, in fact, at all?

Today the chief executive resigned. And nobody saw that coming. Or at least, nobody except maybe Goebbels. And once again, the hardest, most cynical, most seen-it-all hacks in Fleet Street... struck dumb.

Don't get me wrong: I didn't care much for her myself. I barely saw her in the flesh, and whenever that was was usually when she'd come onto the floor to give someone the beasting of their lives. But still. She's the chief executive! Her name is synonymous with this paper. She came here as a graduate trainee three decades ago and worked her way up – all the way to the very top. Trainee, reporter, feature writer, deputy features ed, deputy showbiz ed, showbiz ed, news ed, editor, chief exec. It's not a bad career ladder, is it? And the stories you hear about her...

The time she actually went undercover as a reporter on a rival paper – I mean, actually took a job there, just in order to phone in all their stories to us. She got away with it for six months, Martin! Six months in which they couldn't understand why they couldn't get a single exclusive without us getting it first. And when they did find out, she needed a police escort from the building. For her own safety. The editor himself told her if he ever saw her again he'd kill her. She believed him.

The trick she had of leaving a jacket permanently hung on the back of her chair – and of slipping the cleaning staff and the work-experience kids a few quid to ensure that her computer was turned on and a lit cigarette was in her ashtray 24 hours a day… just in case somebody important should pass by. She wanted to make it look like she lived in that office, like that job was her life.

The weird thing is: that job was her life. And so when she appeared on the newsroom floor this afternoon, all power-suited and clicky-heeled, deathly pale and clutching a notepad (some reporters' habits never die) and Goebbels announced with a weird, strangled kind of smile that she wanted to address the troops, what we naturally assumed was that she was about to shut the paper.

Well, what else were we to think? And instead, we got a resignation. A tearful resignation. A taking of the bullet for the team. With her out of the picture, the heat might come off a little. The scandal might follow her, and leave us all behind. That's the plan. And to be fair to her, it's a pretty bloody honourable one too.

But still. Gobsmacked. Struck dumb. All except Goebbels, who just kept smiling that creepy smile, even as she tottered out again, shoulders shaking, to face the camera crews outside.

And naturally it was Goebbels who broke the silence. 'You.' He pointed at me. 'Get me something other than the resignation of our chief executive to lead with on Sunday. Get me it now.'

And that, as they say, was that.

Au revoir!

Dan

From: **Martin.Harbottle@premier-westward.com**
To: DantheMan020@gmail.com
Re: 22.20 Premier Westward Railways train from London Paddington to Oxford, January 26.

Dear Dan

Once again, thank you for taking the time to write and tell me of your recent problems. Your train on January 18 was the victim of a mix-up in our depot, when the earlier service was mistakenly assigned four buffet cars instead of standard-class carriages. Unfortunately, the resulting delay to that service had consequences for several other services throughout the morning, of which yours was one.

On January 21, your evening service back to Oxford was delayed thanks to rowdy passengers threatening a guard who refused to let them use a toilet reserved for first-class customers. Those troublemakers, I might add, were subsequently breathalysed, found to be intoxicated and arrested by the British Transport Police.

I am very sorry you feel that drunkenness – and indeed rioting – are socially acceptable ways of behaving. Perhaps I am old-fashioned but I certainly do not. And even making allowances for the pressures you are under at work and at home, I can't help thinking that perhaps sometimes you should examine your own opinions before being so hasty to pass comment on everyone else. I feel that on occasion you do tend to become rather 'tabloid' in your thinking, and that is a shame.

Martin

Letter 65

From: **DantheMan020@gmail.com**
To: Martin.Harbottle@premier-westward.com
Re: 07.31 Premier Westward Railways train from Oxford to London Paddington, February 1. Amount of my day wasted: 13 minutes. Fellow sufferers: Guilty New Mum, Lego Head, Universal Grandpa.

Woah there, soldier! Easy, tiger! Careful, cougar! What's with all this sudden judgemental stuff?

I'm sorry if you feel I'm a bit tabloid. I am a bit tabloid. I said it to you ages ago, didn't I? In fact, I've just looked back through my email history and found it. Here's what I said:

'I basically think I'm better than everyone else and at the same time worry that nobody else really realises it. It makes me think I'm always right (even when I sort of know, inside, I may be wrong). Because the *Sunday Globe* – it is always right, isn't it? It tells the world what's right – and more often, what's wrong.'

That really is me, isn't it? Oh dear. The thing is, Martin, I've been living like that for years now (at least as long as I've been at the paper, anyway) and, like the paper, I've been doing it with a swagger, a self-confidence that's born out of being part of something that's basically untouchable.

But now. Now the paper has been touched. Now I've been touched (as it were). And I'm not so sure either the paper or me is so right about everything any more. And it's true what you say: rioting isn't big or clever. It's not funny. It's no cause for celebration. I'm just being an idiot pretending it is. I'm just showing off.

I'll be honest with you, Martin. (I'm always honest with you, for good or ill.) I'm having a bit of a crisis right now. I don't know if you've noticed, like, but things are kind of falling apart – and I'm not sure

(OK, I have no idea) what I should be doing about it. Even whether I can do anything about it. All this stuff at work, and all this stuff at home: I'm part of it, it's part of me, but I feel like it's all happening despite me, like it's all happening to me, but like I've got absolutely no influence on what matters. I'm not driving the train, Martin, I'm sitting on the train watching it all happen out of the window, powerless to do anything about where it's taking me or how long it's going to take to get there.

I should get off the train, shouldn't I? I should get off the train and start walking. I should take charge of stuff, determine my own direction, be in control of how long it takes to get there. It's just that… I don't know how to do it.

And what of the train? Who can I see today? Guilty New Mum… I'm beginning to wonder about Guilty New Mum. Choppy waters may run deep, as far as she's concerned.

When she got on the train today, she was in the usual flap, tottering and tripping down the aisle, handbag perilously close to spilling its contents everywhere, one hand clutching her travelcard, the other holding an overflowing cup, coffee sloshing over the sides and dripping along her hand and onto the floor. Her phone was crammed between her shoulder and ear and she was giving it both barrels to him indoors.

'Well of course she's crying,' she said. 'You'd be crying too if you were up all night. Except you weren't; I was the one up all night with her. I feel like crying too. I'd love to have a good old cry. There's nothing I want more, to be honest, than a big cry. What's that? No, I'm not being sarcastic. Far from it. I'm telling the truth. What? When? Have you checked her nappy? What colour was it? No, that's fine, it's always that colour. What's her temperature? Well, why not? Check it now. Has she been too close to the radiator? How many blankets have you put on? Well, I don't know, but that's what it said in the book, didn't it? What do you mean which book? All the books! Gina thingy. That book. Well, yes, I know it also says that but you can ignore that bit. Definitely ignore that bit. Don't leave her crying. Seriously. Don't leave her crying. What? Where? Oh you're joking. Both sets of keys? Well, why were they by the fridge anyway? I never leave them by the fridge? Oh Christ, don't tell me I've left my security card at home again as well…'

And that's when it happened. She was, by this time, ensconced in the seat across the aisle from me, and as she frantically rooted around in her bag, something small and rectangular and plastic dropped out and came skidding across the carriage floor towards me. I picked it up and was about to hand it back without looking when I realised she hadn't noticed its absence. 'Oh for crying out loud,' she was saying, pulling out little fluffy animals and notebooks and dummies and organisers and teething granules and USB sticks. 'I do not need this, not again, not today, not with the meetings I've got, not with the bloody PM on my bloody case…'

And I thought: PM? Hello?

So I took a look at her security card. On the front: her photo (taken pre-motherhood, looking smart, relaxed, confident), her name (double-barrelled!), a barcode. No clues there. But, on the back, this: 'If found, please return to SIS, 85 Vauxhall Cross, Albert Embankment, London', along with the whole Lion and Unicorn *Dieu et mon droit* thing.

85 Vauxhall Cross: I know that building, Martin! Everyone knows that building. It's been in the James Bond films. The Real IRA fired a missile at it not so long ago. It's where the spies are. And SIS: that's another name for MI6. She's a spy, Martin! And judging from some of the conversations she has on that phone, thinking about it again with a bit of hindsight, I'm beginning to think she might be someone pretty senior in the spy world. A Spymaster!

Remember the incident in the Putin meeting? Putin? Putin, Martin! And now the PM? And what was that thing with the G8? Am I sharing my train every day with M? (Or was it Q? No, M. Definitely M. Judi Dench, either way.) Am I sharing my train with the real-life Judi Dench? And is she actually a massive flake?

Anyway, I handed the pass back, and she gave me such a look of gratitude, I only thought: I guess she doesn't know who I am, who I work for. If she did, she would certainly not want me going anywhere near it. A reporter at the *Globe* in possession of M's security pass? No. Good God, no!

And then I thought again: perhaps it's not so great, after all, being swaggering and arrogant and untouchable and unthinkingly right about everything. Not if it means you're not a very nice person. Or not a very nice newspaper.

Or am I just going soft, Martin? Are you making me soft?

Au revoir!

Dan

Letter 66

From: **DantheMan020@gmail.com**
To: Martin.Harbottle@premier-westward.com
Re: 23.20 Premier Westward Railways train from London Paddington to Oxford, February 3. Amount of my day wasted: 11 minutes. Fellow sufferers: No regulars (too late even for Overkeen Estate Agent).

Hey Martin, you want to know why I'm writing to you again? Can you guess? I'll tell you. It's because your train is running late again, I'm stuck on it again, it's late, I'm drunk again, I'm on the way home to my wife, to whom I haven't spoken in a month now, and my daughter, at whom I can hardly look because she breaks my heart for looking so much like her mum, and I promised you I'd write and waste your time every time you waste my time and I've got to write about something after all so I might as well write about what's going on in my life.

OK? Good.

Actually, I'm not going to tell you about what's happening at home. I don't want to talk about home. I don't want to start crying again. Not in public. Not even on this late train of the tired and emotional.

Let's talk about work. Guess how work is? Work is toilet.

You know that business with the chief executive resigning? How she was going to draw the fire away from the paper, take the bullets, distract the world from taking aim at us? Well, guess what? It's not worked. What's happened is, she's just given the whole story new legs. Instead of taking the line that with her departure comes a brave, ethical new dawn for the *Globe*, it seems that everyone's gone and followed the opposite way of thinking.

How bad can it be at this paper, runs the line, when even the chief exec, a woman who has lived and breathed tabloid journalism, a woman whose loyalty to the organ is legendary, cannot stand to stay there any longer? How deep goes the poison when even she didn't know about the nefarious goings on? When even she didn't know about poor little Barry Dunn? When even she feels she'd rather resign than stay there a moment longer? Just how bad must it be at that place?

Hmm. Not, in short, what anyone was hoping for. Not a good result. (Unless she's really super clever, but I doubt that. Really, that would imply a level of deviousness and cynicism even beyond that of the very worst kind of tabloid hack. Nobody could be that smart. Not even her. Right?) In fact, I'd go so far as to say it's exactly the worst result. And it's put everyone in a bad mood.

There's more bad news. Following her departure, following the reaction to her departure, the advertisers have apparently been getting antsy. Those paragons of virtue, the multinational supermarket chains, the banks, the fast-food outlets whose adverts pay for the massive print run and relatively cheap cover price our paper has… they've been making uneasy noises. They're unhappy, apparently. They're unhappy about being associated with such a paper as us. They're worried we might be making them look bad by implication. And they're talking about pulling out. And once the paper starts losing money… well, then the game changes altogether.

At the moment, Martin – what most people don't realise in fact – at the moment we're still selling an awful lot of newspapers every week. We're still outselling the rest of them. We're still the nation's favourite Sunday read. And just so long as it stays that way, just so long as we can ride out these scandals with readers intact, well, then we'll be fine.

But if the advertisers go… if the money goes, everything changes. Without enough advertising, every copy sold becomes another few pence lost. The cover price does not cover the cost of making the paper. And a newspaper without adverts is just a very expensive vanity project.

Our rivals know this, of course. There is no honour among thieves. Here's what one of the other papers ran yesterday:

'Following the hasty resignation of the chief executive, the *Globe* is left rudderless, and, one fears, without any kind of moral compass. Most ethically minded companies have already pulled their advertising from the paper, not wishing to be associated with such scandals as the alleged illegal accessing of murder victim Barry Dunn's private information, and now it seems that many of the remaining advertisers look set to follow suit. Those still on the fence will be watching the conclusion of the six-month court case brought about by various celebrities against the *Globe* with great interest. A verdict on that case is expected within weeks.'

I know the guy who wrote that, Martin. He used to work here. Until today he still had friends at this paper. And now… now he all but incites our advertisers to take away the one thing that's keeping us afloat. Does that make him a better man, or a worse man?

No such moral dilemmas for Goebbels, however. Just straight-up fury. And when someone came back from lunch and mentioned that the man in question was outside with the rest of the pack, he flew out of his seat, stormed down the stairs, shouldered his way past security, marched past the cameras (and they all swung to watch him do so, every lens trained, every finger clicking, every shutter whirring), grabbed him by his throat and literally threw him to the floor. He would have kicked him too, had some of the rest not held him back.

And now, of course, it's all over the TV. Over and over again. Each time as shocking as the last. Goebbels of the *Globe* physically assaulting a rival journalist. Face twisted in rage, spewing out a list of obscenities. The human face of our paper – snarling, thuggish, bullying, brutal.

Perfect. That's going to make everything OK again, isn't it? That's exactly what we needed. Well done. Oh, well done that man.

Au revoir!

Dan

Letter 67

From: **DantheMan020@gmail.com**
To: Martin.Harbottle@premier-westward.com
Re: 07.31 Premier Westward Railways train from Oxford to London Paddington, February 10. Amount of my day wasted: 14 minutes. Fellow sufferers: Guilty New (Spymaster) Mum, Lego Head, Train Girl.

Ooh, another week without delays! Get you! You must be very proud of yourself. Award yourself a bonus, Martin! Give yourself a dividend!

I'm glad things are going well for you. I'm pleased you might be finally getting to grips with this job of yours, because that will at least make one of us.

I am what you might call unhappy at work, Martin. Could you guess? Is it becoming obvious? Unhappy at home and unhappy at work. And it's not the imminent conclusion of the court case against us (that case that started out so sensationally and quickly lapsed into droning legalese… but don't be fooled by that. If we should lose, if the verdict was to come back in favour of our favourite philanderer, it's going to be headline news again all right). It's not the arrests or the resignations. It's not the protestors outside the building, the condemnation of the world or even the betrayal by our erstwhile brother journalists. These things I've been coping with fine, as it happens. No: the problem, my problem, is the descent into madness of my boss. What's making me unhappy is the insanity of Goebbels.

Sunday's paper sees the last of my Narcotics Anonymous scoops – and rather than them getting pushed further up the news agenda, up towards the front of the paper, as I thought, he's been bumping them back. My high court judge is currently on page 23. Twenty-three? What's the point of that? Who cares about what's on page 23 for crying out loud? Not me. Not Goebbels either.

But that's not the issue. The issue is that Goebbels wants me to go after bigger fish than dope-smoking butlers and coke-snorting judges. Even the ketamine-addled clothes heiress wasn't lighting his fire. What Goebbels wants is revenge. He's finally flipped his lid altogether, and he wants to use me to take revenge on the world.

'This is where the worm turns,' he snarled at me this week. 'This is where the dog stops taking the kicks and bites back. This is where the cornered bear charges – and rips off the arms and legs and heads of those who've been after him. This is where we go on the attack. For months we've been subject to every accusation and insult under the sun and we're not going to take it any more. We're going to come out swinging and annihilate the bastards.'

And then he grinned one of those horrible grins – utterly devoid of warmth or humour. Harry the Dog calls it his 'Darth Vader grin'. The sort of grin that sends a shiver down your spine. 'Or rather – you're going to do it. You, my boy, as showbiz editor of the best newspaper in the world, are going to get me the dirt on every one of those lowlifes currently giving us such grief. The whinging celebrities, the bent policemen, the hypocrite politicians. The editors of all those newspapers camped outside our doors every day, the BBC, ITV, CNN. That bloody woman with the dead kid we supposedly hacked. Take her out. Take them all out. Everyone's got a skeleton. Everyone's got a secret they don't want the world to know. Find them. Find them quick and let's slaughter the lot of 'em. Let's show them you don't go to war with the *Globe*.'

And how, I dared ask, was I supposed to do that? Given that everything we're doing right now is subject to ludicrous levels of scrutiny? Given that standard practices (hidden mics, checking the bins, slipping the odd couple-hundred quid here and there) have basically become off-limits? And also – is going to war with the whole world really such a smart idea? Right now especially? Is it… ethical?

And then… and then Goebbels went ballistic. The first thing he threw at me was a notebook. The second was a stapler. Then a barrage of pens, pencils, post-its, bits of paper, whatever he could lay his hands on, before he stood up, picked up his chair and launched that across the desk at me. (It missed – thank Christ.)

'Don't you DARE tell me what to put in my paper, you snotty little SOD!' he screamed. 'Don't tell ME what's smart and what's not! Who are you to tell me ANYTHING? Get out of my sight! Get out of my sight and get me a proper story before I throw you out of that window myself!'

And so now I'm chasing down the very people who've been condemning us. Now I'm trying to dig dirt on the same people who've been saying the way we dig dirt is unethical. Sensible? No. Suicidal? Probably. But that's what Goebbels wants and no matter how crazy he's gone, he's my boss and that's the bottom line. What can I do? This isn't why I became a journalist. This isn't any fun.

And what's worse is I've had to rope in Wee Tim'rous Trainee to help me. The poor girl, so eager to learn, so anxious to impress, smart enough to get those NA scoops and also smart enough to gently rebuff Harry the Dog's advances – I've had to drag her down into the gutter with me. She shouldn't be doing this. She shouldn't be getting her hands so filthy, so quickly. It's not fair on her.

Unhappy at work, and unhappy at home. You know I'm unhappy at home, of course. This isn't news. What is news is that I tried talking to my wife again. After five weeks of silence, last night I tried to look her in the eye and talk to her again. I didn't go to the pub after work for once; I came straight home. I came home to try to talk to Beth.

And the problem was – I couldn't. I walked in the door and hung up my coat and put down my bag and mumbled something, something like 'You all right?' and her face when she looked up at me, all that hope, that sudden, wide-eyed, open, naked hope, unabashed and unselfconscious hope, just pure hope on her face that perhaps I was going to talk to her again, start being nice to her again, that I might forgive her again, that we might be friends again… Martin, it broke my heart. Or rather, it melted my heart.

'Yes thank you, OK, how are you?' she tried, all in a rush. And she took a step forward, towards me. She started to lift her arms, her hands, as if to welcome me back in. As if to welcome me back to her, to us. And I almost forgave her.

Almost. And then, even as I opened my mouth to speak, even as I started – 'I'm…' – I looked at her face again, her eyes, her mouth, and all I could think of were those eyes locked into the gaze of Mr Blair. That mouth kissing his. Her hands, her legs, her body… on his. Skin to skin contact. And my heart stopped melting. It froze again.

How can I forgive her, Martin, when literally everything about her reminds me what she did to me? How can I get past that? I can't look at my wife, Martin. I can't even look at her any more. That face. That open, hopeful face… I couldn't even meet her eyes. And so I turned and walked back out of the door again and went to the pub until I knew she'd gone to bed.

So, am I unhappy? As someone once said: do newborn babies cry? Did Little Red Riding wear a hood? Did the three bears shit in the woods? Was Humpty Dumpty fat? Does the Pope wear a funny hat? Is wrestling fixed?

Au revoir!

Dan

Letter 68

From: **DantheMan020@gmail.com**
To: Martin.Harbottle@premier-westward.com
Re: 23.20 Premier Westward Railways train from London Paddington to Oxford, February 14. Amount of my day wasted: 24 minutes. Fellow sufferers: No regulars.

And she's gone. To her mum's. Yesterday. With Sylvie. She's gone, in tears, hurrying down the street, pushing the pram with her hair all down in her face, shoulders shaking and legs moving too fast, heading for the train station as Sylvie wailed and wailed and drowned out the sounds of her own sobs.

And I watched. I just watched. I didn't say a word, I didn't move a muscle to try to persuade her to stay. I didn't even know if I wanted her to stay. I didn't want her to stay – but I didn't want her to go either. I don't know when she's coming back. I don't know if she's coming back. I don't know when I'll see my baby daughter again.

Happy Valentine's Day, Martin.

Au revoir!

Dan

From: **Martin.Harbottle@premier-westward.com**
To: DantheMan020@gmail.com
Re: 23.20 Premier Westward Railways train from London Paddington to Oxford, February 14.

Dear Dan

I'm so sorry to hear your latest news. Really, genuinely sorry. I'm not sure if you'd like my advice any more, given some of the things you said to me a few letters ago, but for what it's worth, I would urge you to think of your daughter first and foremost. Every marriage has its ups and downs and in every relationship there comes a time when one or the other party might have to swallow their pride in order to make it work. I understand how difficult it must be for you to get past what happened, but perhaps you should ask yourself if you're prepared to lose everything you had before just because of one mistake. And also, whether you're prepared to put Sylvie through all that pain too.

As I said, my advice to you might be completely unwelcome, but I feel that, despite the occasional disagreements we've had over these last nine months or so, we also have built up a kind of 'relationship'. And you did once describe me as 'avuncular'! So I'm urging you, please, don't think of yourself this once, think instead of what really matters.

Also, apologies for the late running of several of your trains recently.

Warmest regards

Martin

Letter 69

From: **DantheMan020@gmail.com**
To: Martin.Harbottle@premier-westward.com
Re: 07.31 Premier Westward Railways train from Oxford to London Paddington, February 17. Amount of my day wasted: nine minutes. Fellow sufferers: Train Girl, Lego Head, Universal Grandpa, Guilty New (Spymaster) Mum.

Hi Martin. Thanks for your letter. I appreciate it. Your trains may be appalling, but you are a gentleman at least. And so thank you for writing back. And thanks for the advice. The giving of the advice, I mean. The actual advice… well, let's just say easier said than done, eh? That's the thing about advice. It's all so simple to give and so much more difficult to take. It's the gift everyone asks for and nobody really wants. Truly, where advice is concerned, the joy is in the giving and not the receiving. Anyone can seem wise, when dealing with other people's problems, anyone can seem sorted when sorting out other people's lives. It's dealing with your own mess that's tricky. It's sorting out your own life that causes such problems.

But anyway. Thanks. I do appreciate it, believe it or not. Even if I can't act on it.

Anyway. I've been taking different advice, from an altogether less avuncular quarter. Train Girl: she wants to take me out. She wants to take me out and get me drunk enough to forget all about it. The way she sees it, what I need to do is take a holiday from my own life for a night or two: if I can't solve the problem, I can at least run away from it, right? And you know what? It works for me. The way I'm feeling right now, it's the only plan I've got.

Because, Martin, I don't mind telling you there's rather a lot I could do with running away from. And it doesn't look like it's going to get any better, either.

But, look, I'm not going to keep banging on about myself. It's just not British, is it? Let's look around. Let's look outside the train and see what else there is to bring us down.

There's riot-payback, of course: a queue of court cases waiting to start, the prisons and police cells and remand centres packed to bursting with kids waiting to hear their fates. The fall-out from the weekend of anarchy in the UK. Those accused of torching cars and buildings, of looting TVs and DVDs and food processors and anglepoise lamps and whatever else they could lay their hands on; the stone-throwers and bottle-smashers; the ringleaders and troublemakers and herd-followers and easily led and led-astray – everyone under the age of 25 in possession of a hood in all greater London, it seems.

And are we expecting full, frank and fair trials for them all? Of course not: they're being pushed through the system at maximum speed, stamped and processed and spat out with optimum efficiency. The hearings start next week, and it's my guess they're not going to reflect well on any concerned. Some of them will deserve to go to jail. Some of them won't, and will go anyway.

And then there's our own little court case.

We'd almost forgotten about that, hadn't we? What with all the other excitement going on, we'd almost forgotten how it started. With the nation's most outraged superannuated club singer.

And now, after all this time and all that expense, the jury has retired to consider its verdict. He's going for a whole load of money, of course, he's after millions in 'damages' – but it's the reputational impact that's the real worry. A guilty verdict coming now, in the midst of all this other stuff, will be a disaster. It will effectively be seen as an endorsement of all the other accusations facing us – as evidence we did what they're saying we did, to him, to all those other celebs who chucked in their two-penneth worth during the trial – but also to the ordinaries, the civilians, the poor little Barry Dunns of this world.

It's going to follow, isn't it? If we were capable of going through our crooner friend's bins, of trailing his personal assistants, of tapping up his friends and associates, of paying for tip-offs from every doorman, maître d, madam and high-class drug pusher we could wave a chequebook at… if we could do all that (and, to be fair, we may well have done, but that's really not the point) then we'd also be capable of hacking into the personal information of a little boy killed by the home counties' most notorious serial killer. Stands to reason, innit.

That's the worry, Martin. That's the implication. That's what's at stake now. That's what a guilty verdict could do.

But on the other hand, if the jury should come back in our favour, if those 12 angry men and women should look past the whited sepulchre of celebrity and see the rotten core underneath, if they should do the right thing – well then, our boy's a dead man walking. Open season. Fair game. All those stories, Martin, all those whispers and rumours: every one of them's going to be front-page news.

And you know what the worst thing might be? I think the worst thing might be that I find myself praying things go the way of the *Globe*, not because I believe we were right so much, but because I want to see the sanctimonious charlatan unmasked good and proper. I'm becoming like Goebbels: I want revenge.

Am I becoming like Goebbels? That would be the worst thing of all. I wouldn't blame Beth for leaving me, if that were the case. I'd leave me too.

Au revoir!

Dan

Letter 70

From: **DantheMan020@gmail.com**
To: Martin.Harbottle@premier-westward.com
Re: 07.31 Premier Westward Railways train from Oxford to London Paddington, February 22. Amount of my day wasted: 12 minutes. Fellow sufferers: Train Girl, Lego Head, Universal Grandpa.

Oh Martin. Oooh, Martin. Ow! Martin! My head. My poor head. My aching head.

My head hurts, Martin. It aches. It bangs and hammers and drills; it thumps and thuds and seems to bulge horribly at each of my temples. My brain doesn't fit any more, my eyes don't feel like they're mine. My nose, my ears, my teeth, my tongue… they're somebody else's. Nothing in my head feels like it fits any longer. I'm like an anagram, Martin: I've got all the right bits, but in some horribly wrong order.

I am, in short, hungover. Hungover? Hungover doesn't begin to cover it. I feel like death. I feel like I've actually died.

And you know what the worst bit of it all is? This is how I feel every morning, now. This is normal. Feeling like my own head isn't mine every day – this is how I am on every one of your trains in the morning. And the feeling lasts until lunchtime or so, when I have another drink and start the sorry cycle all over again.

So obviously you know by now that he won his court case. The prostitute-using, tax-dodging, coke-guzzling, beautifully bewigged flower of Scottish singing: he won his case against the despicable, scandal-hit, scandalous scandal rag I work for. Emphatically. Indisputably. Unanimously.

And the result? Massive damages. Millions. Fourteen of them, in fact. Plus costs of another three mill on top. And worse than that, the ignominy, the humiliation, of having to hear him on every news channel, in every (other) newspaper, preaching about the evils of our organisation. And preaching, it must be said, to a quickly converting congregation.

Oh, and you know what else? (I don't think this has been reported yet, but it will.) His victory – it's not going to be the last. Every other lying, shagging, abusive and abusing actor, singer, footballer, reality star and two-bob celebrity in the country is lining up to follow his suit. They've got the dollar signs in their eyes, of course (can't blame them for that) – but they've also got revenge on their minds. It's a chance to hit back at the people who've exposed them for what they are – and there's not a single one of them ready to pass it up.

The word in the newsroom is 2,000. Two thousand separate claims being filed as we speak. Two thousand court cases upcoming. And after them, the MPs, no doubt. The bent coppers. All the corrupt officials we've stitched up and taken down over our proud history. Followed by the countless others. The ordinaries. All those stories from the shires, the randy reverends and saucy housewives and shenanigans in suburban staff rooms.

And then what, Martin? Assuming we're deemed to have infringed on their rights to a private life too? Who comes next? The actual criminals? All the gun-runners, arms dealers, drug-pushers, rapists and paedophiles we've put away? Where will they draw the line? Where will it end?

Two thousand celebrities jumping aboard the bandwagon could see us tied up in court for the next millennium – literally, if each case takes as long as this first. Two thousand celebrities winning could see us paying out… whatever 2,000 multiplied by £17 million is. (I told you, I'm hungover. And I can never remember the difference between a UK billion and an American billion. Ours is the million million, right? The proper billion.) Billions, though. Definitely billions.

A joke is what it is, all right. And everyone's laughing but us.

Not that I'm in the mood for laughing anyway. Not that I feel like cracking a smile especially. Coming in drunk to an empty house, passing out on the sofa in front of News 24, failing to be woken by any plaintive wailing, any pleading screams, any heartbreaking whoops or squeals or gurgling giggles. Waking up to silence and the detritus of whatever rank food I picked up on the way home; waking up to empty rooms with only the flotsam and jetsam of a beautiful little life to remind me that a beautiful little life once lived here.

I found a dummy in the fridge the other day, Martin. I was looking for something to eat at four in the morning, I was peering at the remains of some mushroom and sniffing at some eggs (can you tell an egg is off by sniffing alone? Who knows?). I was poking around in the fridge in the cold hours before dawn and I found a dummy.

And I thought: what the hell's a dummy doing in the fridge? And then I remembered: Beth used to keep one in there, back in the summer, back when Sylvie used to wake with a fever in the night and Calpol wouldn't calm her down. She used to keep a dummy in the fridge and it was the only thing that would cool our baby daughter's tears at the tail end of last summer.

And I burst into tears. And I stood there, leaning into the fridge at four in the morning, head resting against the shelf, hands turning blue with cold, blubbing and snivelling like a baby myself, wailing and screaming for my little girl. I stood there crying like that until my legs gave way and I fell asleep on the kitchen floor with the fridge door still open and when I woke up what was left in there had definitely gone off and it was time to get up and face another day at the most hated newspaper in the world and I was hungover and nothing felt right any more.

Au revoir!

Dan

Letter 71

From: **DantheMan020@gmail.com**
To: Martin.Harbottle@premier-westward.com
Re: 22.20 Premier Westward Railways train from London Paddington to Oxford, February 23. Amount of my day wasted: 15 minutes. Fellow sufferers: Overkeen Estate Agent.

Martin, I've got a present for you. Look: I've made you a crossword. It's not up to the standard of my dad's, but still, it's a one-of-a-kind, made especially for you. It took me the full hour-plus-15-minute-delay home to do it, but it was worth it. At least I think so. Hope you think so too.

Across:

4. Dad, Pops, the Old Man
6. City of the Blues
9. Indolent animal
10. Me, him, them, and all the other sad sacks
13. The indivisible union of man and woman

15. Verbal justifications for incompetence
17. French for goodbye
18. The ultimate Biblical sin
19. Inevitable additions to any PW journey
20. No man should have a phone this colour

Down:

1. __ Head – the Buddha of the Morning Commute
2. You'll always find me in "C"
3. Affectionate term for the last train home
5. What every celeb has in common
7. The cause of and solution to all of life's problems
8. Popular name for the slow train home
11. The ultimate human sin
12. Horse-riding, computer-geek journos?
14. A belittling psychotherapist?
16. Perfection

Au revoir!

Dan

Letter 72

From: **DantheMan020@gmail.com**
To: Martin.Harbottle@premier-westward.com
Re: 22.50 Premier Westward Railways train from London Paddington to Oxford, February 28. Amount of my day wasted: five minutes. Fellow sufferers: Overkeen Estate Agent.

Breaking news! Even the nonsense that Overkeen Estate Agent is talking cannot distract me tonight ('We're going to baseline that bad girl till she squeals', 'High fives and max respect all round', 'Legendary closing, my friend: stitched like a kipper', etc). Because there's news!

Read all about it! You know those 2,000 court cases currently being brought against the once-mighty but now universally despised *Sunday Globe*? Well, strike one off! Minus one that bad girl till she squeals! Call it 1,999 cases now! Max respect all round!

Why? Who's pulled out? Who's got cold feet and cashed in his chips? Who do you think? Only your friend and mine, England's former golden child, the once-extravagantly gifted and now permanently consigned-to-the-bench Jamie Best.

The boy Jamie and his case for privacy. Saying the nation has no interest in his haircuts (I'm inclined to agree, but he's the one being paid millions by a hair-product manufacturer). Claiming the people do not need nor want to know about the parade of soap girls, models and former high-class escorts on his arm (so why parade them at all? Why encourage them to pose on the red carpets and nightclub thresholds?). Insisting that the whole business with the bagful of Iggle Piggles and the red-handed security footage was either a stitch-up or an intrusion into his personal business or both. He was promising fireworks in court, was Jamie. He was going to give the crowd exactly the thrills he's been failing to deliver on the pitch all season.

And then… yesterday's arrest. In an out-of-town retail park, in the aisles of a vast and cavernous Mothercare. With approximately three dozen six-inch Gruffalos stuffed down his shirt. Thirty-six Gruffalos (Gruffalo? Gruffali? What is the plural?) and all of Our Jamie's case collapses. Because every paper's got the story tomorrow, and the public interest will never have been higher. Silly boy.

One down, Martin, 1,999 to go, right? We can still win this, lads!

Au revoir!

Dan

PS – Sorry about that crossword. It was rubbish, wasn't it? My dad would not have been proud of that effort. Or maybe he would.

Maybe he'd have been proud of any effort, sincerely made. It's funny, you know – I never could second-guess him on that kind of thing. I relied on the odd look, the pat on the shoulder, the regular letters that never really said anything but that always came with a carefully drawn puzzle (always so much better than the sorry effort I sent you). And after he died, I found, under the bed, filed with the same care and attention, all my clippings, all the bylines I'd amassed to that point, every little grubby NIB and showbiz snippet and snatched quote I'd managed to squeeze into the papers. Carefully cut out and stored in photo albums. And he'd never said a word about it. So who knows? Maybe he would have been proud, after all. You just can't tell, in the end, can you?

From: **Martin.Harbottle@premier-westward.com**
To: DantheMan020@gmail.com
Re: 22.50 Premier Westward Railways train from London Paddington to Oxford, February 28.

Dear Dan

I do hope you're well. Thank you for your recent letters and apologies for my late reply. I have been extraordinarily busy, I'm sure you understand.

Your train on February 17 was late leaving Oxford due to an earlier incident with a freight train shedding some of its cargo in the Taplow area. Fourteen Renault Clios were unfortunately written off in the incident – though I should point out that they were all empty of passengers and were being transported from London to Reading at the time.

On February 22, another incident in the same area involving a lightning strike and a fallen tree caused similar delays. As I'm sure you appreciate, neither incident was technically the fault of Premier Westward, but naturally we did our best to work with Network Rail to ensure that our passengers experienced as little delay as possible.

Your lengthy delay on the way home the following day was admittedly due to a fault on one of our trains. I am sorry to say that my job as managing director does not allow me the luxury of time to pursue 'word puzzles' but I am sure that the crossword you were kind enough to create for me was every bit as good as any of your father's.

As far as non-train-related business is concerned, I do hope you are well. You certainly sound much happier of late. Positively buoyant in your last two letters! Have you spoken to your wife yet? And is the fearsome 'Goebbels' happier with your work? I did see Mr Best's arrest on the news. It must be a great relief to all at the *Globe* that he's still such a troubled young man.

Best

Martin

Letter 73

From: **DantheMan020@gmail.com**
To: Martin.Harbottle@premier-westward.com
Re: 22.50 Premier Westward Railways train from London Paddington to Oxford, March 1. Amount of my day wasted: 12 minutes. Fellow sufferers: Overkeen Estate Agent.

Oh, Martin. Have I been getting you wrong all this time? Have I been underestimating you? Are you actually a bit of a sarcastic so-and-so? That last line… that had bite, Martin! That had teeth! And what's with all the buoyant stuff? Are you being deliberately satirical? I'm not buoyant. When I get carried away with the screamers and the superlatives, when I extend my metaphors to metaphorical breaking point, when I get hyperactive with my adjectives… it's not because suddenly everything's OK in my pitiful life again. It's because it's all I've got.

Don't you get it? You're all I've got. You're the only one left to try to impress. My wife's gone back to her mother's (telling tales of drunkenness and cruelty, as the song has it), my beautiful baby daughter's been dragged with her, and my readers, the millions I used to make laugh every week with my cynical asides on the career aspirations and pratfalls of the nation's celebs, well, now they're not sure whether to secretly smile or to tut and frown in disapproval. Even Universal Grandpa's daughter has stopped flirting with me. Or if she still is, he's choosing not to pass the messages on.

So you're it. It's all on you. Even if you are showing a hitherto-unsuspected sarcastic side to your character. Even if you're not that interested anyway. Even if my word puzzles bore you sometimes.

So, to answer your questions: no, I have not spoken to my wife yet. I haven't even tried. She should be the one to call me, right? She's the one who should be trying to build bridges and make amends. She's the one who should be doing whatever it takes to save our marriage, given she's the one who smashed a wrecking ball right through it. It's not up to me to make the first move. I'm the victim here.

And you know what else? I am going to follow the advice of Train Girl. I'm not going to sit around in my empty house crying over dummies in the fridge and bits of shopping lists found in my pocket ('nappies' – how can the word 'nappies' reduce a grown man to tears like that? How can that one stupid word keep me sobbing all night? Was it the word itself, the reminder that I haven't changed a nappy in weeks, or was it the fact it was written by Beth? Can I not even see her handwriting without crying now?). I'm not going to do any of that any more. I'm taking action!

Train Girl and I are going out. We're going to smash up the place. We're going to paint the town red and then paint it black and then paint it red all over again. We're going to enjoy ourselves, like normal people do. The untouchably cool, the effortlessly good-looking, the unutterably sorted Train Girl… and me. The beautiful and the damned.

What was your other question? Something about Goebbels? Is he happier with me? Well, actually, as it happens, since you ask and believe it or not… yes, he is. The mad old nutjob. Do you want to know why?

We're running the teenager-tupping Tory taxdodger story. He said he wanted to go after the people going after us and so we're taking down the elected member who's been most vocal in his criticism. He's spent the last few weeks appearing on every news bulletin, talk show and liberal newspaper – and always spinning the same line, the same uncompromising condemnation of our methods, our madness (his phrase). He has, in short, set himself right up for a fall. And Goebbels wants us to be the ones to knock him over. Poetic justice, he calls it. Also: justice. There ain't no justice – just us.

It's not running this week, but it's down to splash next week. We've got the photos (those girls in their school uniforms, wide-eyed and pouty, perched on the edge of the bed in the swanky hotel room, the champagne and truffles, looking terribly young but also old enough, looking terribly innocent but also not innocent enough…), we've got their words, their breathless confessions, we've got the corroborating receipts, the copies of expenses claims. The lawyers have had a look. We're getting it all double-legalled now. We're going to plaster it all over the front page a week on Sunday and, in the words of Goebbels, 'show them just what it means to go to war with the *Globe*'. It's all going to kick off.

And there will be my name, underneath the headline. There will be my name, under what will be our most-talked-about splash of the year. And what do I think about that? Excited: yes. Terrified: also yes. The story's solid, I'm sure of that… but it's our nuclear option. We're firing our big weapons now. We're launching a full-scale attack and I can't help thinking that the one thing we know about nuclear war is that nobody really wins in the end.

Christ, I do sound a bit buoyant, after all, don't I? I'm not buoyant, Martin. And despite the bluster, I meant what I said. I might be hitting the town with Train Girl again, but I'm still in bits over my wife and daughter. I might be about to score the biggest scalp of my journalistic career, but work is still utterly hellish.

You're all I've got. These letters – they're kind of all I've got. Talking to you is all I've got. And isn't that rather pathetic, in the end?

Au revoir!

Dan

Letter 74

From: **DantheMan020@gmail.com**
To: Martin.Harbottle@premier-westward.com
Re: 22.20 Premier Westward Railways train from London Paddington to Oxford, March 7. Amount of my day wasted: seven minutes. Fellow sufferers: Overkeen Estate Agent.

Oh holy crap, Martin. It's all happened. More unwelcome visitors in the newsroom. Not the police this time, but internal security. A pair of them marched in, all little grey suits and shiny shoes and name badges… they marched in, marched past everyone, entered Goebbels' office without knocking, said something to him, and then stood back as he burst out laughing. And then stood back again as he pushed past them and addressed the whole floor.

'Go on,' he said, still grinning that chilling, humourless grin he has. 'Say that again. Tell the whole paper what you just told me. We could all do with a laugh. Say it again and crack us all up.'

One of them stepped forward. Cleared his throat. Actually adjusted his (clip-on) tie. 'I have been asked to escort you from the building,' he said. 'Effective immediately you are dismissed from your position at this newspaper and are no longer an employee of the company. You're to give me your security pass, your mobile phone, your laptop, and accompany me off the premises. If necessary I've been instructed to make sure these things are carried out by force.'

Goebbels roared with laughter. 'Brilliant, eh?' he shouted. 'Priceless! Perfect! What do you think, team? Isn't that the best joke you've heard in years?'

Utter silence.

He turned back to the security men, no longer smiling. 'Now,' he hissed, 'why don't you piss off back to your little office in the basement and get back to looking at your little CCTV monitors and let me do my job?'

For a second nobody moved. And then they each took an arm, twisted them behind his back and frogmarched him across the floor and out of the door. We could hear his screams all the way down the lift.

And then, almost as one, we turned to the television (the replaced television, replacing the one Goebbels smashed) and the live feed from outside our offices and watched as Goebbels was thrown – literally thrown, slapstick style – out of the building and landed in a heap on the pavement. And then we watched as he charged at the door and bounced back off the glass, landing on the floor again. And then we watched as he got to his feet for the second time, blood streaming from his nose, hair wild, eyes glaring, opened his mouth, screamed like an animal and launched himself straight at the cameramen.

And then the live feed switched back to the studio. And that, I can't help thinking, is the last we've seen of him.

What did we do? We sat there in silence for a while… and then we went to the pub. Later we got an email from someone in the managing editor's office. Goebbels has been sacked following 'an internal investigation into activities surrounding the illegal accessing of civilians' private information'. He's now been arrested too – for that, and for four counts of assault on three journalists from the broadsheets and a News 24 cameraman outside our office.

And so he's gone. It's a hell of a story, right?

Au revoir!

Dan

Letter 75

From: **DantheMan020@gmail.com**
To: Martin.Harbottle@premier-westward.com
Re: 23.20 Premier Westward Railways train from London Paddington to Oxford, March 10. Amount of my day wasted: five minutes. Fellow sufferers: No regulars (Saturday).

Guess what I did today? On the day before my big splash on the tax-fiddling Tory and his teenage totty? Guess what I did, in the offices of the *Globe*?

I hacked into Beth's email. I illegally accessed her private information. Harry the Dog helped me.

'The thing about passwords,' he said, as the pair of us stared at the Gmail log-in page, 'is that they're always simpler than you think. Nobody can be bothered doing all that stuff with mixing up letters and numbers and what-have-yous. People can't remember that stuff. Names, jobs, street names, birthday months, football teams, football players, film stars, pop stars. I'd say 99 percent of passwords fall into one of those categories. And the best thing about webmail is it gives you unlimited chances to guess. All you need is a little persistence.'

I folded my arms and looked at him. 'And you know this how?'

He grinned. 'Everyone knows it, old boy. Everyone who knows what they're doing knows it. Don't tell me you've never got into someone's email before.'

I've never got into someone's email before, Martin. It's illegal. And then today I got into Beth's email.

It took us 17 goes to get it. And do you know what her password was? It was my name.

I know. Don't say it: I know.

Anyway: Harry left then and I had a quick scoot through her email history. Were there any revelations? Well, yes. Were they damning? Did they paint her as the wicked harridan, the fallen woman, the scheming unfaithful wife leading her poor husband up the proverbial garden path? Well, no, actually.

She's been emailing her friend Karen. About us, I mean. About what's happened between us. Here's part of the most recent:

> Kazza, it's awful. Really, properly awful. He's not even called since we came back to Mum's. I know I keep saying it, but I've just fucked everything up so badly. What if he doesn't call? What if he never calls?
>
> Mum says to give him time but all I do is cry all the time. I'm stupid. I'm so stupid. I can't believe I've done this to us. And you know what's really stupid? Dan's being a dick, of course he's being a dick, he's a dick a lot of the time, but that's who he is. He was a dick when I married him. He gets himself into a state over stupid work things all the time, but he's still Dan. He's still my Dan. And I know it sounds crazy but I love him. I love him so much and now I've thrown it all away.

Christ.

Now I feel really bad. And you know what else I realised? I don't even know who Karen is. Martin, what she did – it was wrong. It was terribly wrong. But I don't even know who her best friend is. How can I not even know who my wife's best friend is? What sort of husband does that make me?

And also: am I a dick? I'm not a dick, am I?

Au revoir!

Dan

From: **Martin.Harbottle@premier-westward.com**
To: DantheMan020@gmail.com
Re: 23.20 Premier Westward Railways train from London Paddington to Oxford, March 10.

Dear Dan

Thank you for your recent letters. As I believe I have mentioned before, delays of under ten minutes are not officially classed as delays at all, but I can tell you that your 12-minute delay on March 1 was due to a signalling issue and as a result we had to reroute some services. Unfortunately the 22.50 from Paddington was one of those affected.

I would also like to congratulate you on your 'scoop' in this Sunday's paper. I must confess that following your tip-off I did buy a copy (I hid it inside my usual *Sunday Telegraph* – wouldn't want the neighbours to know, after all!) and I do think you did a splendid job. To carry on like that with his own daughters' friends (two of them!), to claim their assignations on parliamentary expenses! As a father and a tax payer and a right-minded citizen I am shocked at his behaviour. All I can say is that the man is a disgrace and you've done exactly the right thing in exposing him. If only your newspaper always held such high standards you wouldn't be in the mess you are at the moment!

Anyway, well done. I felt oddly proud of you, Daniel.

Best

Martin

Letter 76

From: **DantheMan020@gmail.com**
To: Martin.Harbottle@premier-westward.com
Re: 07.31 Premier Westward Railways train from Oxford to London Paddington, March 13. Amount of my day wasted: ten minutes. Fellow sufferers: Train Girl, Universal Grandpa, Guilty New (Spymaster) Mum.

Oh Martin, I'm blushing. I'm pleased as punch you're proud of me. Truly, I'm not even being sarcastic. Believe it or not, it really does matter to me. Isn't that pathetic? I mean, no offence, but isn't that pathetic?

Anyway. Thank you. Genuinely. And I'm sorry you felt the need to hide my paper in the folds of your downmarket broadsheet rag.

As it turns out you're not the only person to offer congratulations. An email came round from circulation yesterday – our figures were up on Sunday. Up! For the first time in months, we actually sold more copies of the paper than we had the previous week. That's what leading the news agenda does, Martin. That's how you keep advertisers on board: get scoops, sell papers, increase circulation. Old Goebbels, as it turns out, wasn't quite so crazy as he made out. He understood that, at least.

So, all in all, a good day for us. For the paper, and for me. I'm not even worried about the teen-tupping Tory's threats of retribution. The randy old hypocrite's been crucified, pilloried, neutered by the press, thrown out of his own party, threatened with a police enquiry and now kicked out of his own home by his (justifiably furious) family. I reckon that although he's almost certainly seriously angry, he's no longer got the clout to do anything about it. And it serves him right, too.

And, weirdest of all, there were congratulations on the train.

Universal Grandpa – he came up to me on the platform (serious breach of commuter etiquette there!). He shook my hand. He said that I'd done a good job. He said that if I kept up that kind of thing I could leave the 'smutty stuff' behind and 'get a job on one of the qualities'. And you know what? Six months ago I might have had a go at him for saying that. I might have started on about the so-called qualities and the respective levels of journalism and all that other stuff… but I didn't. I smiled back. I shook his hand back. I said thank you. I said: 'It's nice to have written something you've enjoyed as much as your daughter.'

And you know what he said? He said: 'You should know my daughter has learning difficulties.' He smiled as he said it, that twinkly, kind, Grandpa smile. 'She doesn't really understand what you write. She just knows you're being cheeky about her favourite celebrities. And when I read it to her I miss out all the ruder bits.'

And still chuckling, he patted me on the shoulder, got on the train and set off down the carriage.

Um. Crikey! What to make of that! I feel awkward about the flirting thing, now, for a start.

Anyway. That wasn't the end of it. I saw Train Girl this morning. She'd saved my splash again, that same way she did when I did for Jamie Best. Isn't that sweet? Isn't that thoughtful? She produced it with a flourish as she jumped late on the train as usual and barrelled down the aisle. She waved it, she shouted – 'Hey scoop!' – brandishing it above her head, laughing. Christ, Martin, she's a looker though.

Seriously. I know I shouldn't be thinking this (despite everything) but Train Girl's a proper looker. Standing there, waving my paper, her face lit up, her hair pushed back behind her ears, coat off, arms bare, that short skirt, the perfect taper of her legs perfectly outlined in thick black tights… she even makes thick black tights look hot.

And then, when she got to my seat, as I sat slightly bashful and a bit embarrassed, she threw her arms around my neck, planted a big smacker on my lips and laughed, saying 'Look at you, Woodward and Bernstein!' and ruffled the bit on the back of my neck where my hairline ends.

And what did I do? I wasn't sure what to do. Everyone was staring. Guilty New (Spymaster) Mum paused mid-phone conversation and stared at me with an expression of part confusion, part shock, part worry on her face (has she just realised she's been sharing her calls with a *Sunday Globe* journalist?). I just looked at my lap and kind of stammered something about just doing my job, ma'am, and Train Girl laughed again, and sat down too, angling towards me as always, her hand still on my arm, our knees touching.

And then she told me, at some length, most of the way to London (including the ten extra minutes you so thoughtfully laid on to our service today, above and beyond the advertised and scheduled time for the journey), how she had read my story in bed on Sunday morning. Alone. Lying sprawled in only the old East 17 t-shirt she sleeps in (when she sleeps alone), half-in and half-out of the duvet, curled around a cushion… how she had read my story and couldn't help but get excited about it.

'There I was,' she whispered, 'basically naked but for my t-shirt, still all mussed-up from sleep, stretched out in my big bed by myself… and I was reading words you'd written! It was like hearing you speak to me – in bed, in the morning. And I imagined you writing them, I pictured you on the trail of the story, chasing down the leads, nailing down the facts, and I could almost see you directing the photoshoot, those two girls in their sexy little uniforms, I could almost hear you grilling them about exactly what they used to get up to with him…'

And she said all this with a smile on her face, a laugh in her voice, but I knew she wasn't making fun of me. 'Honestly, Dan, I had to take a shower after. The whole thing was just so… hot.'

And then I had to change the subject. Obviously. Of course. We were on a train, there were people standing in the aisles and also, you know, I'm married. I'm a married man. I had to change the subject.

Unfortunately the only thing I could think to change the subject to was to firm up a date for our next night out. So we're going out on Saturday. After work. I would say wish me luck, but I'm not sure whether you would or not. You probably don't approve, do you, Martin? You're probably tutting and shaking your head as we speak. I don't blame you. I am, after all, a bit of a dick.

Au revoir!

Dan

Letter 77

From: **DantheMan020@gmail.com**
To: Martin.Harbottle@premier-westward.com
Re: 22.20 Premier Westward Railways train from London Paddington to Oxford, March 15. Amount of my day wasted: ten minutes. Fellow sufferer: Overkeen Estate Agent.

Back to life. Back to reality. Back to the here and now. You know that sales spike on Sunday – the one led by my lead, the one brought about by good old-fashioned tabloid journalism, the one that heralded the revival of our paper and the point at which we kick against the pricks and start our glorious fightback? Yeah, that one. Well, as it turns out… it's not made a blind bit of difference.

After a day or two going after the dishonourable member, the focus is firmly back on us. The police are promising more arrests. The government are demanding answers. And even after claiming the scalps of the features ed, the showbiz ed, the chief exec and Goebbels himself, the great British public are crying out for more blood. Scapegoats are being sought, Martin, and, as the top copper promised in every daily newspaper today: 'Nobody is safe. From the lowliest cub reporter to the managing editor and every single employee of the company in-between. None of them are safe. We are coming after you and we will find you and we will bring you to justice and we will keep doing so until every last person responsible for the systematic culture of illegality at the newspaper has paid the price before the law.'

And that, I would say, is fairly unequivocal.

But you know what it put me in mind of? You know what that kind of language evoked for me? It conjured up a single word, Martin: 'cleansing'. They want to cleanse the paper. They want to bombard us and batter us and smash us up and tear us down and then they want to bulldoze us all away until there's no trace of the former regime left. They want to cleanse us, same as your man in North Africa is cleansing the old rule and the new rule out over there.

The advertisers – our last barrier against their offensive, the great buffer we had against whatever they threw at us, the enormous safety net which meant we could keep putting our paper out, keep generating profit, every week – the advertisers are pulling out.

Two major supermarkets split yesterday, a multinational department store, a couple of clothes chains and a global restaurant franchise jumped today. There will be more tomorrow. This has got momentum now.

And meanwhile... meanwhile we keep turning up for work. Shouldering our way past the pack outside, ignoring the catcalls and yells from the saddos with placards ('Murderers!' is what one woman screamed at me this morning. Who exactly does she think I murdered?), submitting ourselves to third-degree searches from the same security guards we saw throw Goebbels out of the building...

We keep turning up here, keep sitting down and logging on and trying to get on with the job we're paid to do.

And I'll be honest with you, Martin. It's not much fun, you know? It's really not at all.

Wee Tim'rous Trainee is scared. In the pub after work, with Harry the Dog and Bombshell, she just said it: 'I'm scared.'

Everyone stared at her.

'I'm scared of what's happening at the newspaper. I don't want to get arrested. I hate all those people calling us scum. I hate it. What am I going to do if I get arrested? What will my mum say?'

Harry the Dog put a reassuring hand on her arm. 'Don't worry,' he said, smooth as butter. 'I won't let them arrest you.'

'But what if—'

'Nobody's going to arrest a fucking trainee, darls,' put in Bombshell. 'I mean, seriously, why bother? You'll be fine, serious.' And she clinked Wee Tim'rous Trainee's glass. 'Anyway, so I was in this totes lush bar last night and… where are you going?'

And that was that. Wee Tim'rous Trainee just got up and walked off, right in the middle of a Bombshell anecdote, without saying goodbye, without finishing her drink. Harry and I stared open-mouthed – and then he burst out laughing.

Bombshell fixed her retreating figure with a withering look and then drained the rest of her glass. 'Whatevs,' she said.

Au revoir!

Dan

Letter 78

From: **DantheMan020@gmail.com**
To: Martin.Harbottle@premier-westward.com
Re: 07.31 Premier Westward Railways train from Oxford to London Paddington, March 17. Amount of my day wasted: 14 minutes. Fellow sufferers: No regulars (Saturday).

Hey you. It's date night!

Actually, I lie. Or at least, exaggerate. It's not date night yet. It's the morning before date night. It's Saturday morning, I'm sitting at my desk at the worst place in the world; I'm fresh off one of your terrible trains; I've got a whole bunch of stuff to write on deadline; and instead I'm writing to you.

I didn't see Train Girl on my way in this morning, of course – it's Saturday, and ordinary people don't work on Saturdays. But I'll be seeing her tonight. That's the plan. She was very excited about it yesterday – said she had an outfit planned especially. Something knockout, she said. Something to knock me out.

Do I want to be knocked out, Martin? Is that what I need right now? I've got to confess: a big part of me says yes. But another part of me… I don't know. I kind of think all I want to do is go home and sleep. Maybe call my wife. Maybe not. I'm exhausted.

Anyway. Date night it is. And yes, I did have a shave especially, since you asked.

But first, I've got the whole day to get through. Deadline day. What we do this for, the thrill and the adrenaline of getting the paper out. The energy, the enthusiasm, the white-knuckle ride of writing for the world's most-read English-language newspaper. That's why we're here, right?

Except, like I said in my last letter, the office isn't such a thrilling place any more. Nobody's talking to each other. Nobody trusts each other. All that gossip, the whispers and rumours, the conspiracy theories, black humour, daily sweepstakes and healthy cynicism… that's all gone. We each sit at our desks, in front of our computers and our phones, letting every call go to voicemail where once we'd snatch the headset up on first ring – and nobody speaks. Every time anyone leaves their seat they log off; everyone carries their mobiles and laptops everywhere with them. Everyone's paranoid.

And every time anyone's asked to do anything, to chase a particular lead, to look into a particular story, their first reaction is not the usual (excitement, keenness, anticipation of the breaking story) but suspicion. Why me? Why not him? Or her? What's this really about? Am I being set up?

As for the bosses… since Goebbels left we've been kind of rudderless. The deputy is acting up in his place, but he's as nervy and untrusting as the rest of us. And then there are the big bosses. And they really are freaking everyone out.

For three hours yesterday, Martin, we had no access to our own emails. A (printed) memo was distributed, claiming that 'in accordance with requests from the police', editorial staff were being locked out of all email accounts 'for the foreseeable future and at least until their investigations have been concluded'.

There was nearly a riot. You want to try putting out a newspaper with no email access? People got up and walked out. People threatened to resign on the spot. In the end the acting news ed and all the foreign desk went upstairs themselves to sort it out. And finally, after three hours, the email system came back online. Unbelievable.

And since we're on the subject of incompetence: how about the latest insider knowledge from the fair streets of North Africa? Or rather, not from there (they're anything but incompetent in North Africa right now. Quite the opposite. They're frighteningly competent. Ruthlessly, terrifyingly competent. They know what they're doing, all right. Cleansing the place. The trials, the executions, the public floggings and stonings and hangings. Incompetence is not the word, not by any stretch). No, not from the blood-soaked streets of North Africa. But from the marbled halls and lofty atriums of the United Nations, where the business of North Africa is currently toppermost on the agenda. That's where the incompetence lies.

All the speeches. All those words. Debating back and forth the merits or otherwise of the North African delegation. Discussing just what the official view on the events of the last year over there is. What line they should be taking. Whose side is the right side. The original regime? The brief, inglorious revolution and its ramshackle attempt at order? Or the new regime, the all-too-competent one? All have blood on their hands. No one is innocent.

Why aren't we up in arms about it? Where have all the protesters gone? When the original rebels stood up in the streets, when they unfurled their flags and raised their fists and stormed the citadels, they were hailed as saviours. Speeches were made, bandwagons were jumped upon – they were an example to us all. And now?

Where are the protests? Whither the rioters? It wasn't so long ago they were showing solidarity all across Europe. Maybe they're all exhausted too.

Or is it cowardice? Apathy? Either way it doesn't reflect well on anyone concerned. And you know what: I'm not even talking about North Africa any more. I'm not even talking about the *Globe*. I'm talking about my confusion over tonight's date with Train Girl. I'm talking about my life. When I get worked up about North Africa, when I act like a dick over work, I'm really getting worked up about my life.

Hey, we've got a few minutes left. Do you want some more from Beth's Gmail account? Here's a choice one, from ages ago, from Christmas, from when I first told her about Train Girl.

> The thing is, I know he wouldn't do anything and that's what makes it worse. And it's like I'm punishing him for my stupid mistake. But what can I do? I almost wish he had done something and then we'd be quits, and then I could feel better about being so horrible to him.
>
> I've been horrible twice, Kaz, once for doing what I did and now again for acting like I am over this girl on his train, and I know you keep saying that I need to tell him, but how can I now? Now that I know he wouldn't do to me what I did to him? I'm trapped. All I want to do is say sorry, but I can't. I've got myself into a massive tangle.
>
> And yes, you are right about Dan. I know he wouldn't have done anything with the girl on the train. He's not the cheating kind. He's just not. Even if he wanted to, he's not. I know him better than anyone, and I know that he'd never do it. But is it weird that something so good as that makes me feel terrible?

Remember that, Martin. I'm not the cheating kind. I'm just not. And wish me luck on my date tonight.

Au revoir!

Dan

Letter 79

From: **DantheMan020@gmail.com**
To: Martin.Harbottle@premier-westward.com
Re: 07.31 Premier Westward Railways train from Oxford to London Paddington, March 20. Amount of my day wasted: seven minutes. Fellow sufferers: Guilty New (Spymaster) Mum, Universal Grandpa. (Where is Lego Head? He's not been on the train for ages.)

Good morning, Martin. How was your weekend? Enjoy your sneaky tabloid fix this week? Was it worth the potential approbation of your neighbours? What's that? No? No. You're right. It was not a vintage edition. It was poor. It was pitiful. It had nothing worth the cover price in it. Even my stuff was rubbish.

Sorry about that. Try again next week, eh? That's the great thing about news, about newspapers – there's always the next issue, the next edition, the next story.

Tomorrow, for example, is the budget. Tomorrow everything will be more expensive than it is today. Tomorrow, after the price of booze and petrol has gone up yet again, after the NHS and the DSS have been slashed yet again, after the squeezed middle find themselves squeezed further still and the grindingly poor ground further down… tomorrow, amidst all the misery, it will still at least be tomorrow. And there will be something to report in next week's paper. There will at least be case studies to find (the single parent, the middle-class-two-kids couple, the first-time homebuyer, the nurse, the policeman, the stockbroker, the war veteran) and we'll be able to put out an edition with at least something to read in it.

So, you know, like I say: the sun also rises, right?

Talking of which, Train Girl's not on the train this morning, which I'm actually rather relieved about, so I can give you the full Date Night story without fear of interruption.

OK. Here it is. The whole story. Everything that happened. Get ready, Martin…

Nothing happened.

I didn't go. I stood her up. Well, I didn't stand her up, exactly, I sent her a text to tell her I wasn't going. I said I didn't feel well (true enough, but that wasn't the reason). I cancelled and I went home and I drank a bottle of wine by myself and I went to bed until Monday.

Why did I do that? Why did I choose to drink sad cheap plonk by myself instead of painting the town red with a beautiful, funny, sexy girl who's so obviously (inexplicably) got the hots for me? Well, maybe because she's so obviously (inexplicably) got the hots for me. I got cold feet. I got scared. Because I wanted to… because, when it came down to it, I wanted to. And I know that, despite it all, despite what Beth did, I know I shouldn't want to. Or if I can't help wanting to, I shouldn't do anything about it. I shouldn't be going out painting the town red with beautiful, funny, sexy girls who so obviously (inexplicably) have the hots for me. Because I'm still married. Because my wife is right. I'm not the cheating kind.

Jesus, Martin, I've just re-read that. I'm an idiot, aren't I? What was I thinking of? Going home alone because of my marriage, of all things? I've not even spoken to Beth in God knows how long. I've not even spoken to Sylvie.

Do you think I should try to speak to Sylvie? You're right. I should. If I can't speak to Beth, I should speak to Sylvie. Tomorrow. Tomorrow I'll speak to my baby daughter. Maybe that will stop me crying every night.

Au revoir!

Dan

From: **Martin.Harbottle@premier-westward.com**
To: DantheMan020@gmail.com
Re: 07.31 Premier Westward Railways train from Oxford to London Paddington, March 20.

Dear Dan

Thank you for your recent correspondence. I can tell you that your train on March 13 was delayed thanks to a driver failing to turn up to work on the Tuesday morning. As it was so early, his absence wasn't noticed for some time, and so the knock-on effect continued for some hours. On the morning of March 17, a mix-up in essential engineering schedules meant that a section of track on the Oxford–London line was wrongly improved, resulting in delays across the whole network.

In addition, I would like to add a personal note. Although I understand the temptations of a night out with Train Girl must be manifold, I would still urge you to try to make amends with your wife before you do anything you might later regret. I am not an especially religious man (although I often pray for less trouble from the Network Rail infrastructure!) but nevertheless, I do hold that two wrongs do not often make a right.

I am also sorry that you feel your own situation at work has parallels with the recent war in North Africa. I feel that you may be allowing yourself a little 'poetic licence', however! Although I of course appreciate it is your place of work, it is just a newspaper, and as I'm sure you hardly need reminding, a newspaper that has always been very quick to judge others. And it seems from what I've read that the weight of evidence against some of your newspaper's practices is considerable.

Having said that, of course, I'm sure you have never been involved in any of the illegal activities alleged. I rather think, Daniel, and I hope you don't mind me saying this, that despite your occasional tendency to bluster, you are at heart a rather moral young man. I'm sure you will do the right thing in the end, both personally and professionally.

With warmest regards

Martin

Letter 80

From: **DantheMan020@gmail.com**
To: Martin.Harbottle@premier-westward.com
Re: 20.20 Premier Westward Railways train from London Paddington to Oxford, March 21. Amount of my day wasted: 19 minutes. Fellow sufferer: Sauron Flesh Harrower.

Well, it's been a mixed day. A mixed day – and I'm relatively sober. Look at the time! I'm on the 20.20! For once I didn't go for a drink after work, with the only two people who are still up for any kind of office socialising, Harry the Dog and Bombshell. Even Wee Tim'rous Trainee, the most junior reporter on the whole newspaper, the girl who got me the Narcotics Anonymous scoop, won't drink with us any more; she spends most of the day in a state of permanent terror that she's about to be arrested.

And tonight, I didn't fancy it either. Tonight I came home. Tonight I'm on the train with Sauron Flesh Harrower, for the first time in ages and, from what I can tell, I've missed out on some very important developments. For a start, his hacking and slashing and dragon-slaying days would appear to be over. He's nowhere near a dungeon, or a murky forest, or a barren wasteland or any of the usual haunts. He's not even in the Tavern of the Slaughtered Magi.

He's relaxing in a palace. His palace. He's supine on a *chaise longue* being fed grapes by a suddenly demure-looking Elvira Clunge… and six other women, variously dressed in chainmail bikinis, floaty veils, catsuits and, in at least one instance, absolutely nothing at all. They all seem very attentive, too.

You should see it, Martin. You should be here. (Or better, you should be there.) It would appear that Sauron Flesh Harrower has become some kind of online king – complete with his own online harem. And back in the real world, on this freezing train in the freezing night, crawling through the suburbs near Slough, he's loving it. He's sitting there in his pin-stripe suit, collar undone, middle-aged spread spilling out around the edges, staring at the screen on his lap with a permanent grin, fingers typing frenetically.

And, well, good luck to him, I guess. Whatever gets you through the day. Part of me wishes I could see the conversation he's having with these women, and part of me is rather glad I can't. I'm sure you can imagine what's going on.

Anyway. I've got my own weirdness to deal with. Because it's been a mixed day.

I called Beth's mum's house this morning. I didn't speak to Beth. Her mum answered the phone, said she was in the shower but she could fetch her if I wanted? I said not to bother, not yet… but I wouldn't mind a word with Sylvie.

So she put the little one on the phone. My daughter. My baby daughter. My one-year-old baby daughter Sylvie. One today.

Did I not mention that before? It's her birthday, Martin. She's been around for exactly one year. What a year it's been. When I think back to this time last year, when I cast my mind back to how things were exactly 12 months ago… in the delivery suite, staring at my wife, my amazing wife who'd just done this most amazing thing; staring at my daughter, my amazing daughter, so whole, so complete, so wholly, completely perfect, so total in her total potential… when I think of what I was thinking one year ago today, I…

Actually, you know what? I'm not going to think about that. I don't want to think about that. I don't want to write to you about that. I don't want to lose it in front of Sauron Flesh Harrower, of all people.

So anyway. Today is Sylvie's birthday. And I talked to her on the phone. She said 'Dadda', with only a little prompting from her grandma. She said 'Want Dadda' with a little more. She said 'Wubb you, Dadda' with no prompting at all. And then she started crying. And then as my mother-in-law came back on the phone to reassure me that she was fine and that my card and my present had arrived on time, I hung up, because I didn't want her to hear me crying – and besides, I was nearing work and I didn't want the news crews and the protestors to have the satisfaction of seeing me walk past without my head held high and a defiant look in my eye. Entering the building in tears, right now, could send out the wrong message.

That's how my day started. And then it got worse. (That was the good bit, Martin. That was the good bit of the 'mixed' bit. It was all downhill from then on in.)

I got a tip today. A proper tip. My first good new story in ages. Phoned in, to my mobile (my home mobile, not my work mobile, not the one the police could confiscate at any time, not the one they're no doubt monitoring daily). From an impeccable source. An impeccable source who's also a criminal, but still. He's a useful guy to know – given his connections. He works for a firm providing 'security' in south-east London, and although I don't hear from him often and he doesn't come cheap, when I do it's usually worth it.

Today it was worth it. He had a doozy. A belter. He had proper hold-the-front-page stuff. A girl he knew – or rather, and to be strictly accurate, the daughter of someone for whom he provides security – was in hospital. She'd refused an offer. She refused all offers. She didn't want a place on any reality show or a footballer boyfriend to strut around town with. She didn't even want a recording contract in any factory-assembled girl band or a modelling contract with one of the lads mags. And the people whose offers she refused aren't used to having their offers refused. They don't appreciate ingratitude like that. And that's how she had her accident.

And now, what she wanted was to talk to a journalist. Specifically, a journalist on the scandal-hit and scandalous *Sunday Globe*. She had a story to tell.

Do you want to know why she was being offered Premiership boyfriends and modelling contracts and TV spots and hit singles? Can you guess? Can you, Martin? Can you guess which recently victorious, eminently newsworthy microphone-botherer she might have crossed? Whose offers she might have refused?

Bingo. Give that man a cuddly toy.

Here's what happened. She met our high-moralled and ever-eager singing friend in a nightclub a month or so ago – just about the time he was revelling in his victory over the worst excesses of the gutter press, in fact – and they'd hooked up a few times since. So far, so what? Well... it was then he'd asked her if she ever experimented. You know, with other girls? With threesomes, foursomes, moresomes? Did she party?

She said she wasn't averse to the idea. He said he knew just the place, just the girls.

The place was one of his old haunts near the Elephant and Castle. Somewhere so ludicrously low-rent that discretion (or intimidation) was never going to be a problem. Somewhere dealing exclusively with East European girls. Somewhere dealing exclusively with East European girls of a certain 'innocent' appearance. 'Hungary Hearts', that's what they call themselves. Hungary Hearts. I mean, really.

Our girl took one look at these kids and said she was having none of it. Even his assurances that he'd seen the paperwork and they were all on or around the age of consent failed to convince her. She split. She walked away. And soon after, she was made an offer.

So: lying in a hospital bed with her neck in a brace and her left cheek fractured and three of her ribs broken (a drunk driver – can you believe it, Martin? A drunk driver who was never caught, with no witnesses), she told her daddy she wanted to speak to a journalist. And Daddy said he knew someone who might know someone. And that's how I got the call.

And when I got the call, I swear my heart stopped for a second. 'Gotcha!' I thought. Gotcha! And I burst out laughing – hysterically, gloriously, uncontrollably, the first laughter that's been heard in that newsroom for months. And then I ran – literally, ran – to the acting news ed, pushed him into his office, waved my phone at him and told him everything.

And did he laugh too? Did he punch the air? Did he shout 'Gotcha!'? No. He put his head in his hands and he said 'Oh Jesus'. And then he said he'd have to run the whole thing past the managing editor.

Fair enough, thought I, and it's only Wednesday after all, we've plenty of time. But there's not going to be any doubt about the bottom line. Nailing the man who nailed us? Discrediting every bit of evidence he gave? Gotcha! And so when he called me over later that afternoon, I'd already drawn up the girl's contracts, I'd already loaded up my Dictaphone, I'd already started mentally composing the first three paras – the ones that would go on the front page, under the headline, under my byline.

'Your contact,' he said. 'What sort of security exactly does he provide?'

And so I told him it was best he didn't know.

He shook his head. 'We can't run it,' he said. 'Not if you're getting the tip off anyone with any kind of record. Not if there's even a hint of anything dodgy about any of the people involved. What about the girl's dad? What does he do? And the girl herself? She got any kind of history with the police?'

I couldn't believe it. 'But the facts,' I stammered. 'The facts are the facts! He did it! She says he did it! She's prepared to sign stuff. And what about her face! That's how scared he is of her. He did it! That's the facts!'

He shook his head again and he couldn't meet my eyes. 'We can't use tips off anyone dodgy,' he said. 'Not right now. Especially not where he's concerned. No matter what. Sorry. Really sorry.' And he walked away, leaving me in his office, Goebbels' old office. And I've never felt more like picking up a chair and hurling it at anyone in my life.

But you know what? I'm not even angry any more. Sitting on this useless train, late home again, on my daughter's first birthday, more sober than I'd like to be, watching a middle-aged businessman with thinning hair act out the part of a rampant warrior king being fed delicacies by a harem of barely dressed women, I'm not even especially angry. I just can't help thinking... it's over.

It's over, isn't it, Martin? When we can annihilate the one person who started all this trouble, when we can obliterate him for ever with one golden story... and we bottle out of running it. When the *Globe* bottles it – it's over.

And, like my parents used to say when they wanted me to feel really bad, especially bad: I'm not angry; I'm disappointed. I'm not angry, Martin. I'm disappointed.

Au revoir!

Dan

Letter 81

From: **DantheMan020@gmail.com**
To: Martin.Harbottle@premier-westward.com
Re: 22.50 Premier Westward Railways train from London Paddington to Oxford, March 24. Amount of my day wasted: five minutes. Fellow sufferers: No regulars (Saturday).

Dear Martin

Well, there we go. Another edition to the presses. And it's a budget special, of course. A budget special because in these high-stakes economic times, it's the budget that really matters to people. Ooh, it's a budget special, all right! It's got analysis – pages of it! It's got explanations – for every eventuality! It's got case studies for every possible permutation of reader possible. It's got everything you need, budget-wise.

Of course, what it's not got is the showbiz scoop of the decade, but there you go. What can I say? I'm too tired to complain. You'll just have to amuse yourself for the rest of the delay this letter represents, Martin. Why not pretend you're Sauron Flesh Harrower? I'm sure there are worse ways to pass the time.

Au revoir!

Dan

Letter 82

From: **DantheMan020@gmail.com**
To: Martin.Harbottle@premier-westward.com
Re: 23.20 Premier Westward Railways train from London Paddington to Oxford, March 31. Amount of my day wasted: four minutes. Fellow sufferers: No regulars (Sat again).

What up, Martin? How you doin'?

I hope you're doin' good. I hope you're doing real good. And also, that you're well. I hope you're doing real good and doing real well also.

I could be worse. I'm friends with Train Girl again, at any rate. Did I tell you that? She wasn't too put out that I blew her out the other week. She said she's prepared to forgive me. She said she understands the pressure I've been under. So that's nice. That's nice she understands.

Anyway! We're not here to talk about Train Girl! Why do we keep talking about her?

There was a new email last night. From Beth, to Karen (who is she? I really need to find out just who Karen is!). It was a short one. It went like this:

> Why hasn't he called yet, Kazza? He spoke to Sylvie on her birthday, Mum told me, but he hasn't spoken to me. I keep wanting to call him, but Mum says I should wait for him to call me. She says he needs time. But why hasn't he called me? How can I say sorry properly if he doesn't call me?

I think I should call my wife soon. Really soon. I'll call her really soon and we'll sort it out. Tomorrow, maybe.

Au revoir!

Dan

From: **Martin.Harbottle@premier-westward.com**
To: DantheMan020@gmail.com
Re: 23.20 Premier Westward Railways train from London Paddington to Oxford, March 31.

Dear Dan

I'm sorry to hear of your latest delays. The 20.20 from Paddington to Oxford on March 21 was held up by a suspected sighting of a nesting owl in a signal box near the Hayes and Harlington area. Closer inspection revealed the bird to be merely a pigeon-deterrent placed on the signal by Network Rail, and which they had failed to log correctly, hence our ignorance of its existence and the subsequent confusion.

On another matter, as I believe I've mentioned before, Sauron Flesh Harrower would appear to be a player of MMORPGs, or Massively Multiplayer Online Role-Playing Games, a pursuit both misunderstood and, if I may say so, rather prejudiced against. Your constant sniping against the genre does you no favours. And your insults against him personally even less so. What do you really know about him, Dan? Don't be so quick to judge. For all you know, he may be a perfectly nice fellow. Avuncular, even.

Best

Martin

Letter 83

From: **DantheMan020@gmail.com**
To: Martin.Harbottle@premier-westward.com
Re: 22.20 Premier Westward Railways train from London Paddington to Oxford, April 3. Amount of my day wasted: 19 minutes. Fellow sufferer: Overkeen Estate Agent.

Martin: another tip came in today. Has it made the news yet? I haven't seen a telly since lunchtime, since we walked out, since we all went to the pub. I couldn't face an *Evening Standard* in case they had it too. Has it made the news? Has the latest news on our newspaper made the evening news?

A tip came in to Harry the Dog. From his friend at another paper. Asking for a comment. A comment on the rumour that they were shutting us down. A comment on the rumour that the Big Cheese, the Man Himself, the Old Boy Who Owns the Paper, was flying in tonight. A comment on the fact that when he was presented with the rumour he failed to comment one way or the other. A comment on his failure to deny.

What did Harry the Dog do? He told his friend to get lost. And then he told the rest of us about the rumour, about the imminent arrival of the *Grand Fromage*. And then a delegation went upstairs. And then they came back down again, having also failed to get a denial. And then our phones all started ringing – landline, work mobile, home mobile – and every one had someone on the end wanting a comment on the rumour they were shutting us down or a comment on the failure of anyone to deny the rumour they were shutting us down.

And then we – and I mean the office, the whole office, literally everyone in the office – walked out. Most of us as far as the pub.

Are they going to close us down? Really? Could they actually do that? Would they seriously fold the *Globe*? I know it's been awful there recently, Martin, I know it's been terrible… but really? I mean: really?

Au revoir!

Dan

PS – yeah, yeah, I know, I owe you again. Nineteen minutes. But I'm spending longer spellchecking and autocorrecting than I am actually writing this. I'm sloshed, Martin. I'm sizzled. Sozzled. I'm… gone. Real gone kid.

Letter 84

From: **DantheMan020@gmail.com**
To: Martin.Harbottle@premier-westward.com
Re: 07.31 Premier Westward Railways train from Oxford to London Paddington, April 6. Amount of my day wasted: 15 minutes. Fellow sufferers: Guilty New (Spymaster) Mum, Universal Grandpa.

So then: guess what I've been up to, these last few days since we spoke, since the rumour mill went into overdrive, since the already incredible rise and fall of the *Globe* became a soap opera so farcical, so full of cheap shocks and sensations it kind of began to lose any credibility at all with me? Guess what I've been doing yesterday and the day before, both before and during and after our esteemed chairman jetted into the country and delivered his rumour-quashing, troop-rousing, situation-calming speech?

I've been doing what everyone else at the paper's been doing, of course! (Or at least, what those with any sense have been doing.)

I've been resuming what I started a few months back, when the police first got involved. I've been carefully, methodically, routinely and systematically trying to remove all evidence that I ever put up a story, researched a story, wrote a story, took a tip, passed on a tip, followed a lead, paid a contact, met a contact, talked to a contact, even had any contacts, answered my work phone, answered my work mobile, called anyone on either my work phone or mobile, sent or received a text, sent or received an email, searched for anything on Google, logged on to any other websites, printed anything, photocopied anything, wrote anything down, talked to anyone or listened to anyone. Anything, in short, that might be used against me in evidence, no matter how flimsy, no matter how flaccid.

I've been trying to eradicate all evidence I've ever done anything at the *Globe*, other than sit in my chair, deaf, dumb and blind, seeing no evil, hearing no evil, speaking no evil, writing no evil. (If I could, I'd try to remove the chair too.)

It's not easy, of course. The published stuff I can do nothing about. A byline's a byline: it's there for all eternity. But the rest of the stuff – well, put it this way, I'm doing what I can.

My notebooks – every page covered in shorthand scrawl and scribble, phone numbers and addresses, names and quotes and questions and answers; my notebooks – the vapour trail of my whole career, the physical, tangible paper trail of every story I've ever worked on; my notebooks, the same notebooks we're supposed to keep for ever just in case they're ever needed as evidence… that evidence was the first to go. They came home with me on Wednesday in a couple of carrier bags, were piled up on the allotments across the road in the dark, torched and burned and consigned to ashes before the pubs called last orders.

And the rest of the paper stuff? The invoices, the memos, the printed transcripts and half-finished stories and tip sheets and ledgers? Rather brilliantly, someone brought a portable shredder in. Even more brilliantly, he was charging a fiver for 15 minutes on it, no questions asked. The queue was hours long. He made a bundle. And I got my slot (I paid for a half-hour); I did what I had to do.

The electronic stuff is trickier. Clearing your internet cache, deleting your emails, emptying your trash – that doesn't really cut the mustard, unfortunately. All of that – it's just cosmetic. It's papering over the cracks, it's hiding the damp under a coat of fresh paint. You've not got rid of anything. It's all still there, even if you can no longer see it.

And so me and Harry the Dog got one of the lads from IT up, we bribed him with a couple of hundred quid, and he got a shredding program for us. A virus, basically. A nasty little virtual vandal that gets into your email system and properly scrambles seven shades out of everything you've ever sent or received. Trying to rescue anything legible after this bad boy's been at it, apparently, is all-but impossible. Decoding a single message would take days – working through an entire newspaper's ten-year history of emails would take an army of major tech-nerds a couple of millennia.

And you know what, Martin? This clever, deadly, borderline-legal little beauty is easily available to anyone with a bit of internet savvy and about £50 to spare. Amazing, eh? If it weren't quite so close to home, it would make a great little cyber-shocker feature for the paper.

Anyway. Obviously we installed it. We unleashed it into our servers. We let it do its worst. (Although one old hack on Sport still didn't believe it was enough. He'd seen a documentary, he said, and the only way to wipe a hard drive properly is to physically smash it up. He wanted to take an actual hammer to his workstation. He had to be calmed down quite dramatically.)

As for the rest… well, that was less precise. The work phones were lost, of course, in the Thames, minus their SIM cards, which were also lost, though off a different bridge over the river. The home phones were wiped and lost, and replaced with new Pay As You Go numbers, as before. And before they were wiped, an awful lot of calls were made to an awful lot of people requesting, begging or threatening silence.

And then, in the middle of it, of course, our Leader made his speech. No question of the paper shutting, he said! Just a little restructuring! Corporate housekeeping! Spring cleaning!

What does that mean? I haven't a clue, Martin. So I kept destroying as much evidence of everything I'd done at that paper as possible. And I vowed that, as long as I continued to work there, I would no longer go anywhere near an interesting story again. It's blandsville for me, from now on in. It's strictly the safe stuff.

Which is another way, of course, of saying that I basically won't be doing anything like what they're paying me to do. And barely what you might call journalism at all.

Christ, this train is slow. Train Girl's not on this morning, so I'm writing this delay in real time. (Lego Head's not on either. Lego Head hasn't been on this train for months. After two years in which Lego Head was on the 07.31 every single weekday I caught it, after two years in which he never even seemed to take a holiday, the Buddha of the morning commute has just disappeared. Should I be worried? Should I be pleased? Is it anything to do with you, Martin? Is it anything to do with the incident? *Quo vadis*, Lego Head? Whither goest thou?)

Anyway. Given we're still stuck near Slough, it seems I'm going to have to keep going a little longer.

OK then. Fair enough. I'll tell you what I did last night.

Last night I called my mother-in-law's again. I wanted to speak to my wife. Finally. I called after I knew Sylvie would be in bed; I called when I knew we could talk without the distraction of our baby.

And so what did we talk about? We talked about our baby, of course. About how much she misses me. About how she's a talker, not a walker. About how every day it seems her vocabulary doubles – but how every other sentence is prefixed or suffixed by 'Dadda'. About how she needs me. (Sylvie, I mean. About how Sylvie needs me.) About how Sylvie needs a man around the place.

And that's when I nearly started crying. And so do you know what I did, to stop myself crying? What I did, so my wife wouldn't hear me tearing up and think me weak? I said something stupid.

I said that I was sure Sylvie was getting plenty of male guidance from Mr Blair. I asked how often they saw him, my wife and child, how often he came round. How often he came round to see them, to be with them.

And then Beth started crying. Spluttering and choking through the sobs, pleading with me, telling me she loved me, she was sorry, it had really been a one-off, it was terrible, she hasn't seen him since she told me, she hated seeing him those times she had done since it happened (that Halloween, when we had the argument, when I took him to task in the pub – Christ!), that all she wants to do is move on, that she's worried about me, that she can't stand me being so horrible to her, that I need to realise what I've got and what I'm losing before Sylvie's heart gets broken like our two hearts have been.

And what did I do then? I started crying too. I said I know she still loves me. I said I still love her. But I can't forget. I said I can forgive (because I love her) but I can't forget (because I love her). I said I know I'm a dick, but I can't make things right, I can't move on. Not just yet.

And now we're nearly at Paddington. And that's all you're getting this morning.

Au revoir!

Dan

PS – Martin, I've just realised. It's Good Friday today! How will you be celebrating? Shall we have a crucifixion? Shall we free Barabbas?

From: **Martin.Harbottle@premier-westward.com**
To: DantheMan020@gmail.com
Re: 07.31 Premier Westward Railways train from Oxford to London Paddington, April 6.

Dear Dan

Thank you for your most recent letters. I can tell you that your 22.20 service on April 3 was delayed after a collision between a train and some livestock between Reading and Taplow earlier in the evening. I am very sorry to report that three cows died in the incident, and another disfigured so hideously that it had to be put down as an act of mercy. The disruption unfortunately had a knock-on effect throughout the evening, resulting in many services being delayed.

On April 6 your service was held up after the failure of deliveries for the first-class buffet carriage meant that the train could not depart the sidings until more cream and sugar had been sourced. Thankfully, this only resulted in a delay of 15 minutes, which I think is a huge credit to all concerned.

And on another note, I am familiar with the phrase 'corporate housekeeping'. It is, in business, what you might call, a euphemism. Rarely a euphemism for expansion of a business either, if you get my drift!

And at the risk of appearing unprofessional, it's OK to cry, Dan.

Best regards

Martin

Letter 85

From: **DantheMan020@gmail.com**
To: Martin.Harbottle@premier-westward.com
Re: 23.20 Premier Westward Railways train from London Paddington to Oxford, April 7. Amount of my day wasted: seven minutes. Fellow sufferers: no regulars. (Saturday, innit.)

The police came back today, Martin. We've been watching the detectives. Police and thieves in the street – scaring the nation with their guns and ammunition. They burst in, proper style, old-school rules, all shouting and running, dozens of them. They told us not to move a muscle. They started unplugging and picking up computers even as we'd barely finished typing on them. They swept up notebooks and emptied draws into those big clear bags you see on the cop shows… all without so much as a by-your-leave. A proper raid, Martin!

They waited until the minute after the last pages had gone to press – which is a tad suspicious, don't you think? I mean, if it were a genuine surprise raid, they wouldn't know or care when we went to press. They wouldn't be bothered if we went to press at all. But no… they waited to spring their shock raid until just after we'd all finished for the week.

It's almost as if they'd arranged it with the big brass upstairs, isn't it? It's almost as if the whole thing was done according to some kind of gentleman's agreement ('You can confiscate all the computers, take all the paperwork, arrest who you want… but let us get the paper out first, eh?'). Or am I being paranoid?

Anyway, in they came, shortly after ten tonight. Shouting and running and whatnot, brandishing their plastic bags. And while some of the guys shouted back in return, while some tried to keep hold of their hard drives, tried to stop them taking their notebooks and files and folders, some of us just laughed at them.

I laughed at them, Martin. I heard Harry the Dog laughing too. 'Fill your boots, gents,' he said. 'You'll find nothing there to interest you.' And then they promptly arrested him. And then they arrested one of the guys on Sport (the same one who wanted to smash up his hard drive, which is interesting). And then they looked towards me – and then, and I still have no idea why, they looked past me and arrested poor terrified Wee Tim'rous Trainee. She immediately burst into tears and was led from the floor shaking and sobbing her heart out.

Why didn't they arrest me, Martin? I can't work it out. I'm the new showbiz editor! I'm the one who took down the teen-tax-Tory! I'm the one who fingered the boy Best for his kleptomaniac tendencies! Surely I'm worth at least questioning?

Well, apparently not. I'm trying not to be too offended.

And in the meantime… I came home. They've released everyone on bail, apparently, pending the investigation into all the stuff they seized tonight. I'm not worried about Harry the Dog: he'll be OK, he'll be fine. Harry's one of those people who will always be fine. I'm not even worried about Wee Tim'rous Trainee. She'll be all right. Like me, they've got rid of anything and everything they could.

But as for the paper… that's a different matter. How can the paper survive this? 'Corporate housekeeping' or otherwise: we can't keep going on like this. And now we don't even have any computers. Trust me, Martin, no matter what the *Grand Fromage* says: it's the end of the *Globe*.

Au revoir!

Dan

Letter 86

From: **DantheMan020@gmail.com**
To: Martin.Harbottle@premier-westward.com
Re: 07.31 Premier Westward Railways train from Oxford to London Paddington, April 10. Amount of my day wasted: six minutes. Fellow sufferers: Train Girl, Guilty New (Spymaster) Mum, Universal Grandpa.

Happy Easter, Martin. Well, yes, I know it was Easter Sunday two days ago, but still. Happy Easter!

Actually, that reminds me – I once had to write a feature on Easter Egg packaging, back before I was on the *Globe*, back when I was freelancing and therefore basically up for doing whatever work anyone could put my way. The idea was to take a selection of the six best-selling eggs, disassemble them completely, weigh each part of the whole package separately (the cardboard, the plastic, the foil, the chocolate) and then present the results in as shocking a way as possible (twice as much plastic as cardboard! Twice as much cardboard as foil! Twice as much foil as chocolate!). And you know what? It wasn't an entirely bad idea. It could have worked. Except it didn't. There was more chocolate than cardboard, or plastic, or foil. The whole thing was entirely unshocking. The whole thing was as any sensible person would expect it to be. So what did I do? I lied, of course. I lied, so that I'd still get paid. And after we published it on a double-page spread, and the nation was duly shocked, and the manufacturers disputed it, and we admitted the figures were wrong, and we printed a tiny apology correcting the figures buried near the letters page, I still got paid. That, in reflection, probably was immoral. Perhaps none of us are innocent, after all.

I've been thinking, Martin. On my way to work today, unsure just how much of the office will still be there, will remained unpounded by the cops; unsure of whether there will be a computer to use, or a phone; unsure of how many of my colleagues will remain… I've been thinking – you know what we should do, if they're going to shut the paper? We should run my story. We should nail that Scottish fool for good, once and for all. I've been thinking – I'm going to give that girl a call. I might talk to her anyway. I might line it all up, just in case. Just in case we've got nothing left to lose either way. Just in case we need the Pyrrhic victory to end all Pyrrhic victories.

Or... I could do the sensible thing. And shut up. I could do the smart thing and do nothing at all.

And in the meantime, Train Girl wants to go out again. On the way in this morning, as Guilty New (Spymaster) Mum complained about her childcare ('And I said to her, at that price I'd want my child learning Mandarin! At that price for a morning – just a morning, mind, that's the price for just half a day – I said I'd want my baby playing Grade 8 piano by Christmas...') Train Girl popped the question.

She's giving me another chance, she said. (She said it with a wink.) She's giving me another shot at the prize. And what am I to think about that?

Au revoir!

Dan

Letter 87

From: **DantheMan020@gmail.com**
To: Martin.Harbottle@premier-westward.com
Re: 22.20 Premier Westward Railways train from London Paddington to Oxford, April 13. Amount of my day wasted: 0 minutes. Fellow sufferers: Overkeen Estate Agent.

Shock! Awe! Shock and awe! And also – blimey! It seems I got it all wrong. It seems that someone is doing something good. It seems that someone might be saved after all.

Even what's left of the foreign desk were amazed. Even they didn't see this one coming. (Harry the Dog's not there anymore of course – all those arrested the other night have not been allowed back to work. They're suspended until the police investigation is concluded. However long that takes. And so we are a skeleton staff, working on laptops: the biggest newspaper in the world reduced to resources that would embarrass most student publications. But he's OK, anyway. I spoke to him yesterday: he's sitting at home watching *Antiques Hunt* and *A Place In The Country*. He doesn't seem bothered, either way. I've not been able to get hold of Wee Tim'rous Trainee, though. Seems nobody has. Seems she just isn't answering her phone any more.)

Anyway. Were you as amazed as we were? A full-scale attack! A massive bombing raid! Missiles screaming out of the blue! War in North Africa! And this time, the good guys are involved. This time, for once, somebody's doing the right thing. This time, for once, NATO and the UN have finally shown just what it is they're about, what they can do, what they're supposed to be there for.

I've got to say, Martin, it was rather brilliantly done. Calling the head honcho over to New York like that, summoning him, in his aviator shades and all, to address the leaders of the free world, letting him think it was to welcome him into the fold… and then arresting him. For war crimes. And then launching a full-scale, coordinated, meticulously planned, fully thought-through and entirely top-secret attack on his newly won positions in North Africa.

Amazing. Like I say: amazing. Amazeballs. Shocking. Awesome.

Is it legal? Oh, who cares? There were no referendums, Parliament was not consulted, there were no debates and public deliberations. They just thought it up themselves, decided it themselves and then did it. And that's fine by me. That's what they're there for – and finally, they've done something good, something worth the name.

So: today, the arrest, the air assault. And, we learn, armadas heading that way too. Artillery, tanks, ground and sea support. A full-scale invasion in the offing.

Oh – and you know what else? This train isn't even delayed! Isn't that a scream? I started writing because I just assumed it would be, for some reason, and here we are chuffing into Oxford bang on schedule! Even Overkeen Estate Agent seems surprised ('Gotta 86 this convo, captain,' he said just now. 'Seems we're running on time for once. But let's diarise some face-time and do this skin-to-skin? Wicked. Legendary.')

So – sorry about the unnecessary letter! But you know what? You owe me anyway, right? Those other times when I was too drunk or too upset to give you as many words as I should have? Consider this a payment. Settling the score. Until next time.

And in the meantime… News 24 beckons!

Au revoir!

Dan

Letter 88

From: **DantheMan020@gmail.com**
To: Martin.Harbottle@premier-westward.com
Re: 22.20 Premier Westward Railways train from London Paddington to Oxford, April 14. Amount of my day wasted: nine minutes. Fellow sufferers: No regulars – Saturday…

Ah, there we go. Didn't have to wait long, did we? Twenty-four hours, that's all it took.

Twenty-four hours. I've been thinking about time. About what time does. What it does to us, I mean. Time the healer, time the ravager.

This time last year Beth and I were in what we called 'the tunnel'. Beth and Sylvie and I: our little nuclear family, in our little house in Oxford together, happy. Exhausted, of course. Frantic with exhaustion.

Frazzled. Kept awake all night and sleepwalking through the day. Unable to go longer than five minutes without checking Sylvie again, making sure she's all right, making sure she's still breathing, making sure she's still there. In the tunnel.

Do you remember the tunnel, Martin? Those first six weeks or so after the birth when everything's blurred and yet hyperfocused, when you basically live on the sofa and the telly's on 24-hours a day, when you eat what and when you can, bolting it down as quickly as possible, in between bouts of feeding and nappy changes and pacing the living room, up and down, down and up, shushing and cooing and pleading for sleep. We called it the tunnel, because it felt like we were living in a tunnel, emerging from our house once every few days or so for more supplies, blinking and squinting at the sky, the fresh air.

The tunnel. So difficult and yet, so amazing.

I remember the tiredness, most of all. The tiredness and the happiness. The 24-hour exhaustion and the almost-permanent euphoria. I remember the moment I worked out the trick to get Sylvie to sleep – at about five in the morning, it was. After trying literally every idea in every book we could find, I swapped the nursery rhymes and Mozart CDs and sound effects (waterfalls, rain, heartbeat, etc) for one of my old-school trance albums. I mean, proper, tripped-out, arms-in-the-air, processed beats stuff. Dutch, too, I think. Dutch nosebleed techno. I have no idea why I still even own it. And you know what happened? The moment it came on, Sylvie closed her eyes and fell asleep. The hypnotic rhythms, the driving, relentless, repetitiveness of it… her little face relaxed and she drifted off. Amazing. That trick lasted a full fortnight and although the neighbours probably didn't appreciate it, I've never felt happier about any piece of music in my life.

So, that's where I was a year ago. In the tunnel. And, of course, six weeks later, with a little help from old-school Amsterdam trance music, there was, as there is with all tunnels, a light at the end of it. That's the thing with tunnels: there's always a light at the end of them. No matter how long, how dark, there's always a light at the end of the tunnel.

This time last year I was still just a junior reporter on the showbiz desk, recycling press releases and handing over all my tips to others. I was getting stories (I had contacts all right) but by the time they ended up in the paper they rarely had my name on them. I was barely getting bylines. This time last year the *Globe* was only just beginning to get touched by scandal. It was still the biggest newspaper in the world, capable of toppling Premiers and crushing any who dared cross it.

This time last year I could never have dreamed this is where I'd be right now. Beth gone. Sylvie gone. And showbiz editor of the paper as it enters its death throes.

We got a paper out tonight. Unbelievably, with our student rag set-up, our laptops and cheap mobiles, our almost complete lack of original stories and pitiful excuses for scoops, with our skeleton staff and no access to our own archives… we got a paper out. I suppose that's an achievement in itself, but really: it's hardly worth it. I wouldn't bother buying it tomorrow, if I were you. Unless it's just for curiosity's sake.

And you know what else? It was this time last year I started writing to your customer complaints department. They never did write back. Did I ever tell you that, Martin? Your customer complaints department – they never wrote back to explain the delays on my trains this time last year. You might want to have a word with someone about that, eh?

Au revoir!

Dan

Letter 89

From: **DantheMan020@gmail.com**
To: Martin.Harbottle@premier-westward.com
Re: 20.20 Premier Westward Railways train from London Paddington to Oxford, April 17. Amount of my day wasted: eight minutes. Fellow sufferer: Sauron Flesh Harrower.

Here we are again, Martin. We've had quite a run, recently. We've been averaging three delays a week. What's happening? Taken your eye off the ball? Taken your foot off the gas? Or are you just giving up? Have you taken a good long look at the situation, decided it's hopeless and stopped even trying to do anything about it?

Hey, guess what? I'm a little tipsy (obvs) – but then, I kind of feel I deserve it. And after all the nonsense and despair of the last few weeks, I'm drinking (for once) because, believe it or not, I'm in a good mood. Some things have gone right, for once!

I was offered a job today. I think. Well, no, I'm sure, actually. I got a call, on my new mobile (my first question, as it always is these days, was 'How did you get my number?' The answer: 'You tell me. How would you have got your number?' I liked them for that. It was a good answer). The call was from a PR company. The top PR company, as it happens. The one who looks after the interests of the cream of the country's celebrities, the proper A-listers, the sort of people so rich, so famous, they don't need to pay for anything, they don't need to do anything… and anything they do is deemed newsworthy.

They want to talk to me. They've followed my career this past year with interest, they say. They want to have me in for a chat. Because there's a position. A senior position. They need someone to – and this bit wasn't actually said explicitly, but it was implied heavily enough for anyone but an idiot to pick it up – control the press. To make sure that bad news is buried and good news makes the front pages. They need someone to head up that particular department: the 'media management' department. And I've been a journalist long enough, I've had enough battles with PR companies, to know exactly what media management means.

But then, why not? They are the top dogs. And they've been following me with interest! They've been keeping an eye on my career, watching my rise through the paper. They want me – and they want me in a senior position! On serious money!

It's worth a chat, right? It's not journalism – it's kind of the opposite, to be fair, it's a sort of anti-journalism – but then so what? They want me! I'm flattered, Martin. They've made me an offer it's very hard to refuse.

There is one slight drawback. Because do you know who one of their major clients is? Whose interests they look after?

Yep, got it in one.

And could I bring myself to suppress stories on our famous friend? Could I swallow my pride and promote his supposed good works, place pieces about his heart-warming quirks and his charming eccentricities? Could I?

I'll think it over.

But anyway, even that isn't what's staving off the black dog today. There's something else, something apart from work, something away from the rest of the world. I spoke to Beth at the weekend.

And I mean 'spoke', too. There was no shouting, no crying; there were no accusations or recriminations, or resentment or anger. We just spoke. Like two grown-ups. Not exactly like man and wife, not yet… but not like two people who hate each other either. We spoke for about half an hour, after she'd put Sylvie to bed. And when I hung up I realised I was smiling.

Au revoir!

Dan

Letter 90

From: **DantheMan020@gmail.com**
To: Martin.Harbottle@premier-westward.com
Re: 07.31 Premier Westward Railways train from Oxford to London Paddington, April 20. Amount of my day wasted: 11 minutes. Fellow sufferers: Train Girl, Universal Grandpa.

Oh dear, Martin. Are you ignoring me again? At least you've not set up that awful automated reply whatsit, but still. Where are you? Whither goest thou, Martin, in thy shiny train in the night? It must be six times I've written now, since your last reply. Admittedly, one of them was not apropos of a delay at all, but still, even allowing for that, there's a good half-hour or so of unanswered tardiness on the tally.

So, anyway, I saw Train Girl this morning. (I'm writing this at work, on my personal laptop, through my completely impersonal webmail address.) In our usual seats in the middle of Coach C, we chatted our usual chat to London Paddington.

She's looking good, Martin. This warm weather – it suits her. The legs are bare again, the skirt is short, the jacket is off. She's got a tan somehow (that skiing trip can't have done it – you can't get tanned legs on a skiing trip, can you?). She's had a haircut. She's… well, I've said it before, but especially now, she's hot.

Anyway. We chatted our usual chat, shooted the usual breeze, all the way to London town. And then, after we'd got off the train, after we'd followed the crowds down the length of Platform 4 and through the barriers, after we'd walked our usual walk through the cookie shops and the card shops and the Burger King and the information boards to where we usually part – me down the stairs to the Bakerloo line, her up the walkway and onto the street to her bus stop – she stopped me. Put a hand on my arm. And made me an offer.

'Listen,' she said, 'this is, um, difficult. I don't normally do this. Well, I mean I do, but it's not normally me having to say it. Normally the other person says it. But I don't think you're going to say it, so I'm going to have to say it for both of us.'

She smiled at this point. 'That's part of why I like you so much, actually. Because I don't think you'd say what I want you to say. Because you're the only person I'd actually say this to, if you know what I mean.'

I told her I didn't have a clue what she meant. She looked at the ground for a minute, took a breath, swung her bag further back on her shoulder and then took my other arm, holding me, looking straight up into my eyes.

'OK. Dan, listen. I like you. I mean, I really like you. I like talking to you – even when you're moaning about work or the trains or that stupid bloody war on the other side of the world. Even when you get overexcited about ridiculous things no one else really cares about. I like that. It's funny. It's… endearing. I mean, you're a bit of a dick, but I like that.

'And when we go out, we have fun. We have really good fun. It's a laugh, right? And I think you like me too.

'The thing is, Dan, I do keep asking you out for a reason. I want to go drinking with you, and dancing, and having a laugh, and talking nonsense and stuff – but also, I want something… else. Do you know what I mean? Do you know what I'm saying?'

I stuttered something about not being sure, but I'm pretty sure I did. My heart was banging in my chest; I could feel myself flushing.

'Look,' she continued. 'What would you do if I asked you to kiss me now?'

'Um,' I managed, looking around at the commuters, the tourists, the day trippers, the students, the human traffic passing around us.

'Um, well, it's a bit busy and, y'know, someone might see, and, well, it's difficult, and—'

'Dan,' she said. 'Kiss me.'

I didn't kiss her, Martin. I just stood there, stupidly, as she waited, her hands warm on my wrists, her eyes locked onto mine, her face upturned, her lips slightly parted. I stood there, just looking at her. I don't know why I didn't kiss her… but I didn't kiss her.

She looked down again. 'OK. I knew you wouldn't kiss me. I don't really know why you won't kiss me because I'm pretty sure you want to kiss me, but I also knew you wouldn't.

'Anyway. Listen. I'm going to just say it. Dan: I really like you. I want us to be more than we are now. I want you to kiss me. I want you to… do more than just kiss me. I want us to be more than friends. I know you're a bit mixed up cos of your wife and everything, but I don't want to be your girlfriend. I just want us to have fun, whenever and wherever's good for both of us. With no commitments. No hassles. No claims on each other.'

She stood on tiptoes, leaned in and whispered in my ears. 'I want to sleep with you, Dan. I'm offering myself to you on a plate. No questions asked, no strings attached, no guilt involved. A sure thing. It's yours, if you want it. And don't tell me you don't want it. Every man wants it.'

And she kissed me on the cheek and walked out of the station, and I watched her go, the sway of her hips, the swing of her legs. And you know what? She's right. It is what every man wants. And Beth did sleep with someone else first.

So what do I do? If you thought the offer I was made on Tuesday was hard to refuse, that was nothing compared to this.

But shall I tell you why I didn't kiss her? Because she said I was a bit of a dick. And I don't mean that I was insulted by that, but that when she said it, the first person I thought of was Beth. How she said I was a bit of a dick too, in her email to her friend – and how a few words later she said she loved me. How she said 'He's my Dan'.

I am her Dan. She does love me – despite what she did. And I love her too. I couldn't kiss Train Girl because I love Beth. It's as simple as that.

Au revoir!

Dan

PS – Also, why do people keep calling me a dick? Seriously?

From: **Martin.Harbottle@premier-westward.com**
To: DantheMan020@gmail.com
Re: 07.31 Premier Westward Railways train from Oxford to London Paddington, April 20.

Dear Dan

Thank you for your recent letters. Your train on April 17 was delayed when a suspicious package was found in the Southall region, thus bringing about a 'go slow' enforcement in the area. You'll be relieved I'm sure to hear that after a controlled explosion the package was later found to be nothing more sinister than a box of vinyl records somebody had left outside a charity shop.

On April 20, your morning service ran late due to an issue with vandals dropping eggs onto passing services from a bridge outside Slough. The impact of an egg on the windscreen of a train passing at even a moderate speed can be very serious, not least because of the impaired visual effects of yolk on the windscreen, and so we had to take the incident seriously. As I believe I have mentioned before, the safety of our customers is paramount to us.

I'm also pleased to hear that you have been offered a job away from the *Globe*. I really do believe that you would be better suited to work at a more respectable company and given all that's been happening there, I'm surprised you haven't been actively seeking work elsewhere for some time now.

Will you accept the job? Do please feel free to ignore my advice, and I'm sure you know the 'business' much better than I do, but one thing did occur to me. You say this public relations company looks after the interests of the man who recently won his court case against your paper? It's just that several times in your letters you have mentioned his habit of making people offers 'they can't refuse' when their actions prove troublesome to him. As I say, I dare say I don't understand the situation fully and possibly I'm 'jumping the gun', but could it be that you yourself are now being made such an offer? Perhaps you should consider it very carefully.

Best

Martin

PS – I was going to say something about 'Train Girl' too, but I think you already know what my advice would be.

Letter 91

From: **DantheMan020@gmail.com**
To: Martin.Harbottle@premier-westward.com
Re: 22.20 Premier Westward Railways train from London Paddington to Oxford, April 25. Amount of my day wasted: 13 minutes. Fellow sufferers: Overkeen Estate Agent.

Do you want to know where my integrity is, Martin? My integrity – it's all over me like a very expensive suit. Like a very fine aftershave. I'm wearing my integrity like a crown. Integrity is in every fibre of my being today. Integrity is what I am, it's what I do. My name is Integrity, King of Kings. Look on my integrity, ye mighty, and despair!

I said no to Train Girl. Of course I said no. I had to say no. I told her I didn't know why I was saying no, that I was probably mad for saying no, that the Dan of a decade ago would probably take me outside and give me a good kicking for saying no, that if my friend Harry the Dog ever found out I'd been made an offer like this and said no he would definitely take me outside and give me a good kicking... but that I was saying no.

I said no because I couldn't say yes. I wanted to say yes, but I couldn't say yes. I had to say no. I'm just not that kind of person. I can't do uncomplicated, no-questions-asked, no-strings-attached, no-guilt-involved sex. I'm married.

I'm married. And I love Beth. Despite what happened. Despite the fact she and Sylvie have been at her mum's for the last two months. Despite the fact we'd barely been speaking for a month before she went. Despite the fact things haven't exactly been brilliant since Sylvie was born. I love Beth. No matter what.

Train Girl was OK, I think. I don't want to sound like an idiot and say she was gutted, but she didn't seem ecstatic about the situation. She's not the kind of girl who is often turned down. She's not the kind of girl who's used to rejection. Although having said that, what she actually said, when I phoned her on Sunday morning, when I told her, was: 'I knew you'd say that.'

Then she said she wasn't bothered either way, that it was my loss, that we could have had some fun, that she wasn't going to be repeating the offer, that I might just have passed up the best offer of my life, that she hopes I won't be too lonely all these long nights waiting for my wife to come back... and I just said 'yes' to it all. I said 'no' to her offer, and then I said 'yes' to all her reasons why I was an idiot for saying no. But I still said no.

Are you proud, Martin? Are you reassured and relieved that I am the kind of nice boy you hoped I was? I hope so.

And guess what? There's more! More integrity!

I turned down the job. I refused the other offer I couldn't refuse. I won't be leaving the scandalous and scandal-hit and failing and failed (more of that later) *Sunday Globe*. Or at least, not yet. And not to join the most powerful PR company in the country. Not to look after the media interests of the most famous crooner in the land.

Believe it or not, Martin, you were right. I mean, I had my suspicions – but you were right. It took your letter for me to see it, it took your letter to spell it out to me, in black and white (and read all over). They weren't interested in me, were they? They hadn't been following my career since the Jamie Best scoop at all. They didn't want me for my brilliance and insight and tabloid nous. They were just trying to shut me up. They'd got wind of what I've got wind of and they were trying to shut me up.

(Of course, they didn't admit any of that when I told them yesterday that I wouldn't be accepting their generous offer, that I wasn't interested in a (senior) position at their company. They simply told me they were very disappointed. That they wished I would reconsider. That if money was an issue they were sure something could be worked out. And then when I told them the answer was still no, they told me I was an idiot. They told me I was arrogant and stupid and doomed to go down with the rag I worked for.)

And you know what I did, when they told me that? I laughed. I told them they were right. Because I called them minutes after the managing editor had announced to the whole paper that we were going to fold.

That's right. We're folding. The *Globe*, most-read English-language newspaper in the world, scourge of bent politicians and dodgy dealers and liars and cheats and hypocrites worldwide, is going to cease production. Undone by Barry Dunn. Killed by the last victim of the Beast of Berkhamsted. Shafted by a man in a kilt. A victim of corporate housekeeping.

We were all summoned to the main conference room (those of us who are left, that is); we were told together that the paper had become too toxic, too tainted, by the actions of some in the past, to continue as a going concern. 'We are a business,' he said. 'And as a business we have to put aside romanticism and emotions and think like a business. And as a business the truth is we cannot continue.'

The weird thing is, nobody seemed overly bothered. Nobody was shocked. Everyone knew it was coming. Deep down, everyone knew it was only a matter of time. Even me. Especially me.

So, we've got a last day. A final day. A deadline. Sunday May 20. Put it in your diary, Martin, enter it into your Outlook. You've got four more issues of the most famous newspaper in the world to come. And if I am going to go down with the newspaper, perhaps I might go down with some integrity after all, eh?

Au revoir!

Dan

PS – You blew up a bunch of vinyl records? What are you, some kind of Nazi? What's next? Book burnings? You can't go round exploding old albums, Martin. That's our cultural heritage, right there! Where's your integrity?

Letter 92

From: **DantheMan020@gmail.com**
To: Martin.Harbottle@premier-westward.com
Re: 07.31 Premier Westward Railways train from Oxford to London Paddington, May 3. Amount of my day wasted: six minutes. Fellow sufferers: Guilty New Mum, Universal Grandpa, Train Girl.

All right, Martin? Nearly the weekend. Cup Final weekend! What will I be doing this Saturday? Well, I'll be watching the Cup Final too, of course, from the office (they didn't confiscate the TVs at least). As I'm filing copy for the ante-penultimate edition of the

Globe, I'll be keeping an eye on the action. It's the reds for me, but I won't hold it against you.

The word is out, of course, about our closure. They're dancing in the streets outside our office – the placards have changed, from angry and accusatory to jubilant and spiteful. My personal favourite? The same lady who used to wave a cardboard banner declaring: 'You have stolen from the innocent dead' (nicely poetic turn of phrase there I thought – positively Blakeian) now has a new sign. This one reads: 'RIP Tabloid Scum'. Lovely! What a lovely, forgiving woman!

There are changes inside the building, too. Where once we had to submit to pat-downs from our own security staff, now we're getting full-on searches from a couple of embarrassed-looking police officers. Every time we go in or out of the newsroom, we have to go through the same routine. Nip out for a cigarette? Submit to a search. Pop to the loo for a wee? Submit to a search. And when you come back again a minute later? Search. It's ridiculous. What do they expect to find? Anyone with anything to hide, anything to smuggle in or out, will have done it by now.

It's got to the point where we're now nicking stuff just to see if they'll find it. We've got a sweepstake going (our first sweepstake in ages – what with all the arrests and sackings and resignations and hatred and general horror, we've sort of let our office sweepstakes slip a bit): we've got bets on who can smuggle the most office equipment out of the building. I'm in third place at the moment (out of seven of us) – I've only managed three staplers and an A4 pad. The current leader is Bombshell (of course) – she's managed to get eight whole laptops out. Eight laptops! Her technique is to stand square in front of the police officer, power-suited and micro-skirted, balanced expertly on four-inch heels and with her chest thrust out, and looking him straight in the eye, demand he pats her down. Naturally, he doesn't. You've got to love her for that.

She'll be all right, will Bombshell. Word is that she's already had offers from the monthlies. Say what you like about *Amazeballs!* but it's very well thought of in the industry.

Anyway. I've just got time to tell you about something else, something utterly unrelated to lowlife tabloid scum or North African despair or even the low farce of my own life. Something proper: something real.

A lovely thing happened on the train today, as we paused for breath near Didcot, as we took a moment to collect ourselves before the last limp into that station… a magical thing happened. I saw a kite!

Not that kind of kite! Not the Mary Poppins kind, the 'up to the highest height' kind. I mean a Red Kite. A bird of prey. It was massive! It hovered above the cornfields, it paused… and hovered… and paused… and then… BAM! Dropped like a stone! Whoosh! Up it came with something in its claws and flapped hugely away. Martin! It was amazing! Worth six minutes of anyone's time.

Thank you, Martin. Well done. If you'd been running an efficient service I'd never have seen that kite. If you'd been doing your job properly, I'd have missed out on it all. Nature in the raw! I owe you one.

Enjoy the footer! Do give my love to the chief of the Met when you see him at the corporate bar on Saturday!

Au revoir!

Dan

Letter 93

From: DantheMan020@gmail.com
To: Martin.Harbottle@premier-westward.com
Re: 21.20 Premier Westward Railways train from London Paddington to Oxford, May 3. Amount of my day wasted: six minutes. Fellow sufferers: no regulars.

Any ideas, Martin?

Au revoir!

Dan

Letter 94

From: **DantheMan020@gmail.com**
To: Martin.Harbottle@premier-westward.com
Re: 07.31 Premier Westward Railways train from Oxford to London Paddington, May 8. Amount of my day wasted: eight minutes. Fellow sufferers: Train Girl, Universal Grandpa, Guilty New (Spymaster) Mum.

Morning, Martin. How are you?

Look! It's Tuesday again: the start of another working week at the biggest-rising-circulation newspaper in the country, the doomed and damned *Globe*! We've only got two more issues to go now, and, paradoxically, brilliantly, circulation is rising. It's going through the roof. Since the announcement that May 20's paper will be our last, everyone's been eager to see what the fuss is all about. The paper's been flying off the shelves every Sunday. They've had to increase the print run to cope with demand. Whether it's morbid curiosity, a kind of vulture tourism or people snapping them up for their souvenir value, our sales are climbing. Rocketing, in fact.

Isn't that funny? I think it's hilarious. It's ridiculous. It's typical. Each man kills the thing he loves, right? We're fascinated by what repels us. The people wanted the *Globe* dead – and they're flocking to get their hands on it before it goes. They're all slowing down to watch the car crash. How fantastically British.

And here I am, right in the wreckage. Writing this letter to you on a train that's also slowing down (literally slowing down, of course). We were doing so well, too – I didn't need to get my laptop out and start writing until after Slough. But now, on this final approach into London, on these last hurdles, we appear to be stumbling, stalling, stopping. We haven't got the legs to see it through.

I'm not in my usual seat on this service, next to Train Girl, in the middle of Coach C. I'm towards the back, crammed in next to Universal Grandpa. Our knees are touching, but it's not the same. It's really not the same. He's not mentioned his daughter recently; I haven't brought the subject up either. To be honest, we're both a little embarrassed at having to sit together like this – nods and winks and the odd extended greeting on the platform are one thing; the prospect of an hour in each other's company something else entirely. He's currently engrossed in his crossword, though I know from experience he would normally have finished it before Maidenhead.

Train Girl and I haven't spoken since we, well, spoke. She's ignoring me, and though I can't really blame her, I do miss her, oddly. I mean: I miss having someone to chat to, to laugh with, in the morning. I don't miss the sexual tension. I don't miss the constant feeling that every conversation with her presented me with a new dilemma. So perhaps I don't miss her, after all.

Do I miss Train Girl? You know what? I think maybe I don't. There's a turn-up.

Also, I spoke to Beth again at the weekend. Another long chat. Another good chat, with no accusations. I felt like we might be becoming friends again. She told me Sylvie's missing me. I told her I missed Sylvie more than she could know. She told me she was missing me too. And I told her I missed her in return. I told her that in an odd way I felt like we'd been missing each other for a while before she left. She cried a bit at that point, but it was OK. It wasn't angry tears, or hurt tears. It was just… what-if tears. Tears of regret. And if only I could get that image of her and Mr Blair out of my head, I'd have put the phone down and got the first train to her mum's I could and held her until she stopped crying.

But I can't. That's the problem. Beth and I – we may be missing each other, we may be becoming friends again, but I can't lose that awful thought. My wife and Mr Blair, arms and legs entangled, eyes on each other, lips touching… I can't lose it, Martin. God knows I want to, but it's there. It won't go away. How can I make it go away?

But, we did talk. And it was a nice talk. And she said she was worried about me. At the paper, I mean. I told her that things at the paper were better than they'd been for months, weirdly. Because they are, you know. The atmosphere – now the uncertainty's gone, now we know we've lost the battle, the war – is almost euphoric. The only question is: do we go out with a bang? Do we go gentle into that good night – or do we rage, rage against the dying of the light?

What do you think, Martin? What would you do?

Au revoir!

Dan

From: **Martin.Harbottle@premier-westward.com**
To: DantheMan020@gmail.com
Re: 07.31 Premier Westward Railways train from Oxford to London Paddington, May 8.

Dear Dan

Thank you for your recent correspondence and I am sorry that once again you have found our service to be less than excellent. I can tell you that your train on April 25 was held up when a passenger was found in possession of what the guard deemed to be an offensive weapon. Despite the fact that the guard repeatedly told the girl's father that her age was irrelevant and that according to our safety guidelines (available for all to see on our website) he has the power to confiscate anything he might deem to be a danger to himself or the other passengers, the girl's father became aggressive when the guard confiscated the 'Flower Fairy Barbie magic wand' and refused to return it to the five-year-old girl in question. As both father and daughter had to be ejected from the train at the first available station, the service was necessarily held up.

On May 3, a malfunctioning mobile water-heating device in the buffet carriage meant that hot beverages were sadly not available for passengers, and your train was delayed while an engineer was called to service the device in question. Sadly he was unable to rectify the situation, and so I am doubly apologetic if you did attempt to purchase a cup of tea or coffee on that service also.

On other matters, I can't help feeling pleased you turned down your offers from both 'Train Girl' and the public relations firm. Loyalty is amongst the most admirable of virtues, and you have shown commendable loyalty, even to a newspaper whose methods and ethics I can't help but disagree with.

I am glad also that you are patching things up with your wife. Who knows – this time next year you may both laugh about this!

Best

Martin

PS – Yes I did attend the Cup Final, as it happens, though not in the corporate seats. I took my nephew. It was his first ever football match – a seven-goal thriller! I fear he may now expect to go every year!

Letter 95

From: **DantheMan020@gmail.com**
To: Martin.Harbottle@premier-westward.com
Re: 22.50 Premier Westward Railways train from London Paddington to Oxford, May 15. Amount of my day wasted: 14 minutes. Fellow sufferers: Overkeen Estate Agent.

Hey, guess what? I am in an exceptional mood! Despite this horrible, stinking train I'm on, despite the fact it stood still and useless and uselessly still at Paddington for long after its scheduled departure time and now it seems to have the air-con on full despite it being 11 at night and actually surprisingly cold outside for the time of year! Despite all that! Would you like to know why? Of course you would!

It's not the alcohol that's put me in this mood (though that helps, and there has been a lot of it to help, too). It's not even the news from North Africa, the establishment of a proper interim government, organised by the people but enforced by the UN. It's not down to what one might call a 'satisfactory conclusion' to that whole business down there.

Nope. What's put me all of a jangle and a jitter tonight, what's got me fizzing and buzzing and fidgety and, um, buzzing (sorry, Martin, I'm drunk: I've spent the last ten minutes trying to think of another 'b' word that means buzzing... and I can't. You'll just have to let that one pass. Oh! Hang on! Bouncing!), what's got me fizzing and buzzing and fidgety and bouncing is the impending final issue of the super soaraway *Sunday Globe*. It's going to be a whopper! It's going to be a scorcher! It's going to be sin-sational!

Or, at least, it might be. It hasn't been fully decided yet. It hasn't been totally signed off. But it might, you know. It just bloody well might!

There was a meeting today. A conference. Not like a normal conference, though – this conference involved the whole paper. We were all there. The editor: he said he wanted every one of us to have a say in what we put in the last-ever issue and that he wanted every single person who works on it, from the most senior journalist to the lowliest work experience kid, to have a byline. (Not necessarily to actually write something, that would be madness, but to at least get a byline somewhere. If I write, say, five stories for the paper – which is about usual – then I'd give out bylines for four of them to some kids who've written none.)

Nice, eh? Lovely touch, as they say. But that wasn't the exciting bit. The exciting bit wasn't even when we discussed what the front page should be. Our final scoop. Our last splash. Because we don't have one yet. Although we do have options.

I mean, it's not unusual that we don't have a splash just yet. It is only Tuesday. What is unusual is that we have options – options we dare use, I mean. All those stories in the vault – the unprintably litigious, the best-used-for-leverage, the only-ever-half-stood-up and the liable-to-wreck-professional-relationships-for-ever – we could use those. We could use one – or we could use all. We could go out in a blaze of glory, on a hara-kiri high, with a kamikaze final paper that ruins all of our prospects of ever getting work in this town again but would ensure that our name liveth evermore. We could do that.

Or… we could think of something else. But we all agreed that it's essential we do something amazing. Something spectacular. One last historic shocker from the ultimate scandal rag. Which means, of course, that my work's cut out. Five days to get the scoop of my career? Where's that going to come from?

And then the exciting bit happened.

It was decided that as well as giving bylines to every junior researcher and editorial assistant and grad trainee and work-experience kid in the building, we should sneak bylines in for all those who have been arrested. Another nice gesture. A nice two-fingered gesture, in fact.

And that's when I had the Greatest Idea Of All Time.

The Greatest Idea Of All Time, Martin!

So there I am, brow furrowed, pen chewed, tie askew, trying to think of what to do about Sunday's front-page story, of where I might get a good story from, a story good enough, big enough, to deserve the splash on the last-ever *Globe* – and behind me I'm dimly aware of someone saying something about giving bylines to people no longer at the paper… and suddenly everything clicked.

I'm sitting on the best story of my life, Martin! Not only that – I'm sitting on revenge. No: better than revenge – I'm sitting on vengeance. On justice. On a beautiful, perfect, exquisite illustration of what happens to you if you take on the tabloid press. (Do you remember what happens to you if you take on the tabloid press, Martin? You lose. Always. In the end, you always lose. Even if you win today, you'll lose tomorrow. Taking on the tabloid press is an exercise in Pyrrhic arrogance and futility: even your victories will undo you. If you beat the tabloid press, the tabloid press will ensure they beat you back, harder. No matter how long it takes, they'll get you. And if you win big enough… well, then you're asking to get undone completely. You're asking for annihilation. King Pyrrhus could tell you all about it.)

There I was, Martin, sitting in that conference room, scratching my head, trying to think of a good story lead, when at home I've got taped and transcribed the written testimony of a girl who can ensure that the big-mouthed, swinging-sporraned, lushly wiggy man so responsible for taking down this newspaper falls at least as hard and as far as we do.

Running that story in our last-ever issue… well, it would be just too perfect, wouldn't it? It would be poetic. It would be beautiful.

The only problem is, I've been specifically banned from writing it. By the managing editor. If it came out with my name on, my whole career would be finished. Our crooner friend would of course sue, and the managing ed would throw me to the dogs.

But what if someone else were to write it? Someone whose career is already over? Someone currently out on remand but who is almost certainly looking at a prison stretch – if not for the whole Barry Dunn thing, then at least for up to four counts of assault. What if I got Goebbels to write it?

I sent the old psycho a text this afternoon, to sound him out about the idea. I told him it would be his neck on the block if it did happen, but it wouldn't half make for a show-stopping final act. He texted back straight away. I mean, literally straight away. And you know what he said?

He said: 'I'm in 100 percent. Let's take him out.'

Excited, Martin? I'm bouncing! All I've got to do now is work out exactly how we're going to do it.

Au revoir!

Dan

Letter 96

From: **DantheMan020@gmail.com**
To: Martin.Harbottle@premier-westward.com
Re: 07.31 Premier Westward Railways train from Oxford to London Paddington, May 17. Amount of my day wasted: ten minutes. Fellow sufferers: Train Girl, Guilty New (Spymaster) Mum, Universal Grandpa.

Thursday morning, Martin. T minus three to the last issue. And I'm back where I used to sit in Coach C – where I used to sit, before I sat next to Train Girl every morning. Which is to say, pretty much opposite where I sat next to Train Girl every morning.

She's on this train too, of course. I can see her as I type. She's not said anything to me, but as she passed my seat and sat down opposite and across the aisle she did smile. I smiled back. And then tried not to look as she crossed her legs, her skirt hitching up, her thighs bare, as usual. And then definitely tried not to look as she shook her jacket off, tried not to look at the blouse she was wearing, surely too tight, with one button too many undone… and as I tried not to look I could feel her eyes watching me. And when I glanced up (pretending to gaze around the carriage, as you do) she smiled again. And we both knew what that smile meant.

So I ignored it. I ignored her. I am ignoring her. I got out my laptop and I started writing this letter. To tell you the truth, Martin, I have no idea if this train is going to end up delayed or not, whether I'm going to end up sending this letter to you or not, but, well, it's something to do, isn't it? To be honest, I'm really only writing this so I don't have to look at Train Girl and her blatant come-ons.

So: seeing as we are here, seeing as I am writing, what news from the war? Let me think. So… I've been offered another job. Two other jobs, actually. One of them at our leading tabloid competitor, the one owned by the porn baron, the one currently running with the slogan: 'Hacked off with the other papers? We're the Sunday read you can trust!' (See what they did there, Martin?) They want me to be deputy showbiz editor; they're also offering me a TV column on top of the showbiz stuff. They've offered me 15 grand more than I'm on at the moment. They apologised for not having a corporate healthcare scheme they could offer as well, but have promised that as soon as they do I'll have free private medical whatsit. So that's nice.

The other job came from a broadsheet. A daily. One of the broadsheets, in fact, that has been so sternly sanctimonious over our actions this year past. It's not stopping them from casting lots for our staff though, is it? Principles handily put aside on that score.

Anyway, they're offering me dep ed of their culture section. Plus a weekly music column in the Saturday edition. It's less money than the other offer, but more kudos. And a chance, as they so condescendingly put it, 'to really flex my writing muscles'.

What do I do? I suppose I should think them both over. I guess I should take them both seriously. It's just that I can't help wondering what Goebbels would say about them. What would he think of me? Is that mad?

But, like I say, I should think them both through properly. I've got to eat. I've got a mortgage to pay every month. I guess it has to be one or the other.

Oh! Hello, Martin, it seems we are running behind schedule! Looks like you will be getting this letter after all! I've just checked my watch, and although the sweeping esplanades and palatial homesteads of Slough are rolling gently by our windows now, they're doing so a good eight or so minutes later than they should have. Phew! What a relief, eh? I do so hate writing things pointlessly.

All of which leaves me with just enough time to update you on the Goebbels situation. So he's up for The Greatest Idea Of All Time – he's supposed to be writing it up today, in fact. And he's got an idea to make it work. It's a bit risky: it means basically failing to come up with anything else that could work instead, and enduring three days of beasting from the top bods… and then springing the whole thing, fully formed, completely upfront and with no deception at all on them on Saturday afternoon. If nothing else it covers my back – and it might even cover Goebbels' too. Not that he cares that much. If ever a man anticipated revenge, it's Goebbels right now. He's practically slavering. It's at once horrible and simultaneously makes me feel oddly proud. How weird is that?

Ooh, look! Southall, Ealing, Acton. The Eurostar sheds. We're nearly there, Martin! And what are we? Ten minutes late? I timed that one nearly perfectly! That's what tabloid training does for you, Martin. You wouldn't get that at any broadsheet culture section, take it from me.

Au revoir!

Dan

From: **Martin.Harbottle@premier-westward.com**
To: DantheMan020@gmail.com
Re: 07.31 Premier Westward Railways train from Oxford to London Paddington, May 17.

Dear Dan

Thank you again for drawing my attention to some delays on your trains. The 22.50 service on May 15 was late leaving Paddington due to a problem with the heating regulator. The thermostat had stuck on an exceptionally low rating, meaning that rather than maintaining the optimum ambient temperature for the time of year and late hour of the service, the system instead simulated conditions pertaining to early afternoon in July. After several minutes attempting to rectify the situation, the decision was made to run the service anyway, and I'm sure you're most grateful that the team's strong decision-making spared you any further delays.

Today your train was late arriving in London Paddington due to slow running on the line between Oxford and London Paddington.

I would like once again to remind you that being drunk on a Premier Westward train is a criminal offence. Entertaining though your drunken letters may be, if you continue to use our services whilst drunk, I may have no option but to issue you with a formal warning under the relevant section in our Passengers' Charter, freely available to view on our new 'app', available to 'download' on both 'Android' and 'Apple' devices.

And lastly, though part of me hates to say this, run the story. Run the story, Dan! Publish and be damned!

With very best wishes

Martin

Letter 97

From: **DantheMan020@gmail.com**
To: Martin.Harbottle@premier-westward.com
Re: 07.31 Premier Westward Railways train from Oxford to London Paddington, May 18. Amount of my day wasted: six minutes. Fellow sufferers: Train Girl, Guilty New (Spymaster) Mum, Universal Grandpa.

Woo, Martin! Get you! 'Publish and be damned!' Friday morning, on my way in to the best and worst newspaper in the world, the very best paper at being bad, and it looks like you're up for the scrap! (Hang on. What's that *Bugsy Malone* song? The best-at-being-bad one? 'We could've been anything we wanted to be, with all the talent we had. With a little practice, we made every blacklist, we're the very best at being bad!' Ha! I had to Google that, but how brilliant. How totally perfect. They could have written that song for us!)

Don't worry, Martin. I'm not drunk. It's eight o'clock in the morning, for crying out loud. I'm just excited. This is the stuff, eh? I'm waking up in the morning and (metaphorically) chomping at the (metaphorical) bit. I'm up for the scrap too, Martin! I'm up for going out with a bang, not a whimper.

I'm running two offices at the moment. The work office, containing nothing of very much interest – and from which I'm not allowed to remove anything, thanks to heightened security and rather more diligent police searches than previously (you know why they're searching us? I worked it out. It's nothing to do with the investigation or the arrests. It's because they don't want us nicking anything before the paper shuts down. They don't want us making off with company assets. Paperclips. Biros. That sort of thing. Somebody ought to tell them about Bombshell's eight stolen laptops – she's already put three of them on eBay) – and I'm also running a home office.

And it's the home office that has the big story. It's from my home office that I'm co-ordinating Goebbels. It's from there I commissioned him and it's from there I've edited the copy he's filed. And you know what? It's good stuff. It's dynamite! He knows how to write a proper story does that man. He's given it the lot, pushed it to the edge. He's taken what we've got and used it to dredge up every story ever whispered in the newsroom about the false-haired fool. It's just about the nastiest, dirtiest, most scurrilous thing you'll ever see in a national newspaper. It doesn't pull its punches; quite the reverse – it wades in there like a streetfighter, smacking seven shades out of everything in sight.

It's deranged and demented. It's possibly suicidal. It's all true. I could have cried, when I read it last night. I could have cried for how utterly, fantastically insane my former boss is. If this comes out, not only will he never work again, he'll be lucky if any PR, agent, manager, press officer, PA, journalist or editor ever even speaks to him again.

But I will. I told him: I'll visit you in prison, no matter what. 'Thanks, Dan,' he said. 'No offence, but you wouldn't last five minutes.'

So – in short, that's all going to plan. That's got me going to work with a spring in my step, waking up and eager for the day, eager for tomorrow. It's tomorrow, Martin! It's tomorrow when we go to press, when we see which way the chips might fall.

I've got something else on my mind, too, but I haven't got the time or the space to tell you all about it right now. I need another delay, Martin! I need you to slow another train down, bust another heater, burn out another kettle ('mobile water-heating device'? Really? The train was delayed because the kettle didn't work?). I need one of your officious little footsoldiers to confiscate another Flower Fairy Barbie Wand or else I'm not going to be able to tell you properly!

Suffice to say, I spoke to Beth again last night. We spoke about Sylvie. And she said a word, a single word that made my blood run cold. She used the word 'access'. She said that if things continued like this we're going to have to sort out my 'access' to my daughter.

And that made me think, Martin. That made me think hard. I just need to get this weekend out of the way first.

Au revoir!

Dan

Letter 98

From: DantheMan020@gmail.com
To: Martin.Harbottle@premier-westward.com
Re: 07.31 Premier Westward Railways train from Oxford to London Paddington, May 19. Amount of my day wasted: 11 minutes. Fellow sufferers: No regulars (Saturday).

Blimey, Martin. Another delay on the morning train (little surprise there – though three in a row is pushing it somewhat) – but, more to the point, no problems whatsoever on the evening trains! Whatever's all that about? I've had faultless journeys home every night this week since Tuesday. (You should also know, and I'm telling you this deliberately because I can't quite believe that such a thing as a formal warning even exists, that I have been drunk on every evening train I've caught this week. Drunk? I've been steaming. I've been shitfaced, cheesecaked, banjaxed. I've been blotto and bluey. I've been sozzled and sauced and boozed-up and bombed, loaded and looped, smashed and plastered. I've been inebriated, Martin. I've been thoroughly intoxicated. I've been drinking every night after work and I've continued drinking on the train home. And now, could I please have a formal warning?)

Where was I? Oh yes, sober in the morning. Sober as a judge. It's a new dawn, it's a new day and I'm feeling good. A new day? Not any old new day: it's Judgement Day. It's time for the book of revelations!

What's going to happen, Martin? How's it going to pan out? As it stands there is no splash – other than a rather lame 'That's all folks!' effort. Right now there is no big story to go out on, no massive monument to say 'We were here'. Nothing to show we've gone down fighting. Which is good. Which is all part of the plan. And at lunchtime today – in what? five hours or so – I'm going to walk into the managing editor's office with a typescript, a bunch of signed contracts and a mobile phone with Goebbels on the end of it, and I'm going to give him an alternative.

I'm going to suggest running the nuclear option, pressing the nuclear button. I'm going to suggest Mutually Assured Destruction.

And you know what? It's the end of the world as we know it – and I feel fine. My mind's at rest. I lay in bed last night (drunk, Martin, after being really very drunk indeed on a Premier Westward train) and I made all sorts of decisions. I know what I'm going to do, and I'm pretty happy about it. About work and about other stuff too. Important stuff.

I feel brilliant, in fact. I feel… ready. So brilliant, so ready, that I'm gifting you four minutes this morning. Here! Take it! Four minutes, Martin! Use them wisely. Every minute counts, you know. Don't go squandering those minutes – because one day, as you count up the minutes of your life, as you tally up the minutes of your existence, you'll wish you had more gifts like this. Four minutes! You can change the world in four minutes, Martin. You can destroy the world in four minutes, you know. Anything can happen in four minutes!

Au revoir!

Dan

From: Martin.Harbottle@premier-westward.com
To: DantheMan020@gmail.com
Re: First Formal Warning

Dear Sir

I am very sorry to have to tell you that, following reports of your repeatedly boarding Premier Westward trains in a state of intoxication, it is my regretful duty to issue a First Formal Warning, as outlined in our Passengers' Charter.

Should you offend again, you will be issued with a Second Formal Warning. Following a Third Formal Warning, you will be recommended to the Passengers' and Rail Users' Standards Committee, who have the power to issue a First Cease and Desist Notice.

Any customer of Premier Westward who receives three or more Cease and Desist Notices within the course of one calendar month will unfortunately be recommended to the police as a candidate for an Anti-Social Behaviour Order, which may result in their use of the rail network being restricted at some times.

I hope this is all clear, and that this First Formal Warning acts as a suitable deterrent.

Yours faithfully

pp Martin Harbottle
Managing Director, Premier Westward

Letter 99

From: **DantheMan020@gmail.com**
To: Martin.Harbottle@premier-westward.com
Re: 22.50 Premier Westward Railways train from London Paddington to Oxford, May 23. Amount of my day wasted: 15 minutes. Fellow sufferers: Overkeen Estate Agent.

Hey Martin! Oh, Martin. Martin! Marty! Martinho! Good old ridiculous, pompous, avuncular Martin. Tormentor, target, therapist. Maybe even friend, in a weird way. How are you, Martin? How are you doing?

This is the end, Martin. This is the end, my only friend.

This is the last letter I'm ever going to write to you. (That sounds awesome, doesn't it?) I'm kind of gutted I didn't make it to 100, but I wouldn't want to go making up delays just for the sake of a good story, would I? That would be unethical. But still: 99 is a pretty good number. Ninety-nine is better than 100, in many ways.

Do you want to hear one last journalist tip, Martin, before I leave it all altogether? One last tip from the tabloid book of tricks? Odd numbers are better than even. Prime numbers are best of all. Never promote 20 of something, or 50, or ten. Seventeen is better than 20, 49 better than 50, seven better than ten. Ninety-nine is better than 100. If you're going to give competition prizes away, or advertise tips to improve your sex life, or make a list of the best whatevers ever, make it an odd number, a prime number. Don't write 100 letters, Martin: write 99. It looks better. Paradoxically, it reads better. Trust me.

But this is all academic. This doesn't matter any more. Because this is the last time I will ever call your name. I won't be commuting any more. I'm not commuting any more, in fact. I was in London today tying up loose ends – in the pub, with Goebbels and Harry the Dog, before their pre-arranged appointments at the police station tomorrow (I tried to get hold of Wee Tim'rous Trainee too, but she's disappeared. Nobody's heard a thing. I can't help wondering if she'll even turn up at the cop shop tomorrow. I called Bombshell too, but she wasn't interested: 'totes past all that, darls – wouldn't look good now to be seen with the old crew, you do understand…') – and I don't plan on coming into London again anytime soon.

You'll have seen the paper, of course. The final edition. The last splash. You'll have been one of the six million people who queued up to buy it on Sunday. And, no doubt, you'll have been one of the six million who stopped in their tracks, who forgot where they were, who forgot what they were doing, when you read the front page.

They went for it, of course. How could they not? It took them until past 11 at night, it delayed the presses and screwed up the paper reviews and meant the first edition barely made the newsstands in time for Sunday opening hours… but they did go for it. They put their mouths where the money is. They bloody well did it, too.

It was beautiful, wasn't it? It was everything I wanted. It was – it is still – the single most devastating destruction of any individual ever run in any newspaper. We nailed him. We killed him, Martin. And when it was picked up by every news organisation in the country, when it made all the major networks in the US and Europe, when it hit Australia and Asia and South America… Game over. For us and for the man who did so much to take us down. Mutually Assured Destruction. God bless King Pyrrhus.

He was arrested before lunchtime. His career was over before then. Even if he dodges the clink, he'll never work again. He won't even be able to live in this country. Dropped like a stone by all those set up to protect him, his Twitter account shut down by the afternoon, officially the most reviled man in the Commonwealth before dinner. And by bedtime, all those other stories, all those other girls, coming forward, finally prepared to go on the record with their tales. It's been a bonanza couple of days for the dailies. We've gifted them the best run of stories they've had in years.

Everyone at the paper's screwed, of course. Those job offers I had?

Withdrawn. I'm tainted goods, apparently. Toxic. The Goebbels trick worked in a legal sense, in a public sense, but in the industry it was sussed pretty quick. And I am the showbiz editor. It didn't take Woodward and Bernstein to work out who was really responsible.

But that's fine. I'm fine with that. Because you know those decisions I said I'd made? Well, I meant it. I've made them and I'm sticking with them.

I'm packing in journalism, Martin. I'm walking away. And I'm not walking as far as PR, either. I'm walking all the way away, bridges burned, head held high, two fingers left lingering in the air behind me.

What am I going to do instead? I have no idea. I don't care. I'll think of something. I've got a little redundancy payout which will keep me good for a while, but it's not about the money. It's about... life.

Did I ever tell you about the sloth? The way they die? After eating all the food nearest to them, they just can't be bothered moving a few feet down the branch to get any more – they're so indoctrinated in ennui they would rather die than make the tiniest effort to actually live. Well, that's what sitting on a train is, Martin. That's what sitting on one of your stationary trains every morning and evening, gazing pointlessly out of the window at another blank view of Reading and Slough, of Acton and Southall, of Didcot bleeding Parkway every day, is like. That's what it is: sitting still and impotent and watching the world change and your career implode and your family life fall apart and not having the energy, the ambition, the guts to get out of your seat, get off the train and do something about it. That's what commuting is, Martin. That's what my life has been. It's been the slow death of the sloth.

Well, not any more. I'm getting out of my seat. I'm getting off the train. Literally. I'm going to stop looking at life (through a grimy window, on a tired train in the night) and start living.

I'm walking away from my career and I'm going to go and get my wife. I'm going to go see my wife and my beautiful baby daughter.

I'm going to find them and I'm going to say sorry. And I'm going to tell them we can start again. I'm going to tell them that whatever happened has happened, that the past is the past, that yesterday's news is today's chip wrapper. I'm going to tell them that I'm sick of Pyrrhic victories, I'm sick of scoring moral victories but losing what makes me happy in the process.

I have no idea what Beth will say. In a way it doesn't matter. Because I'll keep telling her that, I'll keep repeating the simple facts – I love her, I love Sylvie, nothing else is important, everything else can be dealt with – until she gets it too. And she will get it, sooner or later. Because that's why I married her in the first place. Because that's the girl she is.

And in the meantime? The big wheel will just keep on turning, right? The world will keep on doing what it does. Dealers keep dealing, thieves keep stealing – that's what the song says. Whores keep whoring, junkies keep scoring. Ain't no use in praying, that's the way it's staying, baby. Tabloids will keep on stinging. Scandals will keep on selling. And good luck to them, too.

And your trains, Martin – they'll keep getting delayed. No amount of letters is going to change that. No amount of angry words or absurd excuses will account for the lost minutes, the lost hours, the accumulated days gone for ever, pointlessly, tragically.

And I'm having none of it any more. Don't take it personally. I'm not quitting because of you. And, despite how it may have seemed sometimes, I have enjoyed writing to you. Between you and me, there have been times this year past when writing my angry little letters has been the only thing that's kept me going. So, oddly, and don't take this the wrong way, thank you, Martin. Not for your trains, not for the job you're doing, but thank you for being a gentleman. Thank you for your advice. Thank you for being you. And that's so much more important than any job.

And that's it. I'm gone. Oxford looms through the gloom and our 15-minute delay is almost over. Overkeen Estate Agent has just said the words 'I'm in this womb-to-tomb. I'm 1,000 percent in the trenches on this one. I'm accelerating my bandwidth as we speak, mate. Literally' – and I can't think of a more fitting note to end on than that.

(Actually, there was one thing more, Martin: I was going to ask you something about Sauron Flesh Harrower. Something about something you said about… but perhaps I won't. Perhaps I'll leave it as it is.)

Good night, Martin, and good luck. Not farewell, but fare forward!

Goodbye

Dan

Epilogue

From: Martin.Harbottle@premier-westward.com
To: DantheMan020@gmail.com
Re: Out of Office Reply

Dear Sir/Madam

Thank you for your email dated May 23 this year. I can confirm that Mr Harbottle has received it and will endeavour to respond as soon as possible. Your concerns are of utmost importance to us.

Thank you again for writing to Premier Westward.

pp Martin Harbottle, Managing Director

This is an automatically generated response. Please do not reply

Acknowledgements

Thanks to everyone who made this book possible. There are too many to name, but you hopefully know who you are. (If you're not sure, feel free to ask.)

In addition, however, I'd especially like to thank Heidi, Eithne and Albert, without whom, nothing – and of course Mum, Damian, Kevin, Finola, Gabrielle and Jenny, for the support, the encouragement, the belief.

This book started life as a blog and no acknowledgements would be complete without a mention of that – so to Rachel, Mark, Ellie, Laura and all at *Fabulous* who lived through the whole thing as it happened – thank you (and sorry). Likewise all the friends, colleagues and twitterers who led me to believe there might be something more in it. Also, of course, thanks to everyone who read and enjoyed the blog in the first place – and apologies to Benjionthetrain for nicking Lego Head.

While we're on the subject, thanks to all the fellow hacks whose anecdotes I stole. And, y'know, sorry for stealing your anecdotes.

Should I name someone cool now? Thanks, Joe Strummer. Cheers, Ian Brown. Good on you, all of New Order.

Thanks to Gordon Wise, my brilliant agent, to Catherine Marcus for being the first person to get really excited about the text, and to Charlotte Van Wijk, for her enthusiasm, amazing editing and genius way with a book title – as well, of course, to the whole team at Oneworld for all their hard work and faith in the book. And special thanks to Hannah and Becca Barr for introducing me to Gordon in the first place.

Finally, most importantly, this book wouldn't have happened without Mark and Sue. Thank you especially, Mark. Not for your trains, but for always being a gentleman – and that's got to count for more, in the end.